A HARD DAY'S KNIGHT

A HARD DAY'S KNIGHT

SIMON R. GREEN

ACE BOOKS, NEW YORK

THE BERKLEY PUBLISHING GROUP
Published by the Penguin Group
Penguin Group (USA) Inc.
375 Hudson Street, New York, New York 10014, USA
Penguin Group (Canada), 90 Eglinton Avenue East, Suite 700, Toronto, Ontario M4P 2Y3, Canada
(a division of Pearson Penguin Canada Inc.)
Penguin Books Ltd., 80 Strand, London WC2R 0RL, England
Penguin Group Ireland, 25 St. Stephen's Green, Dublin 2, Ireland (a division of Penguin Books Ltd.)
Penguin Group (Australia), 250 Camberwell Road, Camberwell, Victoria 3124, Australia
(a division of Pearson Australia Group Pty. Ltd.)
Penguin Books India Pvt. Ltd., 11 Community Centre, Panchsheel Park, New Delhi—110 017, India
Penguin Group (NZ), 67 Apollo Drive, Rosedale, North Shore 0632, New Zealand
(a division of Pearson New Zealand Ltd.)
Penguin Books (South Africa) (Pty.) Ltd., 24 Sturdee Avenue, Rosebank, Johannesburg 2196,
South Africa

Penguin Books Ltd., Registered Offices: 80 Strand, London WC2R 0RL, England

This is an original publication of The Berkley Publishing Group.

This is a work of fiction. Names, characters, places, and incidents either are the product of the author's imagination or are used fictitiously, and any resemblance to actual persons, living or dead, business establishments, events, or locales is entirely coincidental. The publisher does not have any control over and does not assume any responsibility for author or third-party websites or their content.

FIRST EDITION: January 2011

Library of Congress Cataloging-in-Publication Data

Green, Simon R., 1955–
   A hard day's knight / Simon R. Green.—1st ed.
      p.   cm.
   ISBN 978-0-441-01970-0
   1. Taylor, John (Fictitious character)—Fiction.   2. Private investigators—England—London—
Fiction.   3. Knights and knighthood—Fiction.   4. London (England)—Fiction.   I. Title.
   PR6107.R44H37 2011
   823'.92—dc22

                                                                                          2010037673

PRINTED IN THE UNITED STATES OF AMERICA

10   9   8   7   6   5   4   3   2   1

A HARD DAY'S KNIGHT

Things you need to know:

1. The Nightside is the dark, secret, brooding heart of London, hidden away from the rest of the world, where magic is realer than you can bear, where lives and souls and everything else you can think of are always up for sale, and all your worst dreams go walking openly in borrowed flesh. It's always dark in the Nightside, always three o'clock in the morning, the hour that tries men's souls. Hot neon burns over rain-slick streets, bars and clubs never close, and gods and monsters go walking hand in hand. You can find anything you ever dreamed of in the Nightside; but watch your back. It might find you first.

2. I'm John Taylor, private investigator. I wear a white trench coat, but don't let that fool you. I don't do divorce work, and I wouldn't know a clue if I fell over it. I do, however, have a special gift that means I can find anyone or anything, no matter how carefully they've hidden themselves. I do my best to find the truth for my clients; but in my experience, the truth won't make you happy, and it won't set you free. Walk the streets of the Nightside, and you'll hear a lot of bad things about me. Most of them are true. I stay in the Nightside because I belong here. With all the other monsters.

3.   Walker is dead. The one and only Voice of the Authorities, the man in charge of the Nightside, inasmuch as anyone was or could be . . . The only man who could make us all play nicely together is dead. I killed him. I had good reason, but he's still just as dead. So I have to be Walker now. Take over his role and act as representative for the new Authorities. The punishment must always fit the crime.

4.   Something very old and very powerful has come to the Nightside. That ancient and legendary sword, Excalibur. *It isn't what you think it is, and it never was.* Puck told me that; but everyone knows you can never trust an elf. They always lie—except when a truth can hurt you more.

5.   And, last of all . . . When I finally got home, after killing Walker, wanting only to slump exhausted into a chair and nurse my bitter soul . . . I found a long, sword-shaped parcel waiting for me on my kitchen table. Some days, you just can't get a break.

ONE

It Came in the Post

I stood in my kitchen, already so tired and used up I would have lain down in a coffin if that was all that was available . . . and considered the brown-paper parcel on the table before me. Suzie came in from the hall and joined me. She slipped an arm round my waist, and I kissed her absently on the cheek. My Suzie, also known as Shotgun Suzie, also known as *Oh Christ It's Her, Run.* My tall blonde Valkyrie in black leathers, a bounty-hunter who always brings them in dead because there's less paper-work that way. My love, my life, my reason for living, who had dropped the biggest bomb-shell into my life in years by accepting this appallingly significant parcel . . .

I moved away from Suzie and walked slowly round the kitchen table, studying the sword-shaped package from all angles. It stubbornly refused to look like anything except a bloody big sword. I had absolutely no intention of touching the thing just yet. Suzie looked at me curiously but said nothing. She could tell I was working. Solving problems is what I do. I leaned over the kitchen table, examining the brown-paper parcel from hilt to point. There were no stamps anywhere, and no address—only my name, in perfect copperplate. Which meant the parcel couldn't have come by regular post. It had to have been delivered by hand.

"When did this arrive?" I asked Suzie.

Her ears pricked up as she caught the seriousness in my voice. "Two, three hours ago. I heard a knock on the front door, looked out, and there it was. Leaning against the wall. At first I thought it must be for me since it's so obviously a weapon; but then I saw it had your name on it, so I put it on one side for you, for when you got home."

"Think about it," I said. "You wouldn't normally bring a strange, unexpected parcel into our home and leave it lying round without running it through a whole series of security checks first, would you?"

"No," said Suzie, in a way that made it clear she hadn't even considered the point before and was wondering rather angrily why she hadn't. "It felt . . . right. Like it belonged here. Why the hell didn't I find that suspicious?"

"Because the parcel didn't want you to," I said.

We both glared at the brown-paper package.

"Could it have some kind of compulsion, or geas, attached to it?" said Suzie.

"I think we're in bigger trouble than that," I said. "I'm getting a distinct feeling of destiny."

"Oh shit."

"Yes, quite," I said. "Next question: how did our mysterious benefactor pass unscathed through all our security systems? The land mines and the floating curses? We spent ages setting up the defences round this house, to protect us from our enemies and discourage the paparazzi. Our regular postie has a special dispensation; this guy shouldn't even have made it to the front door."

"Oh, this has destiny written all over it," said Suzie. "Let's run."

"You didn't see anyone when you picked up the parcel?"

"Not as such, no. And yes, I should have found that suspicious. Bloody parcel must have been messing with my head."

"The parcel, or whoever sent it . . ." I was scowling so fiercely my forehead was aching. "Beware of unseen strangers bearing gifts."

I raised my gift, opening up my inner eye, my third eye, my private eye. I studied the parcel with my Sight, which shows me all the wonders and horrors of the hidden world, and scanned the parcel for booby-traps or hidden messages. I barely had time to assure myself there were no hidden extras when I cried out despite myself and fell back, as what was inside the parcel blazed up fiercely, a magical, spiritual light that dazzled and blinded me. My inner eye slammed shut as my mind flinched away from something it couldn't bear to look at directly.

I grabbed hold of the parcel, glared at it for a moment, then ripped the wrapping away, tearing the brown paper and snapping the knotted string. I had to see it. Had to see what no man had seen for centuries. The legendary sword, Excalibur. King Arthur's sword, from the Golden Age of Chivalry. The scabbard turned out to be six feet and more of tooled leather, with Celtic markings and designs, and a whole bunch of symbols from a language I didn't even recognise. The foot-long hilt of the sword seemed to have been fashioned from a single piece of bone, polished to a fine dark yellow sheen. I brushed the last pieces of torn paper away from it, and the scabbarded sword lay alone on my table, in my kitchen, like an unexploded bomb, or a warning from history.

"That . . . is not just any old sword," said Suzie.

"No," I said absently. "That's Excalibur."

"*What?*" said Suzie. "You mean *the* Excalibur? As in King Arthur? What the hell is that doing here? Hold everything. You knew what this was all along, didn't you?"

"I was told the sword had come into the Nightside," I said. "I never thought it would end up here." ·

"Excalibur," said Suzie. She sounded honestly impressed, which wasn't something that came easily to her. "Damn . . . Aren't you supposed to draw it out of an anvil, set on a stone? I mean, something as important as this, it shouldn't just turn up in the post. Where's the mystical significance of that?"

"This is the Nightside," I said. "We do things differently here. Somebody wanted to make sure I got it; and this was the best way of sneaking it in, under the radar."

"Well, if you don't draw the bloody thing from its scabbard so we can get a look at it, I'm going to," said Suzie. "That is one of the great legendary swords! How can you not want to try it out for size?"

"Because I don't want it to bite my hand off! I'm working up to it, okay? This isn't something you draw and wave round for the fun of it! This is Excalibur we're taking about. It makes history and gives birth to legends. Everything it does, matters."

"Are you afraid there might be a geas attached to it?" said Suzie, looking at the sword with a new wariness. "Like the Old Man of the Sea—easy to pick up but a damned sight harder to put down?"

"I think I would have Seen anything like that," I said carefully. "I think . . . we're back to destiny again. And I have had enough of that in my life. I have been there, done that, and seen my mother banished from reality rather than embrace the destiny she intended for me. I'm my own man; and I won't give that up, even for Excalibur."

"We can't leave it lying there. I was going to start making dinner soon . . ."

6

"I know! I'm thinking . . . I'm trying to think of any-one else I could safely hand it over to . . . Oh hell. Why is it always me?"

I took a firm hold of the polished-bone hilt, set my other hand on the scabbard, and slowly eased the sword out of its sheath. It came easily, almost eagerly: five, maybe six feet of blade that glowed supernaturally bright in the gloomy kitchen. Suzie made a shocked, almost awed sound, and fell back a step. I held the sword out before me, the hilt fitting perfectly into my hand, and the long, golden blade shone brighter and brighter, free at last after centuries of waiting. I swept the blade slowly back and forth, supporting the whole length of it easily with only one hand, and it all felt so nat-ural, as though I'd been doing it my whole life. The long, golden blade seemed impossibly light, almost weightless, moving easily with my hand as though it belonged there.

I stamped back and forth round the kitchen table, thrust-ing and cutting, the golden blade leaping this way and that. The longer I held Excalibur, the more I knew how to use it, how to handle it. Without quite meaning to, I ran through an increasingly complex series of attacks and manoeuvres, jump-ing and pirouetting as I slammed the blade back and forth. Suzie fell back to the kitchen doorway, to give me plenty of room.

"All right, cut it out, I'm impressed!" she said. "Where did you learn to use a sword like that?"

"I didn't," I said, forcing myself to stop. I was hardly even breathing hard. "I've never handled a sword in my life. Excal-ibur is making all the moves; I'm just along for the ride."

"Okay," said Suzie. "Getting a bit spooky now . . ."

"Trust me, you have no idea. Wait a minute . . ."

Suzie's head came up sharply, as she sensed it, too. Without moving or changing in any way, Excalibur was suddenly so much more than it had been. There was a new presence in the room with us, like a third person, uncanny and overwhelming;

7

and it was the sword. Excalibur's presence beat on the air like a breaking storm, like a great bugle sounding a charge that would never end, a cry to battle, for the soul of Humanity. It dominated my small kitchen—a cry from the past, the deep past, wild and glorious and very dangerous.

Suzie had backed half-way out of the kitchen doorway. I would have liked to join her, but I was still holding the sword. I could feel it coming awake, yearning to be used, demanding to be put to the purpose for which it was intended. And I couldn't help remembering that terrible old weapon, the Speaking Gun. That evil device had wanted to kill and kill until nothing was left, and hated the fact that it couldn't do that without its owner's cooperation. Excalibur didn't feel anything like the Speaking Gun, but it still needed me to wield it. To help it fulfil its destiny.

The sword blazed with purpose: of something vitally important that had to be done, that it had been brought back into the world to do. I took a deep breath and let it out slowly; then I picked up the scabbard and slid the sword carefully back into its sheath. It didn't fight me. I placed the scabbard carefully down on the table again and stepped away from it. The sheer effort of will left me shaking and covered in a cold and clammy sweat. But I am my own man, no-one and nothing else's.

"Well?" said Suzie, from the doorway. "Is it destiny?"

"Oh . . . I'd have to give you ninety-five per cent on that, yes. And it wants me."

"I could write you a note, say you're excused destinies."

"Why me?" I said, a bit wistfully.

"Isn't that what everyone says, when destiny comes calling?"

"If this turns out to be connected to Merlin, I swear I will find a way to bring him back from the dead, just so I can kick his arse!"

"Never speak ill of the dead," Suzie said briskly. "Especially when they aren't always as departed as they should be."

I couldn't help noticing that she'd backed right out of the kitchen doorway and was now standing in the hall, looking in. Suzie wasn't scared of anything, but she had a hell of a lot of natural caution and really good survival instincts. I would have liked to walk away and leave the sword, but owning Excalibur is like holding a tiger by the tail. Bad as the situation is, it's even more dangerous to let go. I had hoped drawing the sword would trigger a recorded message that would tell me what the hell was going on and what I was supposed to do about it; but apparently that was too much to hope for.

"We need to get this sword out of our house," said Suzie. "Something that powerful, running wild in the Nightside; who knows what kind of attention it's going to attract?"

I looked at the scabbarded sword; but all sense of its presence was gone, vanished the moment I sheathed it. It looked like any other sword now. But Excalibur was the kind of sword men would kill and die for, for any number of reasons. Suzie came warily back into the kitchen.

"So, does this mean you're the rightful King of all England now?"

"No," I said. "I'm pretty sure that was a one-time-only thing."

"Does it mean you're King of the Nightside, then? Or was the sword sent to you by someone who thinks you should be?"

"I had the chance," I said. "And I turned it down. I'm not about to change my mind. As to who sent it: I have a horrible feeling this might be Walker's last gift to me, taken from the late Collector's legendary collection."

"Hold everything," said Suzie. "The 'late' Collector? He's finally dead?"

"Haven't you been watching the news?"

"I've been busy," Suzie said defensively. "Aimless lounging round won't do itself, you know. What happened to the Collector? Who killed him? I take it somebody did finally kill the thieving old scrote?"

"Walker killed him," I said. "He walked right up to his

9

oldest friend and stuck a knife between his ribs. I was right there, but there was nothing I could do."

"I'll not shed a tear for the Collector," said Suzie. "How many times did he try to kill us? All right, he was a colourful rogue, or a treacherous little turd, depending on how you look at it, but I think the whole Nightside will sleep more peacefully, now that he's gone. You could always rely on the Collector to stir things up, and rarely in a good way. But . . . why did Walker finally kill him, after all these years? I thought they were friends again, after working together during the Lilith War?"

"They were," I said. "It's . . . complicated. Friendships often are."

"Hold everything, part two," said Suzie. "You said . . . Walker's *last* gift. Don't tell me . . ."

"Yes," I said. "Walker's dead. I killed him."

"Why?" said Suzie. "Okay, dumb question. I can think of a dozen good reasons, without even trying."

"It wasn't like that," I said. "He wanted to kill me and take over my life. And he threatened you. I couldn't have that. So I killed him."

"The most important man in the Nightside is dead," said Suzie. "Good." She put a comforting hand on my arm. "I know you and he were . . . close, in some way I never really understood."

"He was my father's friend," I said. "But he was always there when I needed him. He used me for jobs when he needed someone expendable, but he protected me when he could. At the end, when he knew he was dying, he said he wanted to be my father; but I never wanted that. And I don't want his bloody job, either. Oh yes, the man's barely been gone a few hours, and already people are queuing up to tell me I have a responsibility to take over his position and be the new Voice of the new Authorities!"

"If you don't want to do it, don't do it," said Suzie. For her, it really was that simple.

"But . . . there's no-one else."

"That's my John," said Suzie, putting her arms round me. Her black leathers creaked loudly. "Always ready to take the weight of the world on his shoulders. And always convinced no-one else can do the job as well as him. Maybe that's why our mysterious benefactor sent Excalibur to you. Because they know you can be trusted to use it wisely. I'm not sorry Walker's dead. Or that you killed him. I worked for the man, but I never liked him. He played chess with people and never gave a damn about the pieces he had to sacrifice."

"I worked for him," I said. "I respected him, and sometimes I liked him, against my better judgement."

"Were you and he ever friends?"

"I don't know," I said. "It's complicated."

"Two of the Nightside's greatest lights have gone out," said Suzie. "We shall not see any blaze so brightly again in our lifetime."

I gave her a stern look. "You've been watching the History Channel again."

She laughed and let go of me. She started towards the table, reached out to grasp the sword's hilt, then stopped.

"This sword fascinates me," she said slowly. "It's one of the greatest weapons in the world. But as much as I want to, I can't bring myself to touch it. I don't think it wants me to. As though . . . I'm not worthy."

"Hell with that," I said immediately, carefully keeping it light. "If I'm worthy, you're worthy. No, I think it's just . . . we're back to the destiny thing again. It wants me."

"So we're back to the main question," said Suzie, glaring at the sword with her arms folded firmly across her chest. "Why would anyone send Excalibur to you?"

"I think it's my turn to feel hurt," I said. "Are you implying that I am not worthy?"

She snorted briefly. "Don't start getting ideas above your station."

"I am, let us not forget, the son of a Biblical Myth."

"And look how that turned out."

"Good point," I said. It was my turn to look thoughtfully at the sword. "Maybe . . . I'm supposed to hold on to the sword, guard and protect it, until its rightful owner turns up."

"You mean Arthur? King Arthur? *The* King Arthur?"

"Why not?" I said reasonably. "We spent enough time in Merlin's company . . . Dead, but definitely not departed enough for my liking. A lot of people believe Arthur is still out there, somewhere, sleeping in state until the day shall come when he will be needed again, to lead us all in the Final Battle. I used to love all those books when I was a kid."

"This is sounding worse and worse," said Suzie. "If Excalibur's turned up, does that mean we're on the verge of the Final Battle? I've already been through the Angel War and the Lilith War. I think I'm entitled to a little rest between Armageddons."

"I wish everyone would stop talking about those two wars as if they were my fault!"

"Well, they were."

"Only indirectly!"

"Don't shout, or I'll give you a headache," said Suzie. "Still, it has been a little quiet of late. I could use some exercise. It's been a while since I killed a whole bunch of people."

"I'm starting to get a really bad feeling about this," I said.

Suzie looked at me thoughtfully. "How did the sword feel when you handled it?"

"Light," I said. "Almost weightless. Good balance."

"No, John. How did it *feel* . . ."

I thought about it. "Like it could do anything. Like *I* could do anything. Like nothing in this world could stand against us as long as we fought in a noble cause."

On an impulse, I picked up the scabbard and slung it over my shoulder. Leather straps appeared out of nowhere, and I pulled them into place, securing the scabbard on my back.

My hands moved expertly, knowing exactly what to do. I could feel the weight of the sword, hanging all the way down my back, almost to my heels. I could sense the hilt standing up behind my left shoulder, waiting to be drawn. I could feel Excalibur's presence, like a shield at my back that no weapon could ever pierce. Like another pair of eyes, watching out for me. I was so taken up with all these new feelings that it took me a moment to notice that Suzie was looking at me very strangely.

"What?" I said.

Suzie walked round me in a tight circle, examining me from all angles. "The moment you strapped that sword into place, it vanished. Gone. Invisible. Are you sure it's still there?"

"Yes," I said. "I can feel the weight of it, the pressure of its purpose. And it feels like it's got my back."

"You used to feel that way about me," said Suzie.

"I still do!"

"Shouting again . . ."

"I trust you with my life, Suzie. Which is more than I'll say about Excalibur. I can't help feeling that this sword has its own agenda."

"Yes, well, that's magic swords for you," said Suzie. "And destiny, for that matter. I suppose it's too late to mark it RETURN TO SENDER and throw the thing out?"

"Almost certainly," I said. "It's no good, Suzie; I'm going to need help with this one. Very specialised help and advice. And there's only one place I can think of that's a real authority on all things Arthurian. I'm going to have to leave the Nightside and go back out into London Proper. And talk with the London Knights."

"You have got to be kidding. Those arrogant, stuck-up, conceited little prigs?"

"Yes," I said. "That's the ones."

"You are not going anywhere until we've talked this through very thoroughly. You don't have to leave the Nightside,

John. This place is lousy with all kinds of experts, on every subject under the sun, and a whole bunch of other things that can only thrive in permanent darkness. There are people here who know something about everything, everything about something, and . . . there has to be somebody here! There has to be."

"Not this time," I said gently. "Excalibur is too . . . pure for the Nightside. Pure in purpose and nature. It has to be the London Knights. After all: who has a better claim to Excalibur than the last defenders of Camelot?"

Suzie sniffed loudly. Her way of saying that while I might have convinced her, there was no way in hell she was going to admit it. And being Suzie, she immediately attacked from another direction.

"I thought you said you felt a responsibility to take over Walker's position, here in the Nightside?"

"I do," I said. "But that can wait. This . . . is bigger. I'm hoping Excalibur has reappeared to prevent a Final Battle rather than start one. But I can't know for sure, and I won't know what to do for the best until I've talked with the London Knights."

Suzie looked at me for a long moment with her cold blue eyes and her cold, expressionless face. She might be easier with me physically these days, but emotions were always going to be difficult for her.

"You've been gone from London Proper for a long time, John. They didn't treat you at all well, out there in the real world."

"No," I said. "I can't say I was ever happy there. And there are probably still a lot of really nasty people who would love to have another crack at me. Never mind those I still owe money to. But I was hiding my light under a bushel in those days, pretending to be merely another private investigator. I'm so much more than that now."

"Ah well," said Suzie. "If you've got enemies there, that simplifies things. I'll have to go with you. Hang on while I go gather up my guns and grenades."

"You can't come with me, Suzie."

"What? Why not?"

"Because you can't walk round London Proper loaded down with guns and grenades like you do here. The police would arrest you on sight. And you know you wouldn't get on with the London Knights. They're very . . . spiritual."

"You mean superior!"

"Well, yes, that, too. They are knights of the realm."

"Stuck-up pricks . . ."

"Suzie, be reasonable . . ."

"I don't do reasonable! It's bad for my reputation. You are not going back into London Proper without me! Or try and deal with those aristocratic head-cases on your own. They'll talk you into things. Probably persuade you to hand Excalibur over to them because it ought to belong to one of their kind!" She scowled fiercely. "Look at what owning the sword has already done to us. You think now you've got Excalibur, you don't need me to guard your back any more."

"I'll always need you, Suzie . . ."

"Don't you patronise me!"

"I can't let you go with me! Not this time."

"You mean you don't want me to."

"Of course I want you to!"

"Then that's settled," said Suzie. "I'm going."

"No, you're not," I said, hanging on to my self-control as best I could. "Look, Suzie, this has to be a diplomatic mission. The London Knights aren't going to share their most valued secrets with me unless they're convinced I respect their position and authority in these matters. I am going to have to be very diplomatic. And you don't really do diplomacy. Do you?"

There was a long pause. And then Suzie said, very grudgingly, "I could learn . . ."

"Not in time you couldn't," I said, hiding my relief behind a reasonable voice. "I have to do this alone. I'll be fine. Trust me. When I get back, we'll—what the hell is that noise outside?"

"I don't know," said Suzie. "But whoever it is, they've picked a really bad time to annoy me. I am in the mood to take out my displeasure on someone. You check the front door. I am going to load up on guns and grenades."

We left the kitchen. It seemed to me that the noise outside had been building for some time, but I'd only just noticed it consciously. It sounded like a crowd of some size had gathered outside the house, and none of them sounded too happy about being there. I opened the front door and looked out; and the whole street was packed full of people. They took one look at me and went ballistic. The noise level shot right off the scale as they shouted and yelled and hurled abuse, stamping their feet and shaking their fists. I ostentatiously ignored the commotion, knowing that would annoy them most, and looked up and down the street. My house appeared to be under siege by hundreds of people, all of them with one thing on their minds. I could tell that from the loud chant that had gone up.

"*Excalibur! Excalibur! Excalibur!*"

Suzie squeezed in beside me in the doorway and glared out at the crowd. The chanting died away.

"*Get off my lawn!*" said Suzie.

"I think you need grass for it to be a lawn," I said. "And we got rid of that when we laid down the land mines."

"It's the principle of the thing," Suzie said vaguely, scowling indiscriminately at the crowd, who were looking at anything except her. Those at the back started shoving those at the front forward. General pushing and shoving in the crowd increased over who had the better right to approach us and who had the better right to stand at the back shouting orders.

It was mostly groups, along with certain individual protes-
tors, and I recognised quite a few of them. The Salvation
Army Sisterhood were out in force: overmuscled nuns of the
militant persuasion. God-botherers with attitude, they were
always heavily armed, the better to get their point across.
Maintaining a respectful distance from the nuns were rep-
resentatives of the Church of the Riddle of Steel, all the way
from the Street of the Gods. They dressed like Vikings, right
down to the culturally inaccurate horned helmets, and they
worshipped swords. And not in a good way. At least half a
dozen different groups of the *Arthur Is Not Dead Only Sleeping*
persuasion were arguing fiercely with each other over obscure
points of dogma that probably meant nothing to anyone
except them.

Plus, a whole bunch of notorious faces, well-known on
the scene, determined to get their hands on one of the most
dangerous weapons of all time, by whatever means necessary.
Either because they had their own plans for it, or thought
they could sell it to people who did have plans. Most of them
had come armed or with armed body-guards. There was even
a contingent who'd turned up in full armour, riding caparisoned horses with brightly coloured plumes.

And every now and again a voice would rise up from somewhere in the crowd, loudly proclaiming that Merlin was a
louse.

The crowd was getting out of hand, so I stepped forward
and held up a hand to get their attention. Somewhat to my
surprise, the whole lot immediately fell silent. In fact, there
was something very like a breathless hush as they all waited
to see what I was going to say. Which threw me a bit. I wasn't
used to that. I gave them all my very best hard stare.

"What are you doing here?"

They waited to see if I was going to say anything else,
and when it became clear that I wasn't, they all looked at

each other in a confused sort of way. Finally, one of the nuns stepped forward, bobbed a curtsey, made the sign of the cross, and adjusted the Smith & Wesson .45 on her hip.

"Because you've got Excalibur. Haven't you?"

I did consider denying it, just to wind them up a bit more, but I didn't have the energy.

"How did you know Excalibur was here?"

"You drew the sword," the nun said flatly. "You should have known it would blaze so very brightly, in such a dark place. We've all been waiting for the sword to reveal itself. Precogs and oracles have been predicting its arrival in the Nightside for months now, but due to its overwhelming nature, no-one could pin it down. Most groups have been running a countdown to today, ready and poised to spot the sword the moment it made its location clear. Once you drew Excalibur and revealed it to the world, we all came running. The sword of destiny must not be allowed to fall into the wrong hands!"

A great roar of agreement went up from the crowd, which fell apart almost immediately as everyone began arguing fiercely over whose were the right hands. Merlin got called a louse again.

"Okay!" I said, raising my voice to be heard over the general clamour. "That takes care of how. Now would anyone care to take a stab at why?"

"Give us Excalibur!" cried the Salvation Army Sisterhood.

"We demand you turn the sword of destiny over to us!" yelled a rather podgy Viking, who was quite clearly wearing a long blond wig under his horned helmet.

"Only we have the right to Excalibur!" roared a knight in full armour.

"Merlin is a louse!"

"Will somebody please shut him up!"

Then they all fell on each other, the whole crowd fighting for the right to be heard, the right to bear Excalibur, and the right to smite the unbeliever, knock him down, and trample him underfoot. Swords were brandished, magics were unleashed, and punches were thrown when only close quarters would do. There was also a fair amount of gunfire, from the non-traditionalists and those only in it for the money. The crowd had become a mob, surging dangerously back and forth at the bottom of my property. The most enthusiastic groups quickly wiped each other out, and there was then a general tapering off of violence as calmer and more moderate voices made themselves heard, urging that they all work together to take Excalibur from me, by force if necessary. A few self-appointed spokesmen (there are always a few), came right to the edge of my non-lawn and shouted their demands at me. Well, demand, really. They wanted me to hand over Excalibur. Right now. Please.

I shook my head; and before I could even begin to explain why, the whole crowd went apeshit all over again. They surged forward into my garden. Or non-lawn. Or whatever else you wanted to call it. I always thought of it as my first line of defence.

One of the first things Suzie and I did when we moved in was dig up the flower garden at the front of the house and lay down a whole mess of land mines. To keep out the uninvited and ruin an investigative journalist's day. There was a series of loud explosions as the first wave of the crowd hit the first wave of mines, and bits and pieces of people went flying in all directions. Blood splashed everywhere, and black smoke billowed across the property. There were a few brief screams, but that was mostly from those in the second wave, being forced onwards by those behind. The crowd pressed on, and that was when the invisible floating curses kicked in. There was a flare-up of fierce thaumatic energies, and when the black smoke had cleared, the first few waves of intruders had been replaced by a whole bunch of rather resentful-looking frogs. I've always been a traditionalist in these matters.

Besides: the shop had had a sale on.

"We did put up warnings," I said to Suzie. "Didn't we?"

"I am almost sure I meant to," said Suzie. "Can I start shooting people yet?"

"They seem to be taking themselves out of the game quite thoroughly," I said. "Oh look, here comes another wave."

Having used up most of the nuns and the Vikings, the braver and more sensible elements of the crowd were pressing forward, slowly and cautiously and very light-footedly. Most of them were shouting something, if only to keep their spirits up. There were still quite a lot of them.

"John Taylor is the rightful ruler of the Nightside! Excalibur is his! Bow down to King John!"

"Taylor's possession of the noble blade Excalibur is blasphemy! Seize the blade from him, that it might be held in trust for King Arthur! Only we know the way to Avalon!"

"Excalibur belongs to us! Arthur belongs to us! It is prophesised! Kill the unbelievers!"

"Merlin is a louse!"

"Why aren't you dead yet?"

The general advance sort of broke down and went sideways then, as the various elements in the crowd turned on each other, fighting tooth and nail over who represented whom. There was much bandying of Arthur's name, and indeed which King Arthur was the most historical, or accurate, or even most representative. Arguments quickly degenerated into insults, then to hand-to-hand combat. The crowd surged this way and that, churning up the blood-soaked mud of what had once been my garden. I encouraged the general antagonism along with helpful comments like *Are You Really Going to Let Him Talk to You Like That?* and *Look Out! He's Sneaking Up Behind You!*

I do love a good debate.

When the slaughter finally died down, there was a hell

of a lot less of the crowd than there used to be, but the survivors were the really dangerous and determined ones. They
studied Suzie and me thoughtfully and plotted together on
how best to take Excalibur from me now and worry about
what to do with it afterwards. And while I was considering what
to do about that, another branch of the crowd, the really
quiet and sneaky ones, attacked my house from the rear. And
ran straight into the waiting nasty and really very efficient
security devices Suzie and I had set up there, right after we
finished with the garden. Invisible floating mines, shaped
curses, poisoned-shrapnel hedges, and a whole bunch of Suzie's finest incendiaries.

Suzie and I take our privacy very seriously.

A series of explosions filled the night, accompanied by
bright flashes of light, sudden flurries of blood, a whole bunch
of suddenly cut-off screams, and, finally, a severed head
that came flying over the roof like a football. Everyone in
the crowd stopped what they were doing to watch the head
sail through the air, then they all scattered with some really
quite girlish screams as the head finally plummeted down
into their midst. People can get freaked out by the strangest
things. I looked over what was left of my non-lawn and shook
my head sadly.

"This . . . is going to take a lot of tidying up."

"We'll have to get a man in," said Suzie.

"I had hoped the crowd was going to wipe itself out," I
said, "but a discouragingly large number have survived.
Somehow."

"I think we're going to have to talk to them," said Suzie.

"Oh God, has it come to that? Oh well, if we must."

I strode down the garden to confront the crowd, with
Suzie striding ominously along at my side. The thinned-out
crowd immediately stopped arguing and threatening each
other and moved instinctively to stand closer together. Suzie

has that effect on people. There was a brief period of them all trying to hide behind each other, then they turned every weapon they had on Suzie and me. I made a point of walking quite casually, as though I didn't have a care in the world. I didn't need to look round to know that Suzie was carrying her double-barrelled, pump-action shotgun at the ready, in a really quite distressingly casual manner. Those at the front of the crowd tried edging backwards, but those behind them were having none of it. And that was when some poor damned fools decided to launch a surprise attack from above, presumably in the hope that we might be caught off guard.

An armoured knight came swooping down on a huge winged horse, waving a massive glowing sword. Suzie shot him right out of the saddle, and the horse kept on going, disappearing into the night. A distressingly hairy bat-winged harpy plummeted down towards me, her clawed feet thrust out before her. I waited until the very last minute, then grabbed both her ankles, swung her round, and slammed her face-first into the ground. All the fight went out of her as she lay trembling and shuddering in the churned-up mud, struggling to get some breath back into her lungs. I put her out of her misery with a good solid kick to the head. Never let it be said I don't know how to treat a lady. The harpy decided to have a little nap, and I looked round for someone else to vent a little spleen on.

(A part of me was already considering the fact that I never used to be that fast, and that efficient, in a fight. In fact, I usually avoid the hand-to-hand stuff because I'm crap at it. I had to wonder whether just owning the mighty Excalibur was . . . upgrading me.)

A pack of futuristic knights in space-age armour appeared suddenly over the roof, borne aloft on anti-grav backpack units. They assumed a very professional-looking formation and came swooping down with glowing energy blades held out before them. Suzie took up a comfortable stance and shot them out of the sky, one after the other. Her specially adapted ammunition blew great holes through the space-age armour and punched right through their steel helms. The futuristic knights blew apart like so many clay pigeons. Suzie didn't miss one. Dead knights drifted slowly away across the night sky, impelled on by their sputtering anti-grav units. Some bodies had heads; some didn't.

I decided enough was enough. I had no problem with watching murderous religious fanatics carve each other up or come to nasty ends through invading my privacy; but after a while, even justified homicide starts wearing you down. So I stepped forward, raised my hand, and addressed the crowd.

"I am John Taylor. And this . . . is Excalibur."

I reached over my shoulder, took a firm grasp on the invisible hilt, and drew the sword from its sheath with one graceful movement. Immediately, the sword became visible again, the long, golden blade shining with supernatural brilliance. It drove back the night, filling my property with light bright as day. Excalibur's presence filled the air, dominating the scene. And everyone in the crowd before me knelt and bowed their heads to Excalibur. Their respect was entirely for the sword, not the sword-bearer, but still, the sight of so many kneeling before me raised all the hackles on the back of my neck. I was in the presence of history and legend, of a sword that had shaped my country and my culture.

"Anyone here think they can take Excalibur from me, by force?" I said finally. "I bear Excalibur because the sword chose me to do so. Now, for those of you who haven't heard, being a bit obsessed at the moment; Walker is dead. I killed him. I am now the Voice of the new Authorities. So get the hell off my property, every one of you, before I use the Voice to make you do terrible things to yourselves."

The crowd got up off their knees and quietly dispersed.

None of them felt like arguing. I put the sword away, and its light snapped off. Night fell over my non-lawn again. Suzie stood beside me, her shotgun still ostentatiously at the ready.

"You don't have the Voice," she said quietly.

"No," I said. "But they don't know that."

"They're bound to find out. Eventually."

"By then, I plan to be safely distant, in London Proper."

My mobile phone rang. I'm still using the *Twilight Zone* ring tone. Some things feel right and natural. When I answered, Julien Advent was on the other end.

"John, you're needed. Right now. Very urgently."

"This really isn't a good time, Julien," I said. "I'm a bit busy at the moment."

"No, you're not. The Authorities have a mission for you. Did I mention how urgent this is?"

"You want to put me to work already?" I said. "Walker's only been dead a few hours! I haven't even officially accepted the position yet."

"Yes, you have, as of right now. Don't argue with me. This is the kind of problem only Walker could deal with; and since you've made that impossible, it's your duty to take over. There's trouble at the Mammon Emporium. Someone's threatening to blow it up with a soulbomb. And that could threaten the whole existence of the Nightside. So stop arguing with me and get here fast. While there's still a here to get to!"

Julien Advent, the legendary Victorian Adventurer, editor of the *Night Times*, and leader of the new Authorities, doesn't often lose his temper.

"I'm on my way," I said. I put the phone away and smiled uncertainly at Suzie. "I'm afraid I'm going to have to put everything on hold for a while. Sweetie. Big trouble in the Nightside. Now, I really would love to stop and help you clear up all this mess, but you know how it is when duty calls."

She looked at me dangerously. "I do not do housework!"

But I'd already taken out the old gold pocket-watch that used to belong to Walker. I opened the lid and activated the Portable Timeslip inside, and just like that I was off and travelling through the void, on my way to save the Nightside, one more time.

TWO

You've Either Got or You Haven't Got Soul

The pocket-watch locked onto Julien Advent's location and took me straight to him. I have no idea how it does that, but I'm growing increasingly convinced that there's something else inside the gold pocket-watch, apart from the Portable Timeslip. And one of these days I'm going to dig it out with a butter-knife. Walker did so love to keep his little secrets. I arrived in the main bar of the Adventurers Club, where heroes from all over the worlds gather, to test themselves against the challenges of the Nightside. I have never been invited to become a member.

I spent a few moments shaking my head gently until all the bits settled back into place again. Travelling through the Portable Timeslip's interdimensional short cut is never easy. It's dark in there, darker than any night, and cold enough to chill the soul. There are voices in that dark, voices not in any way human, calling out to be freed, promising anything, pleading, threatening terrible things. But then, you can get that walking down any street in the Nightside. A bad trip, though, in every sense. How did Walker stand it? He always appeared out of nowhere, looking cool and calm and collected, as though he were out for a stroll. I had a strong feeling I'd arrived looking like someone who'd just been thrown out of the drunk tank.

I shook the last of the darkness out of my head and looked round. It had been a while since I'd been allowed into the Adventurers Club bar, and I was already rehearsing how many terribly expensive drinks I could demand before I was asked to leave. The place was exhaustingly spectacular and downright lousy with luxury, and the bar itself was a work of art fashioned from gleaming mahogany and brightly polished glass and crystal. Stacked in obsessively neat rows behind the bar was every kind of booze you've ever dreamed of and a few that would haunt your nightmares.

But what really caught my attention was how empty the place was. Normally, you couldn't move for heroes and warriors and would-be legends, fighting for a place at the bar and complaining bitterly over the bartender's inflexible rules when it came to extending credit. This time there was no crowd, no bartender; only a whole lot of silence. You could almost hear the wine aging. And half-way down the bar, Julien Advent sat perfectly poised on a tall bar-stool, drinking pink champagne. With his little finger properly extended, of course.

Julien Advent: tall, dark, and handsome in the old style, the great Victorian Adventurer who fell through a Timeslip in the nineteenth century and emerged in the Nightside in the nineteen sixties. And didn't appear to have aged a day since. Julien is the real deal, a real hero and a complete gentleman. He tends not to approve of me, or my methods—except when he needs me to do something no-one else can.

We're friends, sometimes despite ourselves. I walked over to him, looked briefly but longingly at the bottles behind the bar, so near and yet so far, and nodded to Julien.

"You could offer me a drink, you know. I could be persuaded."

"No, you couldn't," he said calmly. "You don't have time."

"Oh hell," I said. "It's one of those cases, is it? And where is everybody, anyway?"

"Out and about," said Julien. "Doing their best to keep a lid on things. Since Walker died, so very suddenly and unexpectedly, the news has shot round the Nightside. And a great many not-at-all-nice people have been running wild, taking advantage. Seeing what they can get away with until Walker's replacement steps up to dispense law and justice and general beatings. That's you, by the way. But since you weren't immediately available, I deputised everyone in the Club and sent them out into the streets to restore order, by any means necessary, and slap down anyone who looked like getting ambitious."

"I would have got round to it," I said. "I've been a bit . . . distracted."

Julien studied me thoughtfully over the rim of his champagne glass. "There's something different about you though I can't put my finger on it. . . . Either way, it will have to wait. There's trouble down at the Mammon Emporium. The biggest mall in the Nightside is in very great danger of going off bang. But first, John, I have to ask you . . . Did you really have to kill Walker?"

"Yes," I said. "It was necessary. He'd gone too far into the dark."

Julien clearly heard something in my voice because he put his glass down on the bar and leaned forward on his bar-stool. "I never did understand what he saw in you, or you in him. You seemed to work well enough together, when you weren't trying to kill each other. He respected you. I know that."

"I respected him," I said. "Best enemy I ever had."

"He was more than that."

"Of course. He was Walker."

"Well," said Julien, "he was dying, after all, and not in a good way. I suppose you could call his death a mercy killing."

"No," I said. "I don't think you could call it that."

He waited expectantly, but I had nothing more to say. Let Walker take his secrets with him, the good and the bad. In the end, Julien nodded and picked up his glass again, which had mysteriously refilled itself with more pink champagne. One of the perks of Club membership.

"I'll send some of my people to collect the body."

"There is no body," I said.

Julien raised an elegant eyebrow. "Hard core, John."

"Where are the rest of the new Authorities?" I said. Not because I gave a damn but because I felt like changing the subject.

"They're . . . not entirely comfortable with you yet," said Julien. "My colleagues are currently upstairs, arguing over whether or not to accept you as our new representative. Walker wanted you, and I recommended you, but . . ."

"Yes," I said. "But."

I remembered meeting these people before, in a devastated future Nightside, where they were the last human survivors, and my devoted Enemies. Doing their best to kill me in their past before I could bring about the terrible future they were living in. Time travel can really mess with your head. Just say no.

Julien suddenly recognised the gold pocket-watch I was still holding in my hand. "How did you get that?"

"Walker left it to me in his will."

"We haven't even found his will yet!"

I shrugged. "Details, details . . ."

Julien sighed. "And you wonder why nobody trusts you . . ."

"No, I don't. I don't give a damn. However," I said, changing the subject again by brute force, "if I'm going to work for the Authorities, shouldn't I have an official job title? Something big and dramatic, to strike terror into the hearts of evildoers?"

"You do have a title," said Julien. "Walker."

"What?"

"You didn't really think that was his name, did you? I don't think anyone ever knew what his real name was, the one he used in the outside world, when he went home to his family. Henry was real enough, I think. He always looked like a Henry to me. He used it often enough, and he seemed comfortable with it. Especially with his closest friends, like the Collector, and your father. But I couldn't even say for sure whether they ever knew his real surname. To know the true name of a thing is to have power over it, and Henry would never have allowed that. No; he was Walker, like all his predecessors in the job."

"Then Hadleigh Oblivion was a Walker, too?" I said, trying to get my head round the idea.

"Before he went so thoroughly off message, and disappeared into the Deep School, in search of mysteries, and ended up the Detective Inspectre. Whatever the hell that is, and I have a horrible suspicion I'm not going to like it when I find out . . . There have been any number of Walkers, down the years, representing the Authorities as their Voice in the Nightside."

I scowled at Julien. "Why didn't I know this?"

"You could have asked. It wasn't exactly a state secret."

I decided to change the subject again. "Where's Hadleigh now?"

"I'd feel a lot more secure if I knew the answer to that one. No doubt he's out and about in the Nightside, walking up and down in it and disapproving of things in horrible ways. I keep waiting for the other incendiary to drop. Whatever mysteries people learn in the Deep School, it doesn't do much for their sense of tolerance."

"So," I said, "Walker is a title . . . like the Walking Man?"

"Might be a coincidence; might not. That's the Nightside for you. Either way; you're Walker now. Whether you like it or not. But let me be blunt, John . . . The case I'm about to send you on is your first official mission for the Authorities. If you should prove to be . . . not up to the job, the others will ignore my recommendations and appoint someone else."

"Never wanted the job anyway," I said.

"That's why I wanted you," Julien said dryly. "But think on this: you got away with a lot because Walker let you. For his various reasons. You might not do as well with some of the names I've heard proposed."

I smiled briefly. "I handled Walker. And if I could handle him, I can handle anyone."

"That is exactly the attitude that's going to get you killed one of these days. There are . . . things out there that even the mighty John Taylor can't handle. You'd do well to arrange a support team, of people you can trust, to be your backup. Walker had all kinds of useful people on his payroll, to be his eyes and ears in the Nightside, or help him deal with the more specialised problems, and naturally you'll inherit them . . . but there are going to be times when only brute force and massed fire-power will do. Walker had the support of the Army and the Church, when necessary, and he also had the Reasonable Men. You do remember the Reasonable Men, don't you, John? You should; you killed them."

"They annoyed me," I said. "Bunch of stuck-up pricks and bully-boys. I can do better than them. How about Suzie Shooter, Dead Boy, Razor Eddie . . ."

"I meant people my fellow Authorities could approve of! Though admittedly, those appalling friends of yours would scare the crap out of all the right people . . ."

"I think we should talk about the mission," I said determinedly. "What's up with the Mammon Emporium that it might go boom? Someone finally realised how unfair and extortionate the prices are? Profit margins down there are so appalling the business owners have to hire transcendental mathematicians just to do their tax returns. And their returns policy sucks like a hooker when the rent's due."

"You always did have an elegant turn of phrase, John. Some three hours ago, a man walked into the Mammon Emporium and announced that he was there to blow the whole place up. He gave every impression of being full-on crazy, and perhaps even industrial-strength Looney Tunes; but it only took one scan by the mall's security people to reveal he was quite serious. He'd made himself into, or allowed himself to be made into, a soulbomb. I can tell from your expression that you have never heard of a soulbomb. I have, which is probably why I don't sleep as well as I used to.

"When you blow something apart, you get energy, yes? Blow an atom apart, and you get a lot of energy. Blow a soul apart, and you get the kind of energy, the kind of explosion, that can blow holes in reality itself. It has happened in the past. There are those who see it as the ultimate form of suicide. Destroy your soul, and you get to cheat Heaven and Hell."

"So," I said, "we're talking about an explosion big enough to destroy the whole mall?"

"At the very least. The Mammon Emporium is positively crawling with all the very latest kinds of protections, magical and scientific, hopefully enough to contain the explosion. But nobody knows for sure. We could lose the whole district. We could lose the whole Nightside . . . And God alone knows what kind of fallout a soulbomb would produce . . ."

"He's been in there three hours, and he hasn't gone off yet?" I said. "What's stopping him?"

"You are," said Julien. "The soulbomber says he's waiting for you to come and talk with him. Refuses to talk to anyone else and says he'll blow himself up if anyone tries to move him. We sent in specially trained negotiators, but he threatened to detonate immediately if they weren't removed.

Apparently, he became quite hysterical when they didn't leave fast enough. We said we'd send for you, and he quietened down a bit. Now he's sitting there, right in the middle of the mall, sweating heavily and singing sad songs. We've evacuated the Emporium. Wasn't easy. Hell hath no fury like a shopper cheated out of a bargain."

"Was there a sale on?"

Julien glared at me pityingly. "There's always a sale on at the Mammon Emporium. The shop owners didn't want to go, either, and leave their businesses unprotected; apparently their insurance doesn't cover soulbombers. Though I would have thought they were the exact opposite of an Act of God. Anyway, the place is quite empty now. Your mission, should you choose to accept it, and you'd bloody well better, is to go in there, talk to the crazy person, and stop him."

"Stop him what?"

"Stop him anything!"

I thought about it. "Am I empowered to negotiate? What can I offer him?"

"Not a damned thing," Julien said firmly. "We don't give in to blackmail. We can't afford to, or everyone in the Nightside would be trying their luck. Of course, feel free to offer him anything you can think of, as long as it's clearly understood we won't deliver on anything you promise. How convincing a liar are you? Actually, no, don't tell me. I don't want to know. It's up to you, John; talk him down or take him down, by any means you deem necessary. But you have to understand: the soulbomber isn't the real problem."

"Of course not," I said. "That would be far too simple."

"If the soulbomber should detonate, he could destroy some or all of the hundreds of dimensional gateways inside the Emporium, the doors to other Earths, other realities, from which most of the businesses get their stock. Which would seem bad enough, but there are levels of appallingness here.

The explosions could just destroy the gateways, effectively shutting off the doors. The cost of replacing them would be almost unimaginable; the Emporium might very well go out of business, with all kinds of nasty economic repercussions. Let us contemplate the idea of falling dominoes for a moment, then move on.

"That's actually the best option we could hope for if he goes off bang. We could survive that. However, the destructive energies generated by an exploded soul could be enough to blast right through the gateways and cause untold death and destruction on the other sides. The occupants of those other dimensions might well become so enraged that they would invade the Nightside, looking for revenge and compensation. Probably both. Hundreds of armies, from hundreds of dimensions . . . The Angel War and the Lilith War were bad enough . . ."

"They weren't my fault!"

"Yes, they were! Everything's your fault until proven otherwise."

"You haven't finished, have you?" I said. "You're saving the best for last. I can tell. What else could go wrong?"

"The destruction of hundreds of dimensional gateways might be enough to fracture reality and blast open other doors. The kind that lead to places we like to think of as Outside our reality. The kind of door we've done everything but barricade and nail shut from this side. You know the kind of dimensions I'm talking about, John. Where Things from Outside have been waiting for millennia, just for a chance to force their way in and destroy every living thing in creation. Do I really need to say the Names?"

"Better not," I said. "You never know what might be listening. So any or all of these things could happen if the soul-bomber detonates? Wonderful. Terrific. The gift that keeps on giving . . . Let's hope he's only feeling a bit depressed and will respond to a nice hug and some ice-cream. Okay, obvious question. Who stands to profit from something like this? You said yourself, it isn't an insurance scam."

"I have people working behind the scenes," said Julien, "asking those very questions in all kinds of persuasive ways. Never underestimate the Nightside's ability to profit from even the greatest disaster or atrocity. There has to be somebody behind this. It's not a cheap or an easy thing, to turn a man into a soulbomb. Even if you've got a willing fool to work on, ready to sacrifice his entire existence for . . . what? Money? A cause? Revenge? There has to be some plan, some hidden purpose, at the back of this. A pay-off big enough to make the risk acceptable."

"You know, the soulbomber did ask for me by name," I said. "This could all be a trap designed to lure me in."

"It isn't always about you, John," Julien said patiently.

"Maybe not," I said. "But it's the safest way to bet."

"They wouldn't blow up the entire Mammon Emporium, and risk fracturing reality, just to get at you!"

"They might. Depends on who 'they' are. Now I have to go in—if only to find out what the hell's going on and who I've upset this time. Tell me everything you've done so far, so I won't repeat anything."

Julien shrugged. "About what you'd expect. I sent in every professional specialist at my disposal: bomb squad, negotiators, priests, witches, CSI . . . and one of the most experienced and expensive whores in the Nightside, on the chance she might be able to . . . distract him from his purpose and give him a new interest in life. Didn't work. Apparently he blushed a shade of red not normally seen in nature and threatened to blow himself up right there and then if she didn't put all her clothes back on and go away."

I made a mental note to check the mall's CCTV footage later. If there was a later.

"No matter what we say or offer, he just keeps repeating

that he'll only talk to you. John, we really can't afford to lose the Emporium. There's a lot of money at stake here, not to mention a massive loss of prestige and tourists. You wouldn't believe how much tax money the Emporium dumps into our economy every year. We're getting a lot of hard talk from the various business owners to Do Something, along with all kinds of nasty and inventive threats of what they'll do if it all goes horribly wrong."

"So," I said, "no pressure, then. Don't let the mall get destroyed; don't let the dimensional gates get destroyed; don't let the Outsiders force their way into our reality and destroy everything that lives. How the hell am I supposed to talk some sense into someone crazy enough to allow himself to be made into a soulbomb?"

Julien grinned. "I'm sure you'll find a way."

"You can go off people, you know," I said.

The Mammon Emporium is not only the biggest mall in the Nightside, but quite possibly in the world. Opinion is divided over how many floors there are because some of them aren't always there, some only appear on special occasions, and they're always adding more. And yes, the mall is much bigger on the inside than it is on the outside. Such spells come as standard in the Nightside, or we'd never fit everything in. Because of the mall's size, you don't need a map to get round; you need a spirit guide and a compass. The Mammon Emporium specialises in brand-names, franchises, and weird alternatives from any number of different Earths. Just the thing for the Nightside, where tastes and palates tend to grow jaded really quickly; for people who've seen it all, done it all, and produced their own T-shirts to boast about it afterwards.

The Portable Timeslip dropped me off right on the edge of the large crowd that had gathered outside the Emporium. Shoppers who'd been ejected from the mall, much against their will; shop owners mopping the sweat from their brows as they commiserated with each other over loss of trade; and a whole bunch of interested onlookers, quite ready to risk a massive explosion if only for the chance to see something new. There's nothing so popular in the Nightside as a free show. Vendors and street traders already had their stalls up, selling commemorative T-shirts, hastily improvised souvenirs, protective amulets of dubious efficiency, and something wriggling on a stick. (Very tasty! Get them while they're hot!)

I took a few moments to get my head back together before walking calmly and confidently into the crowd. This much I had learned from Walker: look like you know what you're doing, and everyone else will assume that you do. That said, some people in the crowd looked pleased to see me, some didn't, and some took one look at me and started running. Oh ye of little faith.

Half a dozen business owners advanced on me, shoulder to shoulder, and everyone else fell back to give them room. You could tell who they were immediately from their superior tailoring and sense of entitlement. I gave them a thoughtful look, and they all crashed to a halt a respectful distance short of me. The crew drew back even further to let us talk, but not so far they couldn't eavesdrop. There was a lot of glancing at each other amongst the shop owners and a certain amount of pushing and shoving as they tried to agree on a spokesman. None of them wanted to give way to any of the others, but none of them was too keen on talking to the infamous John Taylor. I let them get on with it while I looked them over. They didn't need to identify themselves; I knew who they were. Their names and faces were all over the glossy magazines and the giveaways, trying to persuade me to buy something I knew for a fact I didn't need, at twice the price I wouldn't have paid anyway.

Raymond Orbison, a long drink of cold water in baggy white slacks and T-shirt, supplied musical recordings from other Earths, where music and people had taken surprisingly different directions. Where Marianne Faithfull was the lead singer in the Rolling Stones; Dolly Parton sang opera; and the Elvis Twins sang Country & Western. And Kate Bush fronted Rockbitch.

Then there was Martin Broome, fat and prosperous and perspiring heavily, who specialised in strange food and weird dishes from Earths where human biology was not so much different as downright eccentric. Broome offered dishes with different trace elements and altered isomers; eat as much as you like and never put on an ounce because your body doesn't recognise it as food. Very popular, and very highly priced. And absolutely no warnings about possible side effects, such as bloating, anal leakage, sudden meltdowns in the night, and occasional spontaneous combustion.

And, of course, there was Esmeralda Corr, tall and willowy in flapping silks, who provided exotic perfumes from exotic sources, like moss from the canals of Mars, fungi squeezings from sunken R'Lyeh, and musk glands from extinct animals. They all smelled the same to me, but then, I'm a man.

Orbison finally took the lead and fixed me with his usual watery-eyed stare. "You're who the Authorities sent? You're the new Walker? I can feel my palpitations coming on. Well, don't just stand there! You've got to do something, Taylor! People want to shop! All the time we're standing round here, we're losing money!"

"You'll be losing that finger if you keep prodding it in my direction," I said.

Oribison was overcome with a sudden modesty and insisted on falling back. Esmeralda Corr immediately took his place, hands on hips and pointing her prominent bosoms at me like loaded weapons. "What are you going to do, Taylor? I think we have a right to be consulted before you undertake any operation that might put our livelihoods at risk!"

"I'm more concerned with lives than livelihoods," I said.

"What is that perfume you're wearing? Is it actually legal to smell like that in public? Step back a few paces. A few more . . . Right. I'm here to shut the soulbomb down. That's all you need to know. Now, have any of you upset anyone recently? More than usual, I mean. Someone who might bear a grudge?"

They all looked at each other, and there was much averting of eyes and general shrugging. No-one had to say anything. Business was business in the Nightside, and devil take the hindmost. Sometimes literally. But after a certain amount of nudging, elbowing, and general intimidation, Broome was finally moved to admit that they had no-one special in mind. There had been no advance warning, no threats or ransom demands, and no-one had come forward to claim responsibility. The bomber was a complete stranger to all of them. He'd walked into the mall and threatened to blow up his soul.

They all turned their best business-like glares on me. They'd done all that could be reasonably expected of them, their glares implied, and now it was up to me. So if anything went wrong, it was all my fault. But there was a certain expectant look to them as well because I was the new Walker, and they were curious to see if I was up to it. I was curious, too.

Walker had only been dead for a few hours; but everyone knew. News travels fast in the Nightside, especially bad news.

I walked through the crowd, and it opened up to let me pass. It had all gone very quiet. Except for the bookmakers, who were already offering odds.

I strolled under the huge M and E that marked the main entrance to the mall, and a whole new world opened up before me. Shops and businesses, chains and franchises, speciality stores and perv parlours stretched away before me, for just a bit further than the eye could comfortably see. Corridors and passageways branched and separated, and stilled elevators led up to more floors and even more wonders and marvels, all major credit cards accepted. There was a map floating on the air in the lobby, a huge 3D hologram affair of such complexity that staring at it long enough could start you speaking in tongues. I chose a direction and started walking.

I looked carefully about me, but the whole place was deserted. Thankfully, someone had shut down the piped Muzak, and there wasn't a sound to be heard anywhere apart from the gentle humming of the fierce fluorescent lighting and the distant rumble of the air-conditioning. It could still be a trap. Either for me, specifically, or for whoever took over as the new Walker. Certainly, I'd made enough enemies in my time, and in the Past and Future, too.

Why had the soulbomber demanded to speak to me, and only me? Julien had shown me a photo of the guy before I left; but I didn't recognise him. There was nothing special or striking about him. If anything, he'd looked almost defiantly average. Did he want to lure me in, to be sure of getting me? Did he need to look me in the face, to tell me something important to him, before he could destroy himself? Or had he heard of my ability to work miracles on a budget and drop-kick victory from the jaws of defeat, and was hoping to be talked out of it? Or possibly even rescued if this hadn't been his idea in the first place . . . It's amazing the things a man will do—for money or fame or if his loved ones are threatened.

My footsteps echoed loudly on the quiet, I could actually hear my own breathing, and my heart was hammering in my chest. Malls aren't supposed to be quiet or empty. It felt unnatural. And then I stopped abruptly as I heard footsteps up ahead, coming my way. I slipped my left hand into my coat-pocket and let my fingers drift over certain useful items . . . and then took my hand out again. It was the Nightside CSI—first in, last out, as always. He came round the corner, stopped when he saw me, then smiled and nodded amiably enough. The Nightside CSI is only one man, pleasant enough, calm and easy-going, and very professional. It probably helps that he has multiple personality disorder, with a sub-personality for every speciality and discipline in his profession. (One to handle fingerprints, another to examine blood spatter, or look for magical residues . . .) He's really quite good at his job though he does tend to argue with himself.

Between himself, he knows everything he needs to know.

Each sub-personality has a different voice. Some of them are women. I've never asked.

"Alistair Hoob," I said. "As I live and breathe heavily. No-one told me you were still in here. How are we doing today?"

"As well as can be expected, Mr. Taylor. Not much in the way of evidence to offer you, I'm afraid. (You didn't check for fingerprints!) (What was the point?) (Hush, we're talking.) All the soulbomber brought in was himself, and he wouldn't allow me to get anywhere near him. (Has anyone seen my wetwipes?)"

Alistair Hoob is a big blocky type with a shock of bushy red hair, one green eye and one blue, and a reasonably sane smile that comes and goes according to who's talking. He always wears the same baggy white sweater with holes in it, grubby cream slacks, and cheap knock-off trainers. He carries a battered old briefcase that unfolds and unfolds, to contain all his (very) specialised equipment. I once saw him open it wide enough to pull out a chemical lab, an X-ray machine, and a rather surprised-looking rabbit.

"Have you spoken to our soulbomb, Alistair?" I said.

"Oh, of course. (Seems sane enough, if a bit gloomy.) Bit frustrating, really, as he didn't want to talk to me. (Smells funny.) He was quite insistent that he would only talk to John Taylor; but he wouldn't say why. And he wouldn't let me get close enough to run any useful tests. (Elephant!) (Shut up!)"

"But you are certain he's a soulbomber?"

"Unfortunately, yes. You wouldn't believe the state of his aura. Even sitting still, he's giving off so many negative vibrations he's contaminating his surroundings. It'll take weeks to scour the psychic stain out of the area. Assuming you can talk him down, of course. (Oh, well done, Mr. Tact.) I've run all the usual tests on the Emporium, and I can tell you that no-one else is in here with us. (No life signs anywhere.) (Except for the exotic pet shops on the thirteenth floor, and they're all securely locked down.) (Spiders shouldn't get that big. There ought to be a law. It's unnatural, and it might give them ideas.) So once I'm gone, you're on your own, Mr. Taylor. Best of luck. (Bye-bye.)"

"Are all the dimensional doors and gateways properly shut down and closed off?" I said, when I could get a word in edgeways.

"For the moment, yes. But if the soulbomber should go *boom!* all bets are off. We can't predict the outcome because there's never been a soulbomb explosion next to a dimensional door before. (I checked before I came in here. Went to the Library, and everything.) There was a soulbomb explosion some twenty-odd years ago, in Tokyo's fabled Sinister Zone. Blew it right out of reality. Just a bloody big crater now, with energies radiating in all directions that can mutate your DNA if you even think about going to take a look at it. The Japanese have been throwing all kinds of lizards into it, hoping they'll mutate into giant forms . . . They do love their cinema, the Japanese. (I like the Muppets.) (Has anyone noticed it's getting cold in here? I should have brought a scarf.)"

"Has a soulbomb ever exploded in the Nightside?" I said, frowning.

"Not . . . as such, Mr. Taylor. In fact, I'm really quite curious to observe what might happen here. (From a distance.) (A safe distance.) (Why are we still standing round talking?)

I could learn all kinds of fascinating things. (From a distance.) (Yes, we've established that.)"

"Can you tell me anything about the soulbomber himself?" I said desperately. "What kind of a man is he?"

"Troubled, clearly. (Looney Tunes.) (Bit harsh . . .) The subject is male, middle-aged, no wedding ring. Could be a midlife crisis. (Should have bought a Porsche, like everyone else.) Didn't have much to say for himself, just *Go away* and *Where's John Taylor?* He seemed determined enough, in a quiet way. (Stubborn.) No signs of fear or uncertainty. No hysterics. I couldn't get close enough to run medical scans, but he seemed physically sound."

"Do me one last favour," I said. "Run one last scan of the Emporium; check for mechanical or magical booby-traps."

"Way ahead of you, Mr. Taylor. Done and done. I am a professional, after all. It's all quiet; nothing here that shouldn't be. And I am now leaving the Emporium, while the leaving is good. (I'm gonna leave old Durham town . . .) I may even leave the Nightside, to be on the safe side. Not that I doubt your abilities, Mr. Taylor, but there are limits to how professional I'm prepared to be. If the dimensional doors go down . . . (There are those who say . . .) (No, there aren't; you're thinking of something else.)"

"The Emporium does have a lot of protections in place," I said.

"Oh yes, Mr. Taylor. Absolutely and quite definitely, there are many protections in place. First-class protections, magical and scientific. Unfortunately, someone has shut them all down. Every last one of them. In advance. (Makes you think, doesn't it?) Good-bye, Mr. Taylor. Best of luck. Soulbomber's down that way; keep going, you can't miss him."

"Any last advice?"

"Try not to upset him."

He hurried off, and I was left alone in the Emporium. Just me, and the soulbomber.

• • •

I'd never known the Emporium to be so still, so silent. Like the calm before the storm. I headed for the centre of the mall, following Alistair Hoob's directions. My footsteps seemed to echo increasingly loudly on the quiet, carrying news of my progress. The lights shone as brightly as ever, fierce and characterless fluorescent light, and there were no shadows anywhere. But it felt as though there were. For all the intense illumination, it felt like I was walking into darkness.

I could feel the weight of Excalibur, invisibly scabbarded on my back. It was a comforting feeling, like it was watching my back and holding my hand, a companion in my time of need. But it also felt like it was trying to warn me of something. No words; only this feeling that there was something very bad here, apart from the soulbomber. But sometimes you have to suck it up and walk into the trap if that's what it takes to get to the heart of the matter. I slowed my pace, wandering along quite casually, looking into the shop-windows. Never let them know they've got you worried. I surreptitiously checked every doorway and every side passage as I came to them, just in case; but there was never anyone there.

Some of the goods on display were quite interesting. The Elizabethan Goode Foode Shoppe, offering hedgehog in clay, coney on a stick, hedgerow salad soup (every dish a surprise!), puffin flambé. And jugged venison, in very large jugs. Given what some of our ancestors ate in the past, it amazes me that any of us are here.

The Twenty-Second Century Magik Shop had a special sale on Pickled Pixies, Flying Slippers, Old Ones Repellent, and a new exorcism plug-in for your computer. I lingered a while before the window of a specialist bookshop called Pornucopia, which sold specially bound editions of the private pornography written by famous authors, for their own pleasure, never intended for publication. But once you're dead, it's all fair game, so . . . *Miss Marple at the Isle of Lesbos*, *Lady Chatterly's Gang Bang*, and Barbara Cartland's *Strap-on Frenzy*.

Sometimes I think if it wasn't for bad taste, the Mammon Emporium wouldn't have any taste at all. I made a mental note to look back later. If there was a later.

I realised my path was taking me right past the Emporium's one and only real oracle, so I decided to pay it a quiet visit. On a mission like this, information is ammunition. The oracle doesn't look like much: just a traditional stone-walled wishing well, with a circle of stained glass round it, a patchy red slate roof, and a bucket on a chain. It couldn't be more tacky if it tried. A sign in appallingly twee language invited you to throw a coin into the well, make a wish, and toss your worries away. Whoever wrote that clearly knew nothing about oracles. Officially, it was all a harmless bit of fun for the kiddies. What better disguise for one of the few truly reliable oracles in the Nightside? I had approached it for help once before and knew better than to expect anything actually helpful. Like everyone else in the Nightside, the oracle had its own agenda.

The well knew I was coming before I did. I hadn't even turned the corner when it called out to me.

"Well, well, the one and only John Taylor; which is just as well because I don't think I could stand it if there were more of you. Your entire existence plays merry hell with the timelines. Look over there in the corner; see that woman, crying her eyes out? That's Fate, that is. Hello again, John. Knew you'd be back."

"I never knew an oracle that was so in love with its own voice," I said. "Now do me a favour and keep your voice down. The soulbomber isn't far from here, and we really don't want to upset him."

"I know! I know he's there, and I know why he's there, which is more than you do. I know everything. Or at least, everything that matters, and I fake the rest. I even know what you're going to ask before you ask it, and you really aren't going to like the answers."

"Tell me anyway," I said, leaning heavily on its stone wall. "What can you tell me about this soulbomber?"

"Cross my palm with silver, sweetie, and I shall unfold wonders and marvels . . ."

"Cut the crap. I'm not a tourist. You haven't got a palm, and no-one's used silver coins for years. You get the usual—one drop of blood, and that's it."

"You have no sense of drama."

I pricked the tip of my left index finger with the sliver of unicorn's horn I carry in my lapel to warn against poisons and let one fat drop of blood fall into the dark interior of the well. The oracle made a really disgusting satisfied sound, and I winced despite myself.

"All right, you old ham," I said. "You've had your payment, now answer the question. What do I have to do to stop the soulbomber?"

"There's nothing you can do. The soulbomb will detonate some forty-one minutes from now."

I blinked a few times. "That's it?"

"Afraid so. There isn't a single possible future where the soulbomb doesn't detonate."

"No way of avoiding it?"

"None at all."

"Can't I try talking to him?"

"If you like."

"Will that help?"

"No. Doesn't matter what you do or say: Mr. Soulbomber, he go boom."

"Well, you're a lot of use!"

"Lot of people say that to me . . ."

"All right," I said, searching desperately for some solid ground. "Let's try something else. What can you tell me about Excalibur?"

"You mean that appallingly powerful thing hanging off your back? Burning so brightly I can't even look at it? Well, to start with, it's not really a sword. It only looks like one."

"What is it, then?"

"Reply cloudy, try again later. I told you, it's so potent I can't even get a good look at it. You could cut the world in half with a weapon like that."

"I thought you said it isn't a sword?" I said.

"It isn't. It's much more than a sword. More than a weapon. It's the lever you turn to move the world."

"Can you tell me why it's entered my life?"

"I see you going on a long journey . . ."

"If you tell me I'm going to meet a tall dark stranger, I swear I will unzip right here and now and piss into you."

"You would, too, wouldn't you? Bully . . ."

"Hold everything," I said. "You're predicting a journey in my future. How can I have a future if the soulbomb's going to go off in forty-one minutes?"

"Actually, rather less than that now. But yes, I see your point." The oracle hummed tunelessly to itself for a moment. "Look, your whole existence is so unlikely it gives me a pain in the rear I haven't got just thinking about it. It's hard to be sure about anything where you're concerned."

"Because my mother was a Biblical Myth?"

"That doesn't help, certainly. But it's more that you're involved in so many vital, important, and earth-shaking things, that every decision you make changes not only your life but everyone else's as well."

"It's the destiny thing, isn't it?" I said.

"See that sacred-looking guy over there, with the nervous twitch, trying to comfort Fate? That's Destiny, that is."

"Whatever happened to free will?"

"I do have an answer to that," said the well smugly, "but it would make your head explode. I could tell you a lengthy but complex parable if you like."

"Would it help?"

"Not really."

"But you are completely certain that the soulbomb is going to explode?"

"Oh yes. In thirty-nine minutes."

"I hate you."

"I knew you were going to say that."

I ran through the rest of the corridors to be sure of reaching the soulbomber in time. The oracle is shifty, crafty, and absolutely glories in being spitefully obtuse; but it's never wrong. My only hope was that it had seen some kind of future for me afterwards. Otherwise, I'd have said, *Sod this for a lark*, and legged it for the nearest exit. There had to be something I could do. Contain the explosion, perhaps, using the mall's shields? Throw the soulbomber through one of the dimensional doorways? I told myself I'd think of something, and tried very hard to believe it. After all, I wouldn't lie to me about something like that.

I found him sitting quite casually on the floor, in the very centre of the mall. A balding, dumpy, middle-aged man in shabby clothes, with sad eyes and a tired mouth. Sitting on the floor, doing nothing in particular, waiting for me to turn up. I let him have a good look at me before I moved cautiously forward. I was a bit concerned that the sight of me might be enough to set him off; but he didn't look scared, or angry, or impatient. He just looked . . . relieved, that his waiting was finally at an end. He nodded to me, briefly, and I stopped a careful distance away from him. He didn't look like a terrorist, or a fanatic. Maybe I could still talk him out of it.

"Hi," I said. "I'm John Taylor."

"I know," he said. His voice was reassuringly calm, and normal. "He showed me several photos of you before they sent me in here, so I could be sure it was you. I'm Oliver

Newbury. You won't have heard of me. No-one has. I was an ordinary, everyday guy, and I liked it that way. I didn't ask for much, didn't want much; but the world took it all anyway . . . You wouldn't think you could get bored, waiting to die; but you can. Feels like I've been here for hours. And no; you can't talk me out of this. My wife is dead. I'm crippled with debts I can't pay and a family I can't support any more. This is all that's left—one last act of rage against a viciously unfair and uncaring world. He's promised to pay off all my debts, you see, if I do this thing. He'll see my children are protected and cared for. It's all I can do for them."

"If you're so determined to die," I said, "for revenge, for money . . . why have you waited to talk to me?"

"That was part of the deal," he said, not unkindly. "To lure you in and take you with me when I go. He said you wouldn't be able to resist a trap baited with your name. He said you were arrogant and predictable. And you're here, aren't you?"

"Don't go off bang just yet," I said. "I'm also curious. What's the point of all this? What does your benefactor hope to gain from your suicide?"

"Apparently, when I explode, the energies released will destroy every dimensional door in the Emporium," Oliver said calmly. "Blow them all right off their hinges and allow Things from Outside to come in and destroy the Nightside. And please: yes, I do know what I'm saying. Don't try and appeal to my better nature. I don't care how many people die, or how much of the Nightside gets trampled underfoot by the Outsiders. No-one cared when I lost my wife, and my job, and couldn't look after my children any more. I'm a suicide, Mr. Taylor. My life is over. I volunteered to be made into this awful thing, a soulbomb. It hurt like hell, but it was worth it because I can't feel anything any more, only cold. I'm always cold now. At least this way, my death will mean something. It'll make a difference. I get to show my anger and contempt at a world that let me down, then kicked me while I was down. I get to punish it as it deserves."

"Do you know the kind of Things from Outside we're talking about?" I said carefully. "They exist in dimensions far from ours, far from reality, as we understand it. They're not even life, as we understand it. They hate life, and destroy it wherever they find it. They want to destroy the Light, until there's nothing left but the Darkness they hide in."

"You're saying they're evil?" he said politely.

"They're so different from us they're beyond simple labels like Good and Evil. Those are human beliefs, human concepts. They're bigger than that, beyond that, monstrous beyond anything we can imagine because our concept of evil isn't big enough to encompass the things they do. We call them Outsiders because they're outside anything we can understand or accept: outside morality, or sanity, maybe even Life or Death."

"You're very eloquent," said Oliver. "But I told you . . . I don't care. Let them eat up the Nightside, let them burn it up, let all the people die. Where were they when I needed them?"

"You still care about your children," I said. "That's who you're doing this for, right? You let the Outsiders loose in our world, and they won't stop here. Eventually, they will get to where your children are and make them scream with horror before they destroy them."

"That won't happen," said Oliver. "He promised the Outsiders would be contained inside the Nightside. He made a deal with them."

"And he believed them?"

I was about to try for this particular fool's name when I noticed that Oliver's breath was steaming on the air before him. Mine, too. The mall was a hell of a lot colder than it had been. Fern-like patterns of hoar-frost crept quickly across the shop-windows and spread unevenly across the floor, walls, and ceiling. And though the overhead fluorescent lights were still burning just as fiercely, darkness appeared in all the surrounding corridors, one by one, filling them up, then edging slowly forward until only a narrow pool of light remained, surrounding Oliver and me.

"Something's coming," I said. "Something's draining all the warmth and energy out of our surroundings, from the world itself, so it can force its way into our reality. Something from Outside is coming here, to talk to us."

"But I haven't blown open any of the gateways yet," said Oliver.

"Something as powerful as an Outsider doesn't give a damn about doors," I said. "They come and go as they please. But they can't stay long if they force their way in; reality itself rejects them and forces them back out. This is only a messenger boy, here to announce their coming."

A fountain of vomit blasted up out of the floor, slammed against the ceiling, and rained down, thick and foul. Oliver cried out in disgust and scrambled up onto his feet. I grabbed him by the arm and dragged him out of the way. The foul stuff kept spurting up from the unbroken floor, hitting the ceiling and falling back again, a thick, pulsing pillar of vomit. The stink of it filled the passageway, harsh enough to choke on. Maggots curled and writhed in it. A great face slowly formed itself out of the vomit, its details just human enough to be disturbing. The unblinking dark eyes fixed on Oliver and me, and the ragged mouth stretched slowly in an awful smile.

"Don't let it get to you," I said to Oliver. "It's showing off. Trying to find some form that will scare us, disgust us, give it power over us. Think of it as psychological warfare, with a scratch-and-sniff ingredient."

"This is an Outsider?" said Oliver, past the hand he'd clapped over his mouth and nose to try to keep out the smell.

"No, I told you: this is one of their messenger boys. Hey, you! Yes, you, puke face! Knock off the special effects and take on a more traditional form, or I'll turn the fire hose on you! I am John Taylor, and I don't take no shit from demons!"

I did my best to sound confident, like I knew what I was doing, and the demon must have fallen for it because the horror show disappeared in a moment though the horrid smell still lingered. In its place stood a man in a white trench coat, with a familiar face. It was meant to be me, except it had bulging compound insect eyes, and blood dripped steadily from its ragged mouth. The thick blood fell down onto the white trench coat, leaving stains. Its wrists were stuffed deep into the pockets, and something about the way the figure held itself made me think I wouldn't want to see what it had instead of hands.

I looked it up and down and sniffed loudly.

"I suppose that's an improvement. What do you want?"

Its mouth moved uncertainly, as though it wasn't used to human speech. When it finally spoke, it sounded like it was choking on blood.

"We are coming here, and you can't stop us, John Taylor. Little human thing. When my masters finally manifest, in all their awful glory, the sight of them will blast the vision from your eyes and drive all you little human things howling into madness and misery. And they shall feast upon your suffering and make you worship them until you can't stand it any more."

"Ah," I said. "The usual. What is it about you demons that you always want to be loved and worshipped? Definite self-confidence problems there, and probably abandonment issues, too. Like I give a shit. What brings you to the Nightside?"

"My masters are not coming for the Nightside. They come for the whole world and everything in it. They have been offered an opening here, and they will use it to destroy everything that lives. You disgust us. Your very existence offends us. Meat that dares to think and dream. My masters will tear your upstart flesh apart and eat your souls, and even after you are dead, we will still find ways to make you suffer. Your torment will never end. For ever and ever and ever."

"I never get a straight answer, but I'll try one more time," I said. "Why?"

"Because we can. Because we want to. Because you can't stop us."

"Demons," I said. "I swear, you're worse than five-year-olds. Want want want and stamp your cloven feet if you can't get your own way. But . . . while you talk a good game, I think you're running scared. Your masters wouldn't waste all the power it takes to force a messenger into our reality unless you were worried something might go wrong. You can't come in . . . unless Oliver here blows the doors open; and your masters are shit scared I might talk Oliver out of it. That's it, isn't it? You're afraid his resolve is weakening. You're trying to bully him into serving you. How do you feel about that, Oliver? Now you know what your death would really bring about?"

Oliver took his hand away from his mouth, staring at the messenger with revulsion. "I never knew," he said. "I never even realised things like this existed. What good would it do, to die for my children, if it let things like this into their world? Can you stop this, Mr. Taylor?"

"Oh," I said, smiling easily. "I'm sure I can find a way."

I raised my gift, and it only took me a moment to find the dimensional rift that had let the messenger manifest in our reality. It took a complicated lattice of strange energies to hold the rift open, and it only took me a moment to find a fatal flaw in their arrangement. And then it was the easiest thing in the world to hit those energies in exactly the right place, and the whole thing collapsed. The messenger shrieked once, in shock and horror and surprise, and the collapsing rift sucked it back through and out of our reality. There was nothing left in the mall corridor but bright lights everywhere and the last vestiges of a really nasty smell.

I smiled confidently at Oliver and let myself relax a little, reaching for my psychic second wind. I really hadn't thought it would be that easy.

I took a deep breath and clapped Oliver on the shoulder. "Okay, I've got an idea. If you are going to blow yourself up, there might be a way you could do it for the best."

"Maybe I don't want to blow myself up," he said slowly. "Now that I've seen what that would lead to."

"I'm sorry," I said, and I really was, "but you've been made into a soulbomb. I don't think that can be undone. And since an oracle on the way here told me that you were going to detonate no matter what, I think the man who paid for you to be made over into what you are probably installed a fail-safe, to take the decision out of your hands after a certain time. So that even if you did have a failure of nerve, you'd still go off. But even if you can't decide not to explode, you can still choose when, and why. I need you to detonate when I tell you; and I will channel the blast away through this." I showed him the gold pocket-watch. "I know, it doesn't look like much, but it contains a Portable Timeslip under my control. I can find the dimensional rift the Outsiders will use to come through and turn your detonation away from the other dimensional doors, so that all the energies blast right through the rift as it opens. A soulbomb explosion is enough to hurt even Things from Outside. You can use your death to strike a blow against them. Won't be enough to kill them, but it'll hurt them, and make them back off and think again. How does that sound? You could be remembered as the man who saved the Nightside. How's that for making a difference?"

"How does that help my children?" he said bluntly. "If I don't do as I'm told, my children won't get the money."

I thought quickly. "How about this? I sell your story to the *Unnatural Inquirer*. All right, it's a rag, but they love stories like this. They'll pay top money; and I'll see it all goes to your children. I'll guarantee the paper does right by them."

"How can you guarantee that if I blow up, and you're still here? You can't teleport out; the Outsiders would stop you, wouldn't they?"

He was right. I'd been thinking I could escape the blast through the Portable Timeslip, but the Outsiders would have access to the dimensional short cut I travelled through. After the explosion, they'd be too busy with their own problems to worry about me, but until then . . . I thought some more, then I remembered, and smiled.

"I'll be fine," I said. "Don't worry, Oliver; I'm protected. I carry the sword Excalibur."

He looked at me. "Where? Do you have one of those subspace pocket things?"

I reached over my shoulder, took hold of the hilt, and drew the sword. The long, golden blade flashed brightly. Oliver's eyes widened.

"It's . . . beautiful. Everything I ever thought it would be. Can I touch it, hold it?"

He reached out a hand towards the sword, then immediately stopped and drew the hand back again.

"No. It wouldn't be right. Not with what I've made of myself. Nonetheless, it is good to know that there is still wonder in the world. There is still glory."

"Are you ready?" I said. "I don't mean to rush you, but there's no telling how much time we have left, before . . ."

"I'm ready if you are," he said steadily. "Let's do it."

"One last thing," I said. "Who set this up? Who planned all this and made you into a soulbomb?"

"Bijou de Montefort," he said. "One of the business owners in the mall. Do you know him?"

"Oh yes," I said. "I know him."

One of the Emporium's biggest success stories, de Montefort came from nowhere to make himself one of the richest men in the Nightside. He specialised in awakening demand for things people didn't even know they wanted, then selling it to them for ten times the price they would have paid if it hadn't suddenly been fashionable. But he'd come adrift with his last great idea: the Cloned Celebrity Long Pig franchise. Eat the celebrity of your choice! But he really should have asked permission first; a whole bunch of celebrities got together and sued him over unauthorised use of their image and identity, and they won big. Cleaned him out. Overnight, de Montefort's business empire collapsed, his credit rating was run out of town on a rail, and he was on the brink of losing everything. At which point, one assumes, he was contacted by a messenger from Outside, who offered a bargain. And he accepted, the fool.

I realised Oliver was looking at me. Bad time to be woolgathering. "How did he expect to profit from this?"

"He didn't tell me. All he said was that my death would make him King of the Nightside."

"Idiot. Outsiders never keep their bargains. They don't have to."

"I think we should do it now," said Oliver. "While I'm still . . . firm in my resolve. Good-bye, Mr. Taylor. When you see my children, tell them . . . some comforting lie."

"Yes," I said. "I can do that."

He closed his eyes and seemed to relax completely, as though finally putting down some terrible burden. He gave up the last thing that held him together, and when the explosion came, it was too big to see or hear. A light too bright to bear, and a sound that filled the world. I held Excalibur out before me, between my body and the blast, the point on the floor, the hilt before my face, my hands gripping the crosspiece. When the soul detonated, all I could do was hang on to the sword, blinded and deafened, torn at by forces I could barely recognise. I concentrated on my link to the gold watch in my pocket, using all my mental strength to funnel the energies through the Portable Timeslip and throw them at the Outsiders' dimensional rift. It wasn't difficult: once I started the process, the watch did most of the work. Otherwise, I'd never have been able to do it.

I clung to Excalibur as the storm raged round me, hanging on like a drowning man to a raft. The raging energies seemed to keep on coming, destruction without end, power beyond belief, and myself only the smallest mote in an angry god's eye. But the blast did end, eventually, and the world slowly came back into focus round me. I could see and hear again, left trembling and shaken by the storm that had passed. It took me a long moment to unclench my hands from Excalibur's cross-piece and look slowly round me. The mall seemed perfectly normal, undamaged, safe and sane again. The light was very bright, and there were no shadows anywhere. I reached into my pocket and closed the gold watch.

The Outsiders had been thrown back into Darkness, and Humanity had been saved because one man had given up his soul to do it. But he shouldn't have had to. My mission wasn't over yet. There was still justice to be administered. Justice, and vengeance.

I made my way back through the Mammon Emporium, then took a moment to compose myself before strolling outside to give the waiting crowd the good news. They all looked pretty relieved; presumably, they'd heard something of the explosion inside. I put their minds at ease with a few well-chosen words, and when I told them it was safe to go back inside again, they actually gave me a loud cheer before rushing right past me into the mall to resume their interrupted shopping.

Business as usual, in the Nightside.

As the onlookers in the crowd began to disappear, I raised my voice.

"Is Bijou de Montefort here?"

Everyone looked round, sensing that the evening's excitement might not be over yet. A small group of business owners came forward, half encouraging and half driving forward one Bijou de Montefort. He was an average-size, average-looking man, nothing remarkable about him at all, save perhaps that he was better tailored than most. He looked entirely defiant as he was brought to a halt before me and shook off the encouraging hands.

"I had time for a nice little chat with the soulbomber, before he went off," I said pleasantly. "He had a lot to say about you and how you planned to profit from his suicide. Did you really think you could bargain with the Outsiders and hold them to their agreement? Were you really ready to see us all die, so you could be King of Shit Heap?"

"You can't trust anything that man said," de Montefort snapped. "He was clearly mentally disturbed, or he wouldn't have made himself into a soulbomb." He met my gaze unflinchingly and actually seemed to grow in confidence as he listened to himself. He still thought he could talk his way out of this as he always had before. "You have no proof, Taylor, and no evidence, now that your only witness is dead. And I would advise you to choose your next words very carefully. I can afford the very best lawyers to protect my good name."

"Lawyers?" I said. "We don't need no stinking lawyers! Haven't you heard? I'm the new Walker. And this is Excalibur!"

I drew the sword, and the long blade appeared immediately in my hand, its golden light flaring brightly in the night. Everyone watching gasped and cried out. I slammed one hand onto de Montefort's shoulder and forced him to his knees in front of me. I brandished the sword above my head, and the crowd cried out in awe and wonder. Many of them dropped to their knees. Some of them were crying. De Montefort looked up at me, all the colour dropping out of his face.

"No! You can't do this! It's not fair!"

"It's justice," I said.

And I brought Excalibur round in a swift arc and cut his head off.

The sword sliced through his thick neck as though it were air. For a moment, de Montefort just knelt there, eyes wide; and then blood ran down from the long red cut. He convulsed, and his head snapped backwards and fell away. Blood fountained from the stump of his neck. He fell over sideways, his hands clutching spasmodically at nothing. I looked at Excalibur. There wasn't a drop of blood on the blade. I put it away, and immediately both sword and scabbard disappeared, invisible again. Some of the onlookers cried out again, in voices thick with loss and disappointment.

I walked straight at them, and the crowd fell back and split apart, opening up a wide aisle for me to walk through. I kept moving, not looking at anyone. I was considering what I'd done. I have killed before, in my time, when I absolutely had to; but I'm not an executioner. I'd killed de Montefort coolly and calmly, without even thinking twice about it. And that wasn't like me. It was what Walker would have done . . . but I never wanted to be like him. I had to wonder whether the impulse might have come from somewhere else. Whether merely possessing the sword Excalibur was enough to affect my mind, influence my judgement. I realised I'd come to a halt, and was frowning so hard my forehead ached. People were actually backing away from me. Apart from the one who wasn't.

"Hello, Julien," I said. "Come to see how it all turned out?"

"You killed that man," said Julien Advent.

"Executed him," I said.

"In cold blood."

"You know I don't do things like that. I'm thinking that the sword executed him and used me to do it. I think the sword is changing me . . ."

"Could be," said Julien, unexpectedly. "There are many

stories about Excalibur that didn't make it into the traditional tales of King Arthur. May I see the sword?"

I drew the blade and held it out before me. Julien looked at it for a long moment, his eyes full of the golden glow of the sword. I would have let him hold it if he'd asked because of who and what he was; but he didn't.

"No," he said finally. "I'm not worthy."

"Hell with that," I said. "You're a lot worthier than me, and I'm holding the bloody thing."

"Put it away," he said, and I did. He sighed heavily. "It is tempting; but a man should know his limitations. And not test himself. You need to know more about the sword you bear, John; and you can't learn it here. You're going to have to leave the Nightside, go out into London Proper, and speak with the London Knights."

"That was the plan, before I got interrupted," I said. "The whole replacing-Walker thing will have to wait till I get back."

I was expecting an argument, but Julien nodded slowly. "I understand. It's not an easy thing, to bear a legend like Excalibur. The London Knights . . . are an interesting group. You could learn a lot from them. And, possibly, they might learn a few things from you. If you don't kill each other first. I did work with them a few times, back in the day. Though they've changed a lot since Victoria sat on the Throne."

"Could I get a letter of introduction from you?" I said. "Saying, *This is a good man, despite everything you may have heard, done a lot of good things, please don't kill him?*"

"Ah," said Julien. "I have to admit that the knights and I aren't exactly on speaking terms these days. They don't approve of me since I took up residence in the Nightside. They think I've fallen from the straight and narrow path, and I think they're a bunch of arrogant, stuck-up prigs. But they do know their stuff. They are the last defenders of Camelot, after all."

"No offence, Julien," I said, "but I think I'll pass on the letter."

Julien looked at me seriously. "Watch yourself, John. The London Knights have done a lot of good in the world but strictly on their own terms. They see things very much in black and white, and have no time for any of the shades of grey."

"Then I'll just have to educate them," I said cheerfully.

He sighed. "It's all going to end in tears. I know it."

THREE

The Memory That Bears the Gun Smoke's Traces

I might be going back to the real world, but no-one said I had to feel good about it. London Proper never did feel like home to me. Home is where monsters dwell; home is where someone tries to kill you every day; home . . . is where you belong. I've always known I belong in the shadows, along with all the other shades of grey.

But, in my business you go where the job takes you. So I headed for Whitechapel Underground Rail Station, with Suzie Shooter striding silently along beside me. She stared straight ahead, her face cold and composed and very dangerous, as always, and perhaps only I could recognise how much stress she was under. Suzie's never been very demonstrative, except when she's shooting people. It took her a long time to get on speaking terms with her emotions, and she still wasn't sure what to do with some of them. And now here I was heading off into danger, into a part of my life she'd never known or shared, and I couldn't let her come with me. I couldn't, for all kinds of reasons. She wouldn't lower herself to argue, and she had more pride than to sneak along after me, so she settled for escorting me to the station, to make sure no-one messed with me along the way. I didn't say anything. How could I? I was always proud to have her walk beside me.

Everyone took one look at her face and gave us even more room than usual.

There are those who say Whitechapel was the first Underground railway station to be built in the Nightside, back in Victorian times, linking us to its duplicate in London Proper. Do I really need to tell you why they chose Whitechapel? The man currently known as Mr. Stab, the immortal uncaught serial killer of Old London Town, stuck a knife deep into the heart of the city, and while the blood was washed away long ago, the psychic wound remains. Back before the Underground, it was all hidden doors and secret gateways, and certain rather unpleasant methods provided by very private members-only clubs. Though there have always been weak spots in London Proper, places where anyone could take a wrong turn, walk down the wrong street, and end up in the night that never ends. Sin always finds a way.

"So," Suzie said abruptly, still staring straight ahead, "Walker's dead, and now you're in charge. Didn't see that one coming."

"How about this," I said, as casually as I could. "You're going to need something to keep you occupied while I'm away. So I hereby deputise you to keep the peace while I'm gone. You can be Walker till I come back. Be tough but fair, and try not to shoot too many people."

She turned her cold gaze on me. "You give me the nicest presents, John."

"You can't come with me, Suzie."

"You're going back into the outside world, the London of guns and gangs and knives in the back. You need me."

"I'm all grown-up now, Suzie. I can cope. And I know how to fit in; you've lost that knack if you ever had it. I need to do my work under the radar, so I won't be recognised or bothered by any of the outer world's authorities. Official, or supernatural. Or, indeed, by any of the various enemies from my past who might still wish me ill."

"You're trying to reason with me," said Suzie. "You know I don't do reasonable."

"I still know how to fake being normal, Suzie. You don't."

"I haven't been back to the real world since I first found my way here," said Suzie. "Fifteen years old, on the run from everyone and everything. My dead brother's blood still wet on my hands. Don't know why I waited so long . . . I should have killed him the first time he forced himself on me. You're right, John. I wouldn't know what to do in that world any more. I prefer it here, where I can be the monster I always knew I was."

I stopped, and she stopped with me. I looked her right in the eye, and held her cold gaze with my own.

"He was the monster, Suzie. You did what people are supposed to do: you killed the monster. Now say good-bye and let me go."

"If they kill you . . . I will go out into London Proper, kill them all, and burn the city down."

I smiled. "You say the sweetest things, Suzie."

We hugged each other, right there in the middle of the street, ignoring the people who hurried past. Suzie still had problems with public displays of affection, but again, probably only I could have known that. She kissed me briefly, then turned and strode away. She kept her head up and her back straight, and she didn't look back once. Her way of being brave. I watched her till she was out of sight, then I entered Whitechapel Station, and descended into the Underground.

• • •

The cream-tiled corridors and tunnels were packed with men and women and other things, coming and going, intent on searching out all those pleasures that were bad for them. They didn't talk to each other and made a point of looking straight ahead, not wanting to be distracted or diverted from their chosen paths. Without quite seeming to, everyone gave me plenty of room to move. Having a good, or more properly bad, reputation does have its benefits. I was going to have to learn how to get results without that where I was going. The John Taylor who'd lived in London Proper five years earlier had been a much smaller man.

I hurried down the escalators, ignoring the sweet-talking ads on the walls, and headed for the Outer Line. The usual beggars and buskers were out and about, singing and dancing for their supper. A ghost of a nun sang "Ave Maria," accompanying herself with hand signals for the deaf. Three zombies with skin as grey as their shabby suits performed a careful soft-shoe routine that never ever stopped. Half a dozen clones made up a one-man band, and something from a Black Lagoon crooned old calypso songs as he tended his sushi stall. Recent graffiti on the walls included the Yellow Sign, the Voorish Sign, and an official sign saying all familiars must be carried on the escalators.

Down on the platform, the destinations board offered SHADOWS FALL, HACELDAMA, HAVEN, and WHITECHAPEL. The platform was half-full, with all the usual unusual types. A bunch of cheerful teenage girls in public-school outfits were kicking the crap out of a bunch of thugs in bowler hats, heavy eye make-up, and padded cod-pieces. While a circle of City business types in smart City suits with blue woad daubed thickly on their faces steadily ignored the unpleasantness by immersing themselves in the City pages of the *Night Times*. And a large ambulatory plant thing was taking an unhealthy interest in a tree nymph. She was a pretty little thing, all gleaming bark and leaves in her hair, and I did consider getting involved—until the nymph decided she'd had enough and kneed the plant thing right in the nuts.

I looked away and found myself facing a knight in dark armour. He was standing at the far end of the platform, unnaturally still, looking right at me. His armoured suit was made up of large black scales, moving slowly against each other and sliding over one another in places. Satanic markings had been daubed on his breast-plate, in what looked like dried blood. His squat steel helm covered his entire head, with only a Y-shaped slot in the centre for his eyes and mouth. He carried a sword like a butcher's blade on one hip and a spike-headed mace on the other. I'd seen his type before. He was one of the knights in armour King Artur had brought with him to the Nightside, from Sinister Albion. A world where Merlin Satanspawn embraced his father's work, corrupted Arthur, and made a dark and terrible world for him to rule.

That's parallel dimensions for you. For every heaven, a hell; and for every Golden Age, a kick in the teeth.

The dark knight seemed to be displaying more than usual interest in me, but when I turned to face him squarely, he turned away and gave all his attention to the departures board. I shrugged mentally and put it down to paranoia. Lot of that about, in the Nightside.

A growing roar, a blast wave of displaced air, and the train burst out of the tunnel-mouth, screaming to a halt beside the platform. A long, featureless, silver bullet, pulling windowless carriages because you really didn't want to see some of the places the train had to pass through on its way from the Nightside to the outer world. The doors hissed open, I stepped into a carriage, and everyone else in the carriage got up and hurried out onto the platform. Not so much a mark of respect; more that they didn't want to be round when the trouble started. I settled myself comfortably on the battered

red-leather seat, the door hissed shut, and the train set off smoothly.

The journey itself was remarkably quiet and peaceful; nothing tried to break in from outside, nothing tried to block the tracks, and there wasn't even much of the usual strange noises and threatening voices. Perhaps because this wasn't one of the busy lines. People are always queuing up and even fighting each other to get into the Nightside, but only a few ever go home again. For all kinds of reasons.

When the train finally ground to a halt at London Proper, I took a deep breath, stood up, and walked steadily out onto the platform. It was, of course, quite empty. No-one else left the train. The door behind me hissed shut, and the train went away. I walked slowly down the empty platform. The air was still and stale, and the sound of my footsteps didn't echo far, as though the sound didn't have quite enough energy to make the effort. The walls were utterly bare, no posters or adverts, no graffiti. The whole place had the feel of a stage-set that was only rarely used.

The blank wall stretched away before me, with no sign of an exit anywhere. I finally stopped before a courtesy phone, set on the wall inside a dusty glass shield. I picked up the phone. There was no dial tone. I said *London Proper* and put the phone down again. I stepped back, and the wall before me split slowly in two, pulling itself apart in a series of grinding juddering movements until a long, narrow tunnel fell away before me. Its inner walls were dark red, like an opened wound, and the sourceless light was dim and smoky, smelling of corrupt perfumes and crushed flowers. I walked steadily forward, and mists swirled round my ankles like disturbed waters. Faint voices and snatches of strange music faded in and out, like so many competing radio signals. Far and far away, a cloister bell tolled sadly.

I burst out the other end of the tunnel, and immediately, I was standing on an ordinary, everyday platform, while perfectly normal people hurried past me. None of them seemed to notice that I'd arrived in their midst out of nowhere. I glanced behind me, and the wall was just a wall, with nothing to show it had ever been anything else. Which was as it should be. I joined the crush and followed the crowd down the platform, heading out and up into the real world above.

I left Whitechapel Station and stepped hesitantly out into a London I hadn't seen in years. The real world seemed almost defiantly grey after the relentless sound and fury and garish neon of the Nightside. Everywhere I looked, the street and the people were all remarkably ordinary. And the traffic thundering up and down the road was only cars and buses, taxis and messengers on bicycles, and lumbering delivery trucks. They even stopped for the traffic lights and pedestrian crossings. Mostly.

It was early evening, still quite light, and I wasn't used to that. I felt . . . exposed, and vulnerable, now that I no longer had any shadows to hide in. I stared up at the cloudy grey sky and tried to remember when I'd last seen the sun. I wasn't impressed. Sunlight's overrated if you ask me.

Everything felt different. The pace felt slower, with none of the familiar sense of danger and opportunity, none of the Nightside's constant pressure to be going somewhere, to do something unwise and probably unnatural. London Proper did have its own bustle and air of excitement, like every big city, but it was strictly amateur hour compared to the Nightside.

The real difference between the Nightside and London Proper was attitude. In the Nightside, it's all out and open and in-your-face. From magic to super-science, from the supernatural to the other-dimensional. You can sink yourself into it all, like soaking in a hot bath full of blood. In London Proper, in what we like to think of as the real world, such things are hidden. Behind the scenes, or behind the scenery. You won't even know it's there unless you have the Sight; and most don't. You have to go looking for the hidden world, and even then you probably won't find it if it doesn't want to be found.

I knew I should go straight to Oxford Street, and the London Knights' secret headquarters . . . but it had been a long time since I'd been back, and nostalgia can be a harsh mistress. I felt a need, almost a hunger, to see my old haunts again, to go back to that small grubby place where I had lived and worked, and tried so hard to be normal. So I hopped on a bus, one of the old reliable red London double-deckers, and travelled back into my past.

I got off the bus at a stop no-one else seemed interested in and strolled down the grim, shabby streets to where my office used to be. The whole area looked even grubbier and seedier than I remembered, though I wouldn't have thought that was possible. Narrow streets and crumbling tenements, smashed windows and kicked-in doors. Broken people in worn-out clothes, hurrying along with their heads lowered so they wouldn't have to look anyone in the eye. A cold wind gusting down deserted alleyways, and shadows everywhere because someone had been using the street-lamps for target practice.

Homeless people sitting bundled up in doorways, drinking forgetfulness straight from the can or the bottle. Soot-stained brickwork, darkened by generations of passing traffic. Posters slapped one on top of the other, messages from the past, advertising things long gone, faded and water-stained. When I finally got to the old building that housed my small office, most of the windows were boarded up. There were a few lights on, in the surrounding buildings. People too stubborn to leave, or with nowhere else to go. Rubbish in the gutters, and worse in the alley mouths. And what street lighting there was seemed faded and stained.

I was surprised my old office building was still there. I'd

been half-convinced, half-hoping, it would have been torn down by then. The place had been officially condemned even while I was still living in it. I stopped on the opposite side of the street and looked it over. No lights, no signs of life. People had given up on it, like rats deserting a sinking ship. The front door was hanging open, hinges creaking loudly on the quiet, as the gusting wind gave the door a shove, now and again, to remind it who was boss. I stood there for a while, studying the gloom beyond the door, but I was putting off the moment, and I knew it.

I looked round the deserted street one last time, then walked briskly across the road, pushed the front door all the way open, and strode into the dark and empty lobby. It was dark because someone had smashed the single naked light bulb. The place stank of stale piss. And yet, the place couldn't just be abandoned, or the local homeless would have moved in and claimed it for their own. No light, no heating, no signs of occupation; so why had the front door been left so conveniently open? An invitation—or a trap?

I smiled despite myself. Looked like this might turn out to be interesting after all.

I made my way up the narrow wooden stairway to the next floor. The steps complained loudly under my weight, as they always had. The tenants liked it that way, to give warning that visitors were coming. I paused at the top to look about me, my eyes already adjusting to the gloom; but there was no sign anyone had been here in ages. I moved along the landing, checking the open office doors along the way. Old memories of old faces, neighbours who were never anything more than that. Cheap and nasty offices that had been home to a defrocked accountant and a struck-off dentist, dark and empty now, cleaned out long ago, with no sign left to show anyone had ever used them.

My office was still there, exactly where I'd left it. The door stood quietly ajar, with just enough of the old flaking sign to make out the words TAYLOR INVESTIGATIONS. The bullet-hole in the frosted-glass window was still there, too. I should have had it repaired, but it made such a great conversation piece. Clients like a hint of danger when they hire a private eye. I pushed the door all the way open with the tip of one finger, and the hinges complained loudly in the quiet. I took a deep breath, bracing myself against something I couldn't quite name; but all I smelled was dust and rot, so I walked right in.

My old office was completely empty, abandoned—lots of dust and cobwebs, and a few rat droppings in the corner. Amber light fell in through the single barred window, pooling on the floor. All the furniture was gone, but I could still see it with my mind's eye. The blocky desk and the two functional chairs, the cot I'd pushed up against the far wall when I was sleeping in my office because the landlord had locked me out of my flat, as a gentle hint that he'd like some of the back rent paid. This was the place where I tried to help people even worse off than I was, for whatever money they had. I did my best for them. I really did.

I looked slowly round me. Hard to believe that I'd spent five long years here, trying to pass for normal. Trying to help real people with real problems, in the real world. Burying myself in their problems, their lives, so I wouldn't have to think about my own. I found out the hard way I wasn't that good as an investigator when I didn't have my gift to back me up. I didn't dare use it, not here. The Harrowing would have detected it immediately, known I'd fled the Nightside, and come after me. They could pass for normal, when they had to. They looked like people, but they weren't. They wore plain black suits with neat string ties, highly polished shoes, and slouch hats with the brims pulled low, so no-one could see what they had instead of faces. They'd been trying to kill me since I was a child. They wouldn't have hesitated to come into the real world after me.

One of the reasons why I'd come here. To be free of them. They terrified me. Dominated my life for so long. Gone now, at great cost to me and those who'd stood by me.

They were only one of the reasons I'd left the Nightside. I wanted to at least try to be a man rather than a monster. To live my own life rather than the one planned for me by so many vested interests. I thought I'd be safe, in the real world, as long as I didn't use my gift, or get involved with any unnatural situations. I should have known better. It didn't take me long to discover that, without my gift, I wasn't half the investigator I thought I was. I helped some people, solved my fair share of cases, but made damn all money doing it. I amassed a lot of debts along the way, and made a number of real-world enemies, human monsters. Because even in the real world, no good deed goes unpunished.

Because I wouldn't take bribes, I wouldn't back down, and I was too damned honest for my own good.

I later found out that my once-and-future Enemies in the Nightside had orchestrated the series of tragic events that sent me running from the Nightside with Suzie's bullet burning in my back. Their idea of mercy. A second chance, to not be the person they thought I was, or might become. I did try to take the chance they offered. But it wasn't me. My hand drifted to my lower back, where the scar from Suzie's bullet still ached dully when it rained. A struck-off doctor dug it out of my back while I bit down on a length of cord to keep from screaming. Welcome to the real world.

Suzie hadn't meant to kill me. It was just her way of trying to get my attention. We forgave each other long ago.

I looked round sharply, brought back to the present by the sound of someone approaching. Slow, steady footsteps ascending the wooden stairs, making no attempt to hide themselves. Someone wanted me to know they were coming. I moved quickly over to stand behind the open door. A white trench coat may be iconic as all hell, but it does make it difficult to hide in the shadows. I stood very still, straining my ears at every sound, as the footsteps made their unhurried way along the landing, ignoring all the other offices, heading straight for mine. They stopped outside my open door, then a man walked unhurriedly in. A short, middle-aged, balding man in an anonymous coat, so nondescript in appearance he was hardly there. I relaxed, a little. I knew him. I stepped out from behind the door.

"Hello, Russell."

He turned his head calmly, not surprised or startled in the least. He nodded once, as though we'd happened to bump into each other in the street. Russell was a small grey man, always quiet and polite, always ready to do something illegal. If the price was right. He did some work for me, back in the day. Russell did some work for a lot of people. He was a grass, a runner, and a reliable supplier of dodgy items. He never got his own hands dirty; he made it possible for other people to do what they had to. He knew all the wrong people, drank in all the worst dives, heard it all and said nothing. Until you put money in his hand. No-one liked him, but everybody used him. Russell never complained. He had self-esteem issues.

He hadn't changed much. A little greyer, a little more rat-like. Still giving the impression that he wasn't really there. When he spoke, it was the same old polite, self-effacing murmur that I remembered.

"Well, well. If it isn't Mr. Taylor. Back again, after all these years. How unusual, to find you in this old place again. Most of us assumed that you had shuffled off this mortal coil, or been shuffled off it, with important bits missing. Where did you disappear to, Mr. Taylor? No-one could find you, and some people looked really hard."

"You wouldn't believe me if I told you," I said.

"Wherever you've been, it would seem to have agreed with you, Mr. Taylor. You are looking very well. One might even say prosperous. Do you by any chance have the money you owe?"

"Not on me, no."

"Oh dear. I would have to say, that is most unfortunate, Mr. Taylor. Though after all these years, I would have to say that even if you did have the money, it would not be enough. It's the interest, you see. The emotional interest; it accumulates. Certain people are very angry with you, Mr. Taylor. You are the one who got away. The one who set a bad example . . ."

"Why are you here, Russell?" I said, interrupting a flow that threatened to go on forever. "I mean, even I didn't know I was coming here. It can't be a coincidence, you turning up like this."

"Hardly, Mr. Taylor. Certain people have kept this place empty, but observed, all these years. In case you showed up again."

"Oh, come on," I said. "I didn't owe that much."

"You made certain people *very* angry, Mr. Taylor," Russell said simply. "It's no longer about the money; it's the vengeance. No-one can be allowed to get away with defying the men in charge. It's just not done. It might give people ideas."

"Well," I said, "I'm glad I achieved something while I was here. But having given the matter some thought, I would have to say that I don't give a wet fart what the men in charge want."

"They have been watching and waiting for years, Mr. Taylor, on the chance . . . And here you are! Back again, after all this time. Certain people are going to be very happy about that."

"People have been watching my old office for years? Why?"

"For the reward, Mr. Taylor."

"There's a price on my head? I feel strangely flattered. How big a reward?"

"A significant amount, Mr. Taylor. In fact, I would have to say, quite a substantial reward."

I looked at him thoughtfully. "Is that why you're here, Russell? So soon after my return? For the reward money?"

"Not exactly, Mr. Taylor. But you know how it is . . . And if I'm here, others won't be far behind."

"How long have I got, before word gets out?"

He smiled for the first time. "They're already here, Mr. Taylor."

I moved quickly over to the barred window and looked out at the street below. Several cars were parked outside that hadn't been there before, and more were arriving. Car doors slammed loudly as armed men spilled out onto the street. They didn't care if I knew they were there. The trap had been sprung. The men in the street were large men, serious men with serious intent. They carried their guns like they knew how to use them. I was flattered they saw me as such a dangerous threat. Everyone else was quietly disappearing off the street, including the homeless. None of them wanted to be witnesses to whatever was about to happen. Being a witness wasn't good for your continued health.

I smiled down at the men milling outside the building. It had been a long time since anyone had come after me with only guns to back them up. But, of course, these people only knew the old me, from when I was still hiding my gift under a bushel. I looked forward to disillusioning them. Still, given the sheer number of hard men who'd turned up, it would seem Russell was right when he mentioned a substantial reward. I turned back to look at Russell. He hadn't moved—a small grey presence in a half-lit room.

"It occurs to me," I said, "that the reward isn't for money returned but for me personally. Somebody wants to lay hands on me, and not in a good way."

"Somebody bears a grudge, Mr. Taylor. Someone wants you to pay, in blood and suffering."

There was a gun in his hand, pointing at me. I was actually shocked. I'd never seen Russell with a gun, in all the time he'd worked for me. But the gun didn't look out of place. Something in the way Russell held his gun told me he was used to it.

"You never used to like shooters, Russell," I said reproachfully. "You were never a violent man. First out the pub door when the fight started. What happened?"

"You happened, Mr. Taylor." He was aiming his gun at a spot directly above my groin. A disabling shot but not a deadly one. He didn't want me dead. Not yet. Which gave me the advantage even if he didn't realise it. I raised an eyebrow, to indicate that he should continue, and he couldn't stop himself. The words came pouring out, as though he'd been rehearsing them for years. "After you went away, after you abandoned me, I had to look after myself. Turned out I was really good at it. I never realised how much you were holding me back. I stopped working for other people and went into business for myself. And now . . . I'm the boss. I'm the man. I run things in this territory. I bought up all your debts and put a price on your head. You owe me, Mr. Taylor."

"The money, or for not saying good-bye when I left?"

"You never valued me, Mr. Taylor. Never respected me. Even after all the things I did for you."

"I paid you the going rate, like everyone else. And I treated you better than most. I thought we had fun along the way. Didn't we have fun, rescuing the good people from the bad guys, righting wrongs, and dropping the ungodly right in it? I may not have been the most successful private eye in London, but I like to think I made my mark. With your help."

"Don't talk to me like I was your friend, or even your partner. You used me."

"That's what you were for, Russell. You were an informer, the lowest of the low, despised by all. You had no principles and less dignity. You would have sold your mother's organs for transplant while she was still alive for the right offer. At least I gave you a good purpose in life. Now put the gun down, Russell. It doesn't suit you."

"Oh, but it does, Mr. Taylor. With you gone, and all the

77

enemies you'd made circling like vultures, I had to learn to look after myself. And the first thing I learned was that a gun makes all the difference. A small man can be a big man if he's got a gun, and the guts to use it. Much to my surprise, I found I had. Actually, I enjoyed it. I've come a long way since you were last here, and I enjoyed every nasty bit of it. Kneel down, Mr. Taylor. Kneel down and say you're sorry."

"And if I don't?"

"Then I'll shoot your kneecaps out, for starters. Then . . . I'll take my time. Enjoy myself. I do so love to hear my enemies scream."

"You should never go back," I said. "People are never how you remember them. I'm really very disappointed in you, Russell."

"Kneel down and beg for your life!"

"No," I said. "I don't do that."

I stared into his eyes, holding his gaze with mine, and I saw fear fill his face as he realised he couldn't look away. The hand holding the gun trembled as he tried to pull the trigger and found he couldn't. I stepped forward, holding his will firmly with mine. Blood seeped out from under his eyelids and spurted from his nose. He whimpered once as I took the gun out of his hand and tucked it into my coat-pocket. And then I let him go, and he fell to the floor, shuddering and crying out.

"I'm a whole new man myself these days, Russell," I said easily, turning my back on him as I headed for the door.

"You bastard." I looked back, and Russell had forced himself up onto his knees, so he could glare at me through blood-shot eyes. "You still don't respect me!"

"Yes, well, there's a reason for that, Russell. I've flushed things I respected more than you. Now I really must be going. Important things to be about; you know how it is. A shame it had to come to this . . . Don't let the past define you,

Russell. You can't move on if you're always looking back over your shoulder."

"Bastard!"

Words of wisdom are just wasted on some people. I walked out the door and stepped cautiously out onto the landing. I could hear the armed men milling about in the lobby below. And then Russell raised his voice in a vicious, commanding scream.

"He's up here! Taylor's up here! Get up here and find him! Forget the taking-him-alive shit; I want him dead! Dead! Ten grand bonus to whoever brings me his head, so I can piss in his eyes!"

A whole army of men came clattering up the stairs, heavy feet slamming on the complaining wooden steps. I moved silently down the landing towards them, then slipped into the office before mine and hid behind the open door. Some tricks are classics. A whole bunch of very heavy people moved purposefully along the landing, slamming open each door they came to. I braced myself and took the impact on my shoulder, gritting my teeth to make sure I didn't make a sound. The thug stepped into the doorway, looked quickly round the empty office, and moved on. Not all thugs are brain-dead muscle; but that's usually the way to bet.

I eased forward, peering carefully round the edge of the door. The armed men had come to a halt, clustered before my open office door. Russell was yelling at them, but they simply stood there and took it. Probably part of their job description. Russell looked like he was the sort who'd enjoy yelling at people. All of the thugs were carrying guns, in a very professional way. Mostly pistols, a few sawn-off shotguns. I counted twenty-two armed men, in all; rather a lot, to bring down one man. Especially since I'd never been considered that dangerous, back in the day. Either Russell was taking no chances on me disappearing again, or . . . someone had been talking.

Twenty-two armed thugs. In a very confined space. Oh well, you have to make a start somewhere.

I slowly eased round the office door and padded carefully down the gloomy corridor until I could ease in behind the man at the very back of the crowd. I slipped an arm round his throat from behind and had him in a choke hold before he knew what was happening. I dragged him quickly back into the adjoining office, tightened the hold till he was well out, then lowered him carefully to the floor.

Suzie had taught me a lot of useful grips and holds. Often during foreplay.

I stepped out of the office, strolled casually down the corridor, and tapped the shoulder of the man in front of me.

"Who are we after?" I murmured into his ear.

"Some scumbag called Taylor," said the thug, not looking round. "Word is he owes the boss, big-time."

"Taylor," I said. "That's a name from the past."

The thug shrugged briefly. "Should never have come back. The boss has a real hard-on for this guy."

"What a perfectly appalling mental image," I said. "Is this all of us? Any more coming?"

"No; we're it. But watch yourself; this Taylor's supposed to be a bit tricky."

"Oh, he is," I said. "Really. You have no idea."

Something seemed to occur to the thug, and he turned to look back at me. His eyes widened as he realised who he'd been talking to. He opened his mouth to give the alarm, and I kneed him briskly in the balls. His eyes squeezed shut, and he dropped to the floor. Other members of the crowd before me began to turn round, sensing something was wrong. I took out the sachet of coarse pepper I always keep in my coat-pocket, tore it open, and threw the granules right into their faces. They cried out in shock and pain as fierce tears ran down their faces, blinding them; and then the sneezing and the coughing started, convulsing their bodies as their lungs heaved for air. Never go anywhere without condiments. Condiments are our friends.

I moved quickly forward, forcing my way through the hacking, teary-eyed, almost helpless thugs, handing out nerve pinches, low blows, and the occasional really nasty back elbow when the opportunity presented itself. I slammed thugs against the wall, sent them crashing to the floor, and even tipped a few over the railings. Not one of them even managed to lay a hand on me.

I was actually starting to feel a bit cocky when the men on the furthest edge of the crowd, and therefore furthest away from the pepper, raised their guns and opened fire. The noise was deafening in the confined space, and the bullets went everywhere. Some pock-marked the wall beside me, some hit their own men, but none of them went anywhere near me because I was down on one knee and out of sight. Gun smoke thickened on the air, confusing the situation even more. There was screaming and shouting and general uproar, and I contributed a few *He's over there!*s. Just to be helpful.

I slipped easily through the confused crowd and out the other side, ducking and dodging and bestowing vicious unexpected blows on the unworthy. Nothing like a lot of people in a tight space to put the odds in favour of the lone fighter. Particularly if he's a dirty fighter. I waited at the foot of the stairs to the next floor, until I was sure they knew where I was, then I used one of my favourite tricks, and employed a small but useful magic to take all the bullets out of their guns. The crash of gunfire cut off abruptly, and there was a lot of confused shaking of guns. I took advantage of their confusion to run up the stairs to the next floor. And then I sat down abruptly, by the railings, and gasped for air. I'm not as young as I used to be. I peered cautiously down through the banisters to see what was happening below.

More than half the thugs were on the floor: unconscious, bleeding, shot by their own people, or still recovering from various dirty tricks. Most of them wouldn't be taking any more interest in proceedings for a while, and the rest were too busy cursing their fellows for being such lousy shots. Russell could still be heard screaming orders and abuse, almost incandescent with rage. I never knew he had it in him. Bullet-holes had pock-marked the first-floor wall, and all my frosted glass was gone. The gun smoke was slowly clearing, but there was still only intermittent light from outside. It occurred to me that I shouldn't be able to see all this as clearly as I did . . . And then I pushed the thought aside, as some of the thugs reloaded their guns and started cautiously up the stairs towards me, driven on by Russell's screeching voice.

I could feel Excalibur on my back, a fierce and dangerous presence, nagging at me like an aching tooth, demanding to be drawn and used. The sword would have made short work of the thugs, guns or no; but I didn't want to draw it. I didn't need a legendary sword to see off a few bad guys with delusions of adequacy. I was John Taylor, no longer trying to be normal.

I took a flashbang out of my coat-pocket, primed it, and tossed it lightly down the stairs. I counted off five, then turned my head away and squeezed my eyes shut. The flashbang detonated, filling the stairs with unbearably bright light. The thugs screamed like little girls as the fierce-light-blasted eyes adjusted to the gloom, and they fired blindly ahead of them, peppering the stairs and the walls but not coming anywhere near me. I waited till they stopped firing, then strolled casually back down the stairs, snatching the guns out of their hands and hitting them here and there with vicious intent. One by one, I kicked their unconscious bodies down the stairs and threw their guns after them. I've never cared for the things. One lone thug remained, at the foot of the stairs. He'd managed to avoid the worst of the flashbang, and the pepper, and had his gun trained on me. He looked seriously spooked, though; his hand was trembling, and his eyes were almost painfully wide as he watched me descend the stairs towards him. I'd taken down his entire gang, and I wasn't even breathing hard.

I gave him my best unnerving smile. "Tell you what: you run away now, terribly quickly, and I won't do horrible and upsetting things to your person."

His hand was seriously trembling by then. Sweat was running down his face. I let my smile widen a little, and he made a low, whining noise.

"Boo!" I said, and he turned and ran for his life. *Potentially sensible young man,* I thought.

I went back into my old office. Russell made a small, horrified sound in the back of his throat as he saw me. He backed away, and I went after him. He kept retreating until he slammed up against the barred window and realised he had nowhere else to go. All the colour had gone out of his face, but his wide eyes were still sharp and mean and calculating. If I was stupid enough to turn my back on him, he'd stick a knife in it. I stopped in the middle of the room and considered him thoughtfully.

"How do you like being the big man, Russell?" I said. "Making loans to desperate people, at two thousand per cent interest, then sending round the leg-breakers when they can't keep up with the payments? Taking your cut from all the drugs and the working girls and the protection rackets? Leeching money from all the small people, like you used to be? You were never interested in any of that, back in the day."

"Never had any money, back in the day, Mr. Taylor." His voice was flat and collected, wary rather than frightened. "I'm a whole new man, with a whole new life. I don't need you to protect me any more. And you're out of tricks."

"You think so?" I said.

"Of course; or you wouldn't be standing there talking to

me. Talk all you like, I've put in a call. There'll be more of my people here any minute."

I took his gun out of my pocket and offered it to him. He gaped at me for a moment, then snatched it from my hand and pointed it at me. As his finger tightened on the trigger, I took all the bullets out of his gun and let them fall from my open hand onto the floor, jumping and rattling noisily. Russell made a high, whining noise, and pulled the trigger anyway. When nothing happened, he threw the gun onto the floor and looked at me haughtily.

"I know you, Mr. Taylor. You might have learned a few tricks, but you haven't changed. You won't kill an unarmed man."

I looked at him thoughtfully. Russell would never stop coming after me all the time I was in London Proper. He wouldn't stop until he was dead, or I was. Unless I did something about him. The sword on my back wanted me to kill him, to execute him. My hand rose to the invisible hilt behind my shoulder, then I pulled it back again. I was not an executioner. And all that fighting, all the action stuff, diving into danger with a smile on my face and letting the chips fall where they may—that wasn't me. I have more sense. The sword had been influencing me. And it stopped there. I'd deal with Russell in my own way.

I strode briskly forward, grabbed him firmly by one ear, and dragged him out of my old office, down the stairs, back through the lobby, and out onto the street. I then stripped him naked, quickly and efficiently, and left him hanging upside down from the nearest lamp-post. Tied firmly by one ankle with a handy piece of cord from my coat-pocket. Russell struggled weakly, but there was no way he'd be able to work himself loose. He flopped upside down before me, his skin already grey from the cold, his mouth working weakly.

"I've thrown things back that looked less disgusting than

you, Russell," I said. "And you really do have a remarkably small willy. Which explains a lot. Let's see who'll work for you now, after this. Even the most basic thugs draw the line somewhere. Good-bye, Russell. If I should see you again . . . I'll think of something even worse to do to you."

Enough nostalgia, I thought, walking off down the street. Time to find the London Knights.

FOUR

A Knight to Remember

The late evening was darkening into night as I hit Oxford Street, and I was starting to feel more at home. I could feel that little extra bounce in my step as I headed for a Door that was only there when it felt like it. The street was packed with people coming and going, shop lights blazed, and neon glared, but it all seemed somehow faded and subdued compared to the Nightside. The moon in the sky looked small and far away, and the stars were only stars. As though the real world couldn't be bothered to put on a decent show.

Oxford Street had changed a lot in the years I'd been away. Lots of rebuilding and general cleaning up, tearing down the older and dodgier enterprises to replace them with safer and more comfortable brands and franchises. All the local colour was gone, and much of the character, and cold camera eyes watched every little thing you did. Though the messenger boys darting in and out of traffic and pedestrians on their stripped-down cycles were just as obnoxious.

After living so long in the Nightside, the real world seemed like a foreign place, where even the most obvious and everyday things seemed subtly different. To start with, no-one paid me any attention. I really wasn't used to that. At first I quite liked just walking along, amongst people who didn't have a clue as to who and what I was. Who didn't stare or point, or turn and run. But I soon got tired of that when no-one gave way for me, or stepped aside to let me pass, and even jostled me when I didn't get out of their way fast enough. How dare they treat me like everyone else? Didn't they know who I was? Well, no . . . That was the point. I had to smile, and even tried being polite and courteous for a while, if only to see what it felt like.

When I got to the Green Door, it wasn't there. A bleak expanse of yellowing wall separated two perfectly respectable businesses, with no trace of any door or opening, or indeed anything to suggest there was anything special about the wall. Except, this was perhaps the only stretch of wall in London not covered with graffiti, posters, or dried streams of urine. I raised my Sight and studied the wall closely, and still couldn't See the damned Door. I could See rough markings in dried troll blood, from some Scissorboys gang marking its territory, and a reptiloid alien hidden behind a human mask as it strode briskly past me, but the wall remained stubbornly a wall. The Green Door that provided the only entrance point to the London Knights' headquarters remained thoroughly hidden. Which meant . . . really powerful protections.

I knew the bloody thing was there because I'd once tracked a man all the way to it, back when I was being an ordinary private eye. I thought I had him run to ground and cornered until he said a Word I'd never heard outside the Nightside, and the Green Door appeared before him. He hurried through it, and the Door vanished before I could reach it. And I . . . turned round and went home because I was determined not to get involved in cases of the weird and uncanny any more.

I heard later that the Knights executed the guy. Because he wasn't worthy of their sanctuary.

But things were different now. I wasn't afraid to use my gift any more. I reached deep inside me, concentrating, and my inner eye, my private eye, slowly opened . . . and there was the Green Door, right before me. It could hide from my Sight but not from my gift. My sole inheritance from my Biblical Myth mother. The Door itself looked stubbornly real and ordinary: flat green paint over featureless wood, with no handle, no bell, not even a knocker or a keyhole. It was, in fact, a Door that suggested very firmly that either you knew how to get in, or you had no business even trying.

I tested the Green Door with my gift, searching out its secrets, and it didn't take me long to discover the magical mechanisms that operated it. Very old, very simple, and very well protected. My gift could find them but not reach them. Which was frustrating. So I gave the Door a good kick on general principles, hurt my toe, and walked round in little circles for a while. I glared at the Green Door and seriously considered carving chunks out of it with Excalibur. However, since I'd come all this way to ask the London Knights a favour, open assault on their property probably wasn't the best first impression I could be making. So, when everything else fails, try diplomacy. I put away my gift, dropped my Sight, and addressed the blank street wall in calm, civilised, and very polite tones. While studiously ignoring those passersby who wondered why I was talking to myself.

"Hello, London Knights. I'm John Taylor. From the Nightside. I need to talk to you concerning something that's a lot more in your line of work than mine. If it helps, Julien Advent vouches for me. If it doesn't, I never met the man. Look, this really is something you want to know about. It's Arthurian as all hell, and the words *deep shit* and *approaching fan* should be taken into consideration."

Still nothing. Arrogant bunch of pricks. I was considering the soothing properties of giving the wall another good hard kick when, almost without realising it, my hand rose and took a firm hold on the invisible hilt rising behind my shoulder. And the moment my bare flesh made contact with the ancient bone . . . old, old words came to me.

"I bear Excalibur, the Sword of Morning, the Hand of Albion. In the name of the Lady who has granted me her power, and in the name of the man who last wielded it, the once-and-future King, I demand audience with the last defenders of Camelot."

And the Green Door was suddenly there before me, very real and very solid, as though it always had been there and always would. I took my hand away from Excalibur's hilt, and the Green Door opened slowly before me, retreating silently and not at all invitingly—revealing only an impenetrable darkness beyond. I took a deep breath, held my chin up, and walked right into it. Never let them think they've got you cowed, or they'll walk right over you. The darkness swallowed me up, cold and limitless, and I barely had time to wonder whether I'd made a terrible mistake when a blast of light dispelled the darkness, and just like that I was standing in the entrance hall to a medieval castle.

Which was pretty much what I'd been expecting. The London Knights are firmly steeped in tradition. I looked cautiously about me. There was no-one round to greet me, or any signs of human habitation at all. Only great towering walls of a rich creamy white stone, spotlessly clean, without any trace of decoration. The whole place could have been built the day before. Every separate stone in the massive walls had been set so tightly and so perfectly together that no mortar was needed. And that takes real skill and expert measurement.

I appeared to have the whole great open space to myself. No-one there, and not even any windows or arrow slits through which I could be observed. I took a quick look behind me, but of course the Green Door was gone, replaced by a blank and very real wall. There was an open arch-way straight ahead of me, in the far wall. Silence filled the entrance hall, so complete I could hear my own breathing. A silence that seemed pointedly judgemental. I had no doubt I was being watched. So I stuck my hands in my coat-pockets, slouched, adopted a jaunty air, and strolled towards the open archway as though I had all the time in the world.

The sound of my footsteps hardly seemed to travel at all, not even a hint of an echo, as though the sheer massive size of the hall were soaking up the sound.

It took me a while to cross the long hall, and by the time I got to the archway it was filled with a heavy iron portcullis. I was pretty sure it hadn't been there when I started walking, and I was pissed off enough to take this new snub personally. I glared at the portcullis.

"Lift this bloody thing right now. Or I'll show you all a really nasty trick my mother taught me."

There was a pause, then the iron portcullis rose silently before me, without any sound of straining mechanisms. I love it when a bluff comes together. I stuck my nose in the air and strode haughtily through the narrow stone tunnel into another great hall. The same creamy white stone as before, but richly adorned with hanging tapestries and colourful pen-nants, in sharp vivid shades of crimson, emerald, and gold. Huge silver crucifixes were mounted on the walls, between magnificent stained-glass windows depicting scenes from the lives of the Saints. The flooring was polished marble, with huge mosaics presenting scenes from the past—of knights in their armour, clashing armies, blood and mud and the fight for a dream.

I felt a very real lightening of the spirit, a feeling of calm and burdens lifted; the light was crystal clear, and even the air tasted fair. I relaxed a little, despite myself. I'd seen more impressive places in the Nightside, but not many. As medieval castles went, this one went all the way. But I still couldn't help noting that the splendid crystal-and-diamond chandeliers at each end of the hall contained electric light bulbs rather than the usual massed candles. I stopped to study them for a moment, and when I looked down again, there were a dozen knights in full armour standing before me.

I hadn't heard them come in. In fact, given the sheer weight of the armour they were wearing, I should have heard them approaching half a mile away. Clearly, I was meant to be impressed, so I nodded casually, as though I'd seen it all before, and much better done. My first thought was how . . . practical, and functional, the suits of armour looked. They weren't ceremonial, or works of art, or even symbols; this was battle armour, designed to keep its wearer alive in even the most dangerous of situations. Gleaming steel, from head to foot; expertly fashioned, and completely unadorned. No engraving or ornamentation, not even a coloured tabard over the torso to add a touch of colour. Steel helmets covered their entire heads, with only a Y-shaped slots for the eyes and mouths.

For a moment, I was reminded of the knight in dark armour I'd seen on the station platform, back in the Nightside. The nightmare armour that stood in utter opposition to the forces of chivalry before me.

The knights were still staring silently at me. I wondered whether there was some special password I was supposed to use; I still remembered the Word my quarry had used to get in all those years ago. But considering what had happened to him, I didn't think I'd use it. The knights were trying to impress and/or intimidate me, but they really should have known better. If there was one thing that anyone should know about me, it's that I don't do impressed or intimidated. I considered drawing Excalibur and doing something dramatically destructive with it; but that might make me seem weak, in their eyes. And it seemed to me that the castle would be a very bad place in which to appear weak.

So I struck a casual pose and smiled easily at the knights, as though they were on parade in front of me. "Hi. I'm John Taylor."

"Oh, we know who you are," said an amused voice from within one of the steel helms. "Your reputation spreads a lot further than this."

The knight speaking took off his helmet and tucked it casually under his arm. He had a fresh, cheerful face, with short-cropped blond hair and very blue eyes. The warmth in his smile gave every appearance of being genuine. He had the open, easy kind of charm you tend not to see a lot of in the Nightside. An honest, straightforward agent of the Good; exactly like the London Knights were supposed to be. I was immediately suspicious, but I gave him my best open smile in return.

"Hi!" said the knight, stepping forward and extending a mailed glove for me to shake. I grasped it firmly, and he gave it a good solid shake, like a young clergyman who played rugby on the side. "I'm Sir Gareth. Welcome to Castle Inconnu. I see you've noticed the electric lighting. We are a part of the twenty-first century, you know. We have central heating, indoor plumbing, cable, and broadband. We're traditionalists, not barbarians. Sorry we had to give you a bit of a hard time getting in, but we live in dangerous times. You of all people should know that. You're one of the people who makes these times dangerous. And you really should have known better than to drop the Victorian Adventurer's name. He's been persona non grata round here for years. But . . . you say you have Excalibur. And you knew the old Words . . . So here we are. Despite your really quite appalling reputation."

"Are you by any chance suggesting that I'm not worthy to bear Excalibur?" I said carefully.

"Not on the best day you ever had," Sir Gareth said cheerfully. "But then neither am I, or any of the London Knights. Excalibur is so much more than a sword, or any enchanted blade. Whoever bears Excalibur has the power to shape the fate of nations or change the course of history."

"Is that why you felt compelled to make a show of strength?" I said, glancing at the other knights, standing still and silent and watchful.

"Just being cautious," said Sir Gareth. "And, to show respect. To the sword Excalibur."

"And to the man who bears it?"

"Perhaps. As I said: your reputation goes before you, John Taylor."

"Who are you people?" I said bluntly. "What, exactly, are the London Knights? I know the name, I know the reputation, but I don't think anyone knows exactly what it is you do. And I'm not handing Excalibur over to just anybody."

"Fair enough," said Sir Gareth. "We go to great pains to keep what we do secret. We're not in it for the applause. Now, do you want the long version, or the short version? The short version misses out a lot of fun stuff, but the other version does tend to go on a bit. We have been round for a very long time . . . What say I hit the high spots, and you can ask questions afterwards?"

"Can you guarantee there will be an afterwards?" I said. "One of the few things I have heard is that you people have a tendency to execute those you consider unworthy."

"Oh, we don't do that any more," Sir Gareth said briskly. "Or at least, hardly ever. Only when we feel we absolutely have to. Now then, the London Knights are descended from those original knights who sat at the Round Table in Camelot, serving King Arthur and his glorious dream of justice, of Might for Right. The knights themselves were slaughtered at the final battle of Logres, fighting Mordred's army. All save one. The knights fell, and the dream was over."

"You did win, in the end," I said.

"Nobody won. Arthur and Mordred killed each other, both armies were destroyed, and the land was devastated. All they had built, gone, less than the dust. Good men, the finest of their generation—all that was left were piled-up bodies in the blood-soaked mud. But one knight survived. He gathered up all the families of those who fell and took them to a safe place. To the Unknown Castle. And down the centuries he slowly rebuilt the order of knights and based them here in London. That the might and the glory and the traditions of Arthur's dream might not vanish from this Earth. We maintain the chivalric way, serving the good and battling evil. The London Knights.

"We are warriors. We are the secret army, the hidden force, the men who ride to battle when all else has failed. We don't solve problems, we don't investigate mysteries, and we don't do diplomacy. We fight. We are the steel hand; we are sudden death; we are vengeance.

"Mostly we work behind the scenes, apart from everyday society, that we might not be corrupted by it. We fight our wars on far-off worlds and in hidden places, and no-one knows our triumphs and our losses but us. The London Knights stand firm against evil; that is all you know and all you need to know. We are still a religious order as much as an army, with every knight sworn to give his life and honour and everything else that matters to the cause that never ends.

"We are the guardians of the world. Any questions?"

"Where were you when we could have used you, during the Lilith War?"

"We don't sweat the small stuff," said Sir Gareth.

I glared at him. "All right. Who's in charge here?"

"Our leader is the Grand Master. That last original knight who survived the battle of Logres. Perhaps immortal, certainly very long-lived. He goes on, ensuring we still follow the right path and maintain the old traditions."

I didn't say anything, but I thought I had a pretty good idea of who this Grand Master might be. Though how he was still round was a mystery to me. I met Sir Kae, Arthur's stepbrother, back in the sixth century; sometime after the final battle of Logres. In fact, I bashed his head in with his own spiked mace after he disfigured my Suzie. Hopefully, he didn't still bear a grudge after all these years.

"How is it that your Grand Master is still alive?" I said finally. "I don't remember any immortal knights in Arthur's Court."

Another knight stepped forward, to stand beside Sir Gareth. "Those are our secrets. Ours to know, not yours."

"Allow me to introduce Sir Roland," said Sir Gareth. "Hard-core traditionalist, doughty fighter, and a real pain in the arse when it comes to getting your paper-work in on time."

There was a brief chuckle amongst the other knights, quickly dying away as Sir Roland looked back at them. He carefully lifted off his steel helm and tucked it firmly under one arm, revealing the face of a man in his fifties with close-cropped grey hair, cold grey eyes, and a steady gaze. He looked hard used by life, with deep lines etched into his face, but a small smile kept appearing at the corners of his mouth as though it couldn't quite help itself. There was a sense of barely suppressed energy about the man, of a need for battle or just plain violence, to soothe his inner fires.

"I can't believe the Lady gave Excalibur to a jumped-up thug like you, Taylor," Sir Roland said briskly. "Oh yes, boy, I know all about you."

"He has a subscription to the *Night Times*," said Sir Gareth. "And the *Unnatural Inquirer.*"

"John Taylor, a man who has warred with angels, battled

with immortals, and meddled in more ethically dubious areas than is good for any one man," said Sir Roland. "You choose your enemies well, boy, but your friends are little better. Is it true you and Shotgun Suzie are an item now?"

"Yes," I said, taken aback.

Sir Roland smiled his brief smile. "Well. Never saw that one coming. You have consorted with gods and immortals, the dead and the undead, and worst of all, you spent time with that despicable sorcerer, Merlin Satanspawn."

"He wasn't that bad," I said. "Well, actually, he was . . . but he had his redeeming qualities. And he did go to his final rest rescuing the Nightside from destruction."

"You say that like it's a good thing," said Sir Roland.

"We're not going to get along, are we?" I said.

"Who knows?" said Sir Roland, suddenly all bluff and cheerful. "Early days yet! Now, if you really have got Excalibur . . . show it to us."

"That is why I'm here," I said.

I reached up over my shoulder, taking my time about it. The knights' eyes followed my every move. I grasped the invisible hilt and drew Excalibur from its invisible scabbard with one easy move. The sword flashed into life between us, the golden blade filling the air with its glorious light. It was as though the sun had come down amongst us, to bless us with its life. The sword blazed more brightly in the castle hall than it ever had in the Nightside, as though it was back where it belonged. As though it had finally come home. And one by one, amidst a soft clattering of armour, the last and greatest of all the knights in the world slowly lowered themselves onto one knee, to bow their heads to that most ancient and honourable blade, Excalibur. I stood before them, holding the sword, and never felt less worthy in my life.

I have done good things and bad, great things and terrible, but nothing that justified bearing a sword like Excalibur.

I put the sword away, and the golden light snapped off

in a moment. The knights slowly got back onto their feet again, with a rather louder clattering of armour and a certain amount of leaning on each other for support. Sir Gareth and Sir Roland looked at each other, then at me. They both looked a bit dazed, as though someone had sneaked up and hit them both a good one while they weren't looking.

"It's certainly Excalibur," said Sir Gareth. "No doubt about that."

"To be blessed by its presence, after so many years . . ." Sir Roland frowned and fixed me with a stern look. "How did you get your hands on such a sword?"

I took a certain amount of pleasure in telling him, and a little bit more in watching Sir Roland's face turn an unhealthy shade of purple. His hands clenched the air before him as though he couldn't decide whether to grab the sword away from me, or settle for choking the life out of me on general principles. Sir Gareth looked very much like he wanted to go off on his own somewhere and have an extended fit of the giggles. The other knights gave every impression of being stunned speechless.

"In the post?" Sir Roland said finally, veins bulging in his neck. "You're supposed to have the holy blade bestowed on you by the Lady of the Lake, not simply dropped on your doorstep, wrapped in brown paper!"

"Well," I said lightly, "that's the Nightside for you."

"Would you like to take some of your little blue pills, Roland?" murmured Sir Gareth.

"I could spit soot," Sir Roland said bitterly. "All these years I dreamed of the holy blade returning to us in glory, to the order where it belongs, but this . . . this . . . this is what comes of watching too much television! Excalibur, in the hands of a private eye!"

"You like television," said Sir Gareth. "You never miss *Strictly Come Dancing.*"

"Entertaining though this is," I said, "it would help if

someone here would take the time to explain exactly what Excalibur is and what makes it so important. I'm guessing it's not because the sword comes with its own built-in night-light. Someone told me . . . that it's not what we think it is. And it never was. And while we're on the subject: who or what is the Lady of the Lake? I did do some research before I came here, and I couldn't find two books that would agree on the subject. The best guess seemed to be that she might have been Vivienne Le Fae, sister to the more infamous Morgan Le Fae."

"No," Sir Gareth said immediately. "Not even close. That's what comes of historians who love a good story; they always want everything to tie up neatly. The Lady, and the sword, are much older than that. Older than human history, older than the Fae, old as the land itself. All the other great arte-facts and symbols of Arthur's reign were Christian in nature. We'd only recently put our pagan past behind us, in the sixth century, and we saw Christian significance in everything. And, of course, there was the Holy Grail . . ."

"Do you have it?" I said.

"No," said Sir Roland, and he sounded honestly regret-ful. "The Grand Master has forbidden any of the order to go questing for it. He still believes that was what broke up the original Round Table . . ."

"The Lady," I said. "And the sword . . ."

"They both predate Christianity," said Sir Gareth. "By quite a while. The Lady of the Lake is Gaea. Mother Earth herself. And the sword is her will made manifest in the world. To wield Excalibur is to take the weight of the world on your shoulders."

"Hold everything," I said. "Gaea? As in, the whole world, personified? She's real?"

"You're from the Nightside," said Sir Gareth. "Are you really having trouble getting your head round such a simple concept?"

I really was. Even after everything I'd seen and done, to know for a fact that the world we all lived on was alive and aware . . .

"Given all the damage we as a species have done to her, I'm amazed she's still talking to us," I said, finally.

"She doesn't, much," said Sir Gareth. "But she'll want to speak to you."

"She's here?" I said.

"She visits," said Sir Gareth. "When she feels like it. She's always taken an interest in us, her favoured children."

"When she's not giving us a right bollocking for not doing more," said Sir Roland. "Though, strictly speaking, she's in no position to complain . . . You'd better come with us, boy. And for once in your disreputable life, concentrate on making a good impression. She hasn't actually struck anyone down with a lightning bolt in ages, but there's no point in tempting fate."

All twelve of the knights escorted me through the wide stone corridors of Castle Inconnu. Sir Gareth and Sir Roland led the way, one on each side of me, so I wouldn't get lost. Sir Gareth kept up a stream of cheerful chatter, all of it safely inconsequential. Sir Roland contributed the occasional grunt, and every now and again I caught him looking at me out of the corner of his eye as though he still couldn't quite believe what was happening. Didn't bother me. I've always enjoyed being a disappointment to those in authority.

Little victories . . .

We passed through a number of stone galleries, splendid indoor gardens, and comfortable gathering places, and finally ascended a long, winding stairway that ended in a circular stone chamber that felt like it was some way up in the air. (Since there were still no windows, it was impossible to be sure.) The chamber was wide and airy, and dominated by a great well in the centre of the room. (A well, in a tower. Six impossible things before breakfast . . .) The chamber was a good sixty feet in diameter, and fifty feet of it were taken up by the well. The stone rim was only a few feet high, and when I leaned forward and looked down, all I could see was darkness looking back at me. It reminded me of the oracle I'd consulted in the Mammon Emporium. Except that here, I got a definite smell of the sea, far below.

Sir Gareth took me politely but firmly by one arm and pulled me back from the well. One of the other knights removed his helmet and approached the well. Sir Gareth murmured the knight's name in my ear, Sir Percifal. He was an old man, well into his eighties, with a deeply lined face, sunken eyes, a pursed mouth, and a great mane of pure white hair. His face was grave, even grim, but his eyes were sharp and clear. The hands he placed gently on the stone rim were frail and covered in liver spots, but they didn't shake. I was quietly amazed he could stand upright, carrying that much armour. But you could tell, just from looking: Sir Percifal was still a knight and a warrior, an old soldier in a war that never ended. And there was something about him that suggested he could still be a very dangerous man when the situation demanded. You don't get to be an old solider without learning some very nasty tricks along the way. He bent over the well and called down into it; and his voice was firm and sure.

"Lady Gaea, it is Sir Percifal of the London Knights who calls you. Come speak with us, in Arthur's name, for the bearer of Excalibur has come amongst us. John Taylor of the Nightside is here; and we'd all like to have a few words with you about that . . ."

He straightened up quickly, as from deep in the well there came a great roaring sound, of something rushing towards us, building and building like an approaching tidal wave.

I could feel the pressure of something big coming, of something too large to fit easily into our fragile material world. I looked round and realised that all the knights had backed away from the well, as far as they could go, their steel backs pressed against the stone wall. A few had even retreated into the stairway. I moved quickly back to stand in the doorway. I can pick up a hint if you hit me with it hard enough.

And then a jet of water blasted up out of the well, dark blue-green sea-water, and it slammed against the stone ceiling before falling back as a shower of rain. Drops of water ran harmlessly down the knights' armour. I wasn't so lucky, but there are times when a white trench coat comes in handy. The water fell back into the well, and when I'd wiped the moisture from my face and eyes, a young woman was standing elegantly on the surface of the water filling the well.

An extremely good-looking woman, in a long dark dress with a bright scarlet sash round her waist. And not a drop of water on her anywhere. She smiled brilliantly about her, stepped forward, and set an elegant bare foot on the rim of the well. She reached out a hand to me, so I could help her step down. I took her hand automatically and was quietly surprised at how normal and human her hand felt in mine.

She was human, and she was beautiful, but she was also so very much more than that. She was Gaea. All the world in a woman. You only had to be in her company to know it.

She had a classic face with a strong bone structure, a great mane of night-dark hair, warm blue eyes, and a really nice mouth. She smiled at me, and I realised I was still holding her hand. I dropped it like it was red-hot, and she smiled again, understanding. And then I made the mistake of looking her in the eye. Her eyes were old, ancient, far older than any living thing had a right to be. I felt small, and insignificant, next to her, like I was shrinking away to nothing. She looked away, and the moment was broken, and I could breathe again. I swallowed hard and took control of myself. I have known gods and monsters in the Nightside, but never anything like her.

She felt . . . like the mother I'd never known and always wanted. The mother I dreamed of. And a part of me wondered if Gaea, old as she was, might have known my mother, Lilith. I was tempted to raise my Sight, sweep aside the illusion, and see Gaea for who and what she really was; but I had more sense. Some things in this world shouldn't be seen too clearly. We are not worthy.

The knights bowed to Gaea, and she smiled on them.

"Hello, boys. What's up?"

"Lady Gaea," said Sir Percifal. "You must forgive us on not preparing for your arrival, but . . ."

"Call me Gayle," she said, in a perfectly ordinary, perfectly wonderful voice. "You know very well I haven't used the old name for ages. And I know you boys get off on all these formalities; but really, life's too short. Let's get to it." She shot me an amused glance. "So, John, not quite what you were expecting?"

"Damned if I know," I said, and she laughed. Sir Percifal was trying to say something formal, but she was still looking at me, so I talked right over him. "Are you really the personification of the whole world?"

"I used to be," said Gayle. "But it all got a bit much once Humanity arrived, so I abdicated. In order to understand you, I had to become one of you and live amongst you. So I left much of me sleeping, and became Gayle."

"So," I said. "This . . . understanding Humanity. How's it going?"

"Still working on it," said Gayle.

"Lady . . . Gayle," said Sir Roland, as impatiently as his respect would allow, "why has Excalibur reappeared after all this time? Why weren't we told in advance? And why to *him*?"

"I have returned the sword to Humanity because it has

a duty to perform," said Gayle. "And I have bestowed it on John Taylor because his involvement is necessary. I sent it to the Nightside through the offices of the elf Puck. That one has long owed me a favour, and there aren't many who can say that. Because he usually kills them rather than remain obligated. I'd been holding on to that favour for centuries, not quite knowing why . . . and a good thing I did.

"Only the Puck could smuggle Excalibur into the Nightside, to my chosen bearer, past so many watchful eyes. Too many enemies just now, too many ready to seize the sword for themselves, for good reasons and bad. Too many ready to destroy the sword, for reasons good and bad. And far too many waiting for a chance to take it for themselves, even though it would inevitably destroy them, as not worthy." She looked at me. "I have granted you a special dispensation for this one time only."

"I thought as much," I said. "I keep telling people I'm not worthy, and I should know."

Actually, I felt rather relieved. I'd had a hard time believing I could be so wrong about myself.

"Puck served me well, at least partly because it appealed to his warped sense of humour," said Gayle. She sat down elegantly on the stone rim of the well, crossing her long legs neatly and resting her joined hands on the knees. "No-one can better an elf when it comes to sneaking things round. While you were helping smuggle him through the Nightside, John Taylor, he wasn't only providing a diversion for the elf Peace Treaty. He was also keeping all eyes focused on him because with so much excitement going on, who would notice one small package moving through the mail?"

"Why didn't he just give it to me?" I said.

"Probably because messing with your head was so much more fun," said Gayle.

"But why give the sword to Taylor in the first place?" Sir

Roland said stubbornly. "Why a man like him? Why not one of us? Any one of us would be happy to bear the burden of Excalibur. We would all die for you, Lady!"

"Exactly," said Gayle. "I wanted a man who'd live for me. And, to answer your previous question, I couldn't send the sword here. You're being watched. You must have noticed."

The knights looked at each other. Sir Percifal seized his chance to rejoin the conversation. "We knew. Of course we knew. Our security is second to none. Yes. But for all our skills, and all our sources, I have to say . . . We are currently unable to ascertain who it is that's watching us. Yes."

"We've leaned on all the usual unusual suspects," said Sir Gareth. "And it isn't any of them."

"And given how powerful our resources are," Sir Percifal said doggedly, "it would have to be somebody powerful. Yes. Extremely powerful. And that . . . is a very short list. Oh yes."

"Quite," said Gayle. "Anyway, John Taylor is my choice to bear Excalibur, and no, you don't get to bitch about it. He has a destiny to fulfil."

"Oh bloody hell," I said loudly. "Not another one. I had a hard enough time getting rid of the last one. What have I got to do now?"

"You will give Excalibur to King Arthur. After you have helped bring him back."

There was a long silence. The knights all looked at Gayle, then at me. Sir Percifal looked ecstatic. Sir Roland looked like he might have a stroke. Sir Gareth looked . . . thoughtful. Gayle smiled enchantingly on one and all. I didn't say a word. I hadn't a clue what to say. Sir Roland finally broke the silence, looking like he would explode if he didn't, but his voice was still barely under control.

"Arthur is coming back? King Arthur? Our long-lost King is finally returning, in our lifetime? You never said anything about this before! What are our regular consultations for if you're not going to share important information like this? Why didn't you tell us?"

"Somebody is shouting," said Gayle, to no-one in particular. "And he'd better knock it off if he doesn't want me to slap him with an earthquake."

"Beg pardon, Lady," said Sir Roland. "I fear I am . . . over-excited."

"Better," said Gayle. "I didn't tell you because I knew you'd all act like a bunch of schoolgirls when you found out you couldn't be a part of this. You're too close, too involved. You can't do what's necessary."

"Who has a better right to be involved," said Sir Percifal, "than those who have spent centuries preserving Arthur's legacy, ready for his return? Hmm?"

"It has to be Taylor," said Gayle, not unkindly. "He's the only one who can do this. Get used to the idea, boys. And no, I can't tell you why. Not yet. There are . . . complications. Sometimes, things have to sort themselves out. So make John Taylor welcome amongst you, in my name. Or do my wishes mean nothing to you any more?"

"You are our Lady," said Sir Percifal. "Our lives are yours. Yes."

"Dear Percy," said Gayle. "You were such a handsome boy. Now be good, boys, for goodness' sake. And all things shall be made well."

And then she rose, turned lightly on one foot, and leapt gracefully into the well. She disappeared from sight in a moment, taking all the water in the well with her. Sir Percifal sighed and shook his great head fondly.

"Well, that's one way to avoid answering questions." He looked at me with sharp and piercing eyes. "It would seem there's no getting rid of you. No. That you are . . . necessary. So be welcome amongst us while we work out how best we can aid you in your quest. Yes. Stop rumbling, Roland; the decision has been made. Hmm . . . Sir Gareth; show Mr.

Taylor round the castle. Get to know him. Give him the grand tour but keep him away from anything . . . sensitive. Yes. You might bear Excalibur, Mr. Taylor, but you are not one of us. No. No. Off you go, the pair of you. The rest of us have to go off somewhere private and shout a lot."

Sir Gareth took me on a walking tour of Castle Inconnu. The winding stone corridors seemed to go on forever, passing through halls and chambers and galleries beyond counting. He was happy to point out things of interest and not answer any questions I might have. He was also quite open about the fact that he was keeping me occupied, while the knights decided what the hell they were going to do next. But there were all kinds of interesting things to see, and I had a lot to think about. So I followed Sir Gareth past magnificent murals, through portrait galleries and banqueting halls, and past wonderfully carved fountains, until the sheer scale of things began to depress me. Architecture is all very nice, but you can have too much of a good thing.

"Don't you have anywhere normal-sized in this castle?" I said finally. "Some of these halls are so big, I feel I should be adjusting my watch for different time zones."

Sir Gareth chuckled easily. "Oh sure; these are only the public areas, designed to awe and intimidate the casual visitor. We don't actually use most of this any more, except for the odd game of polo, or the occasional martial re-enactment. We live in the inner quarters, which are built on a far more bearable scale. Much more comfortable; you'd hardly know you were inside a castle. We've got Gameboys and everything. I'm afraid you're not cleared to see the inner quarters yet. Feel free to ask questions, though; and I'll try not to be too evasive."

"All right," I said. "Where is this castle, exactly? It's not a part of the Nightside, or any of London's other hidden worlds that I know of."

"You're not cleared for that information either. Everything about Castle Inconnu is a secret unless you're one of us. And even we don't know everything. We have many enemies, and one of our best safeguards is that no-one knows how to find us. We could be anywhere, any time, and for all I know we are. The Green Door is our only link to London Proper, and you couldn't get through that Door with an enchanted battering ram. And now King Arthur is coming back . . . Well, you can bet everyone up to and including the Grand Master is in major panic mode. Everything we ever dreamed and worked for is finally within our grasp . . . and we're not ready."

"And possibly . . . not worthy?" I said.

"The Lady gave Excalibur to you and not one of us," said Sir Gareth. "That has to mean something. That maybe we've spent too long hidden away from the world. Some of us will be making the case for war; for taking our fight public, for the first time in centuries. If King Arthur is coming back, perhaps it's time for the Final Battle against all the evil in the world, when all things shall be decided, once and for all."

"I've been through a lot of battles like that," I said. "Nothing ever changes."

"This is different," insisted Sir Gareth. "King Arthur reborn and returned will be a major player in everything that is happening, perhaps even the Major Player. Especially the upcoming elf civil war."

"Is that still on?" I said. "What about the Peace Treaty?"

"Didn't work. No-one ever thought it would. Neither side really wants peace—just some breathing space to muster their forces. Both sides want this war, John. Their survival as a race depends upon it. They're dying out. No elven children have been born for ages; either in Shadows Fall, under Oberon and Titania, or in the Sundered Lands, under the returned Mab. They will fight their civil war here on Earth, destroying our civilisation in the process, then the surviving elves will take this world for their own again. And thus restore their . . . vitality."

"Could they really wipe us out while divided amongst themselves?" I said.

"Who knows what a species can do with its back against the wall," said Sir Gareth. "We've always known they had weapons beyond our reach or imagination. Either way, it won't be good for the Earth. Which is probably why the Lady Gaea is getting personally involved for the first time in centuries. I'd be worried if I were the worrying kind."

"I did hear," I said, "that the elves chose to leave this world, all those years ago. That they were running from something, and not us."

"Presumably, things have changed," said Sir Gareth.

"What makes King Arthur so important to the elves?"

"His stepsister was Morgan Le Fae," Sir Gareth said simply.

"But who was she? I mean, yes, obviously, the clue is in the name. But was she an elf, a half-elf, or what?"

"Good question," said Sir Gareth. "If you ever find out, please let us know. We've got libraries full of books, from official histories to personal accounts, and none of them can agree on an answer. So much knowledge was lost . . . after the fall of Logres and the destruction of Camelot."

"Merlin told me . . . he never believed she was really family to Arthur," I said.

Sir Gareth looked at me sharply. "Of course; you had dealings with the Satanspawn, in the Nightside. None of us could ever talk to him; the Grand Master would never allow it. He always said Merlin disgraced himself by not being there at Logres when he was needed the most."

"He did say he regretted that," I said.

"Not good enough," Sir Gareth said flatly. "We do not forget, or forgive."

"I don't think he gave a damn what you thought about him," I said. "He had far more serious sins on his conscience. Anyway, he's dead and gone now."

Sir Gareth looked at me thoughtfully. "Word is you knew him as well as any man could. You must write us a full report while you're here, for our records."

"No," I said. "He and I were never friends, but . . . some things should stay private. You knights made the decision to have nothing to do with him; and I think he'd want me to tell you to go to Hell."

"Yes," said Sir Gareth. "That sounds like him."

We walked on in silence for a while, each of us thinking his separate thoughts. I knew a lot of things about Merlin that I was pretty sure the Knights didn't. I knew Merlin wasn't present for the final battle of Logres because he was obsessed with tracking down and killing the missing Morgan Le Fae for her betrayal of Arthur. By the time he was finished with her, and got back, it was all over; and Arthur was dead. Though Merlin did once admit to me that he wasn't entirely sure Morgan was dead. Could she still be round, and ready to reappear, now that Merlin was gone and Arthur was coming back? One more thing to worry about . . . I couldn't tell the knights any of this; because if Merlin had wanted them to know, he would have told them himself. He must have had his reasons for maintaining his silence.

And I definitely couldn't tell Sir Gareth that I'd met the living Merlin, back in the sixth century, taken his heart, and brought about his death. Or that while I was there, I'd briefly seen the living King Arthur, in his last communication with Merlin; in a sending, a dream walking, that arrived too late. Some things should be kept private.

Especially as I still wasn't sure whether I trusted the London Knights yet. Nothing does more harm than a good man doing good in a bad way.

"I'm surprised you guys know so much about me," I said finally. "I wouldn't have thought I was important enough to register on your radar."

"Don't be disingenuous," said Sir Gareth. "It doesn't suit you. We know who you are, and what you are, and what you've done. We always said we'd have to do something about you if you ever left the Nightside. Some kind of high explosive, probably. There was a lot of talk about whether we should intervene during the Angel War, then the Lilith War; but we held off. Partly because we really hate getting involved with the Nightside, but mostly because we were curious to see what you would do."

"Thanks," I said. "I think."

"And there have always been those amongst us who think we should ride into the Nightside in force and wipe you all out once and for all."

"Well," I said. "You could try . . ."

"Quite. We have been keeping a more than usually close eye on the Nightside, recently. Ever since King Artur turned up there from Sinister Albion. That damned and corrupt dimension where a Golden Age was drowned in blood and horror. The only reason we haven't gone there in force and put everything right the hard way is because we can't find a way in. That Merlin is still alive, and protecting his own little infernal playground. Which is why we were so interested when King Artur appeared. How did he leave his world and enter the Nightside?"

"A Timeslip, presumably," I said. "The Nightside is lousy with the things."

"If so, we haven't been able to find it. And we looked really hard."

I gave him a stern look. "You people have been to the Nightside?"

"Hardly. We wouldn't fit in. We'd be noticed. But we do have certain resources . . ."

"Do you know what happened to Artur?" I said. "He seemed to vanish."

"Haven't a clue. Do you . . . ?"

"No. Do you know why he came to the Nightside?"

"Yes. He wanted to get his hands on our Excalibur and make it his own because the Lady of his world refused him her sword. He was not worthy."

"But what would Artur want with our Excalibur?"

"If he could seize it by force, and make it serve him, Excalibur would make Artur powerful enough to stand up to his Merlin," Sir Gareth said patiently. "Artur might be King of Sinister Albion; but he still bows his head to Merlin Satanspawn if he wants to keep his throne."

"Civil war everywhere you look," I murmured. "Why can't people just get along?"

Sir Gareth looked at me sharply. "Both sides of the Fae, and a great many other interested parties, would very much like to know where King Arthur is sleeping. Where his body lies, hidden and protected. Including us."

"You don't know?" I said, honestly surprised.

"We've never known. Whoever put Arthur to rest, dead or sleeping, went to great pains to hide him from everyone, friends and enemies alike. The London Knights have spent centuries searching, to no avail. And we only wanted to protect him. Many others would give everything they possess to discover Arthur's hiding-place. Because whoever controls him potentially controls everything else. He is the greatest hero and warrior this world has ever known."

"I take it we're not only talking about the good guys here," I said. "The bad guys want him, too?"

"Of course. Artur from Sinister Albion was corrupted by his Merlin. For all his many qualities, Arthur was just a man. He could be swayed, turned, dominated by an outside force. Excalibur was never the most powerful weapon in Camelot; that was always Arthur. And as he goes . . . so goes the world."

"I never know whether we're talking about history or legend when it comes to Arthur," I said. "Most of the stories say he was taken away, to sleep in Avalon."

"What is Avalon?" said Sir Gareth. "Only a name. In the whole existence of our order, we've never found any place or any land called Avalon. No-one knows where Arthur is. And before you ask, no, he couldn't be in Shadows Fall. That's where legends go to die when the world stops believing in them; and the world still believes in Arthur. But now Excalibur has come back into the world, the chase is on. Everyone will be after Arthur; and it's vital for the good of everybody that we get there first."

I didn't say anything. But I did wonder if perhaps certain elements inside the London Knights might not prefer it if Arthur were to stay sleeping, even if found. That they might even take steps to ensure he never awoke. Because if he did, would he approve of what the London Knights had become? Of all the things they'd done, and made of themselves, in the fifteen hundred years since Logres? They may have meant well; but we all know what road is paved with good intentions.

We moved on, into the Hall of Forgotten Beasts. A long hall whose walls were decorated with the severed, stuffed, and mounted heads of fantastical creatures that were no longer a part of history. The only remaining examples of hundreds, maybe thousands, of exotic beasts. I walked slowly past row upon row of glassily staring, slack-jawed heads. Some I recognised, some I'd heard of, and some that were perhaps completely unknown now, outside of Castle Inconnu.

"For a long time, hunting was a central part of knightly tradition," said Sir Gareth. "We don't do it any more, of course. We're all conservationists now. But we still take a pride in this hall. It took brave men to hunt these beasts and bring them down."

I didn't say anything, walking on and on past the dead heads of once-noble creatures. I had no doubt many of them had been man-killers in their day; but it still seemed to me that slaughter, no matter how necessary, shouldn't be something you took a pride in. You did it because it needed doing, not because you had a gap on your trophy wall. It was only a step from there to mounting the heads of your enemies on spikes over your door, where everyone could see them.

A unicorn's head stared sullenly out from the wall, its skin still blindingly white though the curlicued horn was cracked from end to end. A gryphon, with a bullet hole left unrepaired in its forehead; a basilisk with no eyes; and a dire wolf with moulting fur, its jaws forever snarling defiance. And, protruding way out into the hall, a dragon's head, at least fifteen feet wide, its scaled hide a dull bottle-green. The eyes were clearly glass and looked like no-one had dusted them in a while. I finally stopped before one head I didn't recognise, and Sir Gareth stopped with me.

"This is the fabled Questing Beast. It eluded us for centuries though many knights went after it, tracking it all across Europe. Finally brought down by Sir Bors, in 1876. One shot, from four hundred yards."

"How very sporting," I said.

The Questing Beast's head was an odd mixture of beast and bird. And perhaps it was my imagination, but to me the Beast looked old and tired and pitiful, and maybe even a little resigned. It had outlived the time it was meant for, and the menaces it understood, like swords and lances, and finally died from an attack it never even saw coming.

I looked back down the Hall of Forgotten Beasts, and it did not seem a place of pride to me. All I felt was a quiet air of melancholy.

"You have to understand," Sir Gareth said defensively, "every beast here preyed on people. It was a knight's duty back then to hunt these creatures down and protect the innocent from attack. No-one thought about preserving endangered species. These days we only hunt bad guys, the real monsters of the world."

I looked at him thoughtfully. "Lots of monsters in the Nightside. You ever go hunting there?"

"I told you," Sir Gareth said steadily. "We stay out of the Nightside."

"Because Merlin was there?"

"It's all about territory," said Sir Gareth. "You should understand that, John."

We moved on again and came to a long stone gallery where the walls were covered with long rows of framed portraits, reminders of those who'd fallen in service with the London Knights. There were hundreds of them, maybe even thousands, stretching away into the distance. The most recent were photographs, showing men of various ages, all striking the same stiff pose and determined smile. These gave way to black-and-white, then sepia prints, and finally to painted portraits, in the varying styles of the times. The same stiff pose, though, the same determined smile. All the way back to stylised images of the original knights of Arthur's Camelot. Painted sometime after, I assumed, though of course I could be wrong. Merlin's court was famous for its anachronisms. I stopped before one portrait.

"Kae," I said. "Arthur's stepbrother."

"Yes!" said Sir Gareth. "You do get round, don't you?"

"You have no idea," I said. "Really." And then I looked at him as a thought struck me. I looked back and forth, at all the images of the original Round Table. "These knights are all from sixth-century England. So how come they're wearing suits of the kind of plate armour that didn't arrive until hundreds of years later?"

"That was Merlin," said Sir Gareth. "Remember, he could

see the future as easily as he saw the past. He looked ahead, saw the armour, and knew a good idea when he saw one . . . He presented the armourers with plans and designs, and next thing you know King Arthur and his knights had suits of armour that no-one else could match. That's why they won so many victories . . ."

"Is that all Merlin gave the knights?" I said.

Sir Gareth sighed heavily. "Who knows? So much was lost, so much was forgotten, after Camelot fell. By all accounts from that period, Arthur's castle was full of wonders and glories, the greatest knowledge and science of that time, with marvellous devices and amazing inventions. All gone now."

"What did happen, to the original Castle of Camelot?" I said.

"They burned it," said Sir Gareth. "Mordred's followers—in revenge for the loss of their leader. No-one was there to stop them; all the knights had gone off, to fight and fall at Logres. The women and children had just enough warning to get out, before Mordred's bastards arrived. And afterwards . . . the last occupants of Camelot scattered, first across England, and later Europe, telling stories that became legends, of the glory that was Camelot. Nothing of the castle survived, and all too soon no-one even remembered where it once stood."

"You never found it while you were searching for Arthur?"

"We never looked," Sir Gareth said simply. "The London Knights preserve the best of the old, and we live by long-established and revered traditions . . . but we have chosen to look forward, not back. There's enough needs doing in the present without obsessing on the past."

We walked on, talking easily about this and that. It occurred to me that we'd been walking a long time without even a glimpse of the more civilised inner quarters. I was moved to wonder aloud exactly how big Castle Inconnu was.

"Hard to tell," said Sir Gareth. "We've been adding to the old place for centuries, as our order grew larger, and we needed more living space for our wives and families. We're as much a city as a castle when you get right down to it."

"So who else wants to find Arthur?" I said. "Name some names. I might know some of them."

"Personally, or professionally?" said Sir Gareth. "I can remember when the good guys fought the bad guys; now it seems like half the time we end up working together to take down some outside force that can't even tell the difference between good and evil. But, our main enemy at the moment used to be one of our own. Jerusalem Stark, the Knight Apostate—rogue, heretic, and blasphemer. Once our brightest light, our most accomplished warrior, now our greatest failure and most dedicated enemy. He was the best of us until he had his crisis of faith. Now the man who swore to follow our cause all his life has given his life to our destruction. Sworn to see us all dead, down to the last man. And to achieve that, he has shown himself ready to join with the worst there is. Poor Jerry. We tried to help him after it all went wrong; but he didn't want to be helped. If he finds King Arthur first, he'll kill him, if only to spite us."

"Why?" I said. "What happened, to turn him round so completely?"

Sir Gareth paused, considering his words carefully. "We had gone to war, in another dimension. Worlds in the balance, whole civilisations at stake, everything to play for. We fought valiantly, with Jerusalem Stark at our head; and the enemy could not stand against us. So they fought dirty. They took Jerry's wife, Julianne. Turn back, they said, or we'll kill her. But we couldn't turn back; it would have meant throwing away everything we'd gained. So many lives lost for nothing and so many more put at peril. So we pressed on, and they killed her. Jerry argued against it, begged for more time to come up with a rescue plan, but there wasn't any time.

117

"I was there with him when we found the body. After the battle was won. They'd taken their time with her, the bastards. We executed all the leaders, of course; but it didn't bring Julianne back to life. Or undo one small part of what they'd done to her. Jerusalem Stark cursed us all and walked out. From that day on, he was our most relentless enemy, and all our previous enemies his friends. And as if that wasn't enough, he made a deal with . . . forces best not named out loud. They brought Julianne back from the dead, as a ghost. Now Jerry carries her preserved heart in a silver cage on his belt, to hold her to him.

"He still believes that if he can only find powerful enough allies, someone will bring her all the way back to life. The fool. If it was at all possible, we would have done it. We all loved Julianne. She brought such light and warmth into this sometimes dry and dusty place."

"Are there any female knights?" I asked.

"No. Tradition, you see. It shapes so much of who and what we are. The order does change, but only slowly. We are still mostly a religious order . . . but it wouldn't surprise me to see the first female knights ordained in my lifetime. We're not celibate; but it is always understood that our lives and our loyalties belong to the order, first and foremost. 'I could not love thee, dear, half so much, Loved I not honour more . . .' Most of us have wives and children. We keep them here in the castle with us, where they're safe."

"So what do the women here do?" I said. "Act as servants?"

"No," Sir Gareth said patiently. "The castle may be medieval, but we're not. Castle Inconnu is full of airy spirits that do all the necessary things. The knights fight; our women provide all the necessary backup work. Doctors, librarians, teachers, historians, armourers . . . We couldn't do what we do without them. Julianne was our spiritual councillor. Our priest confessor in all but name. That's why she was with us on that fateful battle-field so far from home. We would have saved her if we could. There wasn't enough time. I would have died for her; but we couldn't let so many innocents die for her. And she wouldn't have wanted that anyway."

"How could you know what she would have wanted?" said a harsh new voice. "You never really knew her. You never loved her."

We both looked round sharply. Somehow, our steps had brought us round in a circle, and we were back at the beginning of the portrait gallery. And one portrait had come alive on the wall; the calm and peaceful head-and-shoulders pose replaced by a living image. I didn't need to be told who it was. I never saw a more bitter and haunted face in my life. Jerusalem Stark glared out of his portrait at us, his eyes dark and unblinking, his lips pulled back in a grimace that was as much a snarl as a smile. He had the look of a man who would go anywhere, do anything, for the cause that drove him on. And would never, ever, let him rest. A very dangerous man.

"Hello, Jerry," Sir Gareth said calmly. "It's been a while since you last spoke to any of us."

"As a London Knight, I was granted many privileges," said Stark, still smiling his unnerving smile. "And they cannot be taken back. I will always have access to Castle Inconnu. You can't keep me out. You can't keep the truth out."

"What truth would that be, Jerry?" Sir Gareth said politely. "That you betrayed the cause you swore your life to? Your life and your sacred honour? That you have betrayed good men and true to the monsters you have taken as allies, men who once fought at your side and trusted you with their lives? That you have betrayed the memory of your wife, who would never have wanted to be saved at such a terrible cost?"

"You could have found a way to save her if you'd wanted!" Stark's glare was unwavering, his voice unforgiving. "We had time. There were options. But the Grand Master wouldn't listen. All he cared about was victory, whatever the cost. He sacrificed my love for his triumph. Because that's the knightly way. The truth is, Gar, you serve an inhuman cause, in inhuman ways. You've become the very thing you used to fight."

"You know that isn't true, Jerry." Sir Gareth's voice remained calm, in contrast to the dark passion in Stark's every word. "Come back to us. It's not too late. Come home. We can help you find your way again."

"I have my way. You forced it on me when you let my wife die; and I have embraced it."

"We were friends once, Jerry. It wasn't that long ago. Please. I don't want to have to kill you."

"You see? In one breath you call me friend, and in the other you threaten to kill me. See what the order has done to you, Gar."

" 'I could not love thee, dear, half so much . . .' "

"Shut up! I don't have to listen to that any more! They're just words. I only wanted one thing in my life, only cared for one thing, and you let them take her from me. I will have my revenge, Gareth. I know you have Excalibur."

Sir Gareth carefully didn't look at me. "How do you know that, Jerry? Which of your new friends told you that?"

Stark sneered at him. "I have new allies. Very old and very powerful allies. They want you all dead nearly as much as I do." He turned his cold gaze abruptly to me. "I know you, John Taylor. Get out of here while you still can. Forget whatever you were promised; you can't trust anything they tell you. They'll lie, cheat, and betray, in the name of their precious cause. Don't be fooled by their fine words; they've forgotten what it is to be human."

"I always said you were the most dangerous of our enemies, Jerry," said Sir Gareth. "Because you think you're the good guy."

"I am the good guy." The image in the portrait suddenly

changed, the view pulling back sharply to show Jerusalem Stark in full figure, clad in the same gleaming steel armour as Sir Gareth. And standing beside him was the pale and shimmering image of his dead wife, Julianne. She wasn't much of a ghost; just a semi-transparent shape in a long white dress who wasn't always there. She faded in and out, her details vague and uncertain, her face a blur. Sir Gareth made a low noise of distress.

"Oh don't, Jerry. Don't do this. Let her go."

Stark's hand fell to the spun-silver cage at his belt, and at the touch of his fingers, the image of his dead wife became firm and clear. Her white dress was soaked in blood, all the way down her front. Her face was sharp and distinct now, but it held no expression at all. She looked dead. She turned her head slowly to look at Stark.

"Let me go. If you love me, let me go."

Her voice gave me chills. I've heard the dead speak before, but never like this. Her voice was a whisper, as though it had to travel unimaginable distances to reach us. And it was full of all the despair and suffering in the world.

"I can't let you go," said Stark. "I can't. You're all that matters to me now."

She reached out a hand and took his arm, and Stark shuddered despite himself. The living and the dead aren't supposed to be close.

"Come home, Jerry," said Sir Gareth. "Stop tormenting yourself. It wasn't your fault."

"No. It was your fault. You let her die."

"There must be something we can do for you . . ."

"There is. Give me Excalibur."

"What would you do with Excalibur?" said Sir Gareth. "What possible use could it be to you?"

"I don't give a damn for your magic sword," said Stark. "But my allies want it. And they want it so much, they've promised to bring my Julianne back to life in return for Excalibur."

"They lied, Jerry," Sir Gareth said sadly. "They can't bring her back. No-one can. She's gone. Accept it."

"Never! They can do it, Gar. I've seen them do it. I'm going to take Excalibur from you and give it to them. And then I'll watch and laugh while they wipe you all out, down to the last man. Because that's all you've left me."

The portrait was suddenly only a photograph again. The dark and driven knight was gone and his dead wife with him. There was a distinct chill on the air, and Sir Gareth and I both shuddered a little, despite ourselves.

"New allies," said Sir Gareth, after a moment. "That can't be good. Who the hell could he have found who can bring the dead back to life? Only one man could ever do that, and that was our Lord . . ."

"Well, the dead can return," I said. "As zombies, in various forms. Dead bodies possessed by various beings. Not actually alive but better than nothing."

"Jerry wouldn't settle for that. But, he says he saw proof . . ." Sir Gareth shook his head angrily. "Jerry is out of his depth."

"Who do you think these new allies are?"

"There's someone we've been keeping an eye on . . . Prince Gaylord the Damned, Nuncio to the Court of King Artur, of Sinister Albion. He turned up in the Nightside three days ago by a means we couldn't identify. Apparently, his Merlin sent him to the Nightside to search for Artur after he disappeared. I'm surprised you don't know about him."

"I've been a bit busy the past few days," I said defensively.

"Well, when Prince Gaylord couldn't find King Artur anywhere in the Nightside, he got it into his head that we must have him. He's been trying to find or force a way into Castle Inconnu ever since."

"Could he do that? Is he powerful enough?"

"Who knows anything, where Sinister Albion is concerned? If he has his Merlin's backing . . . maybe."

"Do you have Artur?" I said carefully.

"No. He seems to have disappeared. No-one knows where he is. And given everything that's happening, the last thing we need right now is another major player in the game."

And that was when every alarum in the world went off at once. Bells, sirens, electronic alarms, and what sounded very much like a cloister bell. Sir Roland's photograph on the wall suddenly came alive, replaced by an angry and seriously worried face.

"Castle Inconnu is under attack! Our security has been breached! The enemy is within our walls, dammit!"

"What? How the hell is that possible?" Sir Gareth's face was almost colourless from shock. He looked like he'd been hit.

"It's Stark. Somehow he's used his old access rights to force a way through our outer defences and hold open a door for the enemy. They're inside the walls, Gareth; inside the castle! Stark has brought an army in past all our protections! They've invaded the outer layers, and they're heading inwards!"

"What army?" said Sir Gareth. "Who are they?"

"Elves!" said Sir Roland. "Stark's allied himself with the elves!"

"No . . ." Sir Gareth shook his head dazedly. "No, he couldn't . . . Oh, Jerry, you bloody fool. What have you done?"

"How many elves are there?" I said, pushing in beside Sir Gareth. "What kind of numbers are we talking about? Have they any elven weapons?"

"Hundreds of them," said Sir Roland. "And more flooding in all the time. There's a lot of magical armour, and enchanted swords, but no major weapons that we've seen— no Airgedlamh, or Sword of the Daun."

"Well, that's something," I said. "Do we know which

faction? Who do they serve: Oberon and Titania, or the returned Mab?"

"What the hell difference does that make?"

"I've had dealings with the Puck," I said. "Through him, I might be able to negotiate with Oberon and Titania. But if these elves belong to Mab, we don't have anything they want. Except our deaths. And Excalibur."

"Elves in the castle?" Sir Gareth was abruptly himself again. "John and I will be with you as soon as we can, Roland. Get the knights moving and organised; put up a wall between the invaders and our families; give them time to get to the safety of the Redoubt. Stop them with cold steel and pile their bodies high." He looked at me, and suddenly he was grinning, his face full of the joy of battle. "Stark is here for you, John. He wants the sword you carry. Will you fight alongside us?"

"Of course," I said. "Never could stand elves."

"Good man. Roland, see that our families are safe. And if worst comes to worst, see they have a dead man's switch so they can take the enemy with them."

"Of course," said Sir Roland. And his face disappeared from the portrait.

"Was that last bit really necessary?" I said.

"Yes. You know what elves do to women and children. Death would be a kindness."

I nodded. I knew. "You should never have kept your families here in the castle."

"We thought they were safe here, where we could protect them! No-one's ever got past our defences before! Never! No-one ever anticipated elves inside the castle. Let's go."

"Sir Roland jumped pretty fast there, when you gave him orders," I said. "Are you in charge here, or something?"

"Something," said Sir Gareth. "You didn't think they'd leave you with just anyone, did you?"

• • •

We sprinted back through the stone corridors, and I had to work hard to keep up with Sir Gareth. Even though he was wearing full plate armour, and all I had was my trench coat, he still led all the way. Because he was a trained warrior, in the peak of condition; and I wasn't. But I pounded grimly along after him, and all too soon we heard the sounds of fighting up ahead. We rounded a sudden corner, charged into one of the great open halls, and found it full to bursting with elves and knights in their armour.

Sir Gareth plunged straight in, sword in hand, but I made myself hang back in the archway, so I could study the situation. Excalibur was burning on my back, urging me on, but I'd had enough of that. I wasn't a warrior or a hero, and acting like one would get me killed. If I was going to take on an army of elves, it wouldn't be by running straight at them. I'd do it my own way.

Elves in glowing armour, in vivid shades of gold and crimson and emerald, brandishing shimmering swords and glowing axes, went head to head with London Knights in cold steel armour with solid, deadly blades. The elves leapt and pirouetted, dancing through the chaos with deadly grace, supernaturally quick and vicious, impossibly light on their feet; and the knights stamped and spun, meeting the elves' speed with the practiced skill that comes from years of training. Most of the action was simply too fast to follow, as elf and man slammed together, blades flashing and blood spurting. The air was full of the sound of blade clashing against blade, or clanging against armour, and over all, shrieks and howls and war cries, exclamations of pain and rage and hate.

Given the sheer number fighting in the hall, hardly any were dead yet. The elves' enchanted armour turned aside most sword blows while the knights' armour had its own protection, enough to stand against glowing elf blades. Both sides had to search for weak spots and brief openings; joints in the armour, exposed throats, or the eyeholes in a helm. Blood spurted here and there, and I saw one knight crash to the floor. Immediately, half a dozen elves were stooping over him, stabbing down again and again. Two more knights rushed forward to protect their fallen friend, standing proud and powerful over him, beating aside the elves' blades with sharp precision. The elves danced and leapt round them, horribly graceful, laughing lightly.

Sir Gareth was right there in the thick of it, swinging his long sword with both hands, roaring harsh guttural war cries as he struck down one elf after another. They were quick, and they were elegant, but he was an unstoppable force, moving always forward, throwing elves back through main strength. An elf leaned right over to cut at the back of his knee, but somehow Sir Gareth turned at the very last moment to block the elf's sword with his own. He stabbed the elf in the groin, the tip of his blade finding a brief opening in the glowing armour; and golden blood flowed down the elf's thigh. He fell to one knee, and Sir Gareth brought his sword sweeping round in a long arc that cut right through the elf's neck. The head in its glowing helmet tumbled free, golden blood fountaining from the neck stump; and Sir Gareth didn't even wait to see the body fall before moving on to the next.

I stood in the open archway, watching it all, and knew that none of my little tricks and lateral thinking would work here. I could stay back and let the two forces fight it out amongst themselves. But I couldn't do that. Excalibur made this my business, my problem, and besides, I really don't like elves. In any battle, if you want to know who the good guys are, look to see which side has the elves. And then join the other one. The elves are the enemies of humanity because they chose to be. So I took a deep breath, did my best to ignore the sick feeling in the pit of my stomach, drew Excalibur, and went forward into battle.

Calling myself an idiot every step of the way.

The moment I drew Excalibur, everything changed. Its golden glow leapt forth, illuminating the entire hall; and both sides sent up a great cry, as though its very existence validated their being there. The elves all turned to look in my direction and surged forward, aimed right at me. They were singing now, a sweetly inhuman sound that hurt my ears. The London Knights moved quickly to stop them, putting their steel and themselves between the elves and Excalibur, and the man who bore it. And I moved forward, swinging the great golden blade before me as though it were weightless, an unfamiliar exhilaration filling my heart. I might never be a knight, but I had met both Merlin and Arthur, and at that moment it felt like I had both their blessings.

An elf reared up before me in shimmering silver armour, his blade glowing bright as the sun. I cut him down with a single stroke, Excalibur shearing through his enchanted armour as though it weren't even there. The blade sank deep into his chest. I jerked it out again, and golden blood flew on the air. The elf fell away, and I moved on. I didn't have skill or grace; Excalibur was unstoppable. I stabbed and hacked and cut, and elves died at my hand, and it felt good, so good. I was grinning broadly now, shouting and laughing as I cut my way through the elves, like a gardener through tall weeds.

That wasn't like me, and I knew it even then, but I wasn't in charge any more. The sword was. It knew what it was doing; I was only along for the ride. I swung the sword with a speed and a skill that weren't mine, killing elves. Excalibur was in its element, come home again, to do what it was made to do.

I ran an elf through, the sword punching through his breast-plate and out his back. Golden blood streamed down the armour, but the elf didn't even cry out. He stood his ground and tried to force himself forward, along the blade, so he could get his hands on me. I stared impassively into his contorted face and hauled the sword out of his body in one brutal movement. He cried out then, and I cut his exposed throat. And then I continued the movement, spinning round to block the attack of an elf moving in on my blind side. I hadn't known he was there, but the sword had. The new elf stabbed at me, but I blocked his blade with Excalibur, and the glowing elven sword shattered into a dozen pieces. And while the elf hesitated, startled, I cut him down and moved on to my next victim. I wasn't even breathing hard.

And then I stopped, and looked round me, because suddenly there were no more elves. They were all dead, lying scattered and still across the wide and bloody marble floor. The London Knights sent up a great cry of triumph, punching the air with their raised blood-stained blades, then they turned to me and cried out their praises. I nodded. It didn't feel like I'd done anything. I looked round for Sir Gareth; but he was already racing through the archway and back down the corridor, idly flicking drops of golden blood from his blade. I went after him. He was thinking of the women and children hidden in the Redoubt; and so was I.

I caught up with him more easily this time. Excalibur was providing me with all the strength and speed I needed. He shot me a quick grin. An enchanted blade had opened up a long groove along the armour over his left ribs, and blood had trickled down the gleaming steel. But his eyes were bright, and his smile was infectious. He laughed at the expression on my face.

"Is it not a glorious thing, to be a knight in armour and strike down your enemies? To punish the guilty with your own hands, to be brave and strong and know that everything you do matters? This is what it is, John, to be a London Knight!"

"You speak for yourself," I said. "Trust me; I am not warrior material. It's only the sword that's keeping me going."

"Excalibur couldn't bring it out of you if it wasn't there to begin with. A reluctant hero is still a hero, my friend."

I was still trying to come up with an answer to that when we burst into the Hall of Forgotten Beasts. An elven sorcerer was standing at the far end, clad in sweeping crimson silks. He smiled easily at us, as though we were guests arrived just in time for dinner, then he made one sweeping gesture with a pale long-fingered hand, and every trophied head mounted on the walls opened its mouth and cried out in pain and rage.

They weren't alive; but they were awake and aware, and they knew what had been done to them. They rolled their eyes and snapped their mouths, and strained against the mounting boards that held them to the walls. Great cracks appeared in the stonework round each head, the old stone splitting apart as though some unimaginable weight and pressure had been set against the other side of the wall. And then the heads surged forward, and the rest of their bodies crashed through the stone after them. They were complete again, all the great lost beasts of history and legend, and each and every one of them had revenge and retribution on their minds. They were long and sleek, huge and powerful, swift and deadly; and they only had eyes for Sir Gareth and me. Hundreds of enraged beasts and one really big, really pissed-off dragon.

"Oh shit," I said.

"Couldn't have put it better myself," said Sir Gareth. "Do you think it would help if I explained we're much more into conservation these days?"

"You go ahead and try. I plan on running. Try and keep up."

"Love to join you, John, but unfortunately the way to the

inner chambers, and the Redoubt, lies at the other end of this hall."

"Oh shit."

"Couldn't agree more. So, forward into battle it is. Try and keep up."

Sir Gareth strode forward, sword at the ready, not intimidated in the least by the odds against him. I stayed right where I was. Excalibur seemed almost to leap in my hand, pulling me forward and urging me on, but I rejected its call and put the sword away. Courage is all very well, but sometimes all it can get you is a glorious death. I know overwhelming odds when I see them. I've faced them before. And I know from experience that you don't beat them by meeting them head-on. You win by thinking outside the box, and by blatant cheating.

I still couldn't find it in myself to see these long-dead creatures as a threat. They were the victims here. They hadn't asked to be killed and mounted on a wall, then brought back again by a sorcerer's spell. Poor bastards. So I raised my gift, and used it to find the magic the elf sorcerer had used to haul them back into this world. It turned out to be a series of silver threads, trailing back from the head of every animal to the sorcerer's upraised hand. So many puppets on magical strings. Elves have always preferred to let others do their dirty work and not give a damn about the pawns they use. And so it was the easiest thing in the world for me to sever all the threads in a moment and set the beasts free.

The elf sorcerer cried out in shock and pain, and the psychic backlash from the ruptured spell sent him staggering backwards, clutching at his head. All the undead beasts in the hall dropped to their knees and crashed to the floor, released from their new existence and the undead bodies they never asked for. Finally dead, at last. For with my gift and my Sight raised, I Saw the ghosts of hundreds of ancient beasts rise up, freed at last, and turn away from the world to face a new bright light that called to them. One by one they moved away in a direction I could sense, but not See, leaving the Hall of Forgotten Beasts forever. Going home, at last. Bound to this place no longer.

The Questing Beast was the last to go. It turned its noble head to look at me, with huge, kind eyes. And then it bowed its great head to me briefly before hobbling off after all the others.

Sir Gareth looked about him, his sword drooping unheeded in his hand. He looked at me. "John, did you do this? What did you do?"

I could have told him about the original hunters of his order, who had not only mounted the heads of their kills as trophies but also bound the beasts' spirits to those heads, as a sign of ownership . . . but I didn't. The sins of the past should stay in the past. I smiled at Sir Gareth.

"Sometimes," I said, "try a little tenderness."

"The reports were right," he said. "You are weird. And someone's going to have to clean up all these dead animals, but it isn't going to be me. Come on; we have an elf sorcerer to deal with."

The elf was still leaning heavily against the wall at the end of the hall, trying to get his thoughts back together. Having a major working interrupted is never a good idea. He didn't look up till Sir Gareth and I had almost pushed our way through the piled-up bodies; and then he forced himself upright and glared at both of us. But, being an elf, he still had to strike a dramatic pose before he could throw a spell, and while he was busy doing that, Sir Gareth threw his sword at him. The gleaming steel blade flashed through the inter-vening space and slammed into the elf's thigh, pinning him to the stone wall. The elf didn't cry out. He grabbed at the sword with both hands and tried to pull it out.

He didn't have a hope in hell of shifting the blade before we got to him. The blade had gone right through the meat

SIMON R. GREEN

of his upper thigh and sunk deep into the stone wall behind
him. Golden blood streamed down his leg, and pooled on
the floor. The elf was still tugging stubbornly at the blade
when we got to him. He sneered at us, opened his mouth to
say something, and Sir Gareth cut his throat with a knife. I
had to step quickly aside to avoid getting soaked. Sir Gareth
jerked the sword out of the dead elf's leg with one hard tug.
The body slumped forward, and Sir Gareth stepped aside to
let it fall. I glared at him.

"You didn't have to kill him! He was helpless!"

"He was an elf and a sorcerer," Sir Gareth said mildly. "He
could have cursed us both with just a Word."

"He was in no condition to work magic. He could have
been useful. He could have answered questions."

"What questions?" said Sir Gareth, fastidiously shaking
golden blood off his sword blade. "We know why they're here
and who let them in, and we know what they want. You over-
complicate things, John."

"It's the principle of the thing!"

"Wait. You've got principles? We'll have to update your file."

"You know nothing about me," I said. "Nothing at all."

We came at last to the Main Hall, hundreds of feet long and
half as wide, packed from end to end with a great surging
mass of fighting men and elves. I never knew there were so
many London Knights. The whole place was a battle-field,
with two great armies hammering at each other with not one
ounce of mercy or quarter. Neither side was interested in simply winning; this was a fight to the death. To the last death.
The clash of weapons meeting, the shouts of triumph and the
screams of the dying, made a sound loud enough to fill my
head. It was like watching two great herds of deer slamming
their antlers together in a blind fury. Sir Gareth might talk of
honour and glory in battle; all I saw was butchery.

Elven spells blasted through the air, or detonated in the crush of bodies, but mostly there was only room for one-on-one combat, man against elf, cold steel versus enchanted blades, one implacable force slamming up against another. But one figure stood out for me, walking untouched amidst the chaos, ignored by the elves, disdained by the knights. Jerusalem Stark, looking every bit as haunted and driven as he had in the portrait gallery, striding purposefully through the battle-field as though it weren't there. And perhaps for him, it wasn't. He didn't care about any of it. He was looking right at me, coming straight for me, for what I had that he wanted. I met his gaze across the crowded hall and drew Excalibur. His step didn't even hesitate as he saw the blade's golden light. He kept on coming, and I went forward to meet him. Not for glory, or even for justice, but because some things just need to be done.

I plunged into the battle with Sir Gareth at my side, but Stark and I only had eyes for each other. If an elf got in my way, or a knight got in his, we both cut them down and kept going. Our speed increased as we drew nearer, until finally we were running through the crowd, opening up a way through the crush through sheer force of will. Until, finally, we slammed together, swords hammering against each other, driven with all our strength and all our fury. His blade didn't shatter when Excalibur met it, but he couldn't meet my attack either. I pressed forward, beating his sword aside with Excalibur, and he fell back, step by controlled step. I kept hammering away at him, and he kept retreating, but I couldn't force my way past his defence. I rained blow after blow on him, and he parried and turned and let himself be driven back, on his own terms. The London Knights had trained him well. Against the most powerful sword in the world, he was holding his own. He couldn't stand against Excalibur for long, and both of us knew it, but he only had to get lucky once.

I did try my very best to kill him, there in that hall, but

he was an amazing swordsman and a canny warrior. Excalibur
made me a great fighter, but he already was one. I had power,
but he had experience. I could drive him back, but I couldn't
reach him. And even as I was fighting, striking at him with
all my strength and Excalibur's speed, I still couldn't help
noticing something else. Something that quickly seemed
more important than striking down one sad, embittered soul.
So I stepped suddenly forward, slammed his sword aside,
and shoved two extended fingers into his eyes. He cried out
and fell backwards, lashing blindly back and forth with his
sword, as tears streamed down his cheeks from screwed-shut
eyes. He really should have worn a helmet.

I left him staggering blindly, and went to see what was
happening in the middle of the hall. Some elves tried to stop
me, and Excalibur cut them down with almost contemptuous
ease. Ahead of me, surrounded by protective rings of heavily armed elves, kept separate from the main battle, three
elf sorcerers were killing one of their own. He stood tall and
proud as they cut him to pieces, not raising one pale hand to
defend himself. Golden blood flooded down his naked, mutilated body, until he couldn't stand any more, and collapsed.
The sorcerers crowded in round him as he hit the floor, tearing him limb from limb, carving him up like a side of beef.
And then they took the pieces, and began to build something
with them.

By the time I hit the first protective wall, I'd worked it
out. The sorcerer elves were making a hellgate out of a willing victim. A willing suicide could produce a hellgate so
powerful it would be almost impossible to close. Powered
by necromancy and a suicide's will, the hellgate would suck
every living thing in Castle Inconnu down into the agonies
of the Pit.

I hit the elves before me with Excalibur, and they didn't
stand a chance. Their swords shattered against my golden
blade, and their spelled armour couldn't protect them. I was

moving impossibly fast now, the strength in my arms Excalibur's strength, and nothing could stand against me. I cut the elves down and threw myself against the next protective wall. Meat cleaved and blood flew, and bodies fell to every side; and still the elves fought to stand between me and the hellgate. They knew they were going to die, and they didn't care. They only had to hold me off long enough, and the hellgate would destroy the London Knights forever. Powerful energies were already forming, pulsing in the air. Something really bad was struggling to manifest, something cold and terrible and malignant.

I slammed right through the elves and threw myself at the sorcerers. I cut them down with swift, vicious blows, and they died, still trying to finish their work. The thing they'd built from the dead parts of their willing victim was already glowing and steaming. I kicked the assemblage apart, stamping on bones and grinding flesh underfoot, and the last of the life went out of it.

I looked up to find I was alone, cut off from the knights, with elves on every side. They advanced on me with glowing swords and axes, smiling awful smiles. They were wary of Excalibur, edging forward a step at a time, darting back if I brought the sword to bear on them, while others darted in. I kept circling, lashing out with my sword, looking for a way out; but everywhere I looked, cold elven eyes looked back. They had me. I could hear knights calling out to me; they'd seen what was happening, and they were coming. But they knew, and I knew; they wouldn't get to me in time. Excalibur made me strong, but it didn't make me invincible. It could protect me from an exploding soulbomb, but not a stab in the back from an enchanted sword.

I'd always known this warrior crap would get me killed.

I took a firm grip on Excalibur and smiled at the elf faces before me. There was something in that smile that gave them pause, but only for a moment.

They all pressed forward at once, dozens of swords thrusting towards me; and I raised my gift and found Excalibur. Not the sword; but what it really was. It wasn't like talking with another person or even some kind of being; but there was communication. Excalibur was an extension of Gaea, her will made manifest in the world of men. And for a moment, she bestowed her grace upon me. Instead of the sword urging me on, I took control, and Excalibur blazed up, filling the whole hall with its glorious golden light. The sword had always blazed supernaturally brightly, but this was more, this was the essence of light itself, the light that first blazed across the universe when a great Voice said, *Let there be light.*

The elves screamed, in pain and horror and thwarted rage, and fell back, unable to face the terrible energies radiating from Excalibur. They turned and ran, shoving and scrambling and fighting each other, in their desperate need to escape a light they simply could not bear. The London Knights, dazed and awed by the light, let them go. In a few moments the hall was half-empty, knight after knight lowering his sword and looking round and wondering what the hell had happened. Excalibur's light snapped off, and I shut down my gift and studied the blade thoughtfully. The Puck had been right. *It's not what you think it is. And it never was.*

Sir Gareth came over to stand beside me and clap me on the shoulder. "Well done, John Taylor! Always knew you had it in you. You're full of surprises, aren't you?"

"You have no idea," I said. "Really."

There were dead and injured knights lying the whole length of the hall. Other knights were helping where they could. I saw Sir Roland kneel beside one still form in shattered armour, and Sir Gareth and I went over to join him. Sir Roland had taken off his helmet, and his bare face looked shocked, as though he'd been hit. He'd removed the helmet from the dead knight before him; and in death Sir Percifal looked even older. Certainly far too old to be fighting on a battle-field.

"He shouldn't have been here," said Sir Roland. He sounded confused, as though unable to understand how such a thing could have happened. "He should have gone to the Redoubt, to be with the women and the children. But he was a warrior and a fighter all his life, and he didn't know any other way. Even though he must have known it would bring him here, to this. Sleep well, old friend."

I remembered a wise old voice, saying *Yes* and *No* at regular intervals. A man who shouldn't have been able to stand upright in full armour, let alone fight in it; but there was golden blood on his sword that showed he had. He shouldn't have come here, but he had. Because he knew his duty.

All across the hall, knights were putting away their swords, tending their wounds and each other's, and clapping each other across the back and shoulder, laughing and shouting as they swapped tall tales of victory. Because it did feel so good to be alive after a battle even if old friends were dead. Given how outnumbered the knights had been, they were lucky to be alive, and they knew it. Not many people get to face an army of elves and live to talk about it. Hell, there are those who say the only way to win against an army of elves is to not be there when they turn up.

Many of the knights grinned at me and waved and shouted. I was their hero now. I nodded back. They'd done well. Elves are killing machines, delighting in slaughter and suffering, and the knights had been holding their own even before I turned up. I'd never doubted their reputation. I'd only wondered what drove them.

Sir Roland finally stood up and nodded to Sir Gareth, all business again.

"Did all our families get to the Redoubt in time?" said Sir Gareth.

"Yes. They all made it. I always said those regular panic drills were a good idea. I still can't believe it, though: elves, inside Castle Inconnu. Unprecedented. Stark must have got them in, though I'm damned if I can see how. There'll have to be an inquiry. As long as he's out there, the castle is wide open to attack. We have to do what we should have done long before. We have to go out in force and hunt him down and put him out of everyone's misery."

"He's not in his right mind," said Sir Gareth. "Grief and loss have made him forget his vows. But I still believe he can be saved, brought back to a state of grace."

"Of course you believe that, Gar," said Sir Roland. "You're his friend. I wanted to believe in him. He was the best of us. Best I ever trained. But what happened today changes everything. We must deal with the man he is and not the man we remember. Look round you, at all the dead and the wounded. He caused all this and meant worse. It's time to put him down, like any suffering beast."

"I'm still not sure what this was all about," I said. "Did the elves want to take Excalibur, or was that only Stark? Did they want to destroy the castle and everyone in it, with their hellgate? Or did they have some other end in mind? Do you have any prisoners we can question? I can't help feeling we're missing something here."

"Of course we are," said Sir Gareth. "They're elves. A secret hidden inside a mystery hidden inside an enigma."

"We should never have put you in charge of the library," said Sir Roland.

As it turned out, the knights did have one elf prisoner. Two knights had knocked him down during the battle, then sat on him when all the other elves ran. The elf was currently chained to a wall with a hell of a lot of cold iron. The metal burned his bare flesh where it touched, but the elf wouldn't even acknowledge it. He glared at Sir Roland, Sir Gareth, and me with cold, aristocratic disdain. The kind of blunt contempt that makes you want to punch someone in the face. We didn't. It was what he wanted, so he could feel superior to us. To the elves, humans will always be barbarians. His spelled armour had been stripped off him, revealing a bare pale torso covered in cuts and bruises. He was almost supernaturally slender, his pale skin covered with hundreds of etched, burned, and tattooed signs and sigils. Even chained naked to a wall, he still had that basic elf poise and arrogance, designed to make us mere humans feel base and clumsy.

"Jerusalem Stark brought you here," Sir Roland said heavily. "Why? Talk to me, elf. Are we at war with Oberon and Titania, or with Mab?"

The elf said nothing because that would have interrupted his sneer, which was now so concentrated it was almost a work of art. He stared straight through us as though we weren't worth looking at. I leaned forward, and, to his credit, he didn't flinch. I studied the designs etched deep into his bare hairless chest, and grimaced despite myself.

"I know a few things about elves," I said, straightening up painfully. My muscles were really starting to ache and complain, after the battle. "I know those markings. This one serves Queen Mab."

"Why?" barked Sir Roland, sticking his face right into the elf's. "Why has Mab declared war on the London Knights?"

"He won't answer to threats or intimidation," I said. "He won't even give you his name. He's waiting for the torture to start because that's what he'd do if the positions were reversed."

"We don't torture prisoners!" said Sir Roland. "We are honourable men. And I think . . . we already know everything we need to know."

He drew his sword, raised it high, and brought it swinging down in a long arc so that it sheared right through the main lock on the elf's chains. They fell apart instantly, freeing the elf. Sir Roland stepped back, lowered his sword, and nodded stiffly to the elf. "Off you go. On your way. We give you your freedom."

For the first time, the elf acknowledged Sir Roland's presence. "Why?"

The knight smiled. "Because it's the proper thing to do. The chivalric way. Because we're better than you."

The elf turned his back on us and strode off through the knights, who all made a point of bowing and saluting him. When the elf was a safe distance away, he muttered a Word and disappeared. Because elves always have to have the last word.

And then, all the alarums all went off again. A knight in blood-smeared armour came running up to us.

"We've been breached again! Small-scale, this time. We think Stark's back somewhere inside the castle!"

"Search everywhere," said Sir Roland. "Inner and outer. And send word to the Redoubt for the families to stay where they are. I don't think Stark would stoop to taking hostages, but after today's events, it's clear we don't know him at all any more. The order is given: kill Stark on sight."

He strode off with the other knight, still barking orders. Sir Gareth and I looked at each other. He shrugged.

"Might as well make ourselves useful. Come with me; we'll check the outer layers."

"Do you think Stark has come back?" I said.

"He still wants Excalibur," said Sir Gareth. "Where else can he go?"

So we went walking back through the outer stone corridors and hallways. All was quiet. At the Hall of Forgotten Beasts, the long-dead animal bodies still lay where they had fallen. The stone walls were still cracked and broken, the wall mounts shattered. We made our way slowly between the piled-up dead, and I don't think I ever saw anything so simply sad in all my life.

"We'll clear this all away, when there's time," said Sir Gareth.

"Make sure it's done respectfully," I said.

"Don't worry," said Sir Gareth. "They won't remount the heads. I'll have a word. For a man of your destructive reputation, you can be remarkably sentimental sometimes, John."

We hurried on and came at last to the Portrait Gallery. Excalibur stirred in its invisible scabbard on my back, and I stopped immediately. Sir Gareth stopped with me and looked round sharply.

"I don't see anything," he said.

"Something's wrong," I said. "Excalibur is warning me."

Sir Gareth drew his sword. The Gallery was quiet and empty. And while we were both standing and looking, the portrait behind me, that I hadn't even looked at, came alive; and Jerusalem Stark reached out of his portrait, grabbed Excalibur and its sheath, invisible as they were, and hauled them right off my back. It was all over in a moment. Before I could even cry out, Stark had retreated back into his portrait with his prize, and was gone. And the portrait was only a photo again.

I swayed sickly on my feet. It felt as though part of my soul had been ripped away. Sir Gareth grabbed me by the shoulder to steady me.

"He's got it, hasn't he? He's got Excalibur!"

"Yes," I said. "I don't know if he can hold on to it, but he's got it."

Sir Gareth pushed me away. "Only John bloody Taylor could gain and lose Excalibur in the same day!"

"Don't count me out yet," I said, matching his glare with one of my own. "I can get it back. I have a special gift for finding things, no matter where they are."

I raised my gift, forcing my inner eye open as wide as it would go. It didn't take me long to find Excalibur.

"Of course," I said. "It's back in the Nightside. Only place he could hope to hide it. I'll have to go back and get it."

"I'll go with you," Sir Gareth said immediately.

"No," I said, just as quickly. "I already have a partner in the Nightside. And . . . you're a London Knight. You don't belong there. You wouldn't know how to act, in the Nightside."

FIVE

Sinister Doings in the Nightside

I left London Proper for the Nightside with a certain sense of relief and emerged from the Underground station into a refreshing dazzle of neon noir, amber street-lights under an endless night sky, and a bustling sea of Humanity driven along by unhealthy appetites and bad intentions. It felt good to be back, to leave the London Knights behind me, with their strict morality and uncomplicated sense of good and evil. And it felt even better to dive back into the usual crowd of gods and monsters, saints and sinners, and all the lost and battered souls who couldn't hope to survive anywhere else. I was home again, back where I belonged. And the moment I stepped out of the station, there was Suzie Shooter, waiting patiently for me. I went straight to her, and we hugged each other tightly for a long moment. Then Suzie pushed me away, so she could look me over thoroughly.

"No visible wounds. Blood on your coat, but it doesn't seem to be yours. Kill anyone interesting?"

"No-one you'd know," I said. "I would have brought you back a present, but the knights didn't have anything you'd want."

"The London Knights," said Suzie, sniffing loudly. "Bunch of stiffs. Do they really wear chastity belts under their armour?"

"I'm relieved to say I never got the chance to find out," I said. "Suzie . . . Tell me you haven't been waiting here for me all this time?"

She gave her usual sharp bark of laughter. "You wish. I'm your partner, not your nanny. I dropped into the Mammon Emporium and put a little pressure on an oracle in a well to tell me exactly when you'd be back. It didn't really want to talk to me, but I persuaded it."

"Tell me you didn't drop a grenade in."

"Of course not. That would have attracted attention. I pissed in it."

I sighed, quietly. "You're a class act, Suzie."

She slipped an arm through mine, and we headed off down the street. I was pleased to note that everyone was getting out of my way again. It's the little things you miss the most.

"Did you visit your old haunts in London Proper?" said Suzie, after a while.

"Yes," I said. "A lot had changed, but not enough. Never go back."

"I could have told you that. In fact, I'm pretty sure I did. How did you get on with the London Knights?"

"Hard to tell," I said. "I think I was doing quite well . . . right up to the point where I lost Excalibur."

Suzie gave me a hard look. "How can anyone lose Excalibur?"

"It wasn't easy! And I didn't exactly lose it. More . . . had it stolen while I was distracted."

"Ah," said Suzie. "That's more like it. You always were easily distracted. Do you know where the sword is now?"

"Not yet. But I will. I need the right setting, and preparations, before I fire up my gift."

"And then we'll go get it," Suzie said comfortably. "Will I by any chance get to kill a whole bunch of people?"

"Wouldn't surprise me," I said.

We strolled along, under the night sky that never ends, contemplating justice and violence. Wild things rode the night skies, starlight gleaming on their outstretched wings, while dangerous traffic thundered unceasingly up and down; and something foul and fierce went somersaulting over the vehicles, howling and cackling and spitting sparks in all directions. It was good to be back.

"So," I said, "have you finished dealing with all the suddenly deceased persons who were cluttering up our property when I left?"

"All gone," she said cheerfully.

"I won't ask."

"Best not to. But we're going to have some really big flowers in the garden this time next year."

"You hate flowers," I said, amused.

"All right then, I'll plant some fruit trees. I've always wanted to make my own jam."

"You are an endless source of surprises to me," I said solemnly. "Now, let us away to Strangefellows. I need to pick up something I left there with Alex, sometime back. Something I'd really hoped I'd never need to see again."

And so Suzie and I came to Strangefellows, the oldest bar in the world, and still our favourite watering hole. Quite possibly the sleaziest and most disreputable drinking den in the whole of the Nightside, Strangefellows has the saving grace that no-one there will ever give a damn who or what you were. And most of my enemies are too scared to go in. The perfect place to drink and brood and plan revenges against a manifestly unfair and uncaring world. When Suzie and I clattered down the long, metal stairs into the great stone pit that was the bar proper, the background music was already playing Rick Wakeman's *King Arthur* album. Just the bar owner's little way of letting me know he knew what was going on. Alex Morrisey knows everything, except for when he doesn't; and then he fakes it so convincingly that the world often changes to accommodate him. Because his gossip is always more entertaining than mere facts could ever be.

It was a pretty usual night, for Strangefellows. An unfrocked hair-stylist with a piercing through her left eye-ball was busy shaving complicated patterns into the thick body fur of a teenage werewolf. The things people will put themselves through to appear fashionable. Over in the large open fireplace, a pleasant fire was burning in a miniature Wicker Man, while a group of young business men in smart City suits, each with one eye missing, toasted bread against the flames before dipping it into a vat of steaming goat's-cheese fondue. Alex must be trying to drive the bar up-market again. He'd have better luck with a chair and a whip. Two Japanese teenage girl vampires were draining the blood out of a resigned-looking goat through two straws, racing each other to the middle. And a quartet of fuzzy post-nuclear mutants were showing each other strange alien porn on the televisions they had implanted in their stomachs.

At the bar, the owner, bartender, and tall dark pain in the neck, Alex Morrisey, greeted Suzie and me with a sullen nod. Alex was born under a cloud, which surprised the midwife. He was the world's first clinically depressed toddler, and has only got worse down the years. He only ever wears black, including shades and a beret, mixes the worst martinis in the world, doesn't wash the glasses nearly often enough, and could gloom for the Olympics. Always check your change with Alex, and never ever try the bar snacks. You never know who they might have been. He glared at his pet vulture, Agatha, still perched menacingly on his old-fashioned till and still extremely pregnant. Alex put out a hand to pet her. The vulture fixed him with a malignant look, and Alex pulled his hand back.

"I've lost track of how many months that damned bird has been pregnant," he said bitterly as he poured me my usual wormwood brandy and handed Suzie her bottle of Gordon's Gin. "Has to be well over a year now. I think she's going for the record. Still no idea what the hell she mated with, but it must have been something really brave. Wouldn't surprise me if she ate him afterwards. Or even during. I'm hoping it wasn't a phoenix. You can't get good fire insurance in the Nightside."

"That's always been one of the big riddles," I said. "If the phoenix is always born from the ashes of the previous phoenix, then who fired the first phoenix?"

Suzie stopped sucking at her gin bottle long enough to say "Prometheus," unexpectedly.

Alex and I looked at her, then at each other, and shrugged pretty much in unison.

"What are you doing here, John?" said Alex. "I was beginning to wonder if you'd decided you were too good for us, now you're off hobnobbing with the aristocracy. It'll all end in tears. The London Knights . . . Give me a slippery floor and a can-opener, and I could take the lot of them."

"Pretty sure you couldn't," I said. "I've seen them fight. To be exact, I saw them take on a whole army of elves and make chutney out of them. And since they're currently a bit annoyed with me . . ."

"He lost Excalibur," said Suzie.

"I'm getting it back!" I said quickly. "I'm here to use my gift, while you and Suzie run interference and keep the flies off. I can't afford to be interrupted once I start concentrating."

"All right," said Suzie, setting down her half-empty bottle. "Anyone bothers us, I'll shoot them quietly."

"I'll get a bucket and mop," Alex said resignedly.

"Don't pop off yet," I said. "I need to discuss something with you."

"Let's start with your bar bill," said Alex.

"You know I'm good for it. Listen, remember the . . . object I left here with you after the Angel War? The thing I asked you to hide for me? And never mention to anyone?"

Alex lowered his sunglasses and studied me over them. "Are things really that serious?"

"Could be," I said. "I have a strong feeling things could get extremely unpleasant, then a whole lot worse, before they even look like getting better."

"Situation entirely bloody normal round here," said Alex. "Hang on while I get my special gloves."

He reached under the counter and pulled out a pair of woollen mittens, specially knitted for him by the Holy Sisters of Saint Strontium. Guaranteed to protect his hands from anything up to and including the Holy Sisters. Alex went to the back of the bar and very carefully brought down a slender bottle labelled ANGEL'S TEARS, in Alex's own appalling handwriting. He set the bottle down gently on the bar before us and the liquor inside swelled slowly from side to side, shining with delicate silver light. Angel's Tears was a particularly vicious and brutal liquor that could not only open the doors of perception inside your mind, but blow the doors right off their hinges. Alex could only keep the liquor in stock for so long, then he had to take it out, bury it in unconsecrated ground, and run like hell. Alex broke the heavy wax seal with extreme care and reached inside the bottle with a pair of delicate silver tongs. And from out of the concealing liquor, he pulled a single long feather.

It glowed faintly with its own light, a pure white feather of indescribable beauty and grace. It looked like the first, original feather, which all other feathers are based on. Alex laid it gently out on the bar counter, then put the bottle away. The feather lay there, utterly perfect, with not a drop of liquor on it. The Angel's Tears had disguised its presence all this time but hadn't been able to touch it. Because the feather was the real deal.

"Is that what I think it is?" said Suzie, after a moment.

"Yes," I said. "A feather from an angel's wing. I found a downed angel during the War. Brought down by really serious magics, with its wings ripped off and propped up on bricks. So to speak. I found the feather some distance away, in the gutter, and took it away with me. Because I always thought the time would arrive when it would come in handy."

"All right, it's very pretty," Suzie said grudgingly. "But what use is it? What can you do with it, apart from tickle someone to death?"

"According to the reading I've done on the subject, an angel's feather can protect you from spiritual corruption," I said. "And given that we're almost certainly going to be dealing with Sinister Albion . . ."

"You mean the living Merlin?" said Alex, up to the minute on news as usual and determined not to be left out of the conversation. "Merlin Satanspawn, more powerful than the Merlin we knew and nastier with it? Word is he's here in the Nightside right now, looking for his missing King Artur."

"Not just the living Merlin," I said. "According to the London Knights, we also have to worry about one Prince Gaylord the Damned, Nuncio to the Court of King Artur. He's here, too."

"What's so special about him?" said Suzie.

"I don't know," I said. "No-one knows. That's what's so worrying."

"But . . . it's only a feather," said Suzie.

"No, it isn't," I said. "It looks like a feather to our limited human senses because the reality of it is far too big for us to deal with. This came from a messenger of God, His will made manifest in the material world. It's no more only a feather than an angel is just some guy with wings."

"First Excalibur, then the London Knights, now an angel's feather," said Alex. "Going up in the world, John. Been a long time since anything so obviously good came into the Nightside . . . We could probably get good money for this. And I mean serious money . . ."

I picked the feather up and tucked it into my inside coatpocket. My fingers tingled at the brief contact. "There are some things money can't buy, Alex."

"I know. That's what credit is for."

"What are you going to do with the feather, John?" said Suzie.

"Hang on to it," I said. "And hope some of its essential goodness rubs off on me."

"Good luck with that," said Suzie. "Also, Alex, my bottle is empty."

"Lot of people are talking about Excalibur," said Alex as he handed Suzie a fresh bottle. "Mostly trying to figure out how the hell it ended up with you, John."

"I am not worthy," I said solemnly. "But, I have a special dispensation."

Alex paused, thoughtfully. "When I was younger, and still believed I was descended from Arthur Pendragon, instead of Merlin Satanspawn, I used to dream of wielding Excalibur. What did it feel like?"

"Like I could do anything," I said.

And that was when lightning slammed down into the bar. Huge jagged bolts of blue-white electricity, jumping from ceiling to floor to every metal object in the bar. Sparks jumped and exploded, crackling loudly on the air. I could feel the wild energies tingling on my bare skin, and my hair stood up. The air stank of ozone. The lightning slammed down again and again, filling the bar with brutal, merciless light. Tables and chairs caught fire. The floor suddenly cracked apart, a long, jagged line that ran from one end of the bar to the other, the crack widening and splintering as it tore itself apart. Everyone in the bar was running for the exit. Some were on fire. There was screaming and shouting and all the sounds of pain and horror. I put my back to the bar, and Suzie was right there at my side, shotgun at the ready.

The crack in the floor widened further still, becoming a crevice full of darkness. And up out of that bottomless darkness rose a huge iron throne, its heavy black metal carved and scarred with crawling unquiet runes. And sitting at his ease on that cold iron throne—Merlin Satanspawn of Sinister Albion. The greatest living sorcerer of a realm where evil had triumphed. He smiled on me as the throne came to a halt, hovering over the abyss; and it was not a human smile.

The living Merlin was tall, easily eight feet, and grossly fat from lifetimes of indulging his many appetites. Naked, his skin was flushed, stretched taut with heavy rolls of fat, and covered in ancient Celtic and Druidic tattoos. The designs were hard to make out, stretched and distorted by his huge shape. His face was wide, his arms and legs huge. His eyes were sunk deep into his skull, and his smile showed teeth yellowed with age. There was something in those eyes, and in that smile, that held me where I was like a mouse hypnotised by a snake. The knowledge in that stare, the centuries of experience, the sheer concentrated happy evil . . .

Dried blood had caked under his long fingernails, and more was trapped in the heavy lines round his mouth. Goat's horns curled up from his lowering forehead, and scarlet flames danced up from his eyes, rising and falling as his gaze moved this way and that. *They say he has his father's eyes . . .* And an inverted pentagram had been branded deep into his bare chest. No-one was going to steal this Merlin's heart.

Simply sitting there, on his brutal throne, Merlin's presence was overwhelming. He seemed to curdle the bar's atmosphere and poison the air by being there. Merlin Satanspawn, the Devil's only begotten son, the anti-Christ who'd corrupted and destroyed the greatest dream of all, to make his Sinister Albion.

Anyone else would have been helpless under his gaze. But I had an angel's feather, Suzie had her shotgun, and Alex . . . was Alex.

The bar's muscular bouncers, Betty and Lucy Coltrane, had held their ground when everyone else ran. They stood poised together at the end of the bar, ready for action. They weren't impressed by the living Merlin any more than they had been by the dead Merlin who used to manifest in Strangefellows. In fact, the Coltranes were famous for not being impressed by anyone. Which came in very handy when it came to chucking-out time. They looked to Alex for instructions, and he gestured urgently for them to stay put. Merlin turned his great head slowly to look at the two muscular young women, then he licked his lips slowly. Betty and Lucy both shuddered suddenly, despite themselves. Merlin raised one fat hand, and a rose appeared in it out of nowhere. He offered it to the two bouncers, and they both turned up their noses. Merlin laughed softly, a flat horrid sound with all the wickedness of the world in it. He brought the rose to his mouth and breathed on it, so it withered and died in a moment.

"Big deal," said Alex, his voice steady. "I can do that most mornings. Of course, I am not a morning person."

"Hush," said Merlin. "Be still. I have come to the Nightside in search of my errant King. Pretty little Artur. He is mine, and I will have him again. I do enjoy this Nightside . . . Love what you've done with the place. So delightfully uncomplicated, and unhypocritical when it comes to sin and temptation. I really must come again, when I have the time to properly indulge myself. I do like to play though I'm so big I usually break my toys . . ."

"We're not toys," I said, fighting to keep my voice calm and casual and not in any way impressed. "You may be the big mover and shaker in your world, but we've seen better. And you're not in your world now."

"But my father is everywhere, in all worlds," said Merlin. "And where he is, I have power. Do not think I am weak because I am out of my domain."

He gestured lazily with one plump hand at Lucy Coltrane, and she cried out in pain as her back arched suddenly. Her breath came fast and panicked, her eyes full of horror. Merlin gestured again, and Lucy's chest split apart in a flurry of blood and broken bone. Her heart ripped itself out of the great wound in her chest and flew across the intervening space to nestle into Merlin's waiting hand. Lucy collapsed as all the strength went out of her, blood still spurting from the great wound between her breasts and spraying from her slack mouth with her last few gasps for breath. Betty was there to hold Lucy before she hit the floor, but Lucy was already dead, her wide eyes fixed and staring. Betty lowered her slowly to the blood-slick floor and sat there with her, hugging the dead body to her while she cried silent, angry tears. And Merlin Satanspawn brought the still-beating heart to his mouth and ate it greedily, stuffing the pulsing meat into his mouth. And when he was done, and he'd eaten every last bit of it, he licked all the blood from his fingers like a small child with a treat.

I had to physically stop Suzie from giving him both barrels in the face. I grabbed her arm and held it firmly, pitting all my strength against hers. Even her specially made blessed and cursed bullets wouldn't touch Merlin Satanspawn. And I wasn't ready to lose my Suzie the way Betty had lost her Lucy. Suzie stopped fighting me abruptly, her furious gaze still fixed on Merlin. She lowered her shotgun and nodded briefly. Not giving up; just waiting for a better chance. Behind me, I could hear Alex breathing heavily. I knew he had all kinds of weapons and protections stashed away, but I hoped he had more sense than to try to use any of them. He and the Coltranes had been together for years, but this was no time for grand gestures. This was a time for cold thought, and plans, and eventually some very cold revenge, when the opportunity presented itself. Merlin smiled on us all.

"That wasn't a demonstration of power. That was a little something to get your attention. This . . . is the demonstration."

And Lucy Coltrane sat bolt upright in Betty's arms, drawing in a deep breath of air. The great wound in her chest was gone, her eyes were wide open, and she grabbed on to Betty with desperate hands as she fought to get her breathing back under control again. She had been dead, and now she was alive again; and Merlin Satanspawn chuckled happily.

"I am my father's son, inflicted on the world to do his will; and I can do anything the Lamb could do."

(And I remembered Jerusalem Stark saying that his new allies could bring his dead wife back to life. That he'd seen proof . . .)

"What are you doing here?" I said to Merlin. "What do you want with us?"

"This place called to me. My magic tells me that this world's Merlin spent time here."

"Yes," said Alex. "He was buried in the cellars under the bar. But he's dead and gone now. You missed him."

"Pity," said the living Merlin. "I would have enjoyed showing him what he could have become. If only he'd had more ambition." He considered Alex thoughtfully. "You're of his line, though the blood has been diluted through many generations. I have no descendents . . . I kill them all as soon as they appear. I have no use for . . . competition. But, there's some of me in you, boy. I could just eat you up . . ."

I moved quickly forward to place myself between Merlin and Alex, doing my best to meet his terrible gaze with my best hard look.

"Your King Artur isn't here, and none of us have seen him in ages."

"Oh, I know that," said Merlin. "He came to this Night-side against my wishes, and he has never returned. And I can't have that. Can't have people thinking they can go against my wishes. My magic tells me you have a gift for finding things, and people, John Taylor. I can see your gift, hiding within you. You only think you know what it is. Use that gift for me, find my missing Artur, and you and your friends can live."

"If I'm to find him," I said steadily, "I need to know about him. What is Artur doing here? What is he looking for?"

"A toy, a trinket," said Merlin. "Something I'd already told him would do him no good."

"Excalibur," I said. "He wanted Excalibur, didn't he?"

Merlin looked at me for a long moment, and I could feel my skin crawl, feel my legs shake. My heart was hammering in my chest. He could kill me in a moment, and we both knew it.

"I want my Artur," said Merlin. "Find him for me. Or you . . . are no use to me."

"Don't you threaten him," Suzie said immediately, her shotgun trained on his face again.

Merlin didn't even look at her. "Or perhaps I'll turn your little girlfriend inside out and leave her that way, alive and suffering, forever."

"Did you know I killed this world's Merlin?" I said, my voice like a slap across his face. "Did you know I tore out his heart and watched him die by inches?"

"You're telling the truth," said the living Merlin. "I can

tell. How very amusing. Well, well . . . Who knew such a small thing as you could kill a Merlin? But after all, he turned away from real power when he defied our father. I don't have time for this. Someone else will find my missing King for me; and when Artur is back under my wing again . . . I think perhaps I'll destroy this whole stupid Nightside before I go home again."

He disappeared abruptly, gone in a moment, taking his iron throne with him. I let my breath out in a long gasp and leaned back against the bar for support. My legs were shaking so badly they could hardly support me. It's not every day you outbluff the Devil's only begotten son . . . Suzie slipped her shotgun into the sheath on her back and took a long drink from her bottle. Her face was cold and calm as always, her hands entirely steady. Alex was busy pouring himself a large drink and spilling most of it. The sense of evil and oppression was gone, but some harsh sense of it still lingered, like a psychic stain. The great jagged crack in the floor wasn't there any more—if it ever really had been. Sorcerers deal in illusion as often as not. If only because it costs less magic.

Betty got Lucy back onto her feet and led her away. Lucy's death and rebirth could have been an illusion, too; but I didn't think so. The reality of it was still clear in Lucy's face, in her eyes. She was shaking all over, her hands clasped together on her chest where the wound had been. And this from a woman who'd never backed down from anyone, in all the time I'd known her. Betty looked almost as shocked as Lucy. I had to wonder if either of them would ever get over what had happened.

"I will see that smug bastard hauled down off his long throne, trampled underfoot, and fed to the pigs, for what he did to my girls," said Alex, in a worryingly matter-of-fact voice. I turned to face him.

"Don't," I said. "I mean it, Alex. He is way out of your league. Maybe even out of mine. Dead Merlin was dangerous enough; this version is seriously scary. I'm going to have to do a lot of hard thinking and planning, before I'm ready to go after him."

"But you will go after him?" said Alex.

"Yes," I said. "He threatened me, and my friends, and no-one gets away with that."

"He said he was the anti-Christ," said Suzie.

"Our Merlin rejected his father's plans for him," I said. "He could have been the anti-Christ, but he declined the honour. If only because he wouldn't take orders from any-one. Of course, that was before he met Arthur, and every-thing changed. The Merlin we just met . . . is every inch his father's son."

"I'm going to have to get a bigger gun," said Suzie. "Some-thing heavier, and more . . . spiritual."

"Got to be more useful than an angel's feather," Alex said pointedly.

"We're still here, aren't we?" I said. "Now, we have work to do, and not a lot of time to do it in. It won't take Merlin long to find someone who can take him straight to the miss-ing Artur. There's always someone, in the Nightside. Hell, there are probably already people lining up to sell their souls to him. After speaking to the London Knights, I'm pretty sure Artur came here looking for this world's Excalibur. His Merlin doesn't want him to have it because the sword could give Artur power over him. The Lady of the Lake from Sin-ister Albion wouldn't give Artur her sword because he wasn't worthy. So all that's left to him is to steal some other world's Excalibur. Which makes him Stark's best buyer."

"Who's this Stark?" said Suzie.

"Rogue London Knight. Currently allied with Queen Mab's elves. The man who stole Excalibur from me."

"I hate him already," said Suzie. "Let me kill him for you."

"A nice thought, but not until we've got the sword back from him," I said.

"You really think you can find Stark before Merlin does?" said Alex.

"Of course," I said. "I have a gift; and I know the Nightside better than he ever will."

"Yes, but . . . *he's Merlin*!" said Alex. "Alive and in his prime, after fifteen hundred years of practicing his craft! With all the powers of the anti-Christ! He could probably pull the Moon down out of the sky and crash it into the Nightside for laughs! And I'm not sure there's anyone in the Nightside who could stop him!"

"Do I need to get you a paper bag to breathe into?" I said. "Of course there are people here who could stop him! Off the top of my head, there's the Lord of Thorns. And Hadleigh Oblivion, the Detective Inspectre. And Jessica Sorrow, the Unbeliever."

"You really do know some scary people," said Alex. He made an effort to calm himself. "And there's the whole Street of the Gods, of course. Sorry. It's hard to think of anyone else, when that oversized piece of shit is floating right in front of you, larger than life and twice as nasty. Okay, maybe . . . there are people here who could slow him down, but I'd still want to be several dimensions away when they tried it."

"Speed is our best friend here," I said, trying hard to sound confident and in control. "Get to Stark first and take Excalibur back from him; then Merlin can have his bloody Artur for all I care. Let him take his King home, and we're rid of two people we're better off without."

"What's to stop Merlin from destroying the whole Nightside before he goes home?" said Suzie.

"I will," I said. "Once I've got Excalibur back."

"You think you can stop him?" said Alex. "With a magic sword and a feather?"

"Excalibur is a lot more than a sword," I said patiently. "That's why Artur wants it. And knowing I've got the sword will be enough to stop Merlin coming back again. Now, stand back and prepare to be amazed; it's finding-things time."

I concentrated on my gift and sent my mind soaring up and out, shooting up through the bar and rising high into the dark skies above. My mind rose free, no longer held back by the limitations of flesh, and I could See all across the Nightside. The huge Moon glared more brightly than ever though it had no sun to reflect light from. There is no man-in-the-moon face on the Nightside's Moon; it's a huge dead silver eye that sees everything and cares for nothing. The stars danced all round me. If I listened really hard, I could hear them singing. I looked down across the brightly lit streets and squares, the flares and smears of gaudy colour as the Nightside spun slowly beneath me. Hot neon blazed, and magics dazzled, but I couldn't See the sword Excalibur anywhere. Its nature made it invisible to everyone except the man who bore it, rightly or not. And for the moment, that man was Stark. So I looked for him instead.

My gift found him easily, a beacon blazing in the night. My all-Seeing mental eye plummeted down into the Nightside and shot along the streets like an invisible comet, rocketing in and out of streets and side alleys until finally it settled outside one very familiar building. I drifted slowly forward, cautious of protective spells that might set off an alarm, but my gift was more subtle than anything this place had. Soon I was inside, in one particular room; and my Vision showed me two men talking together. Back in the bar, I reached out to Suzie, so she could take my hand and share what I was Seeing. I felt her fingers in mine, and together we watched, and listened.

I knew this place. I'd been in this building before. They called it the Fortress, the one place you could go in the Nightside where no-one would bother you. A place of sanctuary and protection. Originally established by a self-help group of alien abductees, who decided to get together and set up a safe place, with constant electronic surveillance and a whole lot of guns. And a complete willingness to shoot the shit out of anyone or anything that tried to take them anywhere against their will. Let the aliens come again and see what was waiting for them. Over the years, the Fortress had become a refuge for anyone who needed it. Good place for Artur to run to and hide. And a good place for Stark to do business . . .

The rogue knight stood tall and proud in a pokey little room, facing a man who had to be Artur. The room had only the most basic furnishings and few comforts; the Fortress runs on a very strict budget. They prefer to spend what money they have in constantly upgrading the surveillance systems and buying bigger guns. It isn't paranoia if they really are out to get you and shove probes up your behind.

Not really the proper setting for a King in exile, as Artur's expression seemed to confirm. He was tall and elegant, with a pale, aristocratic face that would have been more than usually handsome, if it hadn't been for the cold, dark eyes and thin-lipped mouth. He held himself like a King, like a man used to giving orders and having them obeyed; but he also looked dangerous in his own right. Like a man who could do his own killing, as and when he felt it necessary. He was wearing a suit of some dark armour; but I couldn't See it clearly. Must have its own built-in protections.

Stark looked suspiciously at the surveillance camera set ostentatiously into the room's ceiling. "Any way of turning that thing off?"

"Apparently not," said Artur. His voice was smooth and cultured, with an undertone of viciousness. "It's for my own protection, after all. There's always someone watching. Anyone tries to attack me, the whole Fortress will turn out to defend me. That is why I came here, after all."

"It doesn't matter," said Stark. He sounded surprisingly tired for someone so close to getting everything he wanted.

"They won't recognise me and probably wouldn't care much if they did. I've committed no sins in the Nightside."

"I never got the chance, unfortunately," said Artur. "I'd barely joined up with Queen Helena and her Exiles, when Walker sent his assassin to kill us all. A very scary young lady; I was lucky to avoid her. I've been hiding out here ever since. If Walker finds me . . ."

"Walker's dead," said Stark. "You're safe from him and his people . . ."

"They say there's a new Walker," said Artur. "A certain John Taylor. Yes, I thought you'd know that name. And the assassin who wiped out all my fellow Exiles is his woman and partner. So pardon me if I feel a little . . . unsafe, even here. Let us make our deal, so we can both get what we want."

"You want Excalibur," said Stark. "I have it. And it's yours, in return for Merlin's raising my wife from the dead."

"I have to have the sword first," Artur said patiently. "Merlin won't do a damned thing for you of his own free will. But owning Excalibur will give me control over Merlin; then I will make him restore your dead wife to you."

"Is Excalibur really that powerful?" said Stark. "I mean, it's just a magic sword."

Artur laughed softly, unpleasantly. "You know better than that, Stark. You've been carrying it long enough to know better. It's made its mark on you. I can see it."

"I am my own man," Stark said stubbornly. "No sword tells me what to do."

"Excalibur is far more than just a sword. You have no idea what it really is. To own the sword, to have control over Excalibur, is to have control over the natural world and everything that lives in it. Merlin may be the most powerful sorcerer my world has ever known, he may even be the anti-Christ he claims to be; but all of that is nothing in the face of Excalibur. Merlin is still a living man, and part of the natural order of things, and Excalibur rules the living."

"I wish I had your confidence," said Stark.

"I wish I had your sword," said Artur.

"You will," said Stark.

I shut down my gift and dropped back into my body, in the bar. I looked at Suzie.

"The Fortress," she said. "Could have been worse."

"We have to get there fast," I said. "Stark's ready to make the deal."

"The Fortress is where we first met, after you came back from London Proper," said Suzie. "And I was so glad to see you again."

"You pick the strangest moments to get sentimental," I said. "But it's time we were moving. Allow me to show you my new toy."

I took out Walker's old gold pocket-watch, opened it, and the Portable Timeslip within whisked us away.

The Timeslip dropped us off right outside the Fortress. Suzie shook her head a little and gave me a hard look but said nothing. She's never been big on surprises. I put the watch away and looked up and down the street; but there was no-one else about. Most people steer clear of the Fortress, to avoid being shot at. The Fortress is always on the lookout for Men in Black. Suzie and I strolled casually down the street as though we just happened to be out for a walk. The Fortress is a massive square building, with all its doors and windows protected by reinforced steel shutters. Heavy-duty gun emplacements all but crowded each other off the flat roof, pointing up as well as down, and the exterior of the building positively bristled with all the very latest surveillance gear. The word FORTRESS had been painted in large letters all across the front of the building, over and over, in every language known to man and a few only spoken in the Nightside. For all those who have good reason to feel threatened, the Fortress is the last safe place in the Nightside.

These days it stands between two new franchises of utter respectability. On the one side stands The Devil Has Designs, where a satanic mechanic will implant black-magic circuitry into your brain, so you can make better contact with the infernal realms. Some people will believe *anything* . . . And on the other side of the Fortress lies Bonsai Dinosaurs. Genetically modified, miniaturised dinosaurs for people who will *buy* anything. Their window display consisted of a playpen full of miniature mammoths, chirping cheerfully together, and a large metal cage full of one-foot-high *Tyrannosaurus rex*, shoving and snapping at each other like vicious puppies. Suzie bent over and tapped on the window to get their attention, making *ooh* and *aww* noises.

"We are not getting a pet," I said firmly. "You know very well you'd never walk it, and I'd end up having to look after it. Besides, you never know how big they'd be when they grow up."

We moved over to stand before the heavily reinforced steel door that was the only entrance to the Fortress. It was, as always, quite definitely shut. You couldn't blast through that door with a bazooka, and people have tried. Cameras set all round the door whirred loudly as they turned to focus on Suzie and me. I stepped forward and smiled pleasantly into the main security camera.

"Hi!" I said cheerfully. "You know who we are, and you know what we'll do if you don't open up. We are not here to cause trouble, for once; we only want to talk to someone. So be a good chap and let us in before Suzie starts feeling unappreciated and does something unfortunate."

There was a slight pause, then there was the sound of many locks unlocking and many bolts sliding back. The door swung open before us, and I walked in like I owned the place, Suzie strolling casually along beside me. She hadn't even drawn her shotgun, which I thought showed considerable restraint. The comfortably appointed lobby was entirely deserted, with only a few overturned chairs to suggest that certain people had vacated the area in a hurry. A single desk clerk stood pale and trembling behind the reception desk.

"Oh God," he said, staring in horrid fascination at Suzie. "Not you again. The last time you were here, you shot up half the building."

"I get that a lot," said Suzie.

"Only because it's true," I said. "Last time I was here, you had half the security staff pinned down behind a barricade."

"That was just business. They shouldn't take these things personally. I would have been ever so much more destructive if it had been personal."

"Somehow, knowing that doesn't help," said the desk clerk. "I was on duty the last time you were here, and I'm still on pills."

"We're here looking for King Artur of Sinister Albion," I said. " Tell us what room he's in, and we'll go away and stop bothering you. Won't that be nice?"

"Room 1408," the clerk said immediately. "Never liked the man. Trouble-maker. Knew it the minute I laid eyes on him. But you must realise . . . the Fortress won't let you walk in and take him. He's entitled to protection even if he is an aristocratic little turd who never tips. You kick his door in and try to haul him away, and everyone in the place will come running with really big guns in their hands."

"Let them come," said Suzie. She smiled, and the desk clerk winced.

"All right," he said. "That's it. I am going to go and hide in the toilets until it's all over."

We took the elevator to the fourteenth floor. It played the Carpenters' greatest hits at us until Suzie blew the speakers

out. The doors finally opened to reveal an empty floor stretching away before us. No-one there, nothing moving, except for
maybe twenty or thirty security cameras, all whirring loudly
as they turned to focus on us. I gave them a cheerful wave.
Every door in the corridor was solid steel and firmly shut. I'd
been half expecting a heavily armed welcoming committee,
but for the moment it seemed everyone was waiting for someone else to make the first move. I looked at Suzie.

"Let's get this done before someone grows a pair and starts
the charge. We don't want a confrontation."

"You speak for yourself," said Suzie. "I love a good confrontation."

"Can't take you anywhere," I said. "Come on. Help me look
for 1408. Like it would kill them to put up signs . . ."

We finally found 1408 right at the end of the corridor,
next to the ice machine. Suzie and I eased silently into position outside the door and listened carefully. I could hear
voices inside: not quite raised in anger but definitely getting
there. I gestured to Suzie, then ducked quickly back out of
the way. Suzie kicked the door in with practised violence,
and in a moment we were both inside the room, Suzie covering Jerusalem Stark and King Artur with her shotgun. Even
though they were both wearing full plate armour, they stood
very still. They really shouldn't have taken their helmets off
so they could shout at each other better.

I shut the door behind me. It wouldn't stay shut after what
Suzie had done to it, so I leaned back against it. I smiled easily at Stark and Artur. They didn't smile back.

"Well?" I said. "Isn't this nice? Old friends bumping into
each other again. You ran away from Castle Inconnu, Stark,
just as we were getting to know each other. Oh, this is my better half, Shotgun Suzie, also known as Oh Just Shoot Yourself
in the Head and Get It Over With, It'll Probably Hurt Less."

"Hi," said Suzie.

"You may have a shotgun," Stark said finally. "But I have Excalibur."

"Bet my weapon fires more bullets," said Suzie. "You even try and draw that sword, and what's left of your head will be dripping down that wall behind you."

"Oh, I like her," said Artur. "She's got spunk."

Suzie looked at me.

"Old-fashioned slang, for someone with guts, courage, knows their own mind."

"Ah. I thought I must have misunderstood," said Suzie. "Now shut up, King, or I'll blow your entitlements off."

"So delightfully vicious! Nice tits, too."

"Shut up, Artur," I said. I gave Stark my full attention. "You have the sword, yes. But have you tried actually drawing Excalibur yet? No, didn't think you had. Now you bear the sword, you can hear it, feel its influence. You draw Excalibur, and it will force you to do the right thing."

"I am doing the right thing," said Stark.

"You're not worthy to bear Excalibur, and you know it," I said.

"Neither are you," said Stark. "I know all about you, John Taylor. It's a wonder touching the hilt didn't burn your hand right off after all the things you've done. I could still control the sword long enough to kill you."

"Try," suggested Suzie.

"Don't think you intimidate me," said Stark. "I have fought barrow trolls and dire wolves, gone to war against dark armies and foul invasions."

"They're not here," said Suzie. "I am."

"I would risk anything, for love," said Stark.

"Let's try talking first," I said. "To see what happens."

"Oh, do let's," said Artur. "I'd really rather not die at the hands of that attractively appalling woman if I don't have to. I have so many plans and ambitions, so many enemies to terrorise and slaughter when I return home in triumph. Sir Jerusalem, you seem to know these people. Would you be so kind as to introduce us?"

"The man is John Taylor, thug for hire. She is Suzie Shooter, assassin and bounty-hunter. You can't trust either of them."

"How very unkind," I murmured. "I am the new Walker of the Nightside, given charge of keeping the lid on things and keeping situations from getting out of control. Suzie is in charge of whatever brutality and retribution I deem necessary."

"I thought I detected a hint of bias in Stark's voice," said Artur. He looked thoughtfully at Suzie. "So you're the one who executed my fellow Exiles. And the reason why I've been forced to hide out in this dreadfully down-market accommodation."

"It was only a job," said Suzie.

"Oh, don't think I necessarily disagree, dear lady. They were a most unpleasant assortment, for all their airs and graces. Did they by any chance suffer horribly at your hands before you killed them? Do say yes and warm the very cockles of my heart."

Suzie glanced at me. "Is he flirting with me?"

"In his own horrible way, quite possibly. Leave the dangerous lady alone, Artur; she's with me."

"But I am a King," said Artur. "What woman in her right mind would settle for anything less?"

"I don't think anyone's ever accused me of being in my right mind," said Suzie. "You silver-tongued devil, you."

Artur smiled easily, apparently entirely unmoved by the threat of the shotgun still steadily menacing him. He did have a certain sleazy charm, born of centuries of courtliness and self-confidence. He was also still wearing his dark armour in his own room, which said something about his paranoia. The armour itself seemed to be made up of polished dark plates that moved slowly all the time, slipping and sliding round and over each other. They seemed almost alive. Somewhere, on the very edge of my hearing, I thought I could hear the faintest of voices, crying out for help. I was almost sure they were coming from the armour. The helmet lay on the unmade bed, next to a sword and a scabbard. The blade had the look of a real sword, a killing tool, made for murder and bloodshed, with nothing ceremonial about it.

"Since we are conversing in such a civilised manner," I said, "tell me about your world, King Artur. Starting with: why didn't your Merlin make your Arthur immortal, like him?"

"An intelligent question, my dear sir," said Artur, smiling a civilised smile that might have convinced anyone else. "Because Merlin was determined he should be the only immortal in his world. He wasn't prepared to risk anyone's becoming as powerful as him. He's never liked the idea of competition."

"So why not make himself King?" said Suzie.

"Because Kings have to work, dear lady. They have duties and responsibilities. You wouldn't believe how much paperwork is involved in running a Kingdom. And you have to do all the work yourself. Because if you start delegating, they'll take over while your attention's elsewhere. Merlin makes all the big decisions; I'm the one who has to make sure they're carried out."

"How did you first learn about the Nightside?" I said.

"Oh, quite by chance, I assure you," said Artur. "You have to understand, it's not easy to leave my world. Merlin's seen to that. No gaoler likes to see his prisoners escape. But then, quite out of the blue, someone from your world turned up in mine. Through something he called a Timeslip. He told me everything he knew about the Nightside until he finally died under questioning; and it did sound such a delightfully decadent place. Merlin was intrigued at the thought of another world to conquer: new challenges, new torments, and all that . . . and he soon learned how to open the Timeslip from our side.

"But then . . . he hesitated. Perhaps because it had been so long since he faced any real challenge. So I went through first while he was still thinking about it. Partly because the Nightside seemed like exactly the sort of place to find a weapon powerful enough to control Merlin, but mostly to see if it was as much fun as it sounded. And it is! Oh, the things I've done here . . . I never dreamed there could be so many new pleasures, so many new sins and temptations!"

"And then you saw your chance to get hold of this world's Excalibur," I said. "A chance to control Merlin and be King in fact as well as name."

"Ah, but that was then, and this is now," said Artur, smiling cheerfully. "To hell with my world. I want to stay here! I will use the sword to take charge of Merlin, and he will then conquer the Nightside with his power, in my name! He will make me King here, and I shall enjoy all your pleasures, and your people, for as long as they last. Why would I want to go back to Hell, when I can be King of Heaven?"

"Oh bloody hell," said Suzie. "Another one."

"What?" said Artur.

"You're not the first to get drunk on the Nightside's pleasures," I said. "And want to grab them all for yourself. We eat would-be conquerors for breakfast and clean our plates with jumped-up dictators. We are bigger and nastier and more dangerous than any of you. So cut the conquering crap and get back to answering questions. Why did someone as powerful as you claim to be need to hang out with Queen Helena and her loser Exiles?"

"Camouflage," said Artur. "My fellow royalty helped hide me from Merlin. And from any others who might come looking for me. I have many enemies in my world, as befits a man of my station. Merlin isn't the only one who wants to kill me or drag me home again."

"Are we," I said, "by any chance talking about Prince Gaylord?"

"Gaylord the Damned, Nuncio to the Court of Camelot," said Artur. "Not really a Prince, but he can call himself what he likes; no-one's going to argue with him."

"What the hell's a Nuncio?" said Suzie.

"Messenger, representative, Voice of Camelot," said Artur. "Basically, it means whatever he wants it to mean. He has authority but no restrictions. Power but no limits. He likes to pretend he serves me, but I think that's mostly to wind up Merlin."

"Who is this Prince Gaylord?" I said.

"No-one knows who or what he really is," said Artur. "Or what's inside the blood-red armour he never takes off. It is whispered, in certain quarters, that he can't take it off. That Merlin summoned something up from Hell, then lost control over it. The two of them have spent the last three hundred years in subtle conflict, struggling for control of Camelot. Merlin sent him here to look for me as a means of getting rid of him for a while; and Prince Gaylord agreed, to suit his own purposes. Perhaps he wants Excalibur, too . . . And if he were to use the sword to control or even kill Merlin, I think what he would do with Camelot would make it Hell on Earth indeed. He would soak the land in blood, laughing all the while. Merlin likes to boast about being his father's son. But he's still a man, with a man's limitations. There's nothing in the least human about Prince Gaylord the Damned."

"Wonderful," said Suzie. "More complications."

"After you wiped out all the Exiles—and once again thank you for that, my dear; they really were frightfully boring types—I had to find a better place to hide while I sought out someone who could deliver me Excalibur. The Fortress has served me very well, but I shall be glad to see the back of it. I really am used to better things. Now, let us talk of all the many rewards that can be yours, if you look away long enough for me to make my deal with Sir Jerusalem."

I turned to look at Stark and gave him my best decent

and honourable look. "You can't really be thinking of giving Excalibur to a man like this."

"I don't care," said Stark.

"He's lying to you! Merlin can't bring your dead wife back to life again! Only one man could do that, and He's long gone."

"You're wrong," said Stark. "Merlin can do it. I've seen him do it."

"Sorcerers deal in illusion," I said steadily. "It's what they do. Think about it, Stark; all Merlin could do for you is what any necromancer could—raise up a zombie. A dead body that moves. And maybe, just maybe, he could trap your wife's soul inside it. Is that what you want for her? Her soul, suffering inside a rotting corpse?"

"I have seen Merlin kill a man, then raise him up again, for the pleasure of it," said Artur. "Sometimes he kills the man over and over again, so he can keep bringing him back. To prove that no-one can escape from him and to see the suffering in the man's eyes as he is snatched back out of Heaven's grasp. Merlin is the anti-Christ, and he can do whatever he wants. Give me the wonderful sword, Stark, and you shall have your wife again."

"And damn your soul in the process?" I said to Stark.

He surprised me then by thinking about it for a moment. "I already damned my soul when I allied myself with Queen Mab and her elves," he said finally. "I let them into Castle Inconnu, so they could attack the London Knights and catch them unawares. I let the elves loose upon those who had been my brothers. But the elves died, and the castle still stands, so it was all for nothing. Unless I give Excalibur to this man. I can't damn my soul any more than it already is. I don't care, Taylor. I don't care about anything, any more, except my Julianne. I want her back, and I will ally myself with anyone, do anything, to bring her back. Excalibur is but the latest in a very long line of bargaining tools."

"Is this what Julianne would want?" I said. "Have you ever

asked her if she wants to come back, at such a price? Go on, call her up, right now. Tell her what you're planning to do, and all the evil that will make possible. Or are you afraid to hear what she'd say?"

"Everything I've done, I've done for her," said Stark. "She understands."

"Prove it," said Suzie.

Jerusalem Stark looked at her, then at me, and his hand fell to the preserved heart in the spun-silver cage at his belt. He caressed the dark purple heart with his fingertips, and his lips moved in Words best not spoken aloud, and suddenly his dead wife was standing there beside him. The hotel room had gone bitterly cold, all the warmth driven out of it by her presence. Julianne looked almost human, almost alive, for as long as Stark's fingers made contact with her heart. But you only had to look at her to know she was dead. Her features were clear and distinct, pretty and delicate; but there was a terrible distance in her gaze, and her face held no human expression. Her long white gown was soaked in blood all down the front, with great tears and rents where the blades went in; and the gown moved slowly about her, as though stirred by some unfelt breeze. Even her long, dark hair moved slowly, drifting this way and that, as though she were underwater. She put a hand on Stark's shoulder, and he shuddered briefly despite himself. Because the dead and the living are not meant to be close.

"I hear everything you say," said Julianne, in a calm, faraway voice. "I am never far, my love. Don't do this for me."

"I have to," said Stark. "I can't live without you. It hurts too much. I can't bear this . . ."

"What you are planning would drive us apart forever."

"I'm doing this for you! For us!"

"No. You're doing it for yourself. To stop your pain. I understand, my love, I do. But you have to let me go. I want you to live, not damn your soul with forbidden actions.

Because if you go to Hell, and I to Heaven, how could we ever be together again?"

She embraced him, pressing her chest against his, resting her head on his shoulder, and he held her back for as long as he could stand it. But in the end he cried out and pushed her away from him, and she faded away and was gone. Jerusalem Stark sat down suddenly on the unmade bed as though all the strength had gone out of him. He bent forward, looking only at the floor, and for a moment I thought he might cry. But he didn't. When he sat up again his face was as cold as his dead wife's had been. We all waited, but he had nothing to say.

"So," I said to Artur, just to be saying something. "What's your world like?"

"Tasty," he said immediately. "So many little treats, so many pleasures for those of refined tastes. If you're of the top rank, of course. For everyone else, well, I don't know what they do. Work, I suppose. I don't care. They're there to be used. It's what they're for. But . . . it can get repetitious. Merlin does so love to play out the same old stories, again and again. That's why I'm Artur, after Arthur. He even made me take a Queen Guinevere, but she didn't last long. I killed and ate her, after I found she'd slept with half my knights."

"There," I said to Stark. "That's Sinister Albion and its King. You still want to give him Excalibur?"

He stood up abruptly, his armour making loud protesting noises. "You don't understand. *I don't care.* I don't care about anything except getting my Julianne back."

"Even after what she said?"

"She will forgive me. She always did."

I turned my attention to Artur. "Sorry, Your Kingship, but this is now officially over. We can't let you take Excalibur. Apart from anything else, we're going to need it to defend us from the elves when they come. And besides, you give me the creeps. I'll see you get safely home, but after that you're on

SIMON R. GREEN

your own. And don't argue, or I'll have Suzie send you there
in a series of small boxes."

"You should come with me," said Artur. "You'd fit in
really well at Court."

"Now you're just being nasty," I said. I looked at Stark,
standing tall and somehow still tragically noble in his armour. "Give me the sword. The world needs it."

"Let all the worlds die," said Stark. "What do I care for the
world if my love is not in it?"

"Bloody knights," said Suzie, unexpectedly. "Always said
there was something a bit off about all that celibacy and putting their women on pedestals. I always thought it was so
they could look up their skirts on the sly. None of you ever
know what to do with a real live woman. Stop worshipping
her memory and let her go. This is all self-indulgence on
your part."

"You know nothing of love!" shouted Stark. Excalibur was
in his hand. It appeared suddenly, the tip of the long blade
only inches from my throat. But the golden sword hardly
glowed at all, only a pale golden gleam, far short of what it
had been. It could have been any magic sword, and a badly
fashioned one at that. Faint wisps of steam curled up from
inside Stark's mailed glove, where Excalibur burned his
unworthy flesh, even through the metal. Stark grimaced, but
his cold gaze never left me.

Suzie was shouting at him, yelling at Stark to get that
sword out of my face or she'd blow his head off; but he wasn't
listening. I was pretty sure she wouldn't shoot while I was in
danger, but it was clear Stark's attention was elsewhere. For
all his knightly experience, Stark was holding the blade like
an amateur. Because Excalibur wasn't helping him, as it had
helped me. It was fighting him for control, and Stark was losing. It was all he could do to hang on to the sword as it fought
and burned him.

And while Stark stood there, fighting a battle inside his

174

head, I stepped quickly to one side, and Suzie lunged forward and slammed the butt of her shotgun into the metal cup protecting Stark's groin. The metal actually clanged as it dented, and the sound the cup made as it collapsed in on itself made both Artur and me wince. The force of the blow bent Stark suddenly forward, all the breath forced out of his lungs, and tears actually flew from his eyes before the lids squeezed tightly shut. He sank to his knees amidst a clatter of armour, and I neatly snatched Excalibur from his numbed fingers. The long, golden blade blazed up immediately, its supernaturally bright light filling the room, and once again I could feel the weight of the invisible scabbard on my back and the presence of Excalibur in my thoughts again.

King Artur snatched up his sword from the bed, and hit Suzie in the side of the head with his armoured elbow while she still had all her attention focused on Stark. She sat down suddenly on the floor, still clinging grimly to her shotgun; but her head hung down, and her eyes weren't tracking. I yelled something foul at Artur, and he turned smoothly to face me, sword at the ready. There was nothing magic or special about his blade; it was a big ugly pigsticker, but he clearly knew how to use it. His every move was polished and professional. He feinted once, then swung the sword in a vicious arc that would have taken my head right off if it had connected; but Excalibur leapt up to block it. And the heavy dark blade shattered into a hundred pieces on contact, and Artur was left standing there with only a hilt in his hand. I pressed the tip of Excalibur against his breast-plate, and the dark pieces actually squirmed back out of its way, hissing and squealing. Artur looked down at the golden point pressed against his suddenly bare chest and opened his hand, letting the hilt fall to the floor. He smiled at me cheerfully and sank down on one knee.

"I offer my surrender. I know when I'm beaten."

"Stay down there," growled Suzie. "It suits you."

She forced herself up onto her feet again. A massive bruise was already forming on one side of her face. And while I was looking at her, Stark surged up onto his feet and threw himself forward, moving almost impossibly quickly for a man in full armour. He tried to grab Excalibur from my hand, but even caught off-balance, I still held on to it. The sheer weight of the man in his armour was enough to push me back, and I struggled to hang on to the sword. And while Stark pressed me back, his harshly breathing face thrust into mine, Artur rose up on what he thought was my blind side and stabbed at me with a concealed dagger.

Suzie gave him both barrels in the face. Artur's head simply disappeared in a red flurry of blood and flesh, bits of splintered bone and grey matter painting the wall behind him. His body sank slowly to the floor, held upright only by his armour, blood jetting from the neck stump. Stark let go of Excalibur and moved quickly to put me between him and Suzie. She grinned nastily as she pumped fresh shells into the chambers.

"Plebs one, aristocracy nil. That's history for you. Still, Merlin isn't going to be pleased I've killed his nasty little King, is he?"

"Almost certainly not," I said.

"Good," said Suzie.

She moved round to get a clear shot at Stark, but he surprised her by holding his ground. His hand fell to the heart at his belt, and Julianne appeared again. Stark yelled at her to embrace Suzie. The ghost looked at Suzie with sad eyes and advanced on her. Suzie gave her both barrels, but even the best blessed and cursed ammunition has no effect on a ghost. The bullets blasted right through Julianne, barely missing Stark and me behind her. The ghost embraced Suzie, who cried out in shock. I lifted Excalibur, to cut at the ghost, and Stark threw himself right through her immaterial form and caught me off-balance again. He hit me in the right biceps with a mailed fist, and my fingers, numbed along with my arm, sprang open, releasing Excalibur. Stark snatched it away from me, and I felt the invisible scabbard leave my back again.

Julianne disappeared the moment Stark took his hand off her heart. Suzie said something really foul and shook herself hard, trying to throw off the supernatural shock. Julianne wasn't just any ghost. Whatever Stark had done to her to keep her with him had made her more terrible than any ghost had a right to be. It was as though she wore Death itself round her, like a shroud.

Stark was already out the door, Excalibur in his hand. I could hear his metal boots slamming down the corridor. I lurched after him, my arm hanging limp at my side, but by the time I was out the door, he was already in the lift. I watched the doors close on his cold face and went back into the room. Neither Suzie nor I was in any condition to chase after him.

She was sitting on the unmade bed, cradling her shotgun to her like a doll. Her eyes were clear, but her face was deathly pale. I sat down beside her, biting my lip against the pins and needles of returning circulation in my arm. On the floor, Artur's headless body was no longer wearing armour. Instead, a large pile of dark scales stood quietly to one side, barely moving. Suzie glared at me.

"How can anyone lose Excalibur twice in one day?"

"It's a gift," I said.

"Well, try your other gift and track the bastard down."

I raised my gift and locked on to Stark almost straight away. My inner eye Saw him run out of the Fortress and onto the street, produce a bone charm, and speak several very dangerous Words over it. A dimensional gateway materialised before him, a rip in Space and Time, brutally simple but effective. The rogue knight had a portable Timeslip of his own. Stark stepped into the dimensional gate and disappeared; but he'd barely been gone a moment before Merlin Satanspawn appeared out of nowhere and threw himself into the gateway after Stark. The Timeslip collapsed in on itself and was gone, leaving the street empty again.

I lowered my gift and brought Suzie up to speed. She frowned, thinking.

"So, where has Stark gone?"

"Sinister Albion," I said. "My gift told me that much. And Merlin went straight through after him. So at least the Nightside is safe, for a while."

"But we still need Excalibur, to face the elves when they come," said Suzie. "So we have to go after them. Don't we?"

"Unfortunately, yes. But Merlin took the Timeslip with him when he left. There's not a trace of it left. And my Portable Timeslip can't track his destination without the right co-ordinates. Which is a bit beyond what my gift can do."

"Are you saying they've got away? There's no way we can go after them?"

I smiled. "This is the Nightside. There's always a way. Do you by any chance remember the Doormouse?"

"Oh bloody hell," said Suzie.

SIX

The Land That Merlin Made

When you absolutely, definitely, have to be somewhere else in a hurry, there's no substitute for the Doormouse and his excellent establishment, the House of Doors. He can open up a Door to anywhere and anywhen; though, of course, getting back again is strictly your problem. My Portable Timeslip took Suzie and me straight to his street, dropping us off, a little short because the Doormouse has very powerful protections. The old place looked pretty much as I remembered it. Still standing between a vampire theme pub, where the waiters snack on the customers, and a branch of the Bazaar of the Bizarre franchise, this week specialising in Necro-tattooing; where the tattooist uses blood instead of ink. Elf blood, werewolf blood, Frankenstein blood—producing images that don't just sit there but get right under your skin . . .

Suzie and I walked up to the Doormouse's place, and the frosted-glass doors swung regally open before us, admitting us to an extensive lobby of really quite remarkable style and elegance. Thick carpeting, huge mirrors, antique furnishings, and all the very latest high tech lying casually scattered round the place. Some of it so determinedly futuristic I couldn't even begin to name it, let alone guess what it was for. The Doormouse is always up to the mark; and, thanks to his Time-travelling capabilities, often more than a bit beyond.

The Doormouse himself came scurrying cheerfully forward to greet us; a six-foot-tall, vaguely humanoid mouse, with dark chocolate-coloured fur under a pristine white lab coat, complete with pocket protector for his colour-coded pens. He had a long muzzle, twitching whiskers, and shrewd, thoughtful eyes. He actually looked quite cute, in an entirely disturbing and unnatural way. He spoke in a high-pitched, cheery, and very human voice, like the born salesman he was.

"Hello, hello, hello there! Welcome to my emporium of Doors! Every destination you ever dreamed of, nowhere too remote or unlikely! Come on in and, oh my God, it's you again."

He stopped dead in his tracks, whiffling his whiskers and staring balefully at Suzie, who glared right back at him. The Doormouse folded his arms across his broad chest and tapped one sandaled foot very quickly.

"She's not going to break anything, is she? Only I still remember the last time you two were here, during the Lilith War. I'd have been safer out on the street with the rioting mobs. It's bad enough you marched in and used one of my best Doors without paying, but the whole shop's ambience was fatally compromised, just by her being here. Took three exorcists and a feng shui specialist to restore the usual happy House of Doors atmosphere."

"We only want to use a Door," I said soothingly. "We

might even pay for this one. Show us what we need, and we'll be on our way and leave you alone. Won't that be nice?"

"She's growling at me," said the Doormouse.

"Yes, well, that's her being her. Suzie doesn't do cute and fuzzy. I think it offends her view of the universe on some level. Don't make any sudden moves, and you'll be fine. Let's see the Showroom."

The Doormouse sniffed loudly, stuck a very pink tongue out in Suzie's direction, then he turned sharply and stomped off, leading us deeper inside. The main Showroom was full of Doors, row upon row and rank upon rank, all of them standing alone and upright and apparently unsupported. Made from every kind of wood and metal, glass and crystal, they all bore individual handwritten labels, describing their destinations: Shadows Fall, Carcosa, Haceldama, and Scytha-Pannonia-Transbalkania.

"A very popular holiday resort, that one," said the Doormouse, bustling busily along. "If you like it old-fashioned and a little odd."

I wasn't really listening. I'd spotted a familiar face—that general fixer and go-to man, Harry Fabulous, lurking further down the Showroom. He took one look at me and disappeared through a Door. I get that a lot. Still, the guilty flee where no man pursueth, and Harry did a lot of fleeing. Suzie elbowed me discreetly in the ribs, and I pretended I'd been paying attention all along.

"Lots of Doors in stock," said the Doormouse, padding along before us. "Lots and lots . . . I'm always expanding, always looking for something new and interesting. I still design all the Doors myself, but I do enjoy tracking down the odd rarity. I nearly got my hands on the legendary Apocalypse Door at an auction in Los Angeles; but someone else got their hands on it first. It can be a cut-throat business in the travel industry, sometimes . . . Where do you want to go this time, Mr. Taylor; and why do I just know I'm not going to like the answer?"

"I don't know," I said innocently. "Maybe you're psychic. I need to get to an alternative Earth called Sinister Albion."

The Doormouse stopped so abruptly I nearly walked right over him. He turned and looked at me thoughtfully.

"Oh. There. . . . Nasty place, by all accounts. But no doubt you know your own interests best. Have you made a will? I have. Very comforting things, wills. So, you want the Alternate Earths Door. This way, this way . . ."

He started off again in a completely different direction, down a long line of standing Doors, until he finally lurched to a halt before a large mahogany door with a complicated brass combination lock inserted right in its centre. The Doormouse patted the gleaming dark wood with one soft paw.

"Remarkable piece of work, this, Mr. Taylor. Remarkable. This Door can give you access to any alternate history track you can think of and a few most people would be better off not thinking of. All you need is the correct co-ordinates. I should point out that you have to be extremely exact when entering the co-ordinates if you want to get the world you want and not one just a bit like it. Now, Sinister Albion. Are you sure you're sure about this, Mr. Taylor?"

"Unfortunately, yes," I said.

"Quite so, quite so . . . I gather from your companion's expression that she's about to start growling again, so I'll get to the point. I don't know the exact co-ordinates for Sinister Albion. Don't know anyone who does. I didn't even know the awful place existed before its inhabitants started showing up in the Nightside: King Artur, Merlin Satanspawn, Prince Gaylord the Damned . . . That last one actually turned up here a few days ago. I locked the doors, pulled down all the shutters, hid in the toilets, and pretended I was out until he gave up and went away. I mean, you have to draw the line somewhere. No, if you want to go to Sinister Albion,

Mr. Taylor . . . you're going to have to provide the co-ordinates. Of course, they say you can find anything . . . Must be a wonderful gift. Very useful. I can never find anything. Can't even find my spectacles most of the time."

"They're on top of your head," I said absently, studying the Door before me. It looked like any other wooden door, but even without using my Sight I could tell it was much more than that. It had a sense of *potential* about it, a strong feeling of possibilities, as though it could take you anywhere at all. And might even snatch you away for standing too long in front of it. This was a Door that wanted to be used.

I raised my gift and let it glide forward and sink into the Door. Beyond it I could see endless scenes, flickering on and off, worlds without end, worlds come and gone in a moment—some familiar, some horrible, and some so utterly *other* I couldn't even make sense of what I was Seeing. I concentrated, frowning, focusing on Sinister Albion. Worlds fanned out before me like a pack of cards; and one world snapped suddenly into focus. I pulled back immediately and concentrated on the brass combination lock on the Door. The mechanism whirled back and forth, spinning rapidly under the impetus of my gaze, then it snapped to a halt, and the Door swung open a little.

Blood-red light spilled out round its edges, bleeding into the cool antiseptic light of the Showroom. The Doormouse fell back a step, his whiskers twitching frantically. A terrible stench of blood and carrion filled the air, wafting out into the Showroom from the world beyond the Door. It was the smell of death and horror, like some gigantic slaughterhouse. The world Merlin Satanspawn had made, to please his father . . .

"You know," Suzie said thoughtfully, "you can be really spooky sometimes, John."

"You're just saying that," I said, shutting my gift down as thoroughly as I knew how.

"I feel it is my duty to remind you," the Doormouse said diffidently, "that while my Doors can take you anywhere in the unknown universe, they are all strictly one-way operations. To be blunt: once you're in Sinister Albion, you're on your own. I cannot bring you back. And no, I don't do travel insurance."

Suzie looked at me. "What about your Portable Timeslip?"

"Only works in this world," I said. "It operates in Space and Time, not dimensions. It's a gold watch, not a TARDIS."

"Wouldn't work anyway," said the Doormouse. "Not where you're going."

I looked Suzie in the eye. "You heard the mouse. This could be a one-way trip. You don't have to come with me."

"Don't make me slap you in front of a mouse," said Suzie. "You can't do this without me, and you know it. Someone's got to watch your back."

I nodded. Suzie's never been very good at the sentimental stuff, but I knew what she meant. There was no way she'd let me go into danger without her, not while she had a say in the matter. I pulled the Door all the way open, and the blood-red light flared up. Suzie and I walked forward into it, into Sinister Albion.

And behind us I could hear the Doormouse crying, "Come back! Come back! You haven't paid yet . . ."

It was dark, even though it was day. The sun burned a sullen crimson through heavy, lowering clouds, turning the sky blood-red. Ashes fell out of the sky as though the clouds were on fire. But it didn't take me long to work out where the ashes were really coming from. In long rows, all along the distant horizon, stood rank upon rank of giant burning Wicker Men. Huge hollow forms, roughly man-shaped, full of men and women burning alive. I couldn't really hear them screaming, from so far away; but it felt like I could. The Wicker Men burned like beacons, illuminating Sinister Albion.

The land round us was churned-up mud, for as far as the eye could see. No fields, no crops, no forests, and no rivers. Thick filthy mud, soaked with old and new blood, punctuated here and there with human body parts and all kinds of scattered offal. Some of the mud had been disturbed in more or less straight lines, tracks rather than roads. The air was hot and sweltering, difficult and unpleasant to breathe. Thick with the stench of burning meat, it coated the inside of my mouth with grease and ashes.

Dotted here and there across the rough landscape were huge concrete structures: featureless blocks with no windows and only the one door. Surrounded by long walks of barbed wire, interrupted here and there with signs warning of mine-fields. This was where the workers lived when they weren't working. I knew that, somehow. This was England as a slaughter-house, as concentration camp. The land Merlin Satanspawn had made, in his father's image. A place of torture and horror and death for the lucky ones. Sinister Albion. The murdered dream of Camelot.

I could see Camelot from where I was. It stood at the top of a hill, not far away, the only castle in this nightmare place. It was all steel walls and thrusting metal turrets, polished and gleaming, with no windows and only the one door. And I had to wonder if it was as much a prison for its inhabitants as any of the concrete workers' blocks. There was no stone or marble to the castle, nothing so . . . soft, or human. I pointed the castle out to Suzie, and she nodded quickly. Her face was as cold and collected as always, but her eyes were fierce and unforgiving.

"You bring me to the nicest places, John," she said finally.

"I think that's Camelot," I said.

"That ugly thing? I've had better-looking bowel movements."

"You see any other castles round here? I told the Door to bring us straight to Excalibur, and this is apparently as close as it could get. And where else would Stark take the sword?"

"I have been in some real shit holes," said Suzie. "And this is definitely one of them. Let's get this done, John. I don't like it here. I think . . . it could be bad for the soul. That something in the nature of this place could rub off on us."

"Sooner we start, sooner we finish," I said. "Cheer up. I'm sure you'll get to kill someone worth killing before this is over."

"Anywhere else, that would be a good thing," said Suzie. "But here—I think if I start, I might not be able to stop . . ." She met my gaze suddenly. "John, whatever happens here, don't leave me here, not in this place. Dead or alive, promise me you'll get me home."

"Dead or alive," I said. "Nothing is ever going to part us."

She nodded once, and we set off through the thick mud, towards the castle on the hill.

We made our way slowly across the dark, uneven countryside, our boots sinking deep into the mud with every step. It took all my strength and determination to keep going, hauling one foot out of the clinging mud with brute strength, only to have it sink in deep again with the next step. On and on, ploughing through the mud with stubborn strength, feeling my stamina leached slowly away by the unending effort. Giant bubbles of carrion-thick gas welled up out of the mud, disturbed by our progress, popping fatly on the already foul air. I cursed the mud and the stench and our slow pace until I ran out of breath and needed all I had to keep going. Suzie struggled on beside me, grimly silent. The oppressive heat left me soaked in sweat, and I had to stop now and again to cough ashes out of my throat. And deep down I knew that none of this had happened by chance. This was a world made to make people miserable, just for the fun of it.

The mud was deeper in some places than others, with never any warning, dropping off suddenly under our feet like giant sucking pits, trying to drag us down. Suzie and I looked after each other and fought our way through. The bottom half of my trench coat was soaked in mud and blood and filth, and Suzie's black leathers didn't fare much better. I kept hoping I'd get used to the stench and stop smelling it. But somehow it was always there, clogging up my mouth and throat and lungs. My eyes ran constantly with tears, from something in the air; I could feel them cutting slow runnels through the encrusted mud and ashes on my cheeks and mouth.

We'd barely made it half-way to the castle on the hill when we slowly became aware that we weren't alone. Suzie stopped and looked sharply round. We moved to stand back-to-back, both of us aware of a threat we could sense but not see. The mud stirred slowly, its surface disturbed by living creatures moving underneath it. The mud was deep here, up to my waist, and things circled slowly round us, leaving long, slow trails in their wakes. Human hands and heads bobbed slowly up through the mud's surface, rotten and corrupt and partially devoured, brought to the surface by what moved below. I still couldn't see anything, nothing had broken the surface yet, but I could follow their progress through the deep mud. Suzie followed the wakes with her shotgun and pumped shells into position, the sound loud and carrying on the quiet. She tracked one particularly heavy wake, took careful aim directly ahead, and gave the creature both barrels.

The blast was shockingly loud but almost immediately drowned out by a vicious, angry screaming, as something large and twisted thrashed back and forth just under the surface. Blood spurted up through the mud, which flew spattering in all directions. Something that might have been a clawed hand briefly showed itself, and a set of massive snapping jaws, then they were gone again. Suzie aimed and fired a second time, and the screams shut off abruptly. The thrashing grew still, and the mud settled down again. A great pool of blood spread across the surface of the mud, but there was no sign of the creature itself. Slowly, the other wakes moved away from us, heading off into the mud. Suzie sniffed loudly, and we set off towards the castle again. Suzie has always favoured the direct approach to dealing with problems.

We moved on, ploughing stubbornly through the rotten and corrupt land, heading for two ranks of trees that formed a corridor, leading out of the mud and towards the base of the hill. I was really tired now, fighting the growing ache in my legs and back with every movement, breathing through gritted teeth to try to keep the falling ashes out of my mouth. As we drew closer to the trees, I slowly realised none of them had any leaves. The branches were twisted and gnarled and completely bare. The bark was a dull matte black, split here and there by some internal pressure, with thick red blood leaking out—as though the tree roots had spent so long in this corrupt ground that the trees no longer had sap in them, only blood. And perhaps no longer had any use for leaves in this world that knew nothing of sunlight.

The mud grew steadily more shallow as Suzie and I approached the corridor of trees, and we finally hauled ourselves out onto something very like proper ground. It was hard and flat and deeply cracked, almost volcanic. It felt good to have solid ground under my feet again, and I walked up and down a while for the pleasure of it. Then I spent some time slapping the hell out of my trench coat, trying to dislodge the caked-on filth; but it clung like tar, and I really didn't want to try to prise it away with my bare hands. I finally gave it up as a job for later, and, hopefully, somebody else. Suzie, typically, hadn't even bothered. She was looking thoughtfully about her, shotgun held at the ready. I followed her gaze, and quickly made out a whole bunch of creatures lurking in the shadows of the trees. Whatever they were, none of them wanted to get too close to us. They watched silently as Suzie and I moved cautiously through the corridor of trees. A few emerged from the shadows long enough to snarl briefly at us and retreat. They were cowed and broken things, with no spirit. What little I could make out of their forms looked rotten, decaying, malformed. Carrion feeders, not predators.

"First trees we've seen," I said, just to be saying something. "Wonder what happened to the great forests here?"

"Cut down, set fire to," said Suzie, sweeping her gun slowly back and forth before her. "Probably for the fun of it."

"You know, you can be really depressing sometimes, Suzie."

"Just trying to fit in."

We came at last to the foot of the hill and stopped to lean on each other for a moment, to get our breath back before we tackled the hill. The dusty grey surface had given way to the first real road we'd seen, a dull yellow clay, winding round the hill on its way up to the castle. It wasn't a yellow brick road, and that that certainly wasn't an Emerald City, but it would do.

A bare wooden door-frame stood at the side of the road, containing no door, merely thick swirling mists that only existed inside the door-frame. Strange lights came and went in the depths of that thick, churning fog. Flames flickered sullenly all round the wooden door-frame, burning and blackening the wood without consuming it. The fires could have been burning for hours or days or even years. The longer I looked into the churning mists, the more convinced I became there was someone or something in there, looking back at me. And then I heard the sound of horses' hoofs, drawing steadily nearer, and I backed quickly away from the door-frame. Suzie moved in beside me, covering the mists with her shotgun. The sound of hoofs grew louder, and a whole company of knights in dark armour came thundering out of the mists, right at us. Suzie threw herself one way, and I went the other, as horse after horse emerged from the mists to form a barricade blocking the road up the hill.

The horses were huge: great black beasts snorting and stamping in the ash-filled air. And on their backs, knights in the same black armour that Artur had worn. Armour made of black scales that hissed and seethed and slid slowly over each other. The dark knights carried huge oversized swords and battle-axes, some so large they had to be strapped to the sides of their horses. Their breast-plates bore ancient satanic symbols, burned right into the armour, and they all carried heavy oblong shields, each marked with the sign of the inverted cross.

And at their head, on the biggest, blackest horse of all, a knight in blood-red armour. His crimson helmet bore a pair of stylised horns but no slit for eyes and mouth—just a blank expanse of gleaming metal. The whole of the knight's armour seemed fused together, made and forged all of one piece, so that even when the great joints moved, there was never any trace of an opening. The armour was a single sealed unit, with no way in or out. Designed, perhaps, to keep something inside from getting out.

I knew who this was, who it had to be. Prince Gaylord the Damned, Nuncio to the Court of Camelot. I wondered if he knew his King was dead. Or, indeed, who had killed him.

Prince Gaylord urged his huge black horse forward until it stopped right in front of me. Suzie was quickly there at my side again, shotgun at the ready. The Prince in scarlet ignored her, the featureless helmet fixed on me. I still hadn't figured out what I was going to say or do, so I made a point of ignoring him and being only interested in his horse. There was something definitely wrong about it.

The horse's body was strangely asymmetrical, everything out of shape and out of balance, and its long head was almost a caricature of what a horse's head should be. Its eyes bulged like a frog's, and its wide, grinning mouth showed pointed teeth. Thin wisps of smoke curled up from its flared nostrils. And when I looked down, I saw the horse had cloven hoofs, with smoke rising from the ground they trod. A very disturbing horse—if it was a horse.

"I am Prince Gaylord," the blood-red knight said finally, his voice echoing inside his crimson helmet. It was a smug and very self-satisfied voice, with a hint of mocking evil. As though he had done terrible things and enjoyed every minute of it but didn't like to boast about it. Effortlessly scary, because it came so naturally. "Welcome . . . to Sinister Albion."

"Ask him if he's got a small companion called Tattoo," said Suzie. She sniggered loudly as I shook my head. Her sense of humour emerges at the strangest times.

"You'll have to excuse Suzie," I explained, "because she'll shoot you if you don't. I am . . ."

"Oh, I know who you are, Lilith's son," said Prince Gaylord. "I've been looking forward to this little chat. We have so much in common."

"We do?" I said politely.

"We both know what it is to have an overbearing parent whose very existence overshadows everything we do. You destroyed yours; and I really would like to learn how you did that."

"How did you know we were coming here?" I said. "Given that even I didn't know half an hour ago."

"I know everything I need to know," said the Prince. "Except for when I don't. I saw you admiring my horses. Aren't they wonderful? So much more interesting than the mere beasts of burden they started out as. Now they all contain followers of mine, brought up out of Hell with me, to serve me in this world. I'm pretty sure that possessing horses wasn't what they had in mind; but I'm not ready to share my glory with anyone. Do you like the black armour my knights wear? My idea, again. Every separate scale contains the imprisoned soul of some innocent slain by the knight. Bound to serve him, forever. Souls are such a marvellous source of power. And so it is my knights are strong and invincible, in such a delightfully ironic way."

"Does like to talk, doesn't he?" said Suzie.

"Living armour?" I said, concentrating on the Prince. "Like the Droods?"

"Copy-cats," the Prince said dismissively.

"Look, what do you want, tomato face?" said Suzie. Her long struggle through the mud and filth had not improved her temper. The company of dark knights stirred dangerously at the open insult.

"Nothing happens here that I don't know about," said Prince Gaylord. "Or in the Nightside, for that matter. Hell is as close to the Nightside as it is to Sinister Albion. You should know that, John. The Griffin says 'hello' . . . And yes, I know the two of you killed my King. Dear little Artur. The King is dead, long live the . . . Well, that's the point, isn't it? You must accompany me to Camelot, John Taylor and Suzie Shooter. You must come with me to the Court of Camelot, then . . . Oh, the things we'll do . . ."

"That's where we were going anyway," I said. "But you're welcome to tag along."

The dark knights laughed—a jeering, cruel, unpleasant sound.

"No-one ever wants to go to Camelot," said Prince Gaylord. "Not given what lies in wait there. Not given what happens there. Many go in, but few come out because Camelot is the worst place there is, on this worst of all worlds. But things can change, even here. You shall be my weapons, dear

John and Suzie, with which I shall bring down Merlin and take his place. And when I am King, I shall truly make this land Hell on Earth."

"Who are you?" I said. "What are you, Prince Gaylord the Damned?"

"I am the Devil's other son, begotten in Hell as my brother Merlin was begotten on Earth. And I am much more my father's son than he ever was or could be."

"Then why did he let you come here?" said Suzie.

"He didn't," said Prince Gaylord. "He couldn't keep me out any longer."

"If your father is the Devil," said Suzie, "what do you need us for?"

"I don't," said Prince Gaylord. "I can take care of my brother. But I want you to remove a certain object, a certain sword that might . . . complicate things. I can't touch it, but you can. You can take it away from my brother and give it to me, to destroy it. Excalibur has no place in this world."

"And if we choose not to get involved in your family squabble?" I said. "If we take the sword anyway and go home?"

"You have no choice," said Prince Gaylord. "Excalibur is too powerful a thing to be allowed to run free. You shall go to Camelot on your knees, and in chains, as my slaves. You will do my bidding, John Taylor, or I will make your woman scream in front of you as I take her apart, piece by piece, until you beg to serve me, to save what's left of her." He gestured, and one of the dark knights urged his horse forward, a set of spiked chains dangling from one black mailed glove.

"Typical bloody stuck-up aristocrat," said Suzie.

She opened fire on the approaching knight, giving him both barrels full in the helmet. The blast smashed the helmet and the head inside it right off, and the headless body slowly toppled backwards off his horse, his arms still failing as blood jetted from the ragged neck aperture. The horse reared up, menacing Suzie with its great cloven hoofs, and Suzie gave it both barrels in its exposed belly. The horse screamed shrilly, in an almost human voice, and crashed to the ground, blood and entrails spilling out of the massive hole in its guts. Suzie turned on the other knights, and picked them off one by one, shooting them right out of their saddles and bringing down their demon horses. Some tried to get to me, and Suzie shot them methodically in the back. I don't know whether it was the blessed or the cursed armour that did the trick; but their armour was no protection against a Nightside shotgun. Soon the ground was covered in headless knights and thrashing horses as fresh blood soaked into the dusty earth. Suzie moved unhurriedly amongst the bodies, finishing off anything that didn't look dead enough. Stopping now and again to reload the shotgun from the bandoliers that crossed her chest.

I had my own problems. Prince Gaylord screamed with fury inside his seamless crimson helmet as the first knight died and urged his demon horse forward to ride me down. I backed quickly away, thinking hard. None of my usual bag of tricks would work against the Devil's other son. Given time, I might have been able to put something together, but he was right on top of me. I couldn't throw pepper in his face, or take bullets out of his sword, or play games with his head. The only actual weapon I had on me was a small ceremonial silver dagger that someone had given me in part payment for an old fee. I only used it for carving magical graffiti into the walls of places I didn't approve of. But after that business with the werewolves the other day, I did find the time to have the silver dagger officially blessed: by the Rogue Vicar Tamsin MacReady, and the Lord of Thorns himself . . . and those were pretty heavy-duty blessings.

So when Prince Gaylord's demon horse reared up over me, cloven hoofs pounding on the air over my head, instead of continuing to back away, as expected, I stepped forward, darted to one side, and sliced the demon horse along its ribs with the point of my silver dagger to see what would happen. The horse screamed like a fire siren, and sulphur-yellow flames burst out, all down the long cut. The horse's hoofs slammed to the ground again, its legs almost buckling from the shock of actually being hurt, so I moved quickly in and jammed the dagger into the horse's bulging eye. I forced it in, all the way to the hilt, ignoring the acidic jelly that splashed over my hand. The horse howled and shook its head savagely at the new pain. I jerked the dagger out and fell back, so that the stream of yellow flames bursting out of the eye socket missed me by inches.

Prince Gaylord was thrown from his saddle, as his horse crashed to the ground and lay still. He landed on his feet, almost elegantly, and laughed unpleasantly inside his sealed helmet. The Prince advanced on me, long butcher's blade of a sword in hand, clearly expecting me to give ground. But I'd had enough for one day. I stood there, silver dagger in hand, and waited for him to come to me.

Prince Gaylord slowed his advance at the last moment, mistaking my bad temper for confidence. If there'd been anywhere to run, I'd have been half-way there already; but as it was . . . Besides, I couldn't leave Suzie. So I stood my ground, waited until Prince Gaylord was towering over me, then feinted one way and dived to the other. I knew his heavy armour couldn't match me for speed and manoeuvrability; thus while he was still reacting to my first move, I was inside his guard, and slamming the silver dagger into his side. Doubly blessed, the leaf-shaped silver blade punched right through his blood-red armour, and Prince Gaylord screamed inside his helmet. He tried to strike at me with his sword, but I ducked the blow easily and yanked the dagger out of his ribs. He screamed again, as crimson fire shot out of his side, like a gas jet under pressure. He clapped one red metal hand over the wound to try to smother the flame, but it shot past his fingers. And while the Prince was busy doing that, I got behind him, jumped on his back, and stabbed the silver dagger right through his featureless metal face, right where the eyes should have been. His scream became a series of horrible noises, and he staggered back and forth. I jerked the dagger free and jumped down again. More flames blasted out of the hole in the front of his helmet.

But while I was preoccupied, his demon horse had been hauling itself along the bloody ground, leaving a long trail of guts behind it. It rose up suddenly, bared its huge pointed teeth, and lunged forward. I spun round and slammed the silver dagger into its one remaining eye. I jammed it in with both hands this time, hot viscous fluids spilling over my bare fingers, but the horse went down and stayed down.

Prince Gaylord staggered this way and that, flames shooting from two great holes in his armour. I circled him silently, looking for another opening. He was howling constantly inside his sealed helmet, words and sounds that made no sense at all. He'd thrown aside his sword and acquired from somewhere a massive double-headed battle-axe. Blood dripped steadily from both blades, and hissed and spat when it hit the ground. Prince Gaylord surged forward inhumanly quickly and swung the axe round in a vicious arc that would have cut me in two if I'd still been standing in the same place . . . But armour exaggerates every move, making it easy to anticipate, and I started moving almost the moment he did. The axe hissed through the air where I'd been standing, and buried itself deep in the ground. And while the Prince stooped over it, trying to pull it back out again through brute force, I stepped in and slammed the silver dagger into his blood-red neck and jerked it all the way across the metal throat, opening up a long, jagged rent, and flames roared out.

I quickly retreated as Prince Gaylord flailed wildly about

with his arms. He screamed again, the volume rising and rising, the sound of it increasingly inhuman. And while he was doing that, Suzie stepped up behind him and let him have both barrels in the back of his head at point-blank range. The whole helmet exploded, and I ducked out of the way as fragments of crimson metal flew on the air. I stood ready to go again, the silver dagger in my hand; but the whole front of the helmet was gone, a great jet of crimson flames shooting out of it. Prince Gaylord was still screaming, but the sound seemed to come from further and further away, until suddenly it was gone. The flames snapped off from all the openings we'd made, and the armour fell forward, hit the ground, and shattered into a thousand pieces.

It was all very quiet. I nodded my thanks to Suzie and put the dagger away. Suzie put her gun away and looked round at all the death and destruction she'd wrought with a quiet air of satisfaction. Dead horses, looking much more like horses now that their possessors were gone; and dead knights in armour, many of them headless. When Suzie finds something that works, she tends to stick with it. I breathed deeply, trying to get my heart rate back to something like normal. I'm really not one for the old hand-to-hand combat thing, especially against heavily armed and armoured demon knights out of Hell. Suzie came over and looked down at the scattered pieces of Prince Gaylord's armour.

"Sent him home with his tail between his legs," she said. "Probably to tell his daddy we were mean to him."

"I think the armour was the only thing that could keep him here," I said. I looked at Suzie. "I could have taken him. I had a plan."

"What were you going to do, whittle him to death? I keep telling you, John, you need to invest in some serious weaponry."

"Don't need them," I said. "I have you."

"Of course you do," said Suzie. "Always and forever."

• • •

We started up the path to the castle, leaving all the mess behind. My heartbeat was almost back to normal, and my hands had very nearly stopped shaking. Suzie pretended not to notice. She seemed perfectly fine and was actually whistling something she clearly thought was a tune. The path made its way round and round the hill, rising slowly upwards. I kept a careful eye on the castle above us. It felt like it was looking back at me, daring me to approach any closer. After a while, I gave in to temptation and raised my Sight, just enough to give me a clear view of what lay ahead, in case there were any hidden defences or booby-traps I ought to know about. I had to limit my Sight; I didn't think I could bear to See this land too closely, for too long.

I checked the path ahead but couldn't See any traps or protections, as though the castle believed no-one in this land could present any threat, any more. All I could See were ghosts, armies of them, filling up the country-side for as far as I could See. All round the hill, angry and desolate faces stared up at Camelot, howling silently. I saw ghostly elves, proud and disdainful even in death, and hundreds of other magical creatures, standing still and silent in ghostly ranks—all wiped out by Merlin. Because he wanted to be the only magical thing in the land. I could See dead dragons, deep in the ground, and the ragged remains of slaughtered elementals, drifting on the sky above. So much death and suffering, so much sorrow, all because of one man.

One anti-Christ down, one to go.

I concentrated on the castle, so I wouldn't have to See any more death, and my Sight stirred my gift, enough to give me a Vision of what was happening, deep inside Castle Camelot. Stark was there, in his armour, talking with Merlin, though I couldn't hear what they were saying. They seemed to be arguing, which was good news. It implied that Stark had yet to make a deal over Excalibur. I couldn't See the sword anywhere in the Vision. It might have been that Stark had enough sense not to bring the sword into Merlin's presence; or it could have been that the sword was still invisible to anyone except its bearer. I felt distinctly jealous. It was my sword, dammit. And then Merlin turned his head abruptly and looked out of the Vision right at me, his blazing eyes widening in recognition. I shut the Vision down immediately, along with my Sight. I'd Seen enough.

I told Suzie about the Vision, and she nodded thoughtfully as we continued up the hill towards Camelot.

"No protections?" she said finally. "No defences at all?"

"Nothing magical," I said. "But who knows how many more dark knights Merlin has at his command, now that he's made himself King."

"And he definitely Saw you, through the Vision? He knows we're coming?"

"Yes. Which could be a good thing . . ."

"Oh, do go on. I can't wait to hear this one."

"If he knows we're coming, it could distract him from making a deal with Stark."

"That's what I love about you, John. Always the optimist."

We laughed briefly together and continued on up the hill. The higher we rose, the further I could see out across the land. The rows of Wicker Men were still burning fiercely, pumping black smoke and ashes up into the sky. Huge bat-winged shapes flapped slowly through the clouds, lean and vicious things. They weren't dragons. Something else Merlin had summoned up from Hell? I pointed them out to Suzie, and she smiled and said something about target practice.

When we finally got to the castle, we found ourselves facing two huge steel doors, great featureless slabs of gleaming metal, thirty feet tall and twenty wide, that were the only way in. I looked the doors over, but there was no knocker or bell-pull anywhere. The blank metal walls on both sides seemed to stretch away forever, towering high above us, without so much as a single arrow slit to relieve the monotony. Suzie did offer to try her shotgun on the door, and I said some very loud things about ricochets. While we were still arguing, the great metal doors swung slowly back, opening wide enough to allow a single knight in dark armour to march out to join us. Suzie and I immediately stopped arguing and glared at him, and he stopped dead in his tracks. Behind the narrow slit in the front of his helmet, his gaze was suddenly uncertain.

"Hi," I said. "I'm John Taylor, and this is Suzie Shooter. Be impressed, or we'll take you apart with a can-opener."

"Doesn't it get hot inside all that armour?" said Suzie. "You can take it off if you want. It wouldn't protect you from us anyway."

"Please don't kill him yet, Suzie," I said. "He's the only guide we've got. I don't want to end up wandering through this bloody place with a map in my hand. You are here to guide us, aren't you? Speak up!"

"Yes," said the knight. "I'm . . . uh . . ."

"Get on with it," I said ruthlessly. "And get a move on. We're expected."

"Merlin Satanspawn demands you attend him in the Great Hall," said the knight, getting the words out in a rush so as to be rid of them as quickly as possible.

"Good," said Suzie. "We want to see him. We have a lot to talk about. Don't stand too close, and you won't get blood and innards all over your armour."

"He's going to kill both of you," said the knight. "And I'll get to watch."

"And you were doing so well," I said.

"How do you take a piss in that outfit anyway?" said Suzie,

looking the armour over critically. "Have you got a trap-door, or something? Doesn't it get rusty?"

The knight turned his back on us and stomped off through the doors. Suzie and I wandered after him, taking our time. The courtyard beyond the gates was full of men, women, and children, all of them impaled on long metal spikes. Hundreds of them, filling the courtyard from wall to wall. All of them still alive, kept alive and suffering. Suzie and I stopped short, and the great metal doors slammed shut behind us. The knight looked back at us, smirking behind his helmet.

"See? Not so funny now, are you?"

Suzie and I surged forward and hit him together, bowling him off his feet and slamming him onto the courtyard floor. Suzie knelt on his chest and stuck the barrel of her shotgun right into the slit opening of his helmet. I put a hand on her arm.

"Don't kill him, Suzie. Not yet." I looked at the knight. "You—arsehole. Tell me what's happening here."

"You wouldn't dare shoot me," said the knight.

"You really don't know her," I said. "Trust me. I am the only thing keeping you alive at the moment. Talk."

"They spoke out, everyone here. Against the way things are. Someone overheard them and turned them in. Now they'll squirm and rot on those spikes forever, kept alive by Merlin's magic. Or at least, until the next batch of traitors get hauled in."

I stood up and looked round me. Sharp metal points protruded from mouths and eyes, and blood and other fluids ran down the poles to pool on the courtyard floor; but all of them were still alive. Dying by inches, over and over, but never getting there. Agony beyond belief . . .

"I can't help them," said Suzie. "I don't have enough ammunition. Please, John. Do something."

I raised my gift, and, powered by my rage and disgust, it

only took me a moment to find the magic that made all this possible. I could See it, hanging across the courtyard like a spider's web, every strand an artery, pulsing as it fed on the pain it made possible. I grabbed the whole web in my mental hand and crushed it. Something far away cried out, in pain and fury, and I smiled. All round me, men, women, and children slumped forward on their spikes, dead at last. I looked at Suzie, still with one knee pressing down on the knight's breast-plate.

"Get his helmet off."

Suzie wrenched the steel helm off and threw it to one side. It didn't travel far in the shit and gore crusted on the floor. The knight's face was pale and sweaty, and very young. Barely out of his teens by the look of him. He tried to glare defiantly up at Suzie, but he wasn't used to being on the receiving end. He couldn't meet the cold fury in her eyes. He was close to death, and he knew it.

"What's your name?" I said.

"Sir Blaise." He licked his dry lips. "I am a knight of the land, and it is death to threaten me."

"Never stopped me before," said Suzie.

"Get him on his feet," I said.

Suzie hauled him back onto his feet again through a combination of brute strength and intimidation. I walked up to Blaise, kicking his helm out of the way. I smiled at him, and he flinched at what he saw in my smile, in my eyes.

"Blaise," I said, "you only think you know scary. Look at me, and look at Suzie. See that gun she's holding? She just killed Prince Gaylord with it. If you say one more word to piss either of us off, she will blow your head right off your shoulders. Won't you, Suzie?"

"Love to," said Suzie.

"Lead the way, Blaise, and don't waste our time with the scenic route."

He led us on, through the courtyard and out the far door. Suzie paused there for one last look at the bodies on their spikes.

"That is it," she said. "Merlin is dead."

"You get a decent chance," I said, "go for it."

Blaise led us into the dark interior of Camelot, and we went with him. Guards in dark armour lined the corridors all along the way, but none of them spoke to us, only sometimes standing aside to let us pass. They looked at Suzie and me as though they were seeing something utterly alien. I don't think they were used to seeing people who still had their pride. Who weren't afraid of them. I felt like killing them all, on general principles, and given the fury that was still burning so very coldly within me, I think I might have used my gift to find a way to do it . . . But I kept reminding myself, that wasn't what I was here for. I had to concentrate on keeping Excalibur away from Merlin, or everything was lost.

"How much further?" I said to Blaise.

"It's a big place, Camelot," said the knight, looking straight ahead. "Don't talk to me. You're nothing but dead men walking. Merlin will make you suffer and die, and there's nothing you can do to stop it. Because that's what happens here."

"Someone's getting snotty again," said Suzie. "Let me shoot him somewhere painful, John, for the good of his soul."

"And death won't be the end of it," said the knight. "No-one stays dead here. No-one escapes Merlin that easily."

Suzie looked hopefully at me, but I shook my head. We still needed a guide.

The interior of the castle grew steadily more awful the further in we went. Camelot was a place of fear and horror and endless suffering. The floors were covered with flayed human faces, there to be stepped on and crushed under metal boots. The faces still had eyes in them, alive and aware, and

SIMON R. GREEN

the mouths moved constantly in whispering pleas for death and an end to pain. More faces had been stapled to the walls, the eyes following us as they passed. The mouths moved, but their tongues had been torn out. Further in, people had been buried alive in stone walls, with their hands left to protrude, still feebly moving. Bloody organs and human viscera hung from the ceilings in intricate displays, dripping blood and other fluids—still alive, pulsing, twitching. I asked Blaise about them.

"Works of art," he said.

I couldn't stop to set them free. There were too many. I had to save my strength for the fight ahead and hope there'd be time later.

Finally, after so many horrors and brutal indignities that I'd actually started to become numb to atrocity, we came at last to the Court of Camelot. And, of course, Merlin had kept the worst till last. Two huge doors of beaten brass stood before us, covered in deeply etched satanic workings and blasphemous designs. Severed hands and feet had been nailed to the doors, in patterns that made no sense. The doors opened slowly before us, and Blaise crashed to a halt. Suzie and I stopped and looked back at him.

"Aren't you coming?" I said. "I thought you were going to watch, while Merlin did nasty things to us."

"I know better than to enter unless invited," said Blaise. "He'll send for me when he wants me."

I looked thoughtfully at the slowly widening gap between the two doors. "What's in there, Blaise?"

"The dead and the damned."

"Ah," said Suzie. "Knew I should have dressed up formal. And brought more grenades with me."

"We'll have to improvise," I said. "Shall we go?"

"Let's," said Suzie.

"But first things first," I said, and punched Blaise right in the face. He reeled backwards, blood spurting from his ruined

204

mouth. Suzie stepped in behind him and cracked him round the back of his head with the butt of her gun. He bent forward, as though he were bowing to me, and I rabbit-punched him. Blaise hit the floor hard and didn't move again.

"Shouldn't have been a mouthy little shit, Blaise," I said.

"Got that right," said Suzie.

We marched into the Court together, smiling cheerfully, our heads held high. It was a huge open space, full of a dull, murky, blood-red light. The smell hit me first; bad as the outside land had been, this was worse. Blood and offal and filth, but concentrated, as though someone had chosen to make perfume out of it. The massive walls were covered with the flayed bodies of all those who had defied or spoken out against Merlin or sought to change the world he'd made. Thousands of them, with their skins sheared away to show glistening red muscle and splintered bone. Pinned to the wall like so many trophies, so many mounted butterflies. Still alive, enduring agonies that should have killed them, maintained on the very edge of death by Merlin's magic. He fed on their pain and was content.

The marble floor was stained with blood and filth and scattered human offal. Some old, some new, piled up here and there, or kicked aside to make rough passageways. From the high beamed ceiling hung massive chandeliers, made from human bone and gristle, with candles fashioned from human fat. They gave off a thick greasy smoke that hung heavily on the air. There were braziers with irons heating in them, and iron maidens with fresh blood round their bases, and all kinds of instruments of torture, ready for us. One man had been recently dissected, all of his parts cut out and separated, pinned to a large display board. His heart still beat, his lungs still moved, and—like all the others—he was still somehow alive.

I knew what all these things were, without having to be told; there was a low-level information spell operating in the

Court. Merlin wanted his visitors to know what happened here. So he could stamp out the last little bit of hope they brought in with them.

Merlin Satanspawn sat on his great iron throne at the very end of the Court. Hugely fat and naked, and happy in his evil. He beckoned for Suzie and me to approach, with one plump, blood-stained hand. I headed straight for him, as though that was what I'd intended all along. I didn't look down at what I was striding through. Suzie stuck close beside me. I made a point of not hurrying. In a place like this, small victories were sometimes all you've got. I took the time to study the woman sitting on the iron throne next to Merlin's. Incredibly tall and inhumanly slender, she was also naked; but her ivory pale skin was marked with intricate tattoos, from her bald head to her clawed feet. Celtic and Druidic designs, mostly. Her ears had points, and her eyes were golden. Elven blood. A halo of flies buzzed round her head.

There were no more knights in dark armour, no guards, not even any courtiers. Merlin wanted no witnesses to see him forced to bargain with Stark for the sword Excalibur.

I came to a halt a wary distance short of the two thrones and nodded casually to Merlin. Suzie sniffed loudly. Merlin smiled happily on both of us.

"Allow me to introduce Morgan Le Fae," he said. "Now I am King, she shall be Queen. Because it pleases me."

"She reminds me of my mother, Lilith," I said. "And not in a good way."

"My mentor," said Morgan, in a harsh, rasping voice. "Long ago, now. And my ancestor, of course. So welcome, cousin. The family can always use an infusion of fresh blood."

"Okay," I said. "That was creepy, on a whole bunch of different levels."

"Are you an elf?" said Suzie, with her usual bluntness. "I thought Merlin killed all the elves here."

"All but this one," said Merlin. "I thought she had . . . potential."

"I never liked the others anyway," said Morgan.

"I'm not here to talk to you," I said. "Stark! Stark, where are you? Come on, I know you're here; I Saw you."

He stepped out from behind Merlin's throne and met my angry gaze impassively. He still wore his fine armour, the helmet tucked under one arm, but the gleaming steel had been fouled with blood and filth and gore. His face was empty, blank of any emotion. There was no sign of Excalibur anywhere about him, and a chill touched my heart as I wondered whether I was too late after all. If he'd already given Merlin the sword . . . But no; Stark wouldn't give up Excalibur without getting what he wanted first. And there was no sign in the Court of his wife Julianne, living or dead.

"You took your time getting here," Merlin said to me. "I've been expecting you."

"You know how it is," I said. "Taking in the scenery . . . things to do, people to kill. You do know we killed King Artur? Suzie blew his head right off, so I wouldn't recommend trying to bring him back."

"His conversation never was that thrilling," said Merlin. "But I take your point. Yes, I knew he was dead the moment it happened. Pity . . . After all the trouble he caused me, I would have enjoyed killing him myself. And the example I would have made of him would have traumatised generations. Still, I would have killed him anyway even if he hadn't run away. I don't need him any more. I've finally grown tired of the old stories. No more Arthurs; none of them were ever as much fun as corrupting the original. Fallen saints always make the best sinners . . . Now I am King, and I have taken Arthur's sister as my Queen. Ah, the progeny we'll have."

"Oh puke," said Suzie.

"Speaking of family," I said quickly, "we met your brother

SIMON R. GREEN

on the way here. Prince Gaylord the Damned. We sent him back to Hell with his tail between his legs."

"Made him cry like a baby," said Suzie. She let her shotgun drift from Merlin to Morgan Le Fae and back again.

Merlin laughed abruptly and clapped his hands together in glee. "Happy news! You have done me a service, John Taylor; I owe you! And since I can't stand to owe anyone anything, your suffering shall be legendary, even in Camelot."

"Big talk," said Suzie, "for a fat man with no clothes on."

"Don't taunt the fat psychopath sorcerer," said Stark, unexpectedly. We all looked at him, but he had nothing else to say.

"Stark will be leaving us soon," said Merlin. "Once we've closed our little deal. And then, through him I shall make contact with Queen Mab and her army of elves and use them to conquer your world. Ah me, a whole new world to play with . . . I can hardly contain myself."

"Try," said Suzie. "It's messy enough in here as it is."

Merlin looked at her. "One more interruption, and I'll turn you into something amusing. Where was I . . . ? Ah yes; the elves. I've often wondered whether I was right to let them stay dead . . . I think they would have appreciated what I've done with the place."

"No," I said. "The elves, for all their differences, have always understood honour."

"And taste," said Suzie. She grinned nastily at Merlin. "Go on. Try something. I've always wanted to be amusing."

I looked directly at Stark, who was staring out across the bloody Court, ignoring us all. "Do you still think you can make a deal with Merlin? After everything you've seen here? This was Camelot, the birth of a wonderful dream. And look what he's done to it."

Stark turned his empty gaze on me. "I'm only waiting because Merlin said he wouldn't close the deal until you two were here to witness it. You fascinate Merlin. He lusts to see you broken."

208

"Nasty man," said Suzie. It wasn't immediately obvious whom she meant.

"Enough," said Morgan Le Fae. She leaned forward on her throne, her face ugly with anticipation. "Break them, my King, with pain and horror and despair. Tear away their insulting pride and make them grovel before us. Make them love us and plead to serve us."

Suzie laughed in Morgan's face. "Not a hope in hell, bitch. We don't do that."

"But you will," said Merlin. "Anyone can be broken. And the more defiant you are, the sweeter my triumph will be."

"Don't shoot him, Suzie," I said quietly. "Not yet."

"Why not?" said Suzie, in a perfectly reasonable tone of voice.

"Because that's Merlin Satanspawn, the anti-Christ, and the most powerful sorcerer, ever. And I don't have nearly as much faith in your cursed and blessed ammo as you do. And because I haven't finished with Stark yet. He has to have his chance, to do the right thing." I turned back to Stark. "You were a London Knight. You led their armies into war against the powers of evil. Did you ever think you'd end up in a place like this, begging to make a deal with the anti-Christ? You swore an oath, upon your life and upon your honour, to fight things like him. How can you see what's happened here and turn your head away?"

"I am sickened by what I have seen," said Stark. "I never knew such corruption, such evil, was possible. But I swore an oath to myself that I would do whatever I have to to get my love back." He turned away from me, to address Merlin. "Your witnesses are here. You can have Excalibur—after you've given me what I want. My wife, alive again, for the sword. So do it. Do it now."

"You have hidden the sword well, Sir Jerusalem," said Merlin. "All my power, and I can't see it anywhere. And that's one of the reasons why I want it. I don't like the idea of anything existing that can defy my power. Let us make our deal. Because nothing can stop us now."

Suzie lifted her shotgun, and I was readying myself to do something. Then we all stopped dead and looked about us because something had changed in the Court. Something was coming. We could all feel it; something coming to Court from a direction I could sense but not name. Merlin sat up straight on his throne, looking round him with a look that was part apprehension and part anticipation. I gathered it wasn't often anything happened in his Court that he didn't expect. Morgan Le Fae had sunk back on her throne, a pale hand pressed to her pale mouth. She was an elf, and Saw more clearly than any of us. And then, Julianne Stark was standing in the bloody Court of Camelot, a ghost come to stand before the throne of Merlin, unsummoned and unafraid. She had fought her way here from the land of the dead because the man she loved was in danger. Because he needed her.

"You can't be here," said Merlin. "I didn't call you. Be gone, little ghost, or I'll show you even the dead can be made to suffer."

"Hello, Jerry," said Julianne, ignoring Merlin with magnificent disdain. "Glad to see me?"

"Always," said Stark. "But the sorcerer is right. You shouldn't be here. I didn't want you to know there could be a place like this. How can you be here when I didn't summon you?" He looked down at the preserved heart in its spun-silver cage at his belt. His hand was nowhere near it, but Julianne looked solid and very real. He smiled at her, and she smiled at him, and the whole atmosphere in the Court changed, as though the sun had finally risen after a long night.

"How could I stay away," said Julianne, "when your very soul is in peril? It was easy to come here, Jerry. This is a world of ghosts."

"Julie, you have to let me do this. I'm doing it for you, for us . . . because I can't bear to go on living like this. Without you."

"I don't want to live again," said Julianne, holding his gaze with hers. "Not at such a cost. To you, and to this world. Listen to me, Jerry. This world can still be saved, the people set free to live their own lives again . . . but not if you give Excalibur to Merlin Satanspawn. With its power he could raise all the dead of this world and torment them forever. And then come to our world to do it all again. I couldn't bear to have that on my conscience; and neither could you. I swear to you, Jerry. If you make me live again, at such a cost, I will kill myself."

"Julie, don't . . . I can't lose you again."

" 'I could not love thee, dear, half so much, Loved I not honour more,' " said Julianne.

She reached out with her ghostly hands and took his living ones in hers; and Stark didn't flinch a bit. "I said that to you once," he said finally.

"I know. That was when I first knew I loved you."

Stark smiled at her, a real smile, the first I'd ever seen from him. "I've missed you so much, Julie. So much, I couldn't see anything else. You always were the sensible one in this relationship."

"How sickeningly sentimental," said Merlin. "I sense your resolve is weakening, Sir Jerusalem, and I can't have that. So give me Excalibur or I'll destroy the heart that hangs at your belt and take control of this whining little spirit for myself. Just because she's dead, don't think I can't hurt her. Don't think I can't make her scream and suffer while you watch helplessly. Haven't you seen enough here to know that even the dead aren't safe from me?"

He gestured sharply, and every broken, mutilated, and skinned corpse nailed to the walls and ceiling came suddenly alive. They raised their flayed faces, strained their wet-muscled arms against the pins that held them, and screamed in agony. The horrid sound was deafening. Bodily fluids rained down from still-working organs exposed to the air, and a thousand raw and desperate voices called out for rest and mercy and death. And Merlin Satanspawn and Morgan Le Fae sat on their iron thrones and laughed.

Stark strode forward to stand before the two thrones, Julianne drifting along beside him; and something in Stark's face stopped the laughter.

"You really shouldn't have threatened my wife," he said.

He reached over his shoulder and drew Excalibur from the invisible scabbard on his back. The sword flashed suddenly into existence, the long, golden blade shining supernaturally bright, its golden glow forcing back the murky light of the Court. Merlin and Morgan both flinched away from the sudden new light and raised their hands to protect their eyes.

"You had the sword all the time!" said Merlin. "How could you keep it from me, here in my place of power?"

"It's Excalibur," said Stark. "What else do you need to know?"

Merlin jerked his fat hand down and made himself glare into the golden light. "Artur might have had power over me with that sword, but he was the rightful born King of this land. That gave him authority. You're only a thief with a magic sword. And I have killed so many of those in my time."

"You might be right," said Stark. "I'm Knight Apostate. Not worthy to bear Excalibur. But luckily, I know a man who is."

And he turned and threw Excalibur to me. The sword seemed to hang on the air, turning end over golden end, and I had all the time in the world to reach out and grasp the hilt as it came to me. I snatched the blade out of mid air, and the blade blazed up even more brightly, a terrible, piercing light that filled the whole Court from end to end. I swept the sword back and forth before me, then looked Merlin full in the eye. He stood up abruptly from his iron throne and shoved one hand out at me. Magic blazed and crackled on the air, rewriting reality itself as it forced its way towards me . . . and the sword absorbed every single bit of it. Sucked it right out of the air. I grinned at Merlin and cut suddenly at his extended hand. The golden blade flashed through the air, and Merlin snatched his hand back barely in time to avoid losing it. I stepped forward and thrust Excalibur straight at his heart; but the blade couldn't reach him. It slammed to a halt a few inches short. I cut at him again and again, grunting with the effort I put into every blow, but brightly as the sword blazed, it still couldn't pierce his protections.

Stark and Julianne stood to one side, hand in hand, watching patiently.

Morgan Le Fae raised a hand to fire magic at Suzie, who gave the elf both barrels of cursed and blessed ammo at point-blank range. The bullets slammed to a halt against an invisible shield, and fell harmlessly to the floor. Suzie took a step forward and fired again and again, working the pump action with smooth precision, and every time the bullets got that little bit closer.

Eventually, Morgan ran out of defences, and the blessed and cursed ammunition smashed right through her pale chest and out the back of her throne. Blood flew on the air, and Morgan's face held a long expression of shock and surprise before she slumped forward over the wreckage of her chest, golden blood spilling from her mouth. She twitched a few times and was still. Suzie turned to help me, but I'd already had another idea.

Maybe Excalibur on its own wasn't enough to kill Merlin Satanspawn. But I still had my ace up the sleeve. I raised my gift and sent it out to find the spirits of all those people who should have died here in Camelot's Court. And I took the magic that bound their souls to their dead bodies and broke it in my hands. Thousands of men and women cried out in one great exultant voice, and their souls rose out of their broken bodies, shining bright as the sun, free at last, leaving only mutilated corpses hanging from the walls and ceiling. And all those thousands of spirits, with a single will, gave themselves freely to Excalibur, filling up the ancient blade, until it blazed so brilliantly even I had to turn my face aside. Merlin cried out, afraid at last, and rose from his throne as if to run; but I stepped forward and blocked his way, and ran him through. Burning bright, Excalibur thrust aside all his protections and shattered the inverted brand on his chest, slamming his body back and pinning him to his throne. He cried out at the last like an angry child who's had his toys taken away from him. I twisted the blade in his chest, destroying his heart, and he slumped in his throne, dead at last.

Just another bloody sorcerer, in the end.

I jerked the sword free and held myself ready for any last surprises; but there was nothing. The Court was still and silent. Merlin and Morgan lay dead on their thrones. Merlin's blood dripped quickly off Excalibur, leaving the golden blade clean again.

"Not the first Merlin I've killed," I said. "But definitely the most satisfying."

Suzie moved quickly forward and looked me over, checking me for damage. It was her way of showing concern. And then I looked round sharply, because the Court was full of ghosts. Thousands of men and women, standing in long, shimmering rows, looking at me and smiling. Freed at last from their torment. I saluted them with Excalibur. Because it was more their fight than mine and because I couldn't have done it without them. One by one, the ghosts disappeared, leaving this world behind, and I put Excalibur away. Every now and again, I feel like I've actually done some good, something that matters. It's a good feeling.

Even though I'm not worthy and never want to be.

"I tried so hard to be a villain," said Stark. "But in the end, I didn't have it in me. Once a London Knight, always a London Knight. So, Julianne, Mr. Taylor; what do I do now?"

"You could go back," I said. "I'm pretty sure they'd take you back."

"No," he said immediately. "Not after all the things I've done. Not after letting the elves into Castle Inconnu. My brother knights might forgive me, but I never could. I need . . . to redeem myself. To atone for all the wrongs I've done."

" 'I could not love thee, dear, half so much . . .' " said Julianne.

"Loved I not honour more," said Stark.

"Then stay here," I said. "This world needs a King to lead it out of darkness. Who better than a man who knows the darkness in himself? It won't be easy; not after centuries of ingrained corruption and evil. But the sheer number of bodies nailed up here shows that Merlin didn't have it all his own way. You could spend a lifetime in this land, trying to put things right. Surely that's enough atonement for anyone."

"You could be right," said Stark. He looked at the two iron thrones. "But I'm damned if I'm sitting on one of those ugly things."

We all looked round sharply at an unexpected noise; and there, in the middle of the Court, a fountain sprang up. Clear, bubbling freshwater, rising a good twenty feet into the air, falling down to wash away all the years of accumulated blood and filth on the floor. And out of that clear water stepped a tall young woman in a long blue gown, with dark hair and a face I immediately recognised. Gaea, mother of the world. It only took me a moment to realise this wasn't the same woman I'd met in Castle Inconnu; this Gaea was gaunt and harried and had nothing of Gayle's easy humanity. This was the Queen of all the Earth, free at last of Merlin's domination, come walking amongst us.

She smiled on us all and nodded easily to me. "You're still

not worthy, but my sister chose well when she granted you dispensation to bear Excalibur. Be grateful. It's not every man who gets to be the world's champion." She turned to look at Stark. "The land needs a King," she said bluntly. "You have my blessing. You do know who I am, don't you, Jerusalem Stark?"

"I know who you must be, Lady," he said. "But . . . I must be honest with you. I don't know anything about being a King."

"Best kind," Gaea said briskly. "It's always the ones from long lines of succession who cause no end of problems. They have so much to unlearn. You can do this, Jerusalem. But you won't have to do it alone."

She turned her gaze upon the ghost Julianne. "You're not nearly as dead as you think, my dear. You soul was bound to your heart; you are dead but not departed. And so I call you back, to the man and the world that needs you."

Julianne cried out as she suddenly snapped into focus; real and solid, flesh and blood, and very much alive. She breathed deeply and clapped her hands to her chest, to feel her heart beat and her lungs move; then she laughed aloud and threw her arms round an unbelieving Stark, and the two of them hugged each other like they'd never let go. Gaea looked on them fondly.

"Don't you love a happy ending?" said Suzie.

"It's not over yet," I said.

Suzie looked at me. "What?"

SEVEN

Return of the King

"What do you mean, it's not over yet?" said Suzie. "Who is there left to kill that needs killing?"

"We still have to find a way home," I said, in that calm, kind, and very reasonable tone I happen to know drives her absolutely batshit. "The Door we came through doesn't exist in this dimension, and my Portable Timeslip doesn't work here."

Suzie sniffed. "When in doubt, go to the top. Why don't you ask Gaea? Maybe she could . . . ring up her opposite number. Or something."

"Full marks for optimism," I murmured. "But any port in a storm . . . I really don't feel like walking home."

"Not through all that mud," said Suzie. I can never tell when she's joking.

So we went over to Sinister Albion's Gaea, and I bowed politely and explained the situation. Gaea started nodding half-way through and actually interrupted me before I could finish.

"I know who you are," she said. "And how and why you came here. I know you because your world's Gaea knows you. We're all aspects of the same person, or personification. It's complicated."

"Really," I said. "You do surprise me."

"You want a slap?" said Gaea. "Then pipe down and pay attention. Of course I can get you home. All Earths are linked, on all kinds of levels. From the Dreamtime to the Chronoflow, you can always find some Door to open if you knock loudly enough. Ah . . . It's good to be back! I have been asleep for far too long, John Taylor, and you are responsible for waking me. It was the presence of Excalibur in this land that brought me back, you see, an Excalibur that wasn't mine. I came here to investigate and found that you and your friends had already brought down Merlin Satanspawn and Morgan Le Fae, and set free all the trapped souls of this world. If I'd known it was that easy, I'd have done it myself centuries ago. Ah well . . . Now that I'm back, I think I'll stick round for a while to see what happens next. Stark and Julianne seem capable enough, and there's a lot to be done. I am . . . weakened by Merlin's long centuries of abuse, but I am still Mother Earth, and all this land's secrets are an open book to me.

"Now I have to talk to you, John Taylor, about the sword you carry, the Excalibur of your world. It was given to you because you have a destiny."

It was my turn to interrupt her. "If you're about to tell me that it is my duty to be King of the Nightside, you can forget it. I've already turned that down once. I didn't want it then, and I don't want it now."

"Good," said Gaea. "Because you're not worthy."

"You want a slap?" said Suzie. "Or failing that, two barrels of blessed and cursed ammo right between the eyes?"

"Please don't upset the planetary personification," I murmured. "Particularly one who's about to provide us with a ride home."

"Don't get sassy with me, little miss," said Gaea. "Or I'll give you a period you'll never forget." She gave me her full attention. "You were given your special dispensation to bear Excalibur, for a time, because it is your duty and destiny to deliver the sword to King Arthur. The once-and-future King of your world. You get to do this because you are one of the few people who wouldn't be tempted to hang on to the sword for yourself. You have already faced greater temptations and did not yield. You have no idea how rare that is."

"All right," I said. "Putting aside for the moment a whole bunch of questions and denials, why Arthur? And why now?"

"King Arthur is the only one who can stop the coming elf civil war," said Gaea. "Which will quite definitely devastate your world, and destroy all of Humanity, when the elves use the Earth as their battle-field. Both sides have had centuries to prepare for this war; and they have more powerful weapons, both magical and scientific, than all of the human nations put together. The elves will tear your world apart, fighting over it. Only King Arthur can prevent this."

I considered Gaea thoughtfully. "Wouldn't the Gaea of my world prefer the elves in charge rather than Humanity? After all the ecological damage my people have done?"

"The elves would be worse," Gaea said flatly. "The elves don't have Humanity's conscience or restraint."

"We beat the elves before," said Suzie.

"No, you didn't," Gaea said crushingly. "You outbred and outnumbered them. And you had the Droods on your side. They found the Sundered Lands for the elves, when asked to by the elves. By that time, they wanted to leave the Earth. There are lots of theories as to why, but nobody really knows.

Not even my other self. In fact, some of the elves were so . . . concerned, they hid themselves away in Shadows Fall, because they thought that would be safer. But the elves did not prosper, in either of their new homes, and now they wish to return and claim the Earth for themselves again. Whoever or whatever they might once have been afraid of, apparently that isn't so any more."

"I spy a small but subtle hole in the whole destiny thing," I said. "How am I supposed to get Excalibur to King Arthur when nobody knows where he is? Even the London Knights don't know, and if the London bloody Knights don't know . . ."

"Use your gift," said Gaea. "Find him."

"Ah," I said. "Now why didn't I think of that?"

"Because it's all a wild goose chase?" said Suzie.

"There is still the problem of how we get home," I said to Gaea, in my very best polite and respectful tone.

"Walk into my fountain," said Gaea. "I am still the Lady of the Lake, and all waters are mine."

She smiled at me, ignored Suzie, turned her back on us, and strode away to talk with Stark and Julianne. Suzie and I turned to look at the fountain through which Gaea arrived. It was still shooting a good twenty feet into the air, its cool clear waters bubbling noisily. There was an increasingly large area of clean marble floor round it. I hoped the Court had good drainage.

"It's a fountain," said Suzie. "Great big bubbly water thing. It doesn't even look like a Doorway."

"It's not like we're loaded down with options," I said. "Maybe the Doorway's *behind* the water."

Suzie walked round it twice. "Not a sign."

"You can be so literal, sometimes," I said.

I walked into the fountain, and Suzie strode quickly along beside me, her head held high. I grabbed her by the hand, so that whatever happened we wouldn't be separated, and barely had time to take a really deep breath before the water closed over both of us. My first thought was of how cool and refreshing the water felt after so long in the filth and stench of Sinister Albion, then the floor dropped out from under my feet, and I was falling helplessly. I clamped down hard on Suzie's hand, and she held on to me just as tightly, but I couldn't see her anywhere. There was nothing but the water, rushing past me as I fell and fell into endless depths. My lungs strained for air, and I hoped Suzie had thought to take a deep breath, too. We sank down and down, then suddenly, without actually changing direction, we were rising, forced up by the pressure of the rushing water, until finally Suzie and I broke the surface together. A low stone wall appeared before me, and I grabbed on to it with my free hand. Suzie was right there beside me, and we hung on to the wall together, gasping like beached fish. It was only then that I realised we were in the oracle wishing well, in the Mammon Emporium.

Suzie and I clung to the stone wall while the oracle made loud coughing and hacking noises and complained bitterly about frogs in its throat. My lungs were working overtime, my heart was hammering in my chest, and I was soaked right down to the skin; but still, it was good to be home. I grinned at Suzie, and she smiled briefly back. We'd survived another one.

"Where the hell have you been?" screeched the oracle. "And what in God's good Earth have you been treading in? I'm never going to get this taste out of my mouth. And oh my God, it's that woman again. You peed in me, you bitch! Just for that, I'm going to tell everyone who asks me about their future that they can be King of Everything if only they'll kill you first."

"One more nasty word out of you," I said, "and I will have you filled up to the brim with concrete. The Mall owes me a favour."

"Bully," muttered the oracle.

After a while, Suzie and I hauled ourselves up and out of the wishing well, then stomped in circles round it, trying to wring the water out of our clothes. But you can't really wring water out of a trench coat—or, indeed, black leathers. Besides which, despite our complete immersion in Gaea's marvellous waters, our clothes were still incredibly filthy. And disgustingly smelly. The bottom half of my trench coat had turned a completely new and revolting colour, from dried blood and mud and other things I didn't want to look at too closely. And I didn't even want to think about what was squelching inside my shoes. Suzie's leathers were caked in a kind of nasty-smelling crust, and she was leaving a trail behind her.

"We need a cleaner," I said firmly. "I am not walking round the Nightside looking and smelling like this. Even Razor Eddie doesn't smell this bad, and he sleeps in doorways. People would point and throw things."

"Not twice, they wouldn't," said Suzie.

We ended up at Unconventional Solutions, a twenty-four-hour emergency cleaners that boasted it could handle absolutely anything, from dragon's blood to Martian slime. *If you can beat it down with a stick and wrestle it through the door, we can make it shine and sparkle!* promised the sign over the door. So Suzie and I walked in, and a moment later, everyone else rushed out. It might have been because they recognised Suzie and me, or it might have been because of the smell, which was so intense it practically had its own colour. The girl trapped behind the counter, wearing a smart white outfit, and a badge that said HI! I'M TRACY, glared at both of us with open loathing.

"Well, thanks a whole bunch for the loss of custom. Though if I weren't pinned behind this desk, I would also be legging it for the nearest horizon. What is that *smell*? It's worse than the toilets at a vegetarian restaurant. It's like tear gas! My eyes, my eyes . . . *What is that?*"

"Trust me," I said. "You really don't want to know. Can you do anything with these clothes?"

Tracy sniffed loudly. "How about shooting them, then burying them at sea?"

"You do know who I am, don't you?" said Suzie.

"Of course. They put warning posters about you all over the Mall."

"You really want me to get cranky?"

"You wouldn't like her when she's cranky," I said solemnly.

"Strip it all off and stick them in the bags provided," Tracy said resignedly. "I suppose you want the Emergency Special Biohazard Deep Clean While You Wait service?"

"Sounds good to me," I said.

Tracy pointed to the changing cubicles, and Suzie and I chose one each. Togetherness is all very well, but the smell was bad enough on its own. Combined together in a small space, it would probably have blown the door off the cubicle. I removed my trench coat with great care, looked at the state of the clothes underneath, gulped, and took it all off. I bundled everything up, being very careful what I touched, packed it into the black plastic garbage bag provided, slipped on the complimentary dressing gown, and stepped out of the cubicle. Suzie was already there waiting for me, with her own bulging bag. She was also wearing a dressing gown. Mine was a smart navy blue, hers was a shocking pink. She looked at me.

"One wrong word at this moment, and you will never see me naked again."

"Perish the thought," I said gallantly.

We took our bags over to the counter, and Tracy accepted them from us while wearing heavy-duty rubber gloves. She held the bags at arm's length, pulled a variety of faces, none of them good, and glared at Suzie and me.

"Did you remember to empty everything out of the pockets?"

"Don't worry about the trench coat," I said. "It can take care of itself. Suzie?"

"I already removed the weapons," said Suzie. "They're in another bag, back in the cubicle. Don't let anyone touch that bag if they like having all their fingers."

Tracy slapped two customer numbers on the counter before us and disappeared out the back with the bags. There was a pause, followed by some loud if rather muffled bad language. Suzie and I moved away from the counter and went to sit in the chairs provided and read the nice magazines. I settled down with the Nightside edition of *Empire*, and read what Kim Newman had to say about the latest films: *Butch Cassidy and the Cthulhu Kid*, Clive Barker's *Transformers*, and the rediscovered Orson Welles classic, his Batman movie, *Citizen Wayne*. Sometimes it's nice to sit back, put your feet up, and enjoy a little light reading. Suzie had *Which Magazine: Weapons of Mass Destruction, A Consumer's Guide*.

I could still feel Excalibur in its invisible scabbard on my back. Removing my clothes hadn't disturbed it in the least.

Our clothes were back inside half an hour, spotlessly clean and impressively immaculate. My trench coat was so white it practically glowed, while someone had taken the time to polish every last bit of metal on Suzie's outfit, from the rivets to the steel toe-caps to all the remaining bullets in her bandoliers. Suzie and I took our clothes back into the cubicles, and I soon emerged feeling like a new man. And able to breathe through my nose again. Suzie stepped out of her cubicle, fussing with the two bandoliers so they crossed right over her bosom. She never looks impressed with anything, on general principles, but she didn't seem too displeased. Tracy beckoned us back to the counter and slapped the bill down before me. I took a look. I didn't know numbers went that high. For a moment, I actually considered telling her to put all the filth back on. Instead, I shook my head and smiled condescendingly at Tracy.

"I have decided I don't need to pay any of my bills in the Mammon Emporium. Partly because I am the new Walker, and if any establishment annoys me, I can have it shut down on moral health grounds. But mostly because I have recently saved this entire place from being blown up by a soulbomb, and if anyone gets stroppy, I can always bring back the Things from Outside and let the merchants deal with the bloody things. Any questions?"

"Go ahead," said Tracy. "See if I care. They don't pay me enough to deal with people like you."

"There are no people like us," said Suzie.

"Got that right," I said.

Squeaky clean and utterly fragrant, Suzie and I made the long trip out of the Nightside and back into London Proper. Suzie insisted on accompanying me this time, and I didn't have the heart to say no. She stuck close to me at all times, and though she wouldn't give up any of her weapons, she at least kept her hands away from them. People gave us all kinds of funny looks as we strode down Oxford Street, but no-one actually said anything. They didn't want to get involved. We finally came to a halt in front of where the Green Door wasn't, and I struck an impressive pose.

"It's me! I'm back! And I bear important news concerning Excalibur and King Arthur." There was a long pause. The Green Door remained firmly absent. I scowled at the blank wall before me. "Come on! You know who I am!"

"Yes," said a wary voice from nowhere. "We know who you are. But we also know who that is standing beside you. That's Shotgun Suzie, isn't it?"

"She's with me!"

"I know. That's the problem. I'll have to check."

The voice fell silent, and Suzie and I were left standing there, in the open on Oxford Street, for some time. People were starting to pay serious attention to us, and not because I was loudly berating an apparently empty stretch of wall. If anyone looked like they were getting too close, Suzie just looked at them, and they remembered they were needed somewhere else. Suzie's always been good at that. The voice finally came back again, hovering on the air.

"You can both come in, but only as long as you agree to vouch for her behaviour; at all times and under all conditions."

"I promise Suzie won't kill anyone who doesn't need killing," I said.

The voice sighed loudly. "I told them this was a bad idea. I'm going to hide all the good china. Come on in, and remember to wipe your shoes."

"That's the nicest thing you've ever said about me," said Suzie. "There will be special treats for you when we get home."

The Green Door appeared before us and swung slowly open. Suzie and I passed through into Castle Inconnu, and the Door closed quickly behind us. A knight was waiting, in full armour, to guide us through the many stone corridors. Suzie looked about her unhurriedly, being deliberately not at all impressed, as usual. The knight took us by the quickest route, and maintained a steady pace. He didn't bother us with questions, probably because Suzie kept looking thoughtfully at his armour, as though judging exactly how many shotgun blasts it would take to penetrate it. We finally ended up back in the Main Hall again. Sir Gareth and Sir Roland were waiting there for us, still in their full armour, with their helmets clasped under their arms. They nodded to me and gave Suzie a long, thoughtful look. She gave them her best hard look in return.

"So you're Shotgun Suzie," said Sir Roland. "The posters don't do you justice. We've heard a lot about you. Did you really . . . ?"

"Almost certainly," I said. "Take that as read, so we can move on to more important matters. I have spoken with Gaea . . ."

"And she has spoken to us," said Sir Gareth. "You do get round, don't you? It seems you are to give Excalibur to King Arthur, after waking him from his long sleep. You can imagine how that news has gone down here. We always assumed that duty would fall to one of us."

"Yes, well, that's life for you," I said vaguely. "Now, I could use my gift to find him, but I can't help feeling there are bound to be all kinds of difficulties. King Arthur wouldn't have stayed hidden all this time unless he was protected by really heavy-duty defences. And a whole lot of psychic booby-traps. So I'm pretty sure I need to speak with your Grand Master first, and see what he knows, before I try anything."

"Of course you do," said Sir Gareth. "He is the oldest of us all and knows many things. You'd better come with me. If you're really going to raise up the once-and-future King himself, you need to talk with the last surviving Knight of the Round Table."

Sir Gareth led the way through the increasingly crowded corridors and meeting places that led to Castle Inconnu's interior, where the knights and their families lived. The area presented quite a contrast to the far-more-austere outer layers. The interior was much more comfortable, with all modern comforts. Sir Gareth had a smile and a kind word for everyone, and they nodded cheerfully back. They hardly looked at Suzie and me. We passed through large open-plan rooms, full of men and women hard at work, and children playing in the corridors, and a roomful of teenagers with swords, practicing mock duels. They were really good at it.

"Not everyone here becomes a knight," said Sir Gareth. "Only those most suited to it. It's not for everyone. The rest work at maintaining the castle's infrastructure. There's a lot of work involved, keeping a place this size running smoothly. And we are completely up to date, where we need to be. Everyone here knows how to use a computer. Though someone always wants to take it that one step too far. A few years back, one young man spent far too much time watching American television, and began enthusing about the benefits of organised productivity. He drew up plans for cubicle farms, and efficiency officers, and piped Muzak. He works in the sewage-disposal area now, for the good of his soul, and he'll stay there until he's learned the error of his ways."

Sir Gareth finally led us up a long, winding stair inside a tower, opened a locked door at the very top, and ushered Suzie and me into a richly appointed study, with walls of books, tables covered in computers and monitor screens, and one very big heavy-duty Victorian desk, covered with piles of paper. He sat down behind the desk and gestured for Suzie and me to make ourselves comfortable on the visitors' chairs set out before the desk. They were surprisingly comfortable. I was also surprised that Sir Gareth's chair didn't collapse under the weight of his armour, but I supposed all chairs in the castle were heavily reinforced, as a matter of course. Sir Gareth looked at me thoughtfully.

"Are we waiting for someone?" I said. "Only I thought you were supposed to be taking us to meet the Grand Master of the London Knights?"

"I have," said Sir Gareth. He moved his left hand in a certain gesture, and his illusion spell collapsed. The young and easy-going Sir Gareth disappeared, replaced by a much older man with a very familiar face. It was Kae, Arthur's stepbrother, last seen by Suzie and me in the sixth-century Strangefellows. Kae grinned at us, his eyes cold and commanding.

"Were you really expecting someone else?"

A large, blocky man, Kae now wore a simple but expensively cut grey suit. But I knew that under the suit lay the functional, compact musculature that comes from constant hard use and testing rather than regular workouts in the gym. I knew, because I'd seen it at close range back in the sixth century, when he and I went head to head, and he did his best to kill me and Suzie. He had a square, blocky, almost brutal face, marked with scars that had healed crookedly. Sitting there behind his desk, he had an almost overwhelming air of authority; of a man who could enforce his decisions through sheer brute strength, if necessary. His smile seemed friendly enough, but his eyes were watchful.

"Where did your armour go?" I said, just to be saying something.

"It disappears with the illusion," Kae said easily. "It's only there when I need it these days. I prefer suits. Nothing like wearing plate armour for centuries to make you appreciate well-tailored clothing."

"And what happened to Sir Gareth?" I said. "Is he . . . real?"

"Real enough. He's me. A more approachable me that I developed to deal with outsiders." Kae grinned again. "So much less intimidating, you see. And it makes things easier for dealing with everyday matters. Even a knight bloodied in battle can still get surprisingly bashful and tongue-tied round a survivor from the original Round Table, a man who actually knew Arthur and grew up with him. So I pretend to be Sir Gareth, and everyone else pretends it isn't me, and we all get along swimmingly."

"What was Arthur like, as a child?" said Suzie.

"A real pain in the arse," said Kae. "Always running after his older stepbrother, wanting to be involved in everything, and throwing major sulks when he was excluded. Best student I ever had, mind. I taught him everything he knows about fighting."

He stopped for a moment, as one of his computers chirped politely, and he took time out to run through his latest e-mails and make notes.

"The work never stops. Though computers do make things

easier. You have to keep up with the times, especially when you've lived through as many as I have."

"How . . . ?" I said.

"How did I become immortal? Ha! It's a long story, but I think you'll enjoy it. If only because it's steeped in irony. I was made immortal by that bad old, mad old sorcerer, Merlin. All his idea. I never asked for it. I happened to be present at Strangefellows when Merlin died, and yes, John Taylor and Suzie Shooter, of course I remember you. You made quite an impression. Partly because not many have fought me and lived, but mostly because you bashed my head in with my own mace. Luckily for you, I don't bear grudges." He looked at Suzie. "I also remember destroying your face. I felt bad about that afterwards. I'm glad to see it's been repaired. Anyway, the story . . .

"After you left, I woke up to a splitting headache and a hell of a thirst. I found a bottle behind the bar, and only then noticed Merlin, dead in his chair, with his chest split open and his heart missing. Cheered me up no end. I still blamed him for betraying Arthur by not being there when he was needed, at Logres. I leaned over to spit in his dead face; and his eyes snapped open. I all but shit my britches. I jumped back and let out a yell they could have heard on the Moon. Merlin rose to his feet and smiled at me. He was dead, but he was moving. I never knew he could do that.

"But never forget: Merlin could remember the future as easily as he could the past. When he could be bothered. So it shouldn't surprise any of us that he put a great many spells and protections in place to ensure he would still be able to take care of business, even after he was dead. I suppose I should really have got the hell out of there; but I was too angry with him. I still had so much to say . . . So I stayed, and yelled at him, and he stood there and let me rant. He could be surprisingly understanding, sometimes. When I was finally finished, he nodded once, then told me Arthur's story wasn't over yet. And that I still had an important part to play in it.

"He used his magics to bring Arthur's body to Strange-fellows, from where it had been lying in state at Glastonbury. It just appeared before us, out of nowhere. Arthur had been dead for months, but he looked like he was only sleeping. You have to remember, we didn't have much in the way of embalming, back in the sixth century. It was all burn them up or stick them in the ground, before the smell got too bad. Arthur should have been well on his way to rot and corruption. Instead, he looked like he might sit up and start talking at any moment. It was all part of Merlin's advance preparations. *He was the best of us all,* said Merlin. *How could I let death rob us of a man like him? I always knew he had a duty beyond the simple dream I gave him . . . I had a Vision, you see; I saw Arthur leading an army made up of all of Humanity, in one great Final Battle against Evil . . .* I asked Merlin, *Who is he fighting against?* But if he knew, he wouldn't say."

Kae broke off there to look sharply at me. "Is this it? Are you bringing Excalibur to Arthur because the Final Battle is upon us?"

"Not as far as I know," I said. "I'm just the messenger boy in all this. I haven't seen any Signs . . ."

"I can't help noticing Arthur didn't turn up during the Angel War," said Susie. "Or the Lilith War . . ."

"Far too small," said Kae. "The London Knights fight bigger wars than that year in and year out . . . that Humanity never knows of, of course. We deal in matters too great for even those high-and-mighty Droods. They're only secret agents; we're warriors."

I had to ask. "Do the two of you ever disagree over who has responsibility, or jurisdiction?"

"We . . . tend to operate in different areas," said Kae. "Not entirely by accident. Now, on with the story. We're finally getting to the good stuff. Merlin told me to pick up Arthur and follow him down into the cellar under Strangefellows. There wasn't much there; a few barrels of beer, a still, hardly room to swing a cat. Which back in those days was a popular indoor sport. Merlin waved his hand, and suddenly there was a great stone cavern stretching out before us. Merlin looked at my face and laughed; and I didn't care for the sound of it. The dead aren't supposed to laugh.

"I was carrying Arthur in my arms, like a sleeping child, his head pressed against my breast. We might only have been stepbrothers, but Arthur always treated me as though I was his brother by blood, before and after he became King. Many better men than me had his ear; but he always listened to me. I looked after him while he was growing up; and he spent the rest of his life looking after me.

"Merlin had me lay Arthur down, to one side, then had me dig two graves. He could have conjured me up a spade, but no, I had to dig those graves with my bare hands. I don't know how long it took. My fingers were raw and bloody by the end. And all the time I was working, Merlin was crouched down beside Arthur, whispering in his ear. One dead man talking to another. I couldn't hear what he said.

"When the two graves were ready, I laid Arthur out in one while Merlin clambered down into the other. I covered Arthur over with dirt, crying as I said my good-byes to his sleeping face, and when it was done I patted the rough earth down with my bare bloody hands. And then I had to cover Merlin over. He grinned up at me the whole time, staring up at me with unblinking eyes. I thought I'd shit myself all over again.

"That was when he told me he'd made me immortal, so I could guard the secret until Arthur was needed again. Sometimes I think it was Merlin's last gift; other times, his last curse. Merlin also set a geas on the bar Strangefellows, so that it would endure, and his descendents would run it forever, protecting the secret that lay beneath."

"Okay," I said, "Hold it right there. Merlin's *descendents* . . . I've often wondered about that. He never had any children that I know of. Unless Nimue . . ."

"Hardly," said Kae. "But he did have a fling with an immortal called Carys Galloway, the Waking Beauty." He paused to see if I recognised the name, but I had to shake my head. You can't know everyone. "Anyway, she had a child by him, and this established a long line of descendents and bar owners, bound by the geas to Strangefellows, to serve Merlin's will. Arrogant old bastard. Though of course the bar owners were only ever told of Merlin's grave, not Arthur's. No-one ever knew but me."

"Alex is going to freak," said Suzie.

"King Arthur," I said. "*The* King Arthur, the Pendragon himself, is buried under Strangefellows? And always has been? I have no idea what to say to that."

"I do," said Suzie. "But it involves a whole bunch of really inappropriate language."

"I started the rumour about Arthur being taken away to Avalon," said Kae. "It's a made-up name. Never was any such place. I didn't want anyone looking for Arthur's remains, particularly since it looked like he was only napping. I knew he wouldn't have wanted to be worshipped and adored, his unchanging body a relic to be fought over by the various Church factions, as religious currency."

"So . . . is Arthur actually dead, or not?" said Suzie, who always liked to be certain about these things.

"Yes, and no," said Kae. "Let's say . . . not all the way dead. Merlin put an old magical protection on Arthur; though he never told him, because he knew Arthur wouldn't approve. Arthur always liked to say that for all he'd done, he was just a man. That any man could do what he'd done, if he'd only commit himself fully. That was what the Round Table was all about—to show we were all equal. What safer place could there be for Arthur to lie sleeping, than buried next to Merlin, who could still protect him even after he was dead? And, of course, Merlin's sheer presence was still so powerful that it helped to hide Arthur's. And, finally, who would look for King Arthur's grave under a cheap and sleazy dive like Strangefellows?"

I looked at Suzie. "He's got a point." I turned back to Kae. "So now what?"

"Now," said Kae, "we go back to the cellars under the bar and dig up Arthur. How else are you going to give him Excalibur?"

Except, Kae sat there, staring at nothing, making no move to get up. He seemed to be looking at something far away, perhaps far away in the past. It was only too easy to forget I was looking at a man fifteen hundred years old, with a lot of memories to look back on.

"After all these years," he said finally. "Now the time has come, I'm still not sure I'm ready. I still feel guilty that I survived Logres when so many better men did not. That Arthur died, and I didn't. I would have given my life for him."

"He's Arthur," I said. "He knows that."

One long and mostly uneventful journey later, we all ended up at Strangefellows bar. I had worried how Kae would react to the Nightside, him being Grand Master of the London Knights; but he seemed more amused than anything. Strangefellows looked rather better than the last time I'd seen it; Alex had cleaned up most of the damage. But the place was still pretty empty. There was no sign anywhere of Betty and Lucy Coltrane. A few customers had ventured back in. A handful of Burroughs Boys, out on the nod, being roughly gay and talking in cut-up sentences. An alien Grey and a Lizardoid, sitting opposite each other in a back booth, sharing their troubles over a bottle of Mother's Ruination. And a couple of beat cops from some medieval city, waiting patiently for someone. They looked like they could punch their weight. The man had a scarred face and an eye patch, and a bloody big axe. The woman had long blonde hair in a plait that ended in a steel weight, and a really mean attitude. You get all sorts in Strangefellows.

The piped music was playing a selection of Marianne Faithfull numbers; always a sign that Alex Morrisey was in an even worse mood than usual.

Kae looked about him as I led the way to the long wooden bar at the end of the room. "Hasn't changed that much since I was last here. Still a dive. And the ambience is just short of actually distressing. The whole place could use renovating. With a flame-thrower."

By this time, we'd reached the bar. Alex glared at Kae. "I heard that! Would you like to say Hello to Mr. Really Big Stick, who lives behind the counter?"

"Ease off, Alex," I said. "This is a London Knight in disguise."

Alex smirked. "Well, colour me impressed. Nice suit. What does he want me to do, polish his helmet?"

"Yes," said Kae. "This is one of Merlin's line. He thought he had a sense of humour, too."

"What is a London Knight doing here?" Alex said to me, ostentatiously ignoring Kae. "Bearing in mind that I've still got that nuclear suppository the Holy Sisters of Saint Strontium gave me, round the back somewhere."

"Well," I said, "it turns out it wasn't only Merlin who was buried in the cellars under this place. King Arthur's down there, too. And we are here to dig him up, so I can give him the sword Excalibur. Oh, and by the way, this is Kae, step-brother to King Arthur, last surviving Knight of the Round Table."

There isn't much that can throw Alex, so I stood there and quietly enjoyed the way his jaw dropped, his eyes bulged, and he couldn't get a word out to save his life. Suzie took the opportunity to lean over the bar and help herself to a bottle of gin.

"I should have been told!" Alex said, finally, and very loudly. "This is my bar! I had a right to know!"

"You were safer not knowing," said Kae, entirely unmoved.

"Safer?" said Alex. "I live in the Nightside! I've had all Four Horsemen of the Apocalypse in here, playing bridge!"

"He has a point," I said. "Don't be upset, Alex. What we didn't know, we couldn't accidentally let slip, or be made to tell someone else."

"Hell with that," said Alex. "Do you have any idea how much money I could have made, running guided tours? Can you imagine how much tourists would have paid, to take photographs of each other, standing over Arthur's grave? I could have been rich! Rich!"

"And that is why we didn't tell you," said Kae. "Or anyone else of your misbegotten line. You couldn't be trusted. A secret can be kept by two men, but only if one of them is ignorant."

"Did he just call me ignorant?" said Alex, dangerously.

"I'm sure he meant it in a nice way," I said.

Alex sulked. "No-one gives a damn for the poor working-man."

He finally calmed down and let us behind the bar. Suzie was still sucking noisily on her bottle of gin, but Alex had enough sense not to make a fuss. He opened the heavy trap-door that led down to the cellars and lit an old storm lantern he kept handy. Electricity doesn't work down in the cellars. Something down there doesn't like it. Alex held the lantern out over the stone steps leading down, but the pale amber light couldn't penetrate the darkness below. Kae looked over his shoulder.

"Dark," he said. "It was dark then, too. All those years ago. Merlin always did like the dark. Said it felt like home."

Alex looked at me. "John . . . What is he saying?"

"He buried Merlin and Arthur here, fifteen hundred years ago," I said.

Alex surprised me by nodding. "What goes round, comes round. Let's get this over with before my customers rob me blind in my absence."

He led the way down the smooth stone steps, and we all went down after him, sticking close together to stay inside the circle of amber light. The steps seemed to descend a hell of a lot further into the impenetrable darkness than I was comfortable with. I had no idea how deep we were, under the bar, under the Nightside. The air was close and clammy, and there was an almost painful feeling of anticipation. Of something important, and significant, waiting to happen. Waiting to be brought back into the light after fifteen hundred years in the dark.

The steps finally gave out onto a packed-dirt floor. The bare earth was hard and dry as stone. I remembered Kae saying how he'd dug two graves out of this earth with his bare hands. A blue-white glare appeared slowly round us, coming from everywhere and nowhere. Alex put his lantern down at the foot of the steps and looked uncertainly about him. We were standing at the beginning of a great stone cavern, with an uncomfortably low ceiling. Hundreds of graves stretched away before us in more or less neat rows, just mounds of earth with simple, unadorned headstones.

"So many graves," said Kae. "Since I was here last."

"My family," said Alex, quietly, bitterly. "Bound to the bar forever, to serve Merlin's will."

"Trust me," said Kae. "I understand how you feel. Merlin always was a great one for doing what was necessary, and to hell with whoever got caught up in his plans. Even Arthur couldn't escape Merlin's designs, not even after he was dead. A man should be free of responsibilities after he's dead."

He led the way forward, looking this way and that, and

finally stopped before two graves, neither of which had a headstone. One mound of earth had been broken open from within, the grave dirt thrown in all directions, from when Merlin had come out of his grave one last time, to face my mother, Lilith, in battle, and die his final death at her hands. The huge silver crucifix, which had been laid on his grave at some point in the past, to hold him in it, had been thrown carelessly to one side. We all stood at the side of the empty grave, looking down, as though we needed to be sure there was no-one in it. Everyone, except Kae. He only had eyes for the other grave.

"Merlin made sure that Arthur could not be brought back unless Excalibur was present," he said finally. "He placed part of Arthur's soul inside the blade, as a wizard or a witch might place his or her heart somewhere else, somewhere more secure . . . That's why Arthur couldn't be completely killed at Logres. Though that bastard Mordred tried hard enough."

"What did happen to Excalibur, after the battle?" I said.

"I took it," said Kae. "To keep it safe. A sword like that could make anyone King, whether he was worthy or not, just by possessing it. I knew even then that only Arthur could be trusted with Excalibur. Several others had already picked it up off the battle-field; but none of them could hold on to it. They were not worthy. They all but burned their hands off touching the hilt. I wasn't worthy, either, but I still picked the sword up and carried it off the battle-field, in my bare hands. It burned, how it burned . . . but that was my penance. For surviving.

"The Lady of the Lake appeared to me then, in a vision, and called me to bring Excalibur to her at a nearby lake. I walked through thick mists to find it, and when I went back there sometime later, the mists were gone, and so was the lake. I threw the blade out over the still waters . . . No hand came up to grasp it. The sword simply disappeared into the lake and was gone. Didn't even leave a ripple behind it. The Lady had taken it back." He smiled briefly. "Gaea always did have a soft spot for Arthur. While he lived, the King and the Land were one, each empowering the other. And since the sword was always Gaea's, I like to think that all this time Arthur has been sleeping in her arms."

I gave him a moment, then moved in beside him. "What do we do now? Call his name? Summon him back from the great beyond?"

"No," said Kae. "No spells, no ceremonies. Give him the sword. When they are reunited, the King shall rise again."

And yet still he hesitated, scowling thoughtfully down at the earth mound before him. "It's so long since I last saw him. So many centuries, living on and on because Merlin required it of me, keeping the secret, building the London Knights to keep Arthur's great dream alive. And now . . . I wonder what he'll think of me when he sees what I've done with all those years. If he'll approve, or say I missed the whole point. But it doesn't matter. This is what I have waited for. This is my duty; and I've always known my duty. I taught him how to be a warrior; and he taught me how to be a man. Let's do it."

Acting on Kae's instructions, I drew Excalibur from its invisible scabbard on my back. Everyone made some kind of sound as the long, golden blade suddenly appeared, blazing brightly, driving back the dark in the cellars. I thrust the sword deep into the earth at the foot of the grave, and the blade seemed almost to drive on down, pulled by something rather than anything I did. I let go and stood back, and what was left of the blade pulsed with a fierce golden light. And then all the earth was suddenly gone from the grave, gone in a moment, leaving a long hole in the ground with a man stretched out in it. We all crowded forward to look. King Arthur lay peaceful and still, in his shining, spotless armour, his face calm and dignified. And then he opened his eyes and took a deep breath as though it was the most natural thing in the world. He stretched slowly and sat up, in one easy movement. And every one of us there knelt to him. Because some things are just the right thing to do.

Arthur stuck up one bare hand, and Kae grasped it with his and helped Arthur out of his grave. They stood together a while, looking at each other, legendary men, smiling easily. King Arthur was a big blocky man, in armour that gleamed like it had been polished, under heavy bear furs draped round his shoulders. His crown was a simple gold circlet set on his brow. He had a strong, hard, somewhat sad and reflective face, and there was about him a natural authority, a sense of solid and uncompromising honour; a simple goodness, strong and true. He was a man you would follow anywhere because wherever he was going, you knew it was the right way.

He pulled Excalibur from the earth as easily as he had once pulled it from an anvil on a stone, and the sword nestled into his hand as though it belonged there, and always had. The golden light blazed up joyously, filling the whole wide cavern; but now it was a warm, golden glow, with none of its previous fierceness. I felt the weight of the invisible scabbard disappear from my back and wasn't in the least disappointed. A burden may be an honour, but it's still a burden.

Excalibur was destined for great things, Earth-changing things, and I wanted nothing to do with any of it. I never even wanted to be a warrior, never mind a King.

Arthur hefted Excalibur as though it were just another sword, and, perhaps for him, it was. He put it away, the golden glow fading slowly away, and the sword in its scabbard hung openly on his hip. Arthur started to brush some grave dirt off him, and Kae immediately stepped forward to help. The rest of us slowly got up off our knees. Alex had actually taken off his beret, a rare sign of respect, and Suzie had put down her gin bottle. Arthur smiled on us all, started to address Kae in old Celtic, then stopped, looked down at Excalibur, and spoke again, in modern English.

"Kae," he said. "Of course; who else? I always knew I could depend on you, brother. So is this it? The Final Battle?"

"Not . . . as such," said Kae.

EIGHT

Kings and Queens and Worlds Without End

King Arthur lunged forward and embraced his stepbrother Kae, who hugged him fiercely back; and the two men stamped back and forth like two great bears, saying each other's names over and over again. They beat each other about the shoulders, called each other names, and generally carried on like the alpha males they were. Eventually, they let go, and Kae introduced me to Arthur. The once-and-future King towered over me, every bit as large and real and intimidating as he should have been, and I stuck out my hand because I was damned if I was going to do the kneeling-and-bowing bit again. Arthur grinned cheerfully and clasped my forearm with his huge hand, in the old style. It was like being gripped by a mechanical press.

"So! You brought Excalibur to me, John Taylor. I owe you

my thanks, and all my duty. I would not be here now were it not for you and the many travails you have endured. Call on me for anything, and it shall be yours."

"It was an honour," I said, and I meant it.

Arthur let go of my arm, and turned his great smile on Suzie. I took the moment to massage some feeling back into my arm. Arthur had the sense not to try to take Suzie by the arm. She still didn't like to be touched by strangers. Instead, he bowed courteously to her, and she nodded respectfully in return. Arthur then turned to Alex and looked on him thoughtfully for a moment.

"You're of Merlin's line, aren't you? I can see it in you. Merlin was always a good friend to me; I trust you will be, too."

Alex, surprisingly, went all bashful on being addressed by the legendary King, and smiled and nodded quickly. Arthur looked round him, taking in the grim and gloomy stone cellar.

"I have been here too long, sleeping in my grave. Not dead, only sleeping, and all the time . . . dreaming history. I know all that matters of the years that have passed, while I waited to be awakened and set to work again. So many wars . . . In my day I fought to put an end to war, but then, I suppose everyone does. And I have dreamed of such progress, such wonders, so many marvellous creations. I have seen the rise of Science, seen the human imagination given form and substance through incredible machines. I never knew such things were possible. But now I have returned. Tell me why I have been awakened at this time, Kae. What is the work that waits for me?"

"You're needed, Arthur," said Kae. "To do something only you can do."

"Same old story," said Arthur. "People always placed too much faith in me and not nearly enough in themselves." He shrugged and looked suddenly at Kae. "How is it that you are still here, Kae, after all these centuries? Did Merlin put you to sleep, too?"

"No," said Kae. "I had to go the long way round to get here, walking through the centuries day by day, waiting for you. Bastard sorcerer made me immortal."

Kae started to explain what Merlin had done, but Arthur cut him off with a curt gesture.

"The past doesn't matter. I am here, and I will do what needs to be done. I will save the day, one more time, because that's what I do. So where exactly am I? My dreams only covered the high spots; many details were left vague."

"You're in the cellars under Strangefellows, in the Nightside," said Alex.

Arthur grimaced. "The Nightside? What the hell am I doing in that disgraceful shit hole?"

Kae smiled briefly. "Where better to hide the resting place of the noble Arthur?"

Arthur growled, deep in his throat. "Merlin always did have too much irony in his blood. What is my trial this time, Kae? Does it hopefully include burning down the entire Nightside and putting its sinful inhabitants to the sword?"

"Wait just a minute," I said.

"Worse than that," said Kae, ignoring me. "It's the elves."

"Oh bloody hell," said King Arthur. "Of course. It would have to be. It's always the bloody elves. What are they up to this time?"

"They threaten civil war, which would devastate the Earth and wipe out Humanity."

"Civil war?" said Arthur. "That's new. In our day, they fought everyone except themselves. Who leads the factions in this age?"

"Queen Mab of the Sundered Lands, versus King Oberon and Queen Titania of Shadows Fall," I said. "But before we go any further, I want it properly understood that the Nightside is my home, and it is not a shit hole. Well, all right, some of it is; but it is still a place worth defending and the people worth preserving. Mostly."

I hadn't realised quite how fiercely I'd spoken, until I noticed how quiet it got when I stopped. Kae looked to Arthur, who nodded slowly to me.

"Your pardon, John Taylor. It seems I have been away so long I have forgotten my manners. No doubt the Nightside has changed much since my time."

"Not that much," said Kae.

"But it must have changed some, to produce a man like John Taylor, worthy to bear Excalibur," Arthur said firmly. "The elves are the enemy now, so let us concentrate on them. I remember Mab, of course. Magnificent creature. Such a shame, what happened between her and Tam O'Shanter." He saw the blank look on our faces. "I see that not all the tales from my time have survived the ages. Very well; I had not been long on the Throne of England, when it seemed to both Merlin and to me that I needed a Queen at my side, and especially one who would help unite my fractured land. So we settled on Queen Mab of the Fae, in the hope that such a union would put an end to the long enmity between Man and elf, and allow me to concentrate my armies on the lesser human foes that threatened my new-won land.

"Queen Mab let it be known that she was not entirely opposed to the idea; and so I sent an envoy to the Fae, to work out the details. A certain young man, new-come to my Court, one Tam O'Shanter. Not a knight as yet, but he aspired to be one and had already made his name famous throughout the land through many deeds of daring and chivalry. So I gave him this task, to prove himself worthy. Thinking also, that since he was not an actual Knight of the Round Table, and had never drawn a sword against the elves, the Unseelie Court might find it easier to accept him. He was supposed to win them over, with his charm and devil-may-care attitude, so much like theirs. He wasn't supposed to fall in love with the Queen; and she wasn't supposed to fall in love with him.

"It all went wrong so very quickly. They must have known their love was impossible, that it could never be accepted, but that only made them declare it all the more openly. A Queen must marry a King; that is the way of it. Tam, my brave young Tam, duelled with an elf who challenged the Queen over her choice, and killed him. And then that elf's brothers killed Tam, in honour's name. And that . . . was that. Mab was never the same afterwards. She grew increasingly . . . strange, even for an elf, and broke off all contact with Camelot.

"I've never had much luck with women.

"King Oberon and Queen Titania, you say . . . Can't say I recognise the names, but the only contact I had with elves after Mab's rejection was killing enough of them to put them in their place. They had to be stamped on, hard, so I could be free to deal with human enemies. And even that went wrong. I spent so long on the move, away from Camelot, fighting my battles all over England, that my people came to believe I didn't care about them any more. That's how Mordred was able to raise his army. And the land I made was split apart by civil war. Always the worst kind, that sets brother against brother. And father against son."

He stood there a while, his gaze far away, and none of us said anything. We were in the presence of history and legend, something greater even than the Nightside was used to. Eventually, Arthur shrugged off the past and looked directly at Kae.

"So, brother, what have you been doing, all these years?"

Kae explained quickly how he had fashioned the London Knights, to protect the people and keep King Arthur's dream alive. Arthur nodded, and cut him off again.

"Who better to keep a dream alive than the man who inspired it? Brothers, together, fighting for what is right."

"Can I ask?" I said. "Very respectfully, of course, but . . . Why do we need King Arthur, specifically, to stop the elves? I could name any number of people in the Nightside who've fought angels, gods, and other-dimensional entities. Myself included."

"Right," said Suzie. "Elves die as easily as anyone else. If you aim properly."

"But only Arthur can stop the fighting before it starts," said Kae. "He was the only one the elves ever respected, and feared enough, to listen to. They often came to him at Camelot to sort out their disagreements when they couldn't do it themselves. Mab and Oberon and Titania will listen to you, Arthur. They will recognise your authority and your impartiality."

"And my willingness to kill the whole lot of them if I can't get them to see sense," said King Arthur.

"That, too," said Kae.

"I like him," said Suzie.

"My knights are ready and waiting, to do what is necessary," said Kae. "At your command, of course."

"They're your knights, Kae," said Arthur.

"Then command me, Sire," said Kae.

"Where is Merlin?" Arthur said suddenly. "He knows the Fae better than anyone; we could use his advice. I did think he'd be here, waiting to greet me, when I came up out of the grave he put me in."

"Merlin is dead and gone," I said. I looked at Kae. Neither of us had anything more we felt like saying.

"Damn," said Arthur. "He always had the best ideas."

We showed him the other grave, and he stood beside it. "Yes, he was here. I can feel it." He knelt, surprisingly gracefully for a man in full armour, and trailed the fingers of one hand through the grave dirt. "Merlin, couldn't you wait for me, old friend?"

And then he stood up abruptly and stepped back, as his touch triggered a message left behind by the grave's occupant. Merlin appeared before us, a vision of a man long dead, floating on the air above his own burial place. But this Merlin looked young and in his prime, and very much alive. How he saw himself, perhaps. He grinned easily, his hands planted on his hips, as though he'd pulled off the best trick in the world. He looked straight at King Arthur, as though he could somehow see him, even across the years. And given who and what he was, perhaps he could.

"Arthur," he said, his voice seeming to come from a long way away, "one last confer, before I lay me down to rest in the grave that's waiting for me. There are things I know, things I have Seen, of the world that's coming. It isn't what either of us thought it would be, but then, that's life for you. Welcome to the future, Arthur. You won't like it. But don't let it get to you. The details may change, but people are still people. Unfortunately. Stick to the job in hand, and you'll be fine."

"They say the elves will war upon themselves unless I can find a way to stop them," said Arthur. "How am I supposed to reason with the most contrary people that ever were? What if I can't find a common ground for them?"

Merlin smiled briefly, as though he'd heard every word. "Then raise up the armies of Man, Arthur, and lead them in a war against the elves. Wipe them out, down to the last of their kind. There is no other option."

Arthur shook his head stubbornly. "I have seen enough of war, and extinction, down the centuries. I have dreamed history, and much of it was a nightmare. I have fought elves in my time, it was my duty as defender of my people; but I never wanted to see them gone from the world. They had many fine qualities. They were beautiful and brave, magical and marvellous. They were glorious in their day."

Merlin smiled. "You always were the wise one, Arthur. Do as you think best, my King. You always did. Good-bye, old friend. Good-bye."

And he was gone. One last vision, of a man who was so much more and less than he could have been.

"Good-bye, Merlin," said Arthur. "May you know peace,

at last." He turned abruptly away from the open grave to face the rest of us. "Merlin did his best to teach me some simple magics, when I was younger and he was older, though I confess I was never a very attentive student. But I did learn a few useful things. I think it is my turn to show you a vision, my friends, of the elves that were."

He moved his left hand through a series of sudden, abrupt gestures, and a great vista opened up before us. The end of the cellars faded away, replaced by a great green expanse that stretched away to a distant horizon. A huge, dark, primordial forest stood out against the skyline, shadowy and secretive, mysterious and menacing. Untamed. A vision of old England as it was in Arthur's day. Standing between us and the forest was a great elven city: tall towers connected by delicate walkways, gold and silver buildings, shining bright in the sunlight, with vast glowing domes and wide-open chambers, all of it magnificent to the eye. The lines were smooth and flowing, more organic than constructed, grown more than built. The whole city sparkled in the clear light, looking like every fairy tale we ever believed in as children. Breath-stoppingly beautiful, alive and protective, in a way few human cities ever are. Beside the city lay a great natural open harbour, where massive elven sailing ships lay at rest, so intricately made and fashioned that they were works of art in their own right.

The city was full of life, of elves walking in majesty and glory, with a simple grace that Humanity could never manage. They were nothing like the elves I'd known—beaten-down remnants of a once-noble race. There was magic in their every movement and a dignity that bordered on arrogance. Their emotions were larger and purer than ours, and so their faults were greater, too. They were not so different from us, really. The elves . . . were Humanity writ large, with all our virtues and our faults magnified. They moved like walking dreams that could become nightmares.

Other magical creatures accompanied them—whole clouds

of wee winged fairies, flashing through the air, shooting back and forth in patterns too complicated for the human eye to follow, leaving behind them shimmering trails of pure joy. Winged unicorns, of a white so bright it was blinding, flying gracefully down to graze on the great green pastures. There were gryphons and cockatrices and gargoyles, moving openly, with no fear of human hunters. There were trolls and ogres and darker shapes I didn't even recognise, gone from history so long that not even their names remained. They bowed respectfully to the elves, who moved amongst them unconcerned.

And then the marvellous scene was gone, the stone cavern abruptly back again. It felt like waking from a dream of something wonderful, lost. Arthur lowered his hand, looking tired.

"The elves were worth saving, then," said Arthur. "Perhaps they can become worth saving again. Honour requires I give them that chance."

"Never did share your enthusiasm for the pointy-eared bastards," said Kae. "They did things no human being would ever do and gloried in it."

"They were different," said Arthur.

"And Mab was a monster!"

"Grief and loss of her only true love drove her mad," Arthur said flatly. "I sent Tam to her; so part of everything that happened after that is down to me. She never got over Tam's death; and immortals have so much longer to grieve than us. Her rage against the fate that took him became a rage against the world, and all who lived in it. I have known grief and loss, too."

"It didn't make you into a monster," said Kae.

"It might have," said Arthur. "You never did realise how close I came, after I lost Guinevere." He shook his great head again. "There's been too much killing. There's only one way to stop this coming civil war amongst the elves; and that's to find them a new home. All of them. I have dreamed the elves' sad history. They are stagnating in Shadows Fall and dying in the Sundered Lands the Droods found for them. Perhaps that's why the Droods chose it. Always were a bunch of devious bastards. No—both sides need to move to a new world, where they can thrive and prosper again, far from humanity."

"Is this . . . really such a good idea, Arthur?" said Kae, trying hard to sound tactful. "A new, revitalised elven race could be an even greater threat to Humanity. For all your . . . dreams, I don't think you realise exactly how far the elves have fallen. There's nothing left in them but bitterness and hate for everything human. They live to screw us over because that's all they've got left. Only this day, an army of elves broke into my castle and killed dozens of my good knights, simply because they could!"

"And how many of them did you kill, Kae?" said Arthur. "The killing has to stop sometime."

"You always were a dreamer," growled Kae.

"And sometimes I make dreams come true," said Arthur. "Isn't that why you founded the London Knights, to keep my dream alive?"

"I don't know why I ever argue with you," said Kae. "You always could talk rings round me."

"Kae, even Gawaine could talk rings round you. And he only had fifty words, thirty of which were arse."

They both got the giggles, which was somewhat incongruous for such large men.

"I can find the elves a new world," I said, thinking quickly, and they both stopped laughing to look at me. I did my best to sound calm and composed. "There is an establishment here in the Nightside, with many Doors, that lead to every place you ever dreamed of. Doorways to all the worlds that ever were or may be, worlds without end. And one Door in particular leads to a world I think would be perfect for the elves. As long as we're careful to bolt the Door firmly behind them. If I lead you to such a Door, Arthur, can you persuade the elves to go through it?"

"The returned King's authority should be enough to summon both sides to parley," said Kae. "Always assuming a suitable neutral ground can be found."

"Again, I have a place in mind," I said. "I've been there before, and it's probably the one place that would impress the shit out of both sides."

"Good!" said Arthur. "Now, for the sake of all that's good and holy, let us leave this dismal and unpleasant place!"

"Best idea I've heard yet," said Alex. "Come on up to the bar. Drinks are on me."

"Ah!" said Arthur, beaming. "Best idea I've heard so far."

Alex led the way back to the stone steps. I moved in beside him.

"Can't help noticing you were a bit quiet back there."

"What is there to say?" said Alex. "That's King bloody Arthur!"

He had a point. But I've never believed in being over-impressed. Especially not by the good guys.

Up in the bar itself, Arthur took a good look round, and wasn't immediately impressed. The few remaining customers took one look at him and decided to leave right then before the trouble started. Alex moved quickly behind the bar and set about dispensing drinks. Back in his usual position of authority, he was immediately much more at ease, and a lot of his usual caustic manner returned. He even told Kae off for leaning on the wooden bar top in his armour and leaving scratches. Arthur eyed the bar-stools dubiously, and decided to stand. I couldn't help noticing that Suzie was being even quieter than usual and keeping a watchful eye on Arthur.

Before anyone could think to warn him, Arthur reached

out to pet Alex's vulture, Agatha, still squatting balefully on top of the till. He rubbed her head and chucked her under the chin, talking cheerful nonsense to her, and to everyone's surprise the bird sat there and let him do it. She actually looked bashfully at Arthur, and fluttered her eyelashes at him. Anyone else, she'd have had his hand off at the wrist.

"Arthur's always had a way with the beasts and the birds," said Kae. "Never would go hunting with me."

"Barbarian sport," Arthur said briskly. "Killing for necessity is one thing. You're not supposed to enjoy it."

He studied the ranks of drinks available behind the bar and beamed happily. "We never had anything like this in my day, did we, Kae? Mead and uisge, and wines that were always half-way towards vinegar. This looks much more interesting. I want lots of drinks, and I want them now. Start pouring, bartender; I have it in me to try at least one of everything. Nothing like sleeping fifteen hundred years to work up a real thirst."

We all looked on, suitably impressed, as Arthur knocked back the drinks as fast as Alex could produce them, to no obvious effect. Kae smiled proudly, though I noticed he made no attempt to keep up with Arthur. I sipped at a wormwood brandy, to be sociable, while Suzie barely touched her bottle of Gordon's Gin. She was still watching Arthur carefully. After a while, Arthur belched loudly, stretched as unselfconsciously as any cat, and looked at all the empty glasses racked up before him.

"Don't suppose there's anything to eat here, is there?"

"I wouldn't," I said quickly.

Alex glared at me. "I'm sure I could find *something* . . ."

"That's what worries me," I said. "A somewhat merry King Arthur is one thing; a King full of killer *E coli*, bent over a toilet when he should be out saving the world, is quite another."

Alex sulked. "It's been days since we had a real case of food poisoning."

"What about that nun who exploded?"

"Coincidence!"

Kae got Arthur really excited over the concept of cocktails, so I moved off down the bar and left them to it. I paused a moment to murmur in Suzie's ear.

"Why are you keeping such a close eye on King Arthur? He's saying all the right things."

"They always do," said Suzie. "You of all people should know that legends rarely turn out who you expect them to be."

"But this is King Arthur! If you can't give someone like him the benefit of the doubt . . ."

"I have," said Suzie. "I haven't shot him yet."

"But can't you . . . well, just *feel* the nobility pouring off the man?"

"I've never trusted my feelings," said Suzie.

I moved even further down the bar, took out my mobile phone, and contacted the Authorities, to find out what had been going on in the Nightside in my absence. I got put straight through to Julien Advent.

"Where the hell have you been, Taylor? All hell's breaking loose in the Nightside!"

"It always is," I said.

"Not like this! You'd better come straight to me, so we can talk."

"Okay. Where are you?"

"You've got Walker's old watch. He programmed it to bring him right to me, in times of need. Open it and say my name, and it'll lock on and bring you here."

He hung up on me. I took the gold watch out of my pocket and looked at it thoughtfully. I had to wonder what else Walker might have programmed into it. He always was a great believer in little surprises, and leaving nasty booby-traps for the unsuspecting. I looked back down the bar at the others.

"I have to pop out for a minute. Arthur, don't touch the bar snacks. Suzie, don't let Alex put any of this on my bill. I'll be back soon, then we can set about stopping the elf civil war and saving all Humanity if you're not too busy."

"There's time," said Arthur expansively. "If there's one thing sleeping for centuries teaches you, it's that there's always time. Now, Sir Alex, more of that peach brandy, I think. Yes. I like the peach brandy. Off you go, John Taylor. Don't mind us. Lots of drinking still to do. Never face an elf sober; they'll just take advantage."

I opened up the gold watch and got the hell out of Strangefellows before I said something someone might regret.

The Portable Timeslip delivered me straight to Julien Advent, dropping me off right on the top of Griffin Hill. I arrived standing on the edge of the great pit where Griffin Hall had once stood, before the Devil himself appeared to drag it down into Hell, along with the Griffin himself and his awful wife. He really should have known better than to make a deal for immortality. No matter how good a contract you have, the Devil is always in the details. I turned my back on the pit, and looked down the long, sloping hillside that led eventually to the Nightside city streets. The strange primordial jungle was still there, still horribly alive and active, thrashing violently as parts of it went to war with the rest. One of these days, the jungle is going to advance down the hill and march on the Nightside, and it will take a lot more than weed-killer to stop it.

I'd put my money on industrial-strength flame-throwers and napalm.

Julien Advent had his back to me, looking out over the

Nightside streets, but I had no doubt he knew I was there. The great Victorian Adventurer had been dodging assailants and assassins for longer than I'd been alive. He could spot a ninja in a darkened room two houses away. I moved over to join him.

"Hello, John," he said, not looking round. "So good of you to join me at such short notice. Hell of a view from up here."

"Why are we here?" I said. "You know this place has bad memories for me."

"This is where Walker died, isn't it?" he said, still not looking at me.

"Yes," I said. "He tried to kill me. I had no choice."

"Did he die well?"

I thought about it. "He died in character," I said finally. "He was himself, right to the very end."

Julien shrugged. "I suppose that's the best any of us can hope for. Look out there, John. Look what they've done to the Nightside."

I looked down at the city, that great sprawl of blazing streets and hot neon. The night was full of fires and explosions, strangely coloured flames and magical flare-ups. Buildings were burning like bale-fires in the night, and every now and again an entire block would vanish, to be replaced by something worse. I watched barricaded holdouts detonate, sending burning shrapnel up into the night sky like so many fireworks. There were vivid lights and horrid sounds, and here and there certain landmarks quietly disappeared, running off to hide in some safer dimension.

"The elves have come to the Nightside," said Julien Advent. "A whole army of the vicious little bastards, bursting out of new and old Timeslips, all across the city. I didn't know there were so many elves left in the world. They're killing everyone they encounter, butchering and slaughtering, and laughing all the while. I've got all of my people out on the streets, doing what they can; but things are bad down there. Almost as bad as the wars you started."

"I did not start the Angel War, or the Lilith War," I said, a bit tetchily. "I wish people would stop saying that."

"If it quacks like a duck, stick an orange up its bum," Julien said vaguely. "The elves are killing people, apparently to get themselves in the mood for their coming civil war. A chance to stretch their muscles and try out new weapons. They have a lot of new weapons, John—magical and scientific. Awful weapons, doing awful things. The elves are running wild in our streets, simply for the fun of it, looting ancient treasures and objects of power, and anything else that catches their eyes. We have to stop them, John. While we still can."

"Do we know whose elves they are?" I said. "Which faction they belong to?"

"Does it really matter?" said Julien, looking at me for the first time.

"It might. We've always been able to negotiate with Oberon and Titania. Mab . . . is another matter since she returned from Hell."

"We don't know whose elves they are," said Julien. "They're not interested in talking to us. The rest of the Authorities are down there now, fighting to regain control of the streets. Jessica Sorrow is walking up and down the Nightside, disbelieving in the elves till they disappear. The Unbeliever may be on our side now, but she still scares the crap out of me. Annie Abattoir has been using some really nasty magics, some so bad they even shocked the elves. And Larry Oblivion has been using his magic wand to good effect. Yes, I know about that. Please don't tell him I know; it would only upset him. He likes to think he can keep things secret from me. And Count Video and King of Skin are working together, for once, doing really horrible things to all those elves who don't get out of their way fast enough.

"They aren't alone. I have a lot of people down there, fighting for control of the streets. But we've been through so much, lately, John; we're all tired and worn-out. By the time we gain the upper hand and drive the elves from the Nightside, I'm not sure how much of the Nightside will be left. We're still rebuilding from the last two wars. We're not as resilient as we used to be.

"I should be down there with them, leading and inspiring the troops. But I wanted to talk to you first. They say . . . you have Excalibur."

"I did have," I said. "I handed it over to the returned King Arthur. He's back, Julien. King Arthur has come back to us."

"Any other day, that news would have gladdened my heart beyond measure," said Julien. "But what can one man, even such a man, do against a whole army of elves?"

"Well," I said, "he may not have an army of his own, but he knows a man who does. In fact, I've had a really good idea. Do what you can to buy me some time, Julien; and I'll come back with reinforcements that will really make your eyes pop."

"Taylor!" said Julien, as I flipped open the gold pocket-watch. "Don't you dare disappear on me! You're the Walker now!"

But I was already on my way, back to Strangefellows.

When I reappeared in the bar, Kae was leading everyone in a really quite appalling drinking song, "'Twas on the *Good Ship Venus.*" Complete with hand gestures. Arthur looked like he was having the time of his life. Alex was beating out the rhythm of the song on the bar top with both hands. Suzie was doing her best to join in, even though she has a singing voice like a goose farting in a fog. Even the vulture was dancing excitedly on top of the till.

I did my best to get them all to shut up and pay attention, but when that failed, I had no choice but to give Suzie

one of our little secret signals. She immediately stopped singing, drew the shotgun from its holster on her back, and fired
both barrels into the air. The song cut off abruptly in mid
verse. In the sudden silence, bits of the ceiling fell down.
Arthur and Kae swung round to face me, their hands on
the swords at their sides. Alex hid behind the bar, and the
vulture hid behind the till. I gave Arthur my best I-mean-
business glare.

"The elves have come to the Nightside. They're out there
right now, killing people, while you're having a party. And
these are not the elves you remember so fondly, Arthur.
They're hunting and butchering people for the sport of it."

"Then we must stop them," Arthur said immediately.
"Kill them all for daring to war on Mankind. And to send
whoever may be behind this invasion a very definite message. It's always best to negotiate from a position of strength
and vindictiveness. Kae, are your London Knights ready for
battle?"

"Always," said Kae. "Simply say the word, Sire."

"The word is given, my brother. If the elves want war, we
shall show them what war really is."

"But I have to get back to Castle Inconnu, to raise my
army," said Kae. "And we don't have time to go by any of the
usual routes."

Everyone looked at me.

"The Portable Timeslip won't take us past all the protections you've put in place," I said. "Which means, we're going
to have to ask a certain someone for help. A certain individual
with a great many Doors . . ."

"Oh bloody hell," said Suzie. "Not the Doormouse again."

Arthur gave me a hard look. "Am I to understand we have
to beg assistance from a mouse?"

"He's a very nice mouse," I said.

Kae was already grinning broadly. "Oh, I think you're
going to like this one, Arthur."

● ● ●

The Portable Timeslip took all of us to the Doormouse's excellent establishment. Alex stayed behind, to lock up and barricade the bar against any passing elves who might decide they had a bit of a thirst on. The rest of us appeared right outside the shop, and Arthur looked round interestedly. He'd never seen the Nightside itself before. Half the street-lights had been smashed, and a few dead bodies lay here and there; but otherwise, it was pretty quiet. Many of the shops were closed and boarded up, but the neon lights still blazed brightly. It could have been just another Saturday night. Arthur sniffed.

"A bit gaudy, for my tastes." He looked round sharply as a whole building at the end of the street exploded. His hand went to Excalibur on his hip.

"Let's get the army first," I said quickly. "And, let's get inside before anyone sees us."

"I do not run from the enemy," Arthur said sharply.

"You do if they outnumber you thousands to one," said Kae.

"Oh well, in that case," said Arthur. "Good to see you stayed awake during some of my strategy classes, Kae."

"You were a rotten teacher, Arthur. Rotten. And I really hated those snap tests."

"They were good for you."

"So is cod-liver oil."

"Do they still use that?"

I glared them both into silence, then led the way into the shop. It hadn't changed. The Doormouse came bustling cheerfully forward again, doing up the front of his white coat and checking that his pens were lined up in the proper order in his top pocket. Then he saw Suzie and me and stopped dead in his tracks. He made the sign of the extremely cross and started to say something really cutting; but then he saw King Arthur and Kae in their armour, and ran out of breath.

His large brown eyes grew even larger, his back straightened, his long whiskers twitched excitedly . . . and then he charged forward and threw himself into Arthur's arms. The Doormouse hugged him tightly and rubbed his furry face against Arthur's.

"It's you! It's really you! You've come back, you've come back! We've been waiting so long for your return, Your Majesty! I mean, I'm just an old hippy in a mouse body, but I've read every book about you I could find. And seen all the films! Welcome back, King Arthur!"

The Doormouse pressed his fuzzy face against Arthur's breast-plate and looked up at him adoringly. Arthur clung to what was left of his dignity.

"Does anyone happen to know whether this mouse I'm holding is male or female?"

The Doormouse let go immediately and scurried backwards to bow repeatedly. "Sorry! Sorry! Got carried away there, a bit. Sometimes I can't help feeling I'd have been better off as a badger. They handle their emotions so much more properly. King Arthur, what brings you to my humble establishment? Everything I have is yours! Except you can't actually take anything with you, of course. The Doors don't move. As such. Am I babbling? It feels like I'm babbling, and that big scary woman is growling at me again."

"Do you, by any chance, happen to have a Door that will transport us inside Castle Inconnu?" I said.

"Oh poo," said the Doormouse, his whiskers drooping. "Someone told you."

"It's hard to keep a secret in the Nightside," I said. "Though actually I was guessing. Jerusalem Stark had to get those elves into the castle somehow, and your Doors seemed the safest bet."

The Doormouse sighed. "Knew that one would come back to bite me on my furry arse. In my defence, he did pay me an awful lot of money."

Kae glared at the Doormouse. "You created a secret backdoor into Castle Inconnu?"

"I build Doors for people," the Doormouse said quickly. "What use they put them to is none of my business. I'm only a craftsman. Craftsmouse."

"You're about to be a dead craftsmouse," said Kae. "You'll make an excellent rug for my office."

"No, Kae," said Arthur. "He has agreed to help us. Haven't you, Sir Mouse?"

Kae was still glaring. "Where's the Door?"

"In the display area, of course. My Doors are always here. I make them, and people make use of them, but they never leave my shop. Far too dangerous. I do have scruples, you know, even if you can't see them past all the fur."

"And when were you intending to inform the London Knights that you possessed a secret backdoor into their Castle?" said Kae.

"I'm almost sure I would have got round to it," said the Doormouse. "Eventually."

"Okay, that's it," said Kae. "It's rug time."

"Take it easy," I said to Kae. "You can't expect morality from a mouse."

"Well quite," said the Doormouse. "That's why I became one."

"Take us to the Door," I said.

The Doormouse bobbed his head quickly, to all of us, and several times to King Arthur, then scurried away into the deeper recesses of his shop. The Doors were still standing there, in their ranks, waiting to be used. I kept an eye out for one particular Door I'd seen earlier and stopped before it. The others stopped with me. The Doormouse came hurrying back to see what we were all looking at. It was a Door like all the others, except for the brass combination lock in its centre.

"This is the Door that leads to alternate Earths," I said.

"All the different histories, all the ways the Earth might have gone. Can it really open onto any possible Earth, Doormouse?"

"Oh yes. You just have to enter the right co-ordinates. Of course, many of the more extreme iterations are completely uninhabitable, but . . . What kind of Earth did you have in mind?"

"A completely empty Earth," I said. "An Earth where sentient life never did develop, in any form. A living breathing Earth, where only the beasts and the birds flourished."

"Of course," said King Arthur. "I see where you're going. An excellent solution for a very tricky problem."

The Doormouse produced an impressively large book from somewhere about his person and flipped rapidly through the pages with his furry paws, muttering querulously to himself. He finally stopped at one particular page, ran a fuzzy finger down a long list of entries, then squeaked happily. He made the book disappear and advanced on the Door, muttering a bunch of numbers under his breath, before spinning the brass combination lock back and forth with practiced dexterity, then flinging the Door open with a triumphant flourish.

Beyond the Door, endless grasslands stretched away under a perfect blue sky, with no sign of civilisation or cultivation anywhere. A gentle breeze wafted through the Door, smelling of every sunny day we ever dreamed of. I could hear birds singing, and the far-away sounds of animals on the move. But otherwise, it was a very quiet, very peaceful world. We all crowded together, peering through the open Door.

"So peaceful," said King Arthur. "Like Eden itself, before the Fall, untouched by human hand."

"What better place for the elves?" I said. "What better place for a new start?"

"If they'll take it," said Suzie. "They don't think like we do or value the things we do. They're not human."

"They want the Earth," said Arthur. "And this is an Earth.

Only without all those irritating humans to get in the way. They'll take it."

"But if they don't?" said Kae.

Arthur looked suddenly tired. "You heard Merlin. If the elves cannot be made to see sense . . . then raise the Armies of Man and lead them against the elves, until one or other of us is gone forever. I would prefer to avoid that if I can."

"But would the elves prefer to avoid it?" said Kae. "There is a part of them that has always loved war."

"They love survival more," Arthur said shortly.

He gestured sharply to the Doormouse, who quickly shut the Door and spun the brass lock. He looked at King Arthur.

"I can't recall anyone ever wanting to visit that Earth before. Calm and quiet and peaceful aren't the kind of things people usually look for in the Nightside."

"Their loss," said Arthur. "Understand me, Sir Mouse; no-one is to have access to this Door until I return. Is that clear?"

The Doormouse bobbed his head in a perfect frenzy of agreement. "Of course, Your Majesty, of course. I'll put an OUT OF ORDER sign on it. Shall we now proceed to the Castle Inconnu Door? We're almost there, and the other large armoured gentleman is growling at me."

"Don't scare the mouse, Kae," said Arthur. "That's my job."

We finally came to the Door, and the Doormouse opened it. Kae led the way through because it was his castle, after all. We appeared in a fairly unremarkable side corridor, with no-one round, and the Door slammed shut behind us and disappeared. Kae growled something under his breath, then led us quickly to the nearest communication point. Which turned out to be a simple office, filled with computers. Arthur was fascinated with all the technology and bumbled around, having a good look and touching things he shouldn't, while Kae put out a general alert, ordering everyone to appear in the Main Hall, right then, no exceptions. Sir Roland appeared, on the run, and stuck his head through the door. His eyebrows practically jumped off his head when Kae introduced him to King Arthur, and he was down on both armoured knees in a moment, bowing his head to the returned King.

"Up, up, my good friend," Arthur said easily. "You are my knights, sworn to serve my cause and my dream. I should kneel to you, for keeping it alive all these centuries."

Sir Roland clambered quickly to his feet again and glared at Kae. "Would it have killed you to have given us a little advance warning? We could have prepared a proper welcome!"

"Such things can wait," said Arthur. "The elves have brought war to the Nightside, and we are going to ride forth and teach them a lesson in manners. Lead the way to the Main Hall, Sir Roland. I would have words with the London Knights."

Sir Roland bobbed his head quickly in a way that reminded me irresistibly of the Doormouse, and led us all to the Main Hall of Castle Inconnu. He was clearly bursting with questions he wanted to put to King Arthur, but Kae kept him busy with questions about the readiness of the knights to go to battle at such short notice. Sir Roland was still answering questions when we got to the hall. Suzie and I brought up the rear. I was starting to feel left out, as though having delivered Excalibur, my part in the story was over. It was Arthur's story now, and Suzie and I were bit players. Except, the story wasn't over yet, and I didn't think Arthur was going to find things as easy as he thought. He was going to fight elves in the Nightside; and neither the elves nor the Nightside was anything like what he remembered of them.

Arthur might have dreamed England's history; but the Nightside has always been outside history.

When we finally hurried into the Main Hall, it seemed like everyone in the Castle was already there, waiting for us.

The knights in their armour, arrayed in solid shining ranks, along with all the other people who made the castle run, and their families. Because no-one wanted to miss this. The Main Hall was packed from wall to wall, with women and small children peering in through the open doorways because there wasn't room for them. When King Arthur stepped up onto the empty platform at the end of the hall, a great roar went up from everyone. They cheered and shouted, they slammed their hands together and stamped their feet on the floor, all of them grinning so hard it must have hurt their faces. The King had returned, something they had dreamed of all their lives but never really believed would happen in their life-times. The knights drew their swords and thrust them into the air, again and again. And still the cheering went on, as though it would never stop.

King Arthur stood at the front of the platform, look-ing out over the crowd, nodding in approval at the ranks of armoured knights. Kae stood at his side, smiling proudly at his brother, gesturing for quiet so the King could speak. Suzie and I stood at the back. This wasn't our moment.

"Want me to fire my shotgun into the ceiling?" Suzie said innocently into my ear. "That should quiet them down."

"Better not," I said. "It might be misinterpreted."

King Arthur thrust one hand up, and immediately all the sound stopped as though someone had thrown a switch. The whole hall fell silent, to hear what he had to say. King Arthur lowered his hand and nodded solemnly.

"It's good to be back," he said. "But I'm not here to bask in your adulation. Later, maybe. For now, there is work to be done. An army of elves has gone to war against Humanity, in the Nightside, indulging in their love of brigandry and slaughter. This cannot be allowed. They must be stopped. I ride out. Who rides with me?"

Everyone there roared approval and agreement, and the

knights thrust their swords into the air again. No-one questioned him. He was King Arthur, and they were his. And as simply as that, the London Knights went to war.

Sir Roland happily took over the logistics of getting so many people ready for action, while Arthur and Kae discussed how best to get their army to the Nightside. I saw a chance to be useful again. If only because I didn't like the idea of a whole army of men in armour on the loose in the Nightside. I wanted to be sure everyone understood that only the elves were the enemy. King Arthur immediately saw what I was getting at, but I kept my eyes on Kae. Arthur might be King, but Kae was Grand Master of the London Knights. And the knights and the Nightside have never been on the best of terms. We had so little in common.

"My knights will behave themselves," Kae said flatly. "We're there to save people from the elves, not trample everyone underfoot indiscriminately. Any one of my people steps out of line, I'll have his balls."

"All right," I said. "How are you planning to get your knights into the Nightside? You'll never get all your horses through the Underground stations, and there's a limit to how many I can transport through my watch."

I stopped because Kae was looking at me in a very superior way.

"We have our own dimensional doorways, Mr. Taylor. For when we ride to war on other worlds, in other dimensions. They won't work anywhere on Earth because that's Drood territory. But the Nightside isn't on Earth, technically, so we can be there in moments."

"If you can enter the Nightside anytime you choose," I said slowly, "why haven't you?"

"I told you," said Kae. "We deal with bigger issues. We fight our wars across all Space and Time, to protect Humanity from the Forces that threaten it. We're not here to spank people because they misbehave. We're only getting involved now because of the elves, and because Arthur wants it. Personally, I could watch the whole Nightside burn to the ground and not shed a single tear. Nasty little place."

"Kae!" Arthur said immediately. "My knights have always defended those in need, wherever they may be! Or have you only kept alive those parts of my dream that suited you?"

"Sorry, Arthur. But this is the Nightside we're talking about . . ."

"It's the elves," Arthur said flatly. "Nothing else matters."

"Of course, Arthur. You're right, as always."

"You are talking about our home, Kae," said Suzie, and something in her voice drew Arthur's and Kae's attention immediately. I've always admired the way Suzie can become very dangerous, very quickly, often without even having to raise her voice. She gave Kae her best cold glare, and he stood very still as she addressed him in her cool, calm, and really quite deadly tone. "The Nightside is necessary. It serves a purpose, for those of us who can't all be perfect. I wouldn't live anywhere else. And, I want to make it very clear that I don't have any patience for *To save the village we had to destroy it* tactics. The knights go in, they kick the crap out of the elves, then they get the hell out. Or I will take it very personally. Is that clear?"

"You can't speak to the King like that!" said Kae, honestly shocked.

"Kae," said Arthur, and Kae immediately shut up again. Arthur smiled on Suzie. "There can't be much wrong with the Nightside these days if it can produce warriors like you and John Taylor. We ride out to rescue your people as well as punish the elves. Will you walk with me and discuss the best tactics to use in the Nightside? You know the situation better than any of us."

They moved off together, cheerfully discussing death and destruction. Kae and I wandered after them.

SIMON R. GREEN

"You know," said Kae, "that is one seriously scary girl-friend you have there."

"You have no idea," I said. "Trust me."

Not all that long afterwards, we were all assembled in a massive courtyard the size of two or maybe even three football fields, surrounded by tall stone walls, open to a starless and moonless night sky. I wasn't sure whether we were outside or not. I wasn't even sure if we were still in the castle. The knights were readying themselves for war with practiced ease and easy camaraderie. They wore brightly coloured tabards over their armour, with various stylised symbols on their chests and backs to identify which groups they belonged to. Their horses waited patiently, huge muscular brutes, tossing their proud heads and snorting loudly, armoured and caparisoned, with brightly coloured plumes on their foreheads. A small army of grooms bustled round them, fussing over them and seeing to their needs. Armourers moved amongst the knights in much the same way, checking their armour and weapons. Suzie, surprisingly, was enchanted by the huge horses and moved happily amongst them, feeding them bits of carrot and murmuring happy nonsense to them. Girls and their ponies . . .

Kae gave the order to mount up, and the knights were quickly in their saddles. And despite what we've all seen in films, they didn't need little step-ladders, or have to be lowered onto the backs of their horses. The London Knights had spent most of their lives learning how to move easily in their armour. They mounted their horses as though it was something they did every day of their lives, and for all I know, they did. They put on their plumed helmets and immediately became anonymous and coldly intimidating. The

270

horses bore the weight easily. Many of them were stamping their hoofs on the cobbled ground, impatient to be off.

Suzie and I had been given our own horses, so we wouldn't be left behind. I'd been assured they were very old, very calm horses, with excellent manners. I got up into the saddle with a little help from a groom who happened to be passing. Suzie vaulted up with more enthusiasm than grace, and looked round her proudly. Kae steered his horse in beside me, on his way to somewhere more important. He was in full armour, and it suited him far more than the grey suit ever had.

"Try to keep up and don't get in the way."

He was gone before I could come up with a suitably cutting rejoinder. I took the reins in a firm grasp to show the horse I knew what I was doing. He turned his great head all the way round, gave me a long, thoughtful stare, and turned his head away again.

"You have to let him know who's in charge," said Suzie.

"I think he already knows," I said.

Kae brought forward a massive white charger for Arthur, almost half as big again as all the other horses. Arthur smiled and patted the horse on its muzzle, and I swear the horse actually bowed its head to him. Arthur had that effect on everyone. He swung easily up and onto the saddle, took the reins in one mailed hand, and then raised his free hand. Immediately, every sound in the courtyard cut off. Even the horses fell silent.

"It is time," said Arthur. "Open the gateway, Kae. We ride to battle."

Kae stood up in his stirrups and made a series of quick, abrupt mystical gestures at the far end of the courtyard. He looked every inch the brutal warrior who'd come so close to killing Suzie and me, back in the sixth-century Strange-fellows. I trusted Arthur, but I still wasn't entirely sure about Kae. I'd liked him a lot better when he was pretending to be Sir Gareth. I missed Gareth; I felt I understood him a lot better than I did Kae. But was Sir Gareth a mask worn by Kae; or was it possibly the other way round? I'd find out soon enough. Nothing like going to war to show you who people really are.

Arthur urged his horse forward, Kae right there at his side. The many ranks of mounted knights moved silently after him; and Suzie and I brought up the rear. Everyone else had disappeared from the courtyard. They'd done everything they could. The only sound was the steady rumble of thunder as hundreds of horses moved across the cobbled ground. A giant doorway stood before us, a simple door-frame some thirty feet tall and twenty wide, full of swirling mists, exactly like the one Prince Gaylord the Damned and his dark knights used, back in Sinister Albion. I think I would have said . . . something, but Arthur drew Excalibur from its scabbard, the long blade blazing brightly against the gloom. He urged his horse forward and plunged into the open doorway, and all the army went with him.

And that was how the London Knights went to war with the elves in the Nightside.

A thousand knights in armour thundered through the streets of the Nightside, leaning out of the saddle to strike at the startled elves, caught by surprise in midslaughter. The doorway had delivered us right into the heart of battle, and the knights rode the elves down, trampling them under their horses' hoofs. Long swords cut off heads and hacked elves down with vicious speed and accuracy. Some elves turned to fight, but it was already too late for them. The London Knights had come to the Nightside for blood, and the elves didn't stand a chance.

Suzie and I were the last through the gateway, which immediately disappeared behind us. It was all I could do to stay on my horse, and Suzie couldn't free a hand to draw any of her guns. I didn't feel like I was in charge of anything any more, and that always worries me.

The Nightside was a mess. Buildings were burning all round us, flames leaping up into the smoke-filled sky. The street was littered with the dead, and the gutters ran thick with blood and gore. The elves had been busy. Bodies had been mutilated and strung up from street-lights by their own intestines. There were neat little piles of hands and feet and hearts. The elves do so love to play. And these were the elves I'd planned to save. The elves I'd found a new home for. Right then, if I could have pressed a button and sent every elf there ever was to Hell, I would have done it.

We slammed through elves caught off guard in the street, leaving them dead and dying behind us. We pressed on, charging through the streets in an unstoppable tide, carrying all before us. We soon caught up with the real action. People had set up barricades across a main street, improvised from anything handy, including bodies, and had fought the elven forces to a halt. The traffic had disappeared from the roads, moving along hidden by-ways until the fighting was over. There were dead men and dead elves everywhere, and some of them had died with their hands locked around each other's throats. There was blood and offal and charred corpses, and bodies turned inside out by horrid magics. Both sides looked round startled, as the London Knights came thundering towards them.

The mounted knights slammed into the massed hordes of the elves before them, throwing them aside and trampling them under hoof. Some elves turned quickly to face the new threat, brandishing all kinds of glowing weapons. They danced and capered amongst the bodies of those they'd slain, mocking the approaching knights, defying them to do anything about all the horrid things they'd done and the worse things they planned to do. They wore strangely designed brass-and-silver armour, crackling with protective spells, and their pale faces were tattooed with hideous designs. They were delighted to be fighting their old enemy Man again. They had forgotten how much they enjoyed killing people and playing their vicious games with them. The knights rode straight at them, roaring war cries booming inside their steel helmets, and the elves darted aside at the last moment, laughing and leaping high into the air, to pull the knights out of their saddles. Elves and knights went blade to blade, both sides eager for blood and honour and the vicious joys of battle.

The elves threw spells that exploded harmlessly against the knights' armour. They had their own built-in protections. The elves came howling, bearing strange alien weapons and devices, and wild destructive energies spat and crackled in the air; but still they couldn't pierce the knights' armour. So the elves drew their glowing swords and cut and hacked at the knights; and even the most modern armour was sometimes no defence against such ancient weapons.

The elves jumped onto the backs of horses, hugged the knights to them, and forced their blades into the gap between helmet and breast-plate. Blood jetted into the night air, the knights fell from their horses, and the elves leapt away, laughing breathlessly. Some of the elves ducked in low, to cut at horses' throats and legs, and were mostly met with a forceful hoof in the face. These were war-horses, trained for battle.

From the shadows some elves fired strangely glowing arrows that nothing could stop.

The knights' advance was quickly slowed, then halted. And they hacked and cut about them with their great swords and axes, and most of the time even the best elven armour was no match for cold steel, coldly wielded. The knights leaned out from their horses to cut off heads, or arms, or stab a chest or throat in passing; and golden blood spurted out, to hang on the air and run in the gutters along with redder blood. Two elves leapt up and grabbed a horse's head, forcing it to a halt. The knight leapt out of his saddle, hit the ground running, beheaded one elf, and cut down the other, his blade sinking deep into the elf's chest. He'd barely pulled his sword free when a dozen other elves came running straight at him. Another knight leapt from his horse to guard his brother's back, and the two knights stood together and killed every living thing that came at them.

Some knights had other weapons. Strange magical and scientific devices I didn't even recognise. The London Knights were traditionalists in everything that mattered, but they were right up to date and beyond when it came to weapons.

The elven forces began to fall back, slowly at first, then they broke apart under the impact of the knights, and fled through the Nightside streets. And the London Knights went after them. A great cheer went up from the Nightsider barricades, and King Arthur briefly saluted them with Excalibur before returning to the fight. His armour was dripping with golden blood, and the sword blazed brightly against the night.

The elves hadn't expected such opposition. And they hadn't expected to die so easily at the hands of men.

Suzie let her horse have its head while she used her shotgun. The horse didn't seem to mind the noise of the gun at all. Suzie picked off elves as she saw them, dealing with targets the knights ahead had missed. Her blessed and cursed ammo blasted right through the elves' armour, and when it didn't, she blew their heads right off. When she finally ran out of shells for the shotgun, she slipped it back into its holster and tossed grenades and incendiaries round where they'd do the most good. Many an elf who'd thought himself hidden in the shadows went flying suddenly through the air with body parts missing, and often on fire. And when she ran out of explosives, Suzie drew the two heavy pistols from her hips and carried on taking care of business. She looked calm and relaxed, cool and easy, in her element and loving every moment of it.

I kept close to her, watching her back, using my gifts to find elves who'd hidden themselves a little more thoroughly than the others. Even the best elf glamour is no match for my gift. I only had to point out a particularly dark shadow where there shouldn't be one, and Suzie would open fire; and something dead would fall out onto the street. We've always worked well together. I've never thought of myself as a fighter, and now that Excalibur was no longer on my back, urging me on, I was quite happy to leave the real fighting to the knights. I'd seen enough violence and had enough blood on my hands.

And, of course, while I was busy brooding about that and feeling sorry for myself, an elf came running up on my blind side, leapt onto the back of my horse, grabbed me from behind with one arm, and set a knife at my throat. The horse started to rear, upset by the unexpected new weight, and I yanked harshly on the reins to hold him still. The edge of the blade gently parted the skin above my Adam's apple, and I could feel a slow runnel of blood trickling down my throat. The elf giggled in my ear.

Suzie saw what was happening and spun her horse round to face me, one pistol already targeting the elf.

"I don't think so!" the elf said cheerfully. "One wrong move, and I will cut your lover's throat! I know the infamous John Taylor when I set eyes upon him, and I know a way out of this trap when I see it. You shall be my passport out of here, John Taylor; and your woman shall be my guide."

"Hell with that," said Suzie, and shot him between the eyes.

The elf's head snapped back, golden blood seeming to hang on the air for a moment before he fell backwards off my horse. Some of the blood spattered my neck and the back of my head. I quickly put my hand to my throat, but it was still intact, apart from the one slight cut. The horse stood calmly, waiting patiently to be told what to do next. I looked back into the street, where the elf lay very still with half his head missing. What was left of his face looked surprised. I looked at Suzie.

"You could have negotiated with him!"

"No, I couldn't," said Suzie. "I don't do negotiation."

"You might have missed!"

"You know me better than that."

And, of course, I did. She didn't ask me how I felt because she was confident in her abilities and confident that I was, too. And if I told her how upset I was, at having to be rescued, she genuinely wouldn't have understood. But I really was mad as hell. I'd allowed myself to be shoved to one side, intimidated by King Arthur and the London Knights, and in my home-town, too. I felt a distinct need to do something, to show all of these big armoured alpha males that this was my territory, and I could do things here that all of them put together couldn't even dream of. I'd seen too many deaths, from the Nightside to Sinister Albion and back again, and I'd had enough. I might not be a warrior knight or a legendary King, but I was still John Taylor. I concentrated and raised my gift, and it only took me a moment to find King Arthur and Kae, riding with their knights, still driving the elves before them.

This is John Taylor. Having found them, it was the easiest thing in the world to put my voice in their heads. *Round up the remaining elves and return to me. There's been enough killing. I have something more constructive in mind.*

I shut down my gift and waited. Suzie steered her horse in beside mine and waited patiently with me. She always assumed I knew what I was doing, and I loved her for that. I've never had the heart to disillusion her. Mostly I make this shit up as I go along. I hadn't known I could make direct mental contact with people just by finding them. But then, I'd never tried before. Never been this angry, before. King

Arthur and Kae came riding back to join me. They'd left the knights behind. Presumably because they didn't want them to see me yelling at their King. Golden blood had soaked their tabards, and more ran down their armour. They seemed well pleased with themselves. King Arthur reined his horse in before me and studied me with cool, thoughtful eyes.

"You don't have to shout, Mr. Taylor."

"And you do not give orders to your King," said Kae, reining in beside Arthur. Suzie studied him coldly, both her pistols in her hands.

"You're the King of England," I said to Arthur. "But this is the Nightside; and we do things differently here. I brought you here to put an end to the slaughter, not start one of your own. These elves are broken; there's no excuse to hunt them through the streets like vermin."

"They're elves," said Kae.

"And we are supposed to be saving them," said Arthur. "My knights are now containing them, as you suggested, Mr. Taylor. You are right. I'd forgotten how much the joy of battle can take a man over. But what are we to do with these captured elves, Mr. Taylor?"

"Kill them all," said Kae. "Send a message to whoever sent them."

"Hush, Kae," said Arthur. "Mr. Taylor?"

"Watch," I said. "And learn."

I raised my gift again, and it rose blazing to the surface immediately, driven by the anger that still burned in me. My inner eye opened wide, travelling across all Space and Time in a moment, and I found Queen Mab in her Unseelie Court, in the Sundered Lands. In the Nightside, everywhere is as close as anywhere else; but even so, I was quietly impressed with myself that I'd been able to find and reach her so easily. Maybe I should get mad more often. I looked upon Queen Mab, sitting on her Ivory Throne, and used my gift to find a connection between the Nightside and the Sundered Lands.

A great opening appeared, hanging in mid air, and shimmering light from the elven Court spilled out into the night. I could see right into Caer Dhu, the last great Castle of Faerie, taken with them when the elves walked sideways from the sun and left the Earth behind. Queen Mab sat bolt upright on her Throne, set on a raised dais before a massive Court full of elves. She looked out at me, through the opening I'd made, surprise and outrage in her unearthly pale face.

Queen Mab was greater in size and scale than any other elf. Ten feet tall, supernaturally slender, and glamorous, naked save for blue-daubed sigils glowing fiercely on her pearlescent skin. She was beautiful beyond bearing, terrible beyond any hope of mercy, alien, inhuman. Her ears were pointed, her eyes were pure gold without a trace of pupil, and her mouth was a deep crimson; the red of heart's blood, red as sin itself. Queen Mab was a first-generation elf, impossibly ancient and magnificent, and it showed.

She leaned forward on her Ivory Throne to fix me with her unblinking gaze. "What poor damned mortal dares disturb me in my Court?"

"That would be me," I said cheerfully. "John Taylor of the Nightside, not in any way at your service. Ah, I see you've heard of me. That saves time. And here with me is the returned King Arthur, of Camelot. He calls you to parley with Oberon and Titania, that we might avert the coming civil war between the elves, and to discuss something more . . . interesting."

Queen Mab looked past me at Arthur. He nodded courteously to her, and she actually bowed her head to him.

"Arthur," she said. "It has been a while, has it not? You haven't changed."

"Neither have you," Arthur said gallantly.

Mab made no comment, still studying Arthur's face. "So, it seems I am not the only one to return to trouble this world again. If things had gone differently, if we had wed, what

SIMON R. GREEN

a world we might have fashioned together. But there was Tam, my lovely Tam, and nothing was ever the same again, after that."

She turned abruptly to face me, fixing me with her intense golden stare. "If any other mortal had insulted me in this way, John Taylor, I would have ripped the meat from his bones with my own bare hands for such effrontery. But you have brought me a face I never thought to see again. That buys you some time. I am . . . intrigued. Arthur's presence changes everything. Yes, I will parley."

"You sent the elves into the Nightside, didn't you?" I said.

"Youngbloods," said Queen Mab. "They wanted so much to prove themselves in battle, and who was I to deny youth its chance?"

"Most of them are dead now," said Kae. "The London Knights hold the survivors captive. Their continued survival depends upon your good behaviour."

"Kill them all," said Mab. "Let them all die, for failing me. I am Mab; and I will do what I will do."

I decided to press on, while she was still in what passed for a good mood. I raised my gift again and sent it searching; and this time I found King Oberon and Queen Titania in their Unseelie Court, in Shadows Fall. I found another connection and opened up another gateway; and more light fell into the Nightside as I connected one hidden place with another.

Oberon and Titania sat side by side on two great Thrones made of bones. Strange shapes and sigils and glyphs had been cut deep into the hundreds of interlinked bones that made up the two Thrones, detail upon detail, in a design complex beyond hope of human understanding. Oberon was easily ten feet tall and bulging thickly with muscles, wrapped in a long blood-red cloak to better show off his milk-white skin. His hair was a colourless blond, hanging loosely down around a long, angular face dominated by piercing blue eyes. He looked effortlessly noble, regal, and perversely intelligent. Oberon

280

had come to his Throne through intrigue and violence, and it showed.

Titania wore a long black dress with silver trimmings, and wore it with a careless, heart-breaking elegance. She was lovelier than any mere mortal would ever be, and she knew it, and didn't give a damn. She was a few inches taller than Oberon, with a skin so pale that blue veins showed clearly at her temples. Her hair was blonde, cropped short and severe, and her night-dark eyes were calm and cold.

Nobility hung about them both, like a cape grown frayed through long use.

"We know you, John Taylor," said Oberon, in calm, bored voice. "Why do you trouble us?"

"King Arthur's back," I said briskly. "That's him, right there. Isn't he marvellous? He and his knights have kicked the crap out of the elves Queen Mab sent to devastate the Nightside. He has asked her to parley, to find a way to avoid the forthcoming elf civil war, and she has agreed. He now asks you to parley, in the same cause, and swears he has another, viable option to propose."

"There still exist ancient pacts, of honour and blood, between the Unseelie Court and Camelot," said Arthur. "Tell me the elves have not forgotten honour."

"No," said Oberon. "The elves still remember honour."

"But what if we do not want peace?" said Titania. She did not move at all, her rich and sultry voice seeming to hang on the air.

"Would you rather face extinction?" I said. "You know that once the war has started, you'd all fight to the end, to the very last of your forces, rather than admit defeat. You'd use any tactic, any weapon, die to the very last elf and take all Humanity and the Earth with you, before you'd let your hated rival win. Arthur is offering you a way out—a way for the elves to survive as a race, with honour. And if you can't trust King Arthur of Camelot, whom can you trust?"

Oberon smiled slightly. "Why not? If nothing else, this process should prove . . . illuminating. I see you, Mab. What say you, to this offer of parley, and a possible solution to our dispute?"

"No-one summons me anywhere," said Mab. She turned her unblinking gaze on Arthur. "You don't have Merlin any more. And without him, your forces failed at Logres."

"Who needs Merlin?" I said. "We have Arthur and the London Knights, and I can call upon the Lord of Thorns, Jessica Sorrow the Unbeliever, and Razor Eddie, Punk God of the Straight Razor. I could even give the Droods a call . . . Do you really want to fight one more useless battle; or shall we try something different for a change?"

"If a suitable neutral ground can be found and agreed on," said Mab, "I will attend. But only because it has been such a long time since I have seen you, Arthur. One does miss . . . old friends."

I turned back to Oberon and Titania, in their Court at Shadows Fall. But before either of them could speak, another figure appeared suddenly from behind the two Thrones of bone, a face I already knew. A short, stocky figure, almost human-sized, though the sheer scale of the King and Queen made him appear smaller. His body was as smooth and supple as a dancer's, but the hump on his back pushed one shoulder down and forward, and the hand on that arm was withered into a claw. His hair was grey, his skin the yellow of old bone, and he had two raised nubs on his forehead that might have been horns. He wore a pelt of animal fur that melded seamlessly into his own hairy body, and his legs ended in cloven hoofs. He smiled a lot, but it wasn't a pleasant smile.

I knew him. He had led me a merry dance across the Nightside, all to protect a Peace Treaty he never had any faith in. He brought me Excalibur. He was Puck, the only elf that was not perfect.

He lounged artlessly against the arm of Titania's Throne,

and she patted his head fondly as he grinned out of the opening in the air.

"And so the call to parley comes, from an old and yet respected human King; and who are we to say no to such a courteous summons? I say, let us go, and talk, for talk is cheap and therefore costs us nothing. After all, nothing shall be decided, nor considered binding, unless both Courts agree on it. And how likely is that?"

"Dear Puck," said Queen Mab. "Still so wise and so provoking."

"Let's do it," said King Oberon. "For the hell of it. It has been so dreadfully dull round here, lately."

"But no more than us," said Queen Titania. "Just us, and no-one else."

"Of course," said Queen Mab. "We might want to say and admit things our people would never approve of." She looked at me. "Assuming, again, that you can find a neutral ground where we cannot be overheard. And how likely is that?"

"Oh, I've got somewhere in mind," I said. "Somewhere that will impress even the King and Queens of Faerie. Certainly a place where I can guarantee no-one will overhear you."

And driven by the anger that still hadn't let go of me, I raised my gift again and found the place I'd been thinking of. I used my Portable Timeslip to transport Oberon and Titania and Puck, Arthur and Kae, Mab, Suzie, and myself out of the Nightside and into the future. To the Nightside at the end of the world, the devastated future that I had helped to bring about.

Everyone looked round, startled at their sudden arrival. They hadn't known I could do that, and until I tried, neither had I. I was deathly tired, all the energy gone out of me, and my head pulsed with a sick pain. Overusing my gift has its price.

Suzie was quickly at my side, so I could lean on her if I needed to, without anyone else noticing. I forced myself to stand upright and smile unconcernedly about me. I couldn't be weak now, not when so much depended on me. Not when I still had so much left to do.

Arthur and Kae moved instinctively to stand back-to-back, staring wildly about them. Oberon and Titania and Mab had also moved together, perhaps for mutual support. And while they towered over us mere mortals, the stark and terrible setting they found themselves in made the elves seem smaller. There's nothing like the end of the world for putting things in perspective.

I had brought them to a dark place, where the Moon was gone from the night sky, and only a handful of stars still gleamed dully. For as far as any of us could see, the Nightside lay in ruins, broken buildings and scattered rubble, endless silence and a bone-piercing cold. Smashed and abandoned vehicles littered the empty streets, but there were no bodies, anywhere. I could have told them why, told them what happened to all the bodies; but they wouldn't have thanked me for the knowledge. What light there was came from distant glares and strange lights out in the ruins. The night had a purple cast, as though it were bruised. We all looked round sharply, as some great shape raised itself briefly on the horizon, then it was gone again.

"What the hell was that?" said Arthur. "John, what is this place? Where in God's name have you brought us?"

"Not so much where, as when," I said. "This is the future of the Nightside, and London, and Earth. Or, at least, one of its many possible futures. I've done everything I can to make this future as unlikely as possible; but the fact that it's still here suggests it's not utterly impossible. Nothing lives here now, except the insects. This . . . is the end of everything."

I let them look round some more, let the cold seep into their bones and into their souls. Arthur and Kae were clearly horrified, and even the elves couldn't help looking impressed. Oberon and Titania held each other's hands, Mab drew herself up to her full height, and even the Puck had stopped smiling. I could have told them that I was responsible for all this: that this was the world I murdered, in one future time-line. But I didn't. I didn't want them distracted from the main issue.

"Welcome to the future," I said, harshly, and they all looked back at me. "This is what the world will look like when all the wars are over."

"Am I back in Hell?" said Mab. "Such desolation of the spirit . . ."

"This is a dead world," said Puck. "There is no life here, only . . . things like life."

"Oh yes," I said. "When we've all finished killing each other, the monsters will still remain. Listen."

From far off in the distance came the sound of living things as big as houses, moving slowly and dragging themselves through the purple twilight. Enormous silhouettes appeared briefly upon the broken horizon, and something far too huge went stalking between the nearby buildings, tottering on great stilt-like legs, pulling down stonework where it brushed against decaying structures. Something impossibly large rose suddenly, blocking off our view of the horizon. It made a series of loud, wet, sucking noises, and lurched towards us.

"You'd better do something about that," I said. "It sounds hungry."

Oberon and Titania and Mab raised their hands and chanted together, and immediately a shimmering protective circle rose, spreading out to fill all the open space round us. A pale blue-white glare from the screens replaced the bruised purple, and the advancing shape slammed to a halt, some distance from the shimmering screen. It stayed where it was, utterly still, watching from the shadows. It gave the impression that it could wait forever, or at least until the screen went down. Out in the darkness, other great shapes were heading our way, attracted by the light.

"Nice work," I said to the elves. "You see what you can do, when you work together? I do love these simple life lessons. Of course, the screens won't last. Nothing lasts, here. And there are things out there that can break through anything, eventually."

Even as I spoke, a great dark shape slammed up against the shield, on our blind side. What details of the thing I could see made no sense at all. All the shapes were monsters, things left behind because they were too big to be killed by anything except each other. More of them came forward, slapping and grating against the shimmering fields, desperate to get in, to get at us. Driven by many appetites, of which hunger was only one. They wanted to do awful things to us, simply because we were sane and normal and alive. Because we made them remember when the world was not as it had become.

I didn't have to tell any of the others this. They could feel it. I could see it in their faces.

"This is what the world will look like," I said, "when all the wars are over and done with. This is what you would inherit after your civil war, Your Elven Majesties. But this is only one possible future, one possible Earth. There are many others, a whole infinity of possibilities. Tell them, Arthur."

King Arthur had to swallow hard before he could speak, but when he finally did, his voice was calm and reasonable.

"I can offer you another Earth, a new Earth, where Man and Elf never happened. A whole new start, for all the elves. Why fight over our Earth, already overrun by Man and his civilisation, and risk ending up in this future, when you could move to this new world I offer, and never have to see Humanity again? It is a wild fine place I offer you, rich with beasts and birds and possibilities. You could flourish there."

Oberon and Titania nodded slowly. "For all that elves do love a feud and delight in slaughter, in the name of honour . . . the needs of the race come first. We are suffocating at Shadows Fall, and it is known to us that the elves are dying out in the Sundered Lands. There is something in us that is bound to the Earth and will not let us thrive anywhere else. We will forgo our ancient enmity and make peace among our kind, in return for a new Earth. What say you, Mab?"

We all looked at her. She smiled slowly. "You tore me from my Throne and threw me down into Hell. I had to claw my way back, through many sacrifices. You expect me to forget all that?"

"Yes," said Titania. "In the name of the race. Mab, in this new world . . . there could be children again."

"I will not give up my hate," said Mab. "It's all I have."

"Still clinging to the past, Mab?" said Titania. "That always was your failing. That's why you lost the war against Humanity and why we had to replace you. Because you cared nothing for the future."

"Because you never got over what happened in the past," said Oberon. "Will you risk the continuation of our race over the memory of one dead man?"

"He loved me! He truly loved me!" Mab towered over us, radiant with rage. "The only one who ever did; and the elves killed him for it. Let them all suffer, as I have suffered."

"You could have children again, on this new Earth," said Titania. "Have you forgotten how sweet it is, to bear a child?"

"I would sacrifice any elf that ever was, or might be, before I will give up my righteous anger," said Mab. "Nothing else matters."

"All this, for revenge?" said Oberon.

"For honour!" Mab sneered at him openly. "I am the last of

the first-born elves. All who came after were smaller things, with smaller emotions. You were never worthy of us. Let the war come. Those who survive will have been made pure again, through blood and sacrifice. And I will rule them."

"And risk this?" said Arthur, gesturing around him. "What point could there be in winning if all you inherit is this?"

"I will do what I will do," said Queen Mab. "Nothing else matters."

"There was a time when something else mattered," said a cheerful, bright, and jaunty voice. "When someone else mattered, sweetest Mab."

We all looked round sharply at the new voice, and there, striding towards us, was a tall well-built young man, wrapped in a heavy bearskin cloak and simple cloth leggings. He had a broad, open face and an infectious smile, and a shock of red hair under a traditional Scottish cap. He came forward to join us, grinning widely, and Mab . . . let out a single low, shocked sound. Arthur started forward, and Kae stopped him with a hand on his arm.

"Is this your doing?" Suzie whispered in my ear. I shook my head.

"Dear sweet God," said Arthur. "How can this be? Tam . . . Tam O'Shanter, as ever was. You died even before I did. Has some dear magic brought you back, too?"

Tam O'Shanter laughed happily, his eyes fixed on Queen Mab. He stopped before her, cocked his head slightly to one side, and planted both fists on his hips. He looked so alive, so full of life, ready to take on the whole world and bend it to his wishes, for the fun of it.

"Why, this is the land of the dead. Where else should I be? I was needed, so here I am, to see my sweet Mab again. Ah, my bonny lass, how fine you look. Even if I did have to stand on a stool to kiss you, in the old days. It is your need that brings me here, sweet lass, to this dark place. Are you still so mad at all who live because I died, and left you alone? Poor Mab, we could never have had long together, no matter how things worked out. Because it is the fate of every man to grow old and die, and you are an elf. That's why our love was forbidden, among Men and elves."

"I would have found a way," said Mab. "I would have kept you with me forever. I will never stop hating and hurting the world that took you from me."

"Then hold me, my love," said Tam O'Shanter. "Hold me as you once did, when the world was young, and so were we."

He stepped forward and opened his arms, and Mab stepped into them without hesitation, and hugged him fiercely to her. For the first time, she looked happy. She kept on smiling, even when Tam's hand came up with a long knife in it, slid it smoothly between her ribs, and twisted it. Golden blood ran down her side, but she never made a sound. She hung on to him, her eyes closed. He pulled the blade out, and golden blood coursed down her side and spattered on the ground. And then, as though only the blade had been holding her up, she fell suddenly to her knees. Still clinging to her dead love. Her head fell forward on his chest, and he patted her hair fondly before pushing her away from him. Queen Mab fell awkwardly to the ground and lay still. Tam O'Shanter looked down at her, the bloody knife still in his hand. And then he put aside the glamour he'd worn and was himself again.

"Sorry, Mother," said Puck. "But I did owe you that, for making me the way I am. And what better glamour to deceive you than the father I never knew? You should have died when he did and saved us all so much suffering."

He looked up and smiled into our shocked faces.

"It's what she would have wanted. She could never give up. She didn't know how. So I have put her out of her misery, and ours. Now she's gone, all the elves must bow down to King Oberon and Queen Titania, by right of succession. The elves are one people again, with no need of civil war. I must thank you, John Taylor, for making this possible. No-one else could have brought us all together."

"This isn't the ending I wanted," I said.

The Puck shrugged again. "You never did understand elven humour." He looked at Oberon and Titania. "Well, Your Majesties, have I done right in your eyes?"

"Of course," said Oberon. "A most elegant solution. We shall now oversee the passing of our people, from Shadows Fall and the Sundered Lands, to the new Earth that has been promised. But Titania and I . . . will not be going with them. To be a new people, they must leave the past behind. And Titania and I . . . have too much past in us. We are the old way, and the old way must be forgotten. So we shall remain in Shadows Fall, where all things of the past belong."

"Some others will no doubt wish to remain with us," said Titania. "The future is not for everyone. But the race will continue, elsewhere, and that is all that matters."

"I will stay with you," said Puck. "Because there's still far too much mischief to get into in our world to ever give it up."

"Dear sweet mischievous Puck," said Queen Titania. But she was looking at Queen Mab's dead body when she said it.

Sometime later, Suzie and I and Arthur and Kae stood watching through the Door, looking out over the empty Earth, as the Fae came through an endless series of dimensional gateways to claim their new home. Thousands of them, on foot and on horseback, or on other magical creatures, some of which I couldn't even put a name to. The elves came proudly, singing and laughing, and for the first time I thought I saw in them something of what Arthur had always seen. They had their pride back, and their grandeur. They had been Humanity's enemies for so long, we had forgotten their magic and their glory. And perhaps they had, too. Seeing them now, it almost made me sad that I'd never see them again. Almost.

The crossing took a long time, but when it was finally over, Oberon appeared out of nowhere to join us at the Door. He waited patiently for us to recover our self-possession, then he ceremoniously closed the Door, spun the brass combination lock, and said a simple but very binding spell over it. No-one would ever be able to access that particular alternate Earth again. He said nothing, merely bowed briefly to King Arthur, and vanished before Arthur could bow in return. Back to Shadows Fall, leaving history behind, to become legend.

The Doormouse crept up to join us, his whiskers twitching anxiously. "Well, this has all been very interesting, and perhaps even moving, but now that it is all quite definitely over; do you think you could all please get the hell out of my life? You're all too weird, even for me."

Outside in the street, Arthur looked round him, suddenly seeming a bit lost. "What do I do now, Mr. Taylor? It would seem I have done what I was brought back to do, though I can't help feeling you did more than me."

"Couldn't have done it without you," I said, and I meant it.

"Do I have to go back to sleep now? I've seen so little of this brave new world that has such wonders in it. I dreamed centuries of history, but I was never a part of it."

"You must come back to Castle Inconnu, with me," said Kae. "Let me show you what I've built, tell you all the amazing things the London Knights have done, all the marvellous victories we won, in your name and in defence of your dream."

"All these years, and still so desperate for my approval?" said Arthur. He put both hands on Kae's shoulders and shook him slightly. "You've always had my approval, brother. I have always been so very proud of you."

"But you can't stay, Arthur, and you know it," said a familiar voice. "This isn't your time—in oh-so-many ways—and it isn't the Final Battle. That is yet to come."

We all looked round, and there was Gayle, or Gaea, Mother Earth herself, standing in a powder-blue business suit, looking very elegant and very efficient. King Arthur bowed to her.

"Greetings to you, my Lady of the Lake. I should have known you'd turn up. Must I go back to my grave again?"

"No," said Gaea. "The word is out, and already far too many people know about it. I suspect a certain bartender of planning guided tours. Come with me, Arthur, and I will find you a new resting place, with a little more dignity, where you can sleep peacefully until you are needed. And no, Kae, this time you don't get to know where."

"But . . . we've been together such a short time," Kae said to Arthur. "After so many years . . . Will I ever see my brother again, Lady?"

"Who knows?" said Gaea. "Merlin did make you immortal, after all. He must have had his reasons."

"Of course we'll meet again," said Arthur. "You really think I'd fight the Final Battle for all Humanity, without my trusted brother at my side?"

The two men embraced fiercely, then one walked off with the Lady of the Lake, and the other walked off to rejoin his London Knights. And Suzie and I were left standing there in the street.

"Let's go home, John," said Suzie. "It's been a very long day."

"Yes," I said. "Let's do that."

We walked off down the street, Suzie's arm through mine. After a while, she looked at me seriously.

"There's something I've been meaning to tell you, John."

"Oh yes?"

"I'm pregnant."

I stopped dead and looked at Suzie, who looked calmly back at me.

"You're . . . what?"

"I'm pregnant," said Suzie. "I'm going to have a baby."

"How did that happen?"

"Well, if you don't know by now . . ."

"A baby," I said. "We're going to have a baby . . ."

"How do you feel about that?" said Suzie.

I smiled at her. "I couldn't be happier."

We started walking again, her arm tucked companionably through mine, her leather-clad shoulder pressed against my white trench coat.

"We've come a long way," I said, after a while. "We're neither of us the people we used to be."

"Just as well," said Suzie. "They were both very . . . limited people."

"Been through a lot of changes," I said, carefully not looking at her. "And most of them, together. I don't think we could have come half so far, without each other's support."

"We do make a good team," said Suzie.

"Yes," I said. "First as colleagues, then as partners. But now . . . baby makes three. We can do a lot as partners, but I don't think raising a child is one of them. Would you like to marry me, Suzie?"

She looked straight ahead, her face as cold and unreadable as ever. "You always were the romantic one."

"I'm serious."

"I know. I love you, John. As much as anyone like me can love anyone. But I don't want you marrying me out of a sense of obligation."

"You know me better than that."

She looked at me briefly. "Yes. I suppose I do."

"I love you, Suzie Shooter. Much against my better judgement. Because I need you."

"And I need you, John Taylor. If only to watch my back while I'm reloading."

"So you'll marry me?"

"Yes," said Suzie, in her usual cool, collected voice. "As long as it is fully understood; I will not be wearing white."

We walked along some more.

"Can you imagine what our kid is going to be like?" I said. "He'll be running this place before he's twenty."

"Damn right," said Suzie Shooter.

*You are cordially invited to the wedding of
John Taylor and Suzie Shooter.
No guns, knives, or explosives,
by request.*